Summer's
Moon

Summer's Moon

Lacey Baker

St. Martin's Paperbacks

This is a work of fiction. All of the characters, organizations, and events portrayed in this novel are either products of the author's imagination or are used fictitiously.

SUMMER'S MOON

Copyright © 2014 by Lacey Baker.

For information address St. Martin's Press, 175 Fifth Avenue, New York, NY 10010.

ISBN: 978-1-250-01924-0

Printed in the United States of America

St. Martin's Paperbacks edition / September 2014

St. Martin's Paperbacks are published by St. Martin's Press, 175 Fifth Avenue, New York, NY 10010.

10 9 8 7 6 5 4 3 2 1

Summer's Moon

Prologue

Third Week of May

Parker Cantrell woke up in a bed that wasn't his.

He'd been back in Sweetland for about three weeks now, having stayed after Gramma's funeral. His sisters and brothers were also still here. All of them were staying at the B&B. Well, Parker, Quinn, and Preston were staying in the caretaker's suite, while Savannah still had a room on the upper floor. Michelle had her own house down the street, and Raine had moved in with her so they could have the maximum number of available rooms for rental. In the caretaker's suite, Quinn used the bed in the bedroom while Preston had taken one of the couches in the sitting room. There was another couch in the sitting room, and it rolled out to a bed; that's where Parker slept.

It was not a queen-size bed, and it definitely did not have a fluffy pink-and-white paisley comforter on it. Another thing was that the caretaker's suite faced the back of the house, which meant he usually woke up to a lovely shaded morning, as the front of the house received the blazing sunlight at dawn. This morning, however, he cracked his eye open only to receive what felt like a laser of brightness making a direct hit to his pupils. And when he turned to his left to roll out of the bed, he rolled into a body instead.

Now he was fully awake, and his eyes shot open, only to blink a couple of times in confusion. There was a body in bed with him. From what he could see via the stream of light that slipped through the blinds at the window, the body belonged to a female. A naked female with hair tangled around her face and an arm draped over her waist. Her breasts were high, with enticing light brown nipples that apparently were more than ready to greet him. His gaze roamed lower, to the curve of her hips, the V of her juncture, the softness of her thigh.

Dammit!

He at least had the good sense not to verbalize what he was thinking. Instead he rolled to the right, let his feet hit the floor, and stood up so fast that he almost took a tumble right out the window that was not supposed to be there. Someone must have been looking out for him so that he didn't crash through the glass, possibly to his death, because he couldn't remember exactly how high up he was in this bedroom that apparently was not his. That same someone was probably busting a gut laughing as he became tangled in the frothy sheer curtains that hung from said window, his man limbs threatening to tear the soft material that constricted his movement.

On a string of mumbled curses, he managed to break free; then he moved quietly around this foreign room, picking up every article of clothing he thought belonged to him. In less than five minutes, Parker was partially dressed and through the door, standing in a narrow hallway that led to even more narrow steps. He moved through the tight enclosure, pushing through the screened door that had not been locked and almost falling down the three smaller steps that he hadn't known would be there. Just as he hadn't known the screened door would lead him right into the center of the flower shop.

"Great move, Cantrell," he mumbled to himself as he maneuvered his way through wrought-iron carts, white-painted stands, and glass enclosures that all held some form of plant or flower. The front of the store was one huge glass-paned window that received the early morning sunlight as if it were a special gift on Christmas morning.

His eyes instantly revolted, closing without warning so that his next step slammed him right into a wall. Something hit the floor, and the sound ricocheting off the walls of his mind caused a deathly echo that had him clenching his teeth. With steely resolve, he headed toward that damned window and its hellfire of sunlight. The door was to the right. After a minute of fiddling with the lock—which he could barely see, because the more he tried to keep his eyes open, the more determined they were to keep up this game of hide-and-seek they were playing with the sun—Parker stumbled out onto the sidewalk of Main Street and let his curses fall freely from his lips. He did have the forethought to head back to the door so he could lock it. The throbbing in his head was his body's way of protesting, but he ignored it. Once he knew the door was locked, he stood as straight as he could and took a deep breath.

"First one-night stand back in Sweetland," he murmured, then took another wobbly step toward the current love of his life parked at the curb—a black-and-silver Suzuki V-Strom 650. "Welcome home, Parker Cantrell."

The last was said with a good amount of pride and a slight smile, one he figured was too soft to cause any pain from the intense hangover he was currently experiencing.

Chapter 1

Today was the day.

Drew Sidney had decided today would definitely be the day she talked to Parker Cantrell.

It had been months since she'd actually stood still long enough to share more than two or three sentences with him. Of course Parker, being the man that he was, had tried to talk to her at every possible opportunity. She prided herself on being able to resist for as long as she had. Tall—over six feet—built like a linebacker with strong, muscular arms and perfect abs, the darkest brown eyes she'd ever seen, and the best lips she'd ever . . . Saying he was hard to resist was definitely an understatement.

The mere fact that Parker had tried talking to her after their one steamy night of passion was a contradiction of the already established reputation of Sweetland's most notorious player and the prominent half of the Double Trouble Cantrells. He'd been back in town for a little less than five months, and she'd managed to get caught in his trap just weeks after his return. That said a lot about her personality and the resolve she'd sworn to uphold since the fiasco in Stratford, the small town in the city of Havre de

Grace, Maryland, where she'd grown up. Neither of which Drew really wanted to think about at the moment.

If life were only that easy.

If she could simply push to the side all the things she did not want to think about or deal with and continue her forward trek in life, things would be all good, all the time.

Yeah, that was a big crock of bull if she'd ever heard any. With a deep sigh, a relaxing, soul cleansing sigh, Drew closed her eyes and wished for the absolute best out of this day. It was going to be a long one, an emotional one, and definitely a life-changing one.

"Your flowers are blocking the freakin' sidewalk again, Sidney!"

The loud, slurred words poured through the front door just as the wind chimes above the access sang in introduction of a new customer. Or in this case with the arrival of Hoover King, Sweetland's resident drunk, cabdriver, historian, and all-around handyman.

"Mornin', Mr. King," Drew said in her most cheerful voice.

The front door didn't slam, even though she figured that was Hoover's intent. Uncle Walt had installed a pneumatic door closer to keep that from happening, since Drew was afraid her entire front window would shatter if the door to the old two-story building located on Main Street right between Delia Kincaid's Boudoir and Bob Flannery's Timeless Antiques shop slammed hard enough. Just about all of the shops on Main Street had large window fronts, as this was the best form of advertisement to the many tourists who filled Sweetland's streets, not to mention another reason for Sweetland to have some sort of celebration. In a couple of weeks it would be the first of October, and Fall Fest, their first official festival of the new season, would kick off with a window-decorating contest. Drew and Delia would be competing to win that contest. But first, today was the Labor Day Festival, which signified the end of summer and apparently had Hoover's boxers in a bunch.

"It's a morning," Hoover continued, huffing as if he were in desperate search of his next breath. "And the parade's gotta come down Main, which means I gotta run this ribbon all up and down the street to keep everyone on the sidewalk. And your sidewalk's all junked up with these flowers," he informed her, as if she didn't already know each of these points.

He lifted an arm, using it to wipe the sweat from his forehead and the top part of his head that was left exposed by his receding hairline.

"Those buckets of flowers are for the flag float. Mr. Flannery's going to use his pickup truck to haul them down to the dock for this evening's festival," she explained calmly.

But Drew was anything but calm. Her stomach had just rolled and she'd had to pause and take a deep breath in an attempt to hold the nausea at bay. For the past few weeks since it had hit, she'd thought about being annoyed with the intruder, but the thought of what it signified kept the annoyance at bay. And replaced it with happiness that filled her like sunshine and a field of wildflowers—which in Drew's world was the equivalent of unimaginable joy.

"Festival's not till tonight. Why can't you keep those buckets inside until then?" Hoover persisted.

Drew shrugged. "Not enough room. But I can come out and push them up against my front so they're not in your way." Even though Drew was almost positive they weren't really in Hoover's way at this moment.

Since Hoover's wife, Inez, had been busted for embezzlement from the town council and implicated in a bigger drug scheme that stretched up the coast to New York City, Hoover had been wandering around town in a constant state of annoyance. Well, no, that might not be the absolute truth. When Hoover was drunk—which was 91 percent of the time—he wasn't annoyed, but either angry or overly flirtatious, neither of which was one of Drew's favorites. And whenever he was sober, he was sad, which was the sole reason Drew felt sorry for him and excused a lot of the rude and unnecessary things he said to her.

"Naw," he said, waving a hand at her as he walked back and forth in front of the counter where she'd been standing, clipping the ends of a lovely batch of Gerber daisies that Preston Cantrell had ordered for his fiancée, Heaven. "You just sit tight. I'll push 'em back."

Heaven and Preston lived in the cutest little blue house Drew had ever seen, and Heaven loved flowers almost as much as Drew. So Preston made it a point to buy her a fresh bouquet at least once a week. This colorful arrangement was in honor of their kitchen renovation being completed two weeks ahead of schedule. The cheery array of colors would look lovely against Heaven's dandelion-yellow walls that had just been painted two days ago.

"Nonsense, you have other things to do this morning," Drew said, dropping her scissors and wiping her hands down the front of the charcoal-gray apron she wore.

Blossoms was decorated in Drew's favorite colors, lavender and gray. Sheer curtains hung to the floor at the front door and at the two French doors that opened to the back terrace. The walls had been painted lavender with the faintest hint of pixie dust—as she liked to call the iridescent-like overlay. Through the main showroom were carts, tables, trellises, and shelves full of flowers and plants and everything imaginable in between. It was a quaint little place that she'd been falling steadily in love with every day in the last three years she'd been in Sweetland.

Hoover had continued to huff and puff with more complaints as she'd come from behind the counter and headed for the front door right behind him. Stifling air smacked her in the face the moment she was outside, and it was barely ten o'clock in the morning.

"I'll just push 'em back here," Hoover was saying as he lifted a foot and pushed a bucket full of white carnations back up against the wall of her storefront.

Inhaling deeply, she leaned forward and more gingerly moved a bucket full of red carnations back. "I'll go over and see Mr. Flannery now. It's really humid out here and I don't want the flowers to start to wilt."

"Fall over and die is more like what they're going to do out in this heat," a female voice said from behind.

It was a familiar voice, a familiarly negative one that Drew loved for the most part and tolerated for the rest.

"Hi, Mama," she said, turning around to see Lorrayna Sidney stepping onto the curb, sun hat covering the upper portion of her face, a purple silk hand fan in her left hand working overtime to keep her cool.

"Why are you out here in your condition? You should be inside in the air-conditioning," Lorrayna snapped as she came closer.

"Shhhh," Drew hissed, standing to face her mother. "Mr. King can hear you."

Lorrayna's thin lips pressed together in a tight line as she looked over Drew's shoulder to see Hoover kicking more of the buckets against the wall.

"All the more reason you should be inside," she whispered conspiratorially.

Drew could only sigh. Her mother meant well. At least she thought she did. Lorrayna had been the first person Drew had called two weeks ago when she'd returned from an appointment in Easton. She'd had nobody else to turn to. For a minute she'd thought about calling Heaven, especially since Drew had been in Heaven's yard when she'd almost fainted, causing Quinn Cantrell, the town's new doctor and Heaven's soon-to-be brother-in-law, to come and see about her. Luckily, Quinn had referred her to a female doctor and hadn't given any hint as to the reason why to her or to anyone else that she knew of.

"Come on inside. I have some orders to fill before I bring out the umbrella and small table to watch the parade." Drew had walked back into the store and knew her mother was close behind. She could tell by the series of three sneezes that never failed to announce Lorrayna's entry into Blossoms even better than the wind chimes did. They still hadn't figured out what in the shop she was actually allergic to.

"Do you have something to drink? It's blazing hot in here," Lorrayna complained.

"In the refrigerator," was Drew's reply.

Nothing—and by nothing, Drew meant anything short of Arthur Sidney being raised from the dead—was ever good enough for Lorrayna. She'd complain about the sun and how hot it burned, then turn right around the next day and complain about the rain making mud puddles in her backyard. All of which Drew was used to and tried not to be annoyed by—emphasis should be added to the word *tried*.

A few minutes later, Drew heard her mother's sigh and looked up to see her standing near the refrigerated display case. Lorrayna was not as into plants and flowers as Drew was—truth be told, she hadn't been really into anything since her husband's death three years ago—but she always paused at the display case in search of one particular item. The Peace Lily served as a reminder of the day they'd buried Lorrayna's husband, Drew's father. The otherwise peaceful and quietly beautiful plant marked that day in Lorrayna's life as if it had been etched on every calendar from here to forever. And her mother searched for it like a wolf hunting prey.

It was sad, the way she stood in front of that display case staring off into what seemed like oblivion, holding on to a memory that was better left clipped to the nub, as Drew had just done to the Gerber daisy in her hand.

"Your father was so excited when I told him I was carrying you," Lorrayna said quietly.

Drew didn't reply. She didn't want to talk about Arthur Sidney, but that was all Lorrayna ever wanted to talk about.

"I thought he'd want a boy. You know, so he could play ball with and pal around with him," Lorrayna continued. "But then he said he'd rather have a girl. 'A girl that looks and acts just like you, Raynie.' That's what he'd said."

Well, he'd gotten his girl, Drew thought with another quick snip of the stem. But she hadn't been blessed with Lorrayna's curvy frame; instead, she'd taken after her father and his family with height and a willowy build. Her mother also had wide, light brown eyes that once upon a time were filled with expression. Now, the only expression they sported was sadness, and they were either red-rimmed from crying, puffy from crying, or simply downcast. Another thing Drew had inherited from her father was her snappy attitude and impatience, or so her mother would quickly point out.

"He had the perfect family, then," Drew heard herself saying. When the words were out, she clamped her lips down so tight that her temples ached.

"Nothing's ever perfect," was her mother's retort.

"Nothing except Arthur Sidney, right?"

Lorrayna turned away from the display case at that question and glared at Drew. "Don't do that," she said, and it sounded like a hiss through her teeth.

"He's dead, Mama. How long is it going to take for you to accept that?"

"I'm sorry if I'm not as cold and unfeeling as you are, Drew. One day maybe when you find true love you'll know how it feels to lose it and you'll know it isn't as easy as taking out the garbage."

Drew shook her head vehemently. "I'm not looking for love, true or otherwise."

"Really? Then what do you suppose you're going to do about your situation?"

Yes, her "situation." That's what Lorrayna had taken to calling Drew's medical condition. She shook her head as she caught herself calling it a "medical condition" instead of what it really was. A baby.

"I'm going to do just fine on my own."

"Without a father?" Lorrayna asked, raising a thick brow.

Drew sighed, scooped up the daisies, and slowly slipped them into a Waterford crystal vase. "I lived a good portion of my life without a father," she said under her breath. "Or at the very least without a good father."

"When are you going to tell him?" Lorrayna continued, thankfully not having heard Drew's last comment.

"Today," she replied to her mother's stark question.

"Then you'd best fix that sour attitude of yours or he's going to be on the first bus back to Baltimore."

"He's Parker Cantrell, Mama. He's probably already got one foot on that bus back to Baltimore," she quipped.

Chapter 2

"You're disgusting," Savannah squealed, pushing Parker and his sweat-riddled body away.

Parker laughed as his lips finally made contact with his baby sister's perfectly made-up face. One of his biggest childhood joys had come from harassing Savannah. It was amazing that years later he still received the same pleasure from hearing her high-pitched, ultrafeminine scream.

"You love me and you know it," he said, moving away from her for the moment. He went to the sideboard in the dining room, where there was always a pitcher of iced tea or lemonade and iced water for the B&B's guests. He poured himself a glass of water and gulped it halfway down before turning to see where Savannah had gone.

"You think every female loves you," she was saying as she used a napkin to dab at the cheek where he'd no doubt left remnants of his sweat.

"And you're liable to tear your newly built knee apart with all that running you've been doing," she continued.

"Running is good therapy for my knee, thank you very much." He finished his water. "And all the females do love me," he joked.

Savannah frowned, an action that still didn't mar the
pure beauty she'd been blessed with. She was five years
younger than Parker, but he'd been the first of his brothers
to see the change in the little kid they'd all dismissed for
far too long. Everything about Savannah had blossomed at
once; in the span of one summer, she went from the annoying little brat of a sister to the cute and curvy girl who lived
in the big yellow house at the end of Sycamore Road. That's
precisely what he'd overheard Frankie Myers and Tim
Johnson calling her one day when they'd been playing bas-
ketball at the park. By the time Parker finished with those
two, they knew her name was Savannah and that if they so
much as thought about her curvy body again, they would
regret it.

The evolution of Savannah had not stopped that summer. Each day she had seemed to come further into the
woman she was meant to be, and although Parker had
been proud to see her on billboards and in magazines,
the protective brother in him had waited for the moment
some idiot guy hurt her. Because that would be the day
Parker Cantrell, homicide detective, went to jail for
murder.

"You're such a jerk. All guys are jerks!" she said vehemently.

Parker stared at her another second without speaking.
Something told him that day had finally come.

"Are we talking about a particular guy, or jerk, should
I say?"

She'd taken a seat in one of the cherrywood dining
room chairs and crossed her legs so the big skirt of her
dress fanned out around her. She looked as if she were
posing for a picture, the pale blue dress she wore giving
her sun-kissed skin an alluring sheen and those slanted
eyes giving him the once-over.

"No. I am not talking about any jerk in particular. All

of you share your piece of the jerk pie happily," she snapped.

Wow, she was in a mood today.

And if the mood was related to a man, Parker really wasn't the one to talk to Savannah about it. She normally went to Quinn with those issues because, in her words, "he has more class than you and Preston." Parker didn't agree. Although Quinn was the oldest, and he and Preston, as twins, tended to share the same outlook on things such as relationships, he didn't see how that made Quinn better than them. Four months ago, all three of the Cantrells were against formal, long-term relationships. Now, it was Preston and Quinn who were about to take the plunge into marriage. Parker was still holding on to his bachelor card, with a death grip!

"Well, he's an idiot to have done whatever he did to put that look on your face," Parker told her, hoping that would be enough to get this conversation over with.

"Who's an idiot and what look does Savannah have today?" Michelle asked, coming into the dining room with a fresh pitcher of water in her hands.

"Savannah does not have a look and Parker's the idiot for insinuating I did," Savannah huffed.

"Good, because we have a busy day today. The parade starts in an hour, then we have that picnic lunch to deliver to city hall for that big town council meeting with the Redling brothers, and then we need to be down at the pier an hour before the festival begins tonight."

Michelle talked as she moved. She'd pulled a cloth out of her apron pocket and wiped the sideboard down before replacing the water. Then she'd turned and wiped the dining room table, which hadn't really needed any wiping. She was straightening chairs and giving them the rundown of today's schedule all at the same time. A better multitasker Parker had never seen.

"Why do we have to cater the Redling brothers meeting?" Savannah asked with another frown. "They're our competition, remember?"

"For one, they paid us," was Michelle's reply.

"And for two, it's much better to keep your enemy close," Parker added. "What better way to find out what they're up to than to be at the meeting?"

Savannah frowned. "But we're cooking for the meeting, like hired help."

"You don't cook a thing," Michelle told her. "And we're not just cooking, we're also serving, because those Redlings think they're so smart and so much classier than we poor townsfolk are. They wanted a fully catered lunch, table service included. Which means the three of us, me, you, and Raine, will be in the same room with them, serving *and* listening."

"And tomorrow morning she'll cook us waffles, scrambled eggs with cheese, and scrapple as we all sit down to hear your recap of said meeting," Parker added, his stomach growling at the mention of Michelle cooking breakfast.

Parker would have loved his oldest sister anyway since they shared the same blood, but the fact that she was almost as good a cook as their late grandmother earned her a very special place in his heart. If ever he did consider settling down with a woman, she'd have to be able to cook. That didn't make him some kind of chauvinist, he just liked to eat good food and was sadly inept at preparing it for himself.

"I see the breakfast menu has already been made," Michelle announced with a chuckle.

Parker only shrugged. "With Quinn and Preston out of the house, I'm the only man left, so I figure I've moved up on the totem pole enough to make breakfast suggestions."

"You're not the only man here. Mr. Sylvester is right

down the hall doing Lord knows what in that room," Savannah added. "He's been out and about a little more frequently lately. Have either of you noticed that? And when he comes out he smells like some god-awful cologne. I think he bathes in it."

Of course, Savannah was frowning. Parker laughed as he moved closer to tweak her nose. "Nothing's ever good enough for you, is it, sunshine?"

"Leave Mr. Sylvester alone. I think it's good that he's getting out. I was afraid he'd rot away in that back room thinking about Gramma. She wouldn't want that for him. So if he's getting out and living his life, I'm happy for him. And he loves my waffles," Michelle added with a satisfied smile.

Savannah stood, huffing once more. "Yes, everybody loves Michelle's cooking. And they love how wonderful Quinn is with the patients down at the clinic. Drew's mother is even raving about Preston's help in that lawsuit she was trying to pursue. And you, the famous Double Trouble Cantrell brother, can do no wrong, especially since you ran your bike into a tree and busted up your knee. I swear, living in this house is like living under the Sweetland Perfection Umbrella."

She stormed out of the room before Parker or Michelle could say anything to her. Instead they looked at each other in question.

"She's getting worse," Parker said quietly, shaking his empty glass so that the ice cubes clanked together.

Michelle sighed. "I know. If she holds whatever is bothering her in any longer, she's going to explode."

Parker was shaking his head. "And that's not going to be good."

"No. It's not going to be good. And it's not going to be easy. Whatever happened to her hurt her deeply. She's running from something, and she's afraid to confront whatever it is. I can't stand to see her that way," Michelle said quietly.

For all they fought like cats and dogs, Michelle loved Savannah, probably more than any of the rest of her siblings, since she'd practically helped Gramma raise her.

"I know. Raine's worried and frowning because she doesn't know how to help her," Parker said.

Michelle gave a slight smile. "Raine's always worried and frowning, Parker, you know that."

They both chuckled.

"It's good to be back home," he said suddenly.

Michelle stopped moving and folded her arms over her chest. She looked so much like Gramma, Parker couldn't stand to look at her sometimes. Her mocha skin tone, high cheekbones, and warm smile did something to him each time he saw her. It brought back memories, and those memories were painful. He loved his sister, but damn, he wished she looked more like their mother or even their father, just not Gramma.

"It's good to have all of you back home. Now that Preston and Quinn are staying, I can't help but hope the rest of you find your place here."

Parker hadn't said all that. Even though of each of his brothers, he was probably the only one who'd arrived in Sweetland without a definite date to return to the city and his job, and without a longing to do so, either. "I don't know about all that," he told her. "And you shouldn't get your hopes up. Savannah's always wanted to fly away, and I do have a job in the city." For whatever that was worth, he thought.

"I know. But whatever Savannah flew away to before is what hurt her so bad she's scared to leave here now. I'm hoping she'll finally wake up and see she could be happy right here in Sweetland." She moved to stand in front of Parker then, cupping a palm to his still sweat-damp cheek. "And you, there's something going on with you, too. But if there's one thing I know about this brother of mine, it's that he doesn't run from his problems. He faces everything head-on and then pushes it right out of his way. It's just a matter of time before Sweetland opens up a place for you, too. Just watch and see."

Michelle left him alone then, with her words wafting through the air as only homegrown advice can. Michelle was much wiser than her thirty-four years. She was stronger and more independent than any of them had ever had to be. And she'd found her place in Sweetland while the rest of them had moved on. He admired her for that, wanting to know if what she had could be bottled and stored for later use, because right at this moment Parker had no idea where his place was. No idea at all.

The Labor Day Festival was one of Sweetland's more subdued celebrations, if there was such a thing. In comparison with Bay Day and the winter wonderland makeover the town endured for the entire month of December, this was the calmest. For that reason it was also Drew's favorite.

She'd dressed in a comfortable coral-colored sundress that cupped her breasts, then fell loosely to her ankles. Her sandals had a three-inch wedge heel that was both fashionable and easy to walk in. After twisting her hair into a French braid she prayed was neat as well as stylish, she grabbed her small purse, slipped on her sunglasses, and headed out the back door. Because she lived on the floor above her shop, she parked her car in the back driveway. Well, it wasn't actually a driveway since the majority of her yard had been converted into her personal garden, but there was still enough room for her to pull in her old blue-candy-colored Fiesta.

As soon as she started the engine, Drew switched on

the air-conditioning. This summer had been particularly hot in Sweetland, with more than thirty days of consecutive ninety-five-plus-degree temperatures that had forced everyone to spend a small fortune in electric bills trying to keep air conditioners and fans running. It had been especially hard on Drew, as she'd also had to deal with morning sickness. She was secretly hoping for fall to make its appearance with much cooler temperatures.

The drive down to the dock was short, and before she had a chance to really enjoy the cool interior of her car, she was pulling into the parking lot beside The Crab Pot. In her purse she'd put a handkerchief, one that had belonged to her grandfather. She pulled it out and traced her finger lovingly over the black monogram a second before using it to dab at the dampness on her forehead.

After pulling down the sun visor, she flipped the mirror upward to survey her face. "He's going to think you're a sweat-riddled lunatic if you don't cut it out," she warned herself.

Then she took a couple of deep, steadying breaths. She closed her eyes and whispered a silent prayer.

"Just let me get through this. Everything will be fine once I get this over with," she began. "And please, if he's going to be an ass about this, let him keep it to himself." She clenched and unclenched her fists. "I don't know how civil I'll be able to remain if he doesn't."

Before someone could walk by and catch her talking to herself, Drew climbed out of the car and headed down to the dock, where people had already begun to gather. Normally the pier looked slightly deserted, as only three restaurants occupied the space that stretched for almost two miles before dropping off into the Miles River. Charlie's Bar & Grille, The Crab Pot, and Amore Italian Restaurant were the only waterfront places to eat in Sweetland, but Drew suspected that would change soon. Sweetland was growing in both tourism and development. And both were adding to the success of her flower shop, so she wasn't about to complain.

Today the pier was decorated in red, white, and blue. Earlier, Mr. Flannery had brought her and her flowers down, and she'd decorated the U.S. flag float that remained stationary at the east entrance to the pier. Additionally, she'd designed eight large potted arrangements that were placed in measured intervals up and down the wood-planked walkway, with balloon bouquets attached to them. There were also booths set up along the pier so that it looked more like a carnival than a festival. Some booths held games, while others sold corn dogs and fried dough. One booth in particular, which Drew made a mental note to visit at some point this evening, advertised delicious fried sweets. She'd been tempted by their sign, and her stomach had growled—even though she wasn't sure whatever fried sweets they sold were going to sit well with her newly temperamental digestive system.

The day couldn't have been prettier, with picture-perfect sunshine amid a clear, cotton-candy-blue sky. Someone said the weather had cooled down because they were expecting a thunderstorm later that night, but as Drew continued to walk, she couldn't really tell. The air was still stifling, and she suddenly wished for one of those over-the-top fans her mother liked to carry around.

"Aren't you looking pretty as a peach," Marabelle Stanley said as she cut right in front of Drew's path.

Drew had been so focused on tonight's objective and getting to the nearest stand offering the coolest drink, she hadn't even seen Sweetland's gossip duo approach. Huge error on her part.

"Thank you, Mrs. Stanley," she said, mustering up the nicest fake smile she could.

Marabelle Stanley was a short, round woman with

raven-black hair and a buttery skin complexion. She was married to Sam Stanley, an ex-Marine who preferred to spend his twilight years sitting on the back porch of his house rather than traipsing around Sweetland socializing as his wife did. Marabelle's partner in crime was Louisa Kirk—the woman who was now staring at Drew as if she could see right through her sundress to the small protrusion at her waist that had already started to grow, hence the reason she was forced to do what she had to do tonight.

"Actually, you're looking a little pale. Are you feeling all right, dear?" Louisa asked to Drew's chagrin.

Both these women made her uncomfortable. They were old enough to feel justified in saying whatever they pleased, whenever it suited them, and just evil enough to think what they said mattered to whomever they chose to say it to. Normally, Drew avoided them like the plague, and she inwardly berated herself for not being more careful today. She'd known they would be here; there wasn't a function in Sweetland they missed—whether or not they were invited.

"I'm feeling just fine, Mrs. Kirk. And how are you this lovely evening?" Years of living in a town only a fraction bigger than Sweetland had prepared her for the cattiness-with-a-smile mentality here. And in the time since she'd been here, she'd had to put on her own shield only three or four times. And most of those times had been in the company of these two women.

"All our hard work is paying off. It's nice to see the townsfolk enjoying the event they barely have time to plan for," Louisa immediately began. "That's the problem with young folk, they never want to put in the work it takes to make something special. Always looking for the easy way out or a shortcut of some type, never considering that hard work might actually lead to something good. You know what I mean, don't you, Drewcilla?" she asked her pointedly.

Louisa was a couple of inches taller than Marabelle. Her thick, broader build added to her more intimidating demeanor, and her heavily made-up face made for a cooler presentation whenever she was around. She too was married to a veteran, named Granger, who didn't like being with her any more than Stanley did Marabelle.

"I think the town is certainly thriving, Mrs. Kirk. I happen to know for a fact that the Cantrells together with me, Pia Delaney, and Delia Kincaid put a lot of effort into making tonight a success. And we have Mayor Fitzgerald to thank for reaching out to all the new sponsors we received this year. This year's celebration has been a collaborative effort that I'm sure will pay off for the entire town."

There, that should shut her up, Drew thought triumphantly.

"And speaking of the Cantrells, there's the most popular one of them now," Louisa remarked snidely, nodding her floppy-hat-covered head in the direction behind Drew.

Marabelle began to wave her hand excitedly. "Oh, he's such a handsome fella. The best-looking one of the bunch, if you ask me. And that's saying something, since Quinn and Preston are lookers as well."

Cantrells. Best-looking one of the bunch. Quinn and Preston are lookers as well. That left only one Cantrell brother remaining. Drew's heart beat a rhythm that almost matched the one the barbershop quartet down a few booths was singing. Her skin suddenly felt clammy, sweat rolling in slow, annoying lines down her back and between the swells of her breasts. She swallowed deeply and was just giving herself a count of ten to calm her nerves when he spoke.

"Good evening, ladies. It's a wonderful evening for a

carnival. Everything down here looks good," he said to Louisa's and Marabelle's pleasure.

Then to Drew's horror he touched a hand to her waist as he walked around so that he was now standing in front of her.

"Yes, everything here is looking extremely good. . . ." His deep voice rolled over her like a fresh wave of humidity, and Drew clenched her hands at her sides.

"Hello, Parker," she finally managed, because otherwise she would feel like a 100 percent idiot, instead of a 50 percent one.

"Hello, Drew," was his slow and sultry reply.

Dammit, nothing about this evening was going as she'd planned.

Parker smiled down at her, keeping his hand at her waist—and the body that had been going through its own round of changes in the last few weeks changed once more. Her discomfort shifted to warm desire as she continued to stare up at him. The practiced speech melted to nonexistence in her mind as she inhaled his cologne. He was dangerous, she'd known that the night she'd been out with Delia, having drinks at Charlie's. He was too good-looking to be safe, and he was the father of the baby growing inside of her.

To say Drew was screwed was an understatement—a gross understatement that made her temples throb.

Chapter 3

He'd waited months to get his hands on her again. Damn
if those months hadn't seemed like years. And even if the
touch was as simple as his hand on her waist, it was enough
to send blood soaring through Parker's body to rest soundly
in his groin, where an erection was inevitable.

His attraction to Drewcilla Sidney had hit him hard
one night, and he'd presumed it was the result of the trio
of rum and Cokes Charlie had served him. But the next
evening, when he was completely sober and on his way to
the bar, he'd seen her going into The Crab Pot. Of course
he'd followed, he'd had no other choice. Watching her
work that night—bringing drinks to tables, leaning over
said tables to roll out paper for the customers having
crabs, laughing so that her eyes were alight with joy, her
hair hanging in lazy curls down her back—had proven
one point. His desire for her was not alcohol induced, and
it wasn't going away easily.

This evening her hair was pulled back from her face,
giving Parker an unfettered view of pretty brown eyes
and elegantly arched brows. She licked her lips, then nib-
bled on the bottom one for a split second before squaring

her shoulders and looking directly at him. If he weren't a man, a decorated homicide detective at that, he might have said her actions made him just a bit dizzy with desire.

Instead of actually owning up to that, Parker cleared his throat. "You look really pretty tonight," were the words that tumbled from his mouth.

They sounded so juvenile, so spontaneous, and yet possibly contrived. He mentally kicked himself for not coming up with something better. For weeks he'd been waiting for the moment, to not only get his hands on her again, but to have the chance to speak to her without her running away. And now that the moment seemed to have arrived, this was what he'd said?

"Thank you," she said about a second before she took a step back so that his hand fell from her waist.

"You act like you two have never met," Louisa said to Drew. "When I know that can't be true, since I specifically remember seeing you climb onto the back of that noisy monstrosity he drives around here like he owns the town."

Parker was used to Louisa's abrupt candor, or at least he'd become reacquainted with it in the weeks he'd been back. Louisa and Marabelle frequented The Silver Spoon restaurant at least twice a week. He suspected it was as much to fuel more of their gossip as it was for the food. In the times he'd seen them there, he'd also overheard some of their conversations, where no one was exempt. His family was one of their hot topics, so Louisa's comment was no shock to him.

As for Drew, well, the mortified look on her face said she was feeling differently.

"I'm always available to give a young lady a ride home when needed, Mrs. Kirk. You wouldn't have wanted me to leave Drew to walk home alone, would you?" he asked, tearing his eyes away from Drew only long enough to lock gazes with Louisa. If not, the woman would believe she had the upper hand.

Louisa shook her head. "She has a car. A very bright little thing looks like a buggy. She keeps it parked in her backyard all the time, but I see it whenever she zips up Main Street on her way down here to help her uncle out at his crab shack."

And Parker needed to know all that information. It was a good thing he already knew the details Louisa had just divulged about Drew's personal life and an even better thing he wasn't some deranged stalker. If he were, that information could have put Drew in danger. Of course, that was his cop's mind thinking, but that didn't make it any less true.

"I think it's good that a couple have a practical car and then something completely whimsical and a little dangerous," Marabelle said with a smile to Parker. "Besides, that bike of yours is kind of hot."

She whispered the word *hot* as if it might have actually been a sin to say it and if heard, she would justly burn in the fiery pits of hell.

"We're not a couple," Drew stated adamantly, her eyes widening as she looked from Marabelle to Parker pleadingly.

Parker cleared his throat. "She's right, we're not a couple, Mrs. Stanley. But I think my bike's kind of hot, too."

Marabelle smiled at that. Louisa frowned, and Drew, well, she looked as if she might actually faint. A hand went to her neck, fingers shaking, and another brushed past her stomach and then fell to her side. But it was the clammy look of her skin that really concerned Parker and spurred him into action.

"Ladies, it's been lovely visiting with you, but I really need to get Drew alone for just a second." He thought about how that comment would be perceived by these two women and decided to add, "Michelle's looking for her to talk about purchasing more flowers for the inn."

"Oh yes, the bouquets in the church sanctuary are beautiful, dear," Marabelle told Drew. "You two run along, I can't wait to see what you come up with for the inn. Tell Michelle we'll be there tomorrow night for dinner as usual."

"I will," Parker said with a nod. He stepped toward Drew then because she hadn't moved.

"You look sick, Drewcilla," Louisa spoke up from behind Parker. "Maybe you should call your brother over here, Parker. Instead of trying to drag the girl off somewhere."

Drew shook her head then. "No. I'm fine, really I am," she said, attempting to pull away from Parker's grasp once more.

This time Parker leaned in to whisper in her ear. "Either go along with me and make an easy escape from these two, or stand here and try to fight whatever is bothering you and them at the same time. It's your choice."

She clamped her lips shut and swallowed deeply.

"Let's go, Parker. I don't want to keep Michelle waiting," she said finally.

With an arm resting around her waist once more—a position that felt oddly comfortable to Parker—they walked down the pier away from the town gossips. The wind blew and he inhaled the sweet scent of her perfume, a scent he remembered well from their night together. The night he'd dreamt of for the past few months, wondering, hoping, and quite possibly needing a repeat.

Obviously that was not Drew's intention, as she'd been dedicated to keeping her distance from him since that fateful night.

"I'm fine," she said in a soft voice.

So soft that he almost didn't hear her over his own thoughts.

"Let's go over here and have a seat. You were looking a little off, so I just want to make sure you're okay," he told her as he steered them toward a duo of red-painted benches situated on the side of Amore between huge shrubs and a quaint little fountain.

The benches faced the water, so they had a good view of the waning sunlight as they sat. Drew immediately went to the far end of the first bench, resting her elbow on the arm and holding her head down.

Each time, since the first time, that Parker had seen Drew, she'd been laughing or smiling or otherwise looking as if living life were the most precious thing to her. She had this kind of carefree spirit that he'd admired, at first, from afar. Whether it was her uncle Walt or the group of older men who sat at his counter for a good part of the evening, shooting the breeze and joking with her, or Delia and Pia having drinks with her—as they had the night they'd spent together—she'd always looked to be enjoying herself. And others looked as if they enjoyed her company. Parker had wanted to be one of them, to be among those lucky enough to spend time with such an affable and attractive female. Especially since he felt lately as though his life were on a downward spiral.

However, Parker did not like the look Drew had now. She was breathing deeply, as if each breath were a struggle, and tiny beads of sweat peppered her forehead, causing the wisps of hair there to stick. And when she looked up at him, her eyes were wide, excited, but her shoulders sagged as if she were carrying a tremendous weight. He was confused and he was worried and he wanted to know what the hell was going on with her.

Still standing, Parker moved until he was in front of Drew. Squatting, he lifted her hands into his again and spoke softly. "You can tell me what's wrong, Drew. If you're sick, I'll get Quinn or I'll take you to the hospital in Easton. If you just need to get out of here for a while, I can do that, too. Just talk to me," he pleaded.

"I'm fi—" she started to say before standing abruptly. "I need the bathroom."

Her words were strained, and Parker stood with her. "Sure. Let's get you inside." He walked with her, moving quickly.

When they arrived at the small entryway to Amore, he guided her up the steps and into the foyer of the restaurant. Parker held her hand this time, walking right beside her, waving to Salvatore Gionelli, the owner of the restaurant, as they passed by the hostess quickly.

At the doorway to the ladies' room, Drew pulled out of his grasp.

"I said I'm fine, Parker," she told him again with more than a little agitation in her tone.

"You're obviously not fine," he countered, trying to keep his voice down because a few other people had come into the restaurant behind them.

Drew dragged her hands over her face and took another deep breath. "I'm trying to go to the bathroom and you're on my back like you intend to go with me," she said through gritted teeth.

"I'm worried about you," he admitted.

She shook her head. "Don't be. I can take care of myself."

"I know that, but I'm still worried," he admitted, taking a step closer.

"I'm fi—" she started to say once more, but Parker put his hand up to her lips to stop her.

"Don't tell me you're fine again. You definitely are not fine and I'm not leaving you alone until you tell me what's going on," he told her, growing steadily more impatient.

"You want to know what's wrong, Parker?" she asked almost defiantly. Her shoulders had squared, and she was staring into his eyes as if she were ready to haul off and slap him.

"I do," he admitted with more than a little caution.

Parker was almost positive Drew wasn't going to hit him. Physical violence didn't really fit her personality. Still, her eyes were looking a bit wide, her face was still too pale, and she was now clenching and unclenching her fists at her side. But he refused to back down because now, more than ever, he was certain something was going on with her.

"I'm pregnant, you idiot!" were the last words Parker heard her say before she turned and pushed into the ladies' room.

She was the idiot. A raving, nervous, sweating idiot!

Drew wanted to run to her car, to get inside and start the ignition and drive to her house—or possibly off the nearest cliff. She wanted to sink so far into the floor that Parker could never see her again. She wanted to disappear and . . .

Another pressing need prevailed and she moved quickly into the nearest stall, where the nausea she'd been feeling for the last fifteen minutes finally took over. Minutes later, she felt certain she could stand up straight and that there was nothing left in her stomach to revolt and/or escape. Drew stood, then on second thought leaned against the stall door, trying to steady her breathing.

Her words played over in her mind, as did Parker's, and she couldn't help groaning. This was not the way she'd wanted to tell him. It wasn't what she'd rehearsed. In fact, it was just about the worst possible scenario come true.

"If you stand in there any longer, I'm coming in."

Oh hell, was he really talking to her through the ladies' room stall? Of course he was. He was Parker Cantrell, which meant there was nothing that he didn't believe he could do and get away with.

"Perhaps you missed the sign that said LADIES. It's in big white letters on the door," she snapped.

She almost stomped her foot, she was so angry with herself for not following her plan, and at Louisa and Marabelle for holding her up so that she'd run into Parker before she was ready. And, of course, at Parker for . . . well, for being Parker!

"I know what the door says, Drew. What I'm really interested in is getting a replay of what you said just before you barged through the door."

He was speaking in a really calm tone. It didn't have the hint of laughter that his voice normally held. It was still deep and sexy as hell regardless.

A part of her wanted to retract her words and wait patiently until he believed her and left the bathroom before she came out of the stall. There were two problems with that scenario: First, Parker wouldn't believe her; and second, she'd never been a coward before and she wasn't about to start now.

So, taking a deep breath, Drew turned and slid the latch on the stall door to the side. Pulling on the door, she watched as Parker moved his well-built body back two steps, allowing her space to move forward. Drew gratefully took the space and headed directly to the sink, where she switched on the water and leaned forward to rinse her mouth. When she finished she was surprised to look into the mirror and see Parker standing behind her, offering her a paper towel.

For what felt like endless seconds, they only stared at each other. Then she turned to face him, accepting the paper towel and drying her hands and mouth. When that was done, Drew accepted that she had no choice but to look up at him once more.

It really wasn't a great hardship to stare at Parker Cantrell. He had a golden complexion, with hair so close cut that he almost looked bald. His eyebrows were dark, eyes even darker, strong jaw and chiseled arms like a wrestler, chest and abs like a bodybuilder. Today he wore jeans that weren't tight but fit his muscled thighs and legs perfectly and a white T-shirt that hugged all the amazing contours and ridges of his upper body. The short sleeves bared a portion of his biceps and his lower arms, roped with thick veins. He looked like a biker, a bad-ass biker boy who was trying his damnedest to keep a tight rein on his control.

Drew took a deep breath and asked, "Do you remember that night we were together?"

If it was possible, his eyes darkened even more. "I can't seem to think of anything else," was his reply.

She clasped her hands in front of her and, in an effort to hide her nervousness, silently dared them to move again.

"I doubt either one of us will ever forget that night," she said quietly.

"What are you trying to tell me, Drew?"

Parker crossed his arms over his massive chest so that he looked even more opposing. Only Drew wasn't intimidated by him, not in the least. Instead she was more than sorry to realize she was still unabashedly attracted to him.

"I'm trying to tell you that on that night, that hot sultry night . . ."

"We lay beneath that big old oak tree, staring up at the moon, and decided to sleep together," he finished for her.

Drew nodded. That's precisely what they'd done after they'd left Charlie's. He'd driven them down to Fitzgerald Park on his motorcycle. It had rained earlier that evening, so the air wasn't as thick with humidity, but the grass was still damp from the quick summer shower. Parker had carried her shoes in his hands as she'd walked around wiggling her toes against the cool blades of grass. They'd stopped at the oak tree and kissed. The kiss had turned so desperate, they'd ended up falling to the ground in an attempt to get each other undressed. Then she'd cracked an eye open, and that's when she'd seen it. Just over Parker's shoulder, the summer's moon had shone so big and bright. He'd paused to see what had grabbed her attention, and they'd stared up at the moon together.

Then she'd invited him back to her house.

"That night I wished on the summer's moon that you would make love to me," she told him.

"And I did," was his response.

"And we made a baby," she said simply. "I'm pregnant with your child, Parker."

There, she'd told him. Then she held her breath, waiting for his response. Instead the ladies' room door opened and in came none other than Louisa Kirk. Without a word, she raised her arm and slapped Parker over the shoulder with her purse.

"You haven't changed a bit, Parker Cantrell. Still chasing girls into whatever dark corner you can get them in to do your deeds. Shame on you!" she yelled.

Chapter 4

Drew was emotional and moody and speeding as she took the curve off Duncan to Old Towne Road on what felt like only her right-side tires. There was a screeching sound, rubber disagreeing with its intense contact with concrete, she was sure, but she didn't really care. She just wanted to get home, to find something to eat that wouldn't make a command performance that landed her face-to-face with the toilet once more, to take a hot shower and climb into bed to watch a great old black-and-white movie. That's what she really wanted.

What she didn't want was to have Parker Cantrell feeling any sort of pity for her or the baby she was carrying. She definitely did not want Louisa Kirk spreading rumors about her hooking up with Parker in the bathroom at Amore. And she almost certainly did not want to be pulled over by a cop. Not tonight, please not tonight.

As usual, her prayers went unanswered. Drew sighed heavily as she pulled her car over to the curb in acquiescence to the flashing lights on the police cruiser that pulled in right behind her. They were about a block away from her house, a very short block because Main Street had lots of breaks for quaint little alleyways that boasted antique benches, lovely trellises flanked with ivy, and other spaces that Drew considered cubbyholes for the seagulls once they'd found their meal at the dock. They made the town feel even smaller and just a bit more eclectic. A big city would never keep this type of space untouched, not for long, anyway. But here in Sweetland, the townspeople liked everything the way it had been the first day they were born, or so it seemed.

She sat in her car staring straight ahead and could see the swinging post sign in the shape of a clock, with TIMELESS ANTIQUES scribed over its face. As if she'd had no clue as to why she was stopped there, Drew jumped at the knock on her window. With another sigh—because what else was she going to do?—she pressed the button that operated the window and watched as it descended. Deputy Carl Farraway stood on the other side, his oily black hair curling around the edges of his hat and dark eyes assessing her a little too closely.

"Evenin', Drew," he said in a slow drawl.

When she'd first met him, she'd thought maybe he was from the South or maybe his parents were—which was strange, because his father was Sheriff Kyle Farraway and he didn't have any type of accent. Then, after a few months in town and a few times seeing him talking to the guys at The Crab Pot and at Charlie's, she'd realized Carl spoke that way only when he was talking to a female— correction, females in his age range. He spent a lot of time rolling his eyes and repeating "Yes, ma'am" and "No, ma'am" to Louisa and Marabelle.

"Hi, Carl," she said, unable to hide the lack of enthusiasm in her voice. Her stomach was doing some weird revolt thing that she'd never felt before, and her temples throbbed as if someone were poking spikes in them. In other words, she really needed to hurry up and get this over with. "I was speeding, I know. Can you just give me my ticket so I can go?"

He looked a little shocked at her words, so Drew tried to smile, or at least she moved her lips and hoped the action resulted in a smile.

"Well, I wasn't sure I was going to give you a ticket. Thought we'd talk a little about what had you speeding down the street in the first place. Is something wrong? Someone chasing you?"

Did he really just ask her if someone was chasing her? They lived in Sweetland, the land of the perpetual slow and relaxed mood. Nobody would ever chase her here, unlike what she'd gone through in Stratford.

"I'm fine," she replied quickly before memories had a chance to settle in, shifting her already dismal mood to the possible suicidal range. And yes, she was damn tired of telling people that she was "fine" tonight. "Just in a hurry."

But Carl was not.

He leaned over, resting his arm on the hood of her car, pushing his face through the half-open area of her window. Carl had a big head, literally and figuratively. It fit through the window she'd only partially opened, but it filled the space completely, as though it might even get stuck.

"In a hurry to get home? Why? Is someone there waiting for you?" he continued.

She shook her head, unable to reply since she'd been thinking about the unusual size of his head and wasn't sure what might actually come out of her mouth.

"I could give you an escort," he offered.

"Or you can just give me a warning about speeding and let me be on my way," she countered, since he seemed to be in a giving mood.

"Or he can get back into his cruiser and pretend like he never pulled you over," another male voice countered.

A male voice she'd never wanted to hear again. Okay,

not that serious, she just didn't really want to hear it again tonight, but unfortunately . . .

Carl moved back from the car to stare at Parker. Carl was a couple of inches taller than Parker, who was easily more than six feet tall. They stood glaring at each other as if it were a face-off instead of a simple traffic stop, and Drew found herself getting out of her car instead of pulling off as she probably should have done.

She opened her mouth to speak, then closed it so fast and hard that her teeth chattered. She'd been about to tell Parker she was fine and that he could stand down from this Mr. Protector role she assumed he was trying to pull. He hadn't said another word since his comment to Carl, but his partially spread legs, clenched fists at his sides, and that chest—why, oh why, was it so broad and so muscled and so tempting, even in this uncomfortable situation?—spoke volumes.

"She was speeding, almost turned her car over when she took that corner," Carl told Parker. "And last time I checked, I wore the badge in this town."

Parker was a cop, a detective, if she remembered correctly. He worked for the Baltimore City Police Department and had been there since he'd left Sweetland after graduating from high school. Word around town was that he was some sort of big shot in the city, a high-profile crime fighter just like his twin, Preston, who used to be a defense attorney in the city. These days, Preston was spending more time working on the additions to his little blue house than he was in the courtroom. Three weeks ago, when Dale Connor was rear-ended just off I-33, Preston had been the first person he'd called. Drew and a lot of others around town figured it wouldn't be long before Preston officially opened his own firm in Sweetland.

As for Parker, well, as Carl had stated so clearly, he wore the badge in this town.

"That car weighs about as much as she does," Parker told Carl, clearly not giving a damn who wore what around here. "If she goes over thirty, she's liable to tip the damned thing over."

"She was doing well over thirty," was Carl's comeback as he took a step closer to Parker.

Parker didn't move. "You clock her?"

Carl didn't flinch. "I know when someone's speeding in my town."

Parker smiled. No, he smirked. "And that's the most action you've seen in this town, is that about right, Deputy?"

"Speeding ticket or a warning, whatever, but I'd like to get on with it before I'm too old to drive again," Drew finally interrupted.

Both men turned their heads quickly in her direction, as if for the first time realizing she was standing there. The brilliant day had turned into a sultry evening, the streetlights shining bright along the stretch and back around Olde Towne Square. Lightning bugs buzzed around blinking, mosquitoes were on the prowl, and in the center of the street two grown men stood toe-to-toe like high school rivals. Drew wondered if there was some history between Carl and Parker she'd never heard about, then quickly dismissed the notion. She didn't care what was going on between them, she wanted to go home.

"You're not getting a ticket. Get back in the car," Parker instructed her.

Not to be outdone, Carl quickly added, "She is getting a ticket for driving too fast and almost flipping her car over."

"There's no ordinance for almost flipping a car over, Farraway," Parker told him.

Drew suspected he'd purposely switched from calling

him "Deputy" to calling him by his last name. The frown on Carl's face said her suspicion was most likely true.

Now it was Carl's turn to smile, or smirk, or whatever. The action wasn't nearly as arousing on him as it had been on Parker. "It's called reckless driving, Cantrell. I'd think you big-city cops would know your law a little better," Carl said with obvious satisfaction.

And because Parker was not to be outdone, he replied, "I'm a detective, not a traffic cop."

Another second, another couple of words, and Drew figured these two would come to blows. Her money was on Parker, but Carl looked madder than a swarm of bees, so she stepped forward until she was between them, facing Carl.

"Just write the ticket, Carl. I won't contest it," she told him.

"He doesn't have to issue a ticket. He can let you go with a warning," Parker said from behind her.

His hard body had pressed against her back, much closer than she thought when she'd originally come between the two men. Her pulse raced as if on cue, and she swallowed slowly.

"He's right, I was speeding." Although she couldn't recall her exact driving speed, she figured it had to be at least as fast as her heart was beating at this moment. And it was hotter out here. She could feel heat rising right up her spine, settling at the nape of her neck. "I'll just take that ticket now."

"Let her go, Farraway," Parker spoke again.

"Right after I write her ticket," Carl tossed at him before going to his cruiser to get his ticket book.

He hadn't brought the book with him when he'd first come to her window, which made Drew realize he hadn't intended to give her a ticket until Parker had showed up.

"Why are you here?" she asked, whirling around to

face him. "He was going to let me go before you showed up, getting all in his face like some overgrown bully."

"He was going to let you go if you let him follow you home," he replied dryly. "Is that what you wanted?"

"No, it's not what I—" Her words were cut short as Carl returned, tearing a ticket from the pad and handing it to her.

Parker intercepted it. "I'll take care of this," he said to Carl, whose lips instantly tightened into a thin line.

His eyebrows drew close, and Drew thought he was going to spit fire out of his flaring nostrils. Good grief, there must have been some serious feud between these two.

"You got thirty days to pay it, Cantrell. Be sure to do so before you skip town."

Carl didn't stay for another round but turned on his heel and headed to his car. Parker glared at him the entire time, until the police cruiser pulled away from the curb, made a U-turn, and headed back down toward Olde Town Square. While he wasn't paying attention, Drew reached up and snatched the ticket from his hand.

"I'll take care of my own tickets, thank you very much." It was her turn not to wait for a response as she jumped into her car and sped off, praying desperately for mercy.

But when she looked in her rearview mirror, she mumbled a curse. Parker was right behind her on that infamous motorcycle of his, following her like a stalker.

No, not like that. Not again.

Still, he was following her, and she didn't like it.

"There are laws against stalking, Parker," Drew told him after she'd parked and gotten out of her car.

She'd waited while he'd pulled his bike up to park alongside the driver's side before getting out and saying what she'd thought would be her good-bye to him. But, as he suspected, Drew Sidney didn't know him well at all.

"We need to talk," he said simply.

Although she looked resigned to his statement, she replied, "I'm really not up for this tonight. I don't feel well. It's hot and I'm hungry and I'm just way too irritated to talk right now."

"Then I'll see you inside, fix you something cool to drink, maybe get you something to eat," he suggested, knowing she was already searching for another excuse.

She sighed. "You don't have to do this, Parker," she told him. "I didn't tell you about the baby to put any pressure on you. I can handle this on my own."

"Give me your key," he said simply. She looked surprised, as if she were waiting for another response. Of course she was. She hadn't anticipated he'd follow her home from the festival, hadn't assumed he'd give a damn about what she'd just told him. He was Parker Cantrell, after all, the reckless and impulsive Cantrell, the one the members of this town had never expected to amount to anything. For those exact reasons and a few more of his own, Parker stood in Drew's backyard, inhaling the undeniable scent of flowers, lots of flowers, and getting mosquito bites on the backs of his legs. He held his hand out and didn't say another word until she sighed once more and handed him the keys, her house key already singled out.

Parker unlocked the back door and stood to the side to let her go in first. When the door was closed behind him, he followed her up the stairs in what soon became a very familiar trek to her apartment. The last time he'd been here, it had been a hot night just like tonight. The stairway was narrow, so they had to travel single file. At the end of the flight of stairs, there would be two turnoffs. Drew made a right turn, and he followed.

She switched on a lamp and he had to blink to keep his focus. Drew Sidney liked something else as much as she liked flowers—colors. He remembered the walls in the flower shop were some shade of purple, light but still girly. This room was her living room, as evidenced by the futon propped against the far wall with its rainbow array of pillows. There was what he guessed served as her coffee table, sitting in front of the yellow futon. The table was a polar bear lying on its back, its legs holding up a thick slab of stained glass. There was a fluffy yellow-and-white rug on the floor, which was in stark contrast with the red-painted walls. Knickknacks were a popular feature along with shelf after shelf full of DVDs and CDs.

"Do you want something to drink?"

Her voice cut through his perusal of her house, and he nodded. "Sure, whatever you're having will be fine."

"You don't have to take a beer hiatus on my account. I know you like to drink," she told him before she disappeared through another doorway.

Parker used that moment to move to one of the shelves, running his finger along the spines of a section of DVDs. He wasn't a movie buff by any stretch. That would be his younger sister Raine's department. But he recognized some of the names he saw, a couple of the titles, and smiled because he couldn't recollect ever actually watching any of these movies in his lifetime. He preferred watching movies in color and wondered why Drew didn't, considering her decorating tastes. There were pictures on her wall, black-and-white shots of the major city skylines.

"We can talk now if you want," she said, and Parker turned around to see her moving pillows from the futon to sit down.

A quick glance around the room showed him the only other probable seats were a huge black beanbag chair and another black chair with no arms that resembled a rocking horse instead of a piece of furniture. He moved to sit beside her on the futon, being careful not to crowd her because she looked as if she'd had about all she could take for one day.

He was trying to respect that, trying not to push, which was usually his way when he wanted something. At the moment, he wasn't sure why he was taking this route with Drew when he'd never done this with anyone else in his life, but he figured it was the right thing to do regardless.

She handed him a beer, and Parker took a deep swallow.

"That night we were together," he started, then stopped. He really didn't know what to say to her. One would think a thirty-three-year-old man who was not a stranger to women would know how to sit on a couch and talk to one, but right now he was kind of coming up blank. No, that wasn't it. He had things he wanted to say, he just didn't know how to say them or how Drew would react if or when he did.

"I didn't plan to sleep with you, if that's what you're thinking. I'm not trying to trap you," she said.

Shocked at her words, Parker looked over to her. With both hands, she was holding a glass of water filled with ice cubes. Thin wisps of hair were matted to her forehead where she'd begun to sweat from the heat, while the rest of the dark brown strands hung down her back, still twisted in some fashion. Her skin looked creamy, if a bit damp. She stared down at the glass, but from the side he could see her long lashes as she blinked, the tip of her pert nose, the soft curve of her lips.

"I pursued you, Drew, so I know you weren't trying to trap me." He took a deep breath. "And for the record, what I was going to say was that I apologize for not protecting you. I never forget. Ever. But that night."

She began to nod. "I know. I don't usually forget. I mean, I don't do what we did often, but when I do, I don't forget. Ever."

Parker took another drink of his beer, wondering how

his mouth could get so dry so quickly. "I take care of my responsibilities," he said solemnly.

"You don't have to do me any favors," she snapped.

He watched her lean forward and place her glass on the table. Never in his wildest dreams would he have expected her to say that.

"Look, Parker, I'm well aware of who you are and of the type of man you are. I know you have a life in Baltimore and that you were only in town for your grandmother's funeral. I don't plan to ask you for anything for this baby."

"For *our* baby?" he asked, his voice low, his fingers tightening around the neck of the bottle. "You're not asking me to help you take care of our baby, is that what you're telling me?"

She rubbed her hands down her thighs and looked over at him. "That's exactly what I'm telling you."

Parker laughed. He knew it wasn't what she expected. Hell, it wasn't what he expected. None of this was. Since the moment she'd said those words to his face in that bathroom, so many things had been going through his mind. All the women, all the one-night stands, all the nights and then the mornings when he gave some reason to leave if he hadn't done so already. Everything he'd ever thought he knew about himself had come crashing down in that moment. He still didn't know how he felt about that.

But there was one thing he did know—Mary Janet Cantrell hadn't raised a deadbeat. He was a man, and as long as he played in the world doing manly things, he intended to take full responsibility for the repercussions of his actions. No matter what those repercussions were.

"Like I said, I take care of my responsibilities. *Our* baby is *our* responsibility."

He reached for her hand then, not really caring if that was what she was expecting or not. Parker was quickly realizing that life didn't exactly go along as planned, no matter how much you convinced yourself otherwise.

"Right," she said quietly, looking down at their entwined hands as if she were seeing a ghost. "Listen, I'm really tired and I have lots to do tomorrow."

"Tomorrow is Sunday. The flower shop is closed on Sundays," Parker said. He knew this because in the months that she'd been moving around town trying to avoid him at every turn, he had done a little bit of stalking where she was concerned. He knew the hours of the flower shop and the days and times she went down to The Crab Pot to help her uncle. He knew that on Sundays her mother would stop by and they'd end up at The Silver Spoon for brunch. Parker was on puppy duty on Sunday afternoons, so he was rarely in the restaurant when they were, but he'd seen her. He saw her a lot, even when he wasn't looking for her.

"But you do look tired," he conceded, again trying not to push. "So how about we have dinner tomorrow?"

She was already pulling her hand away before he'd completed his question. Standing up quickly, she ran both hands down the front of her dress, then clasped them behind her back as she spoke. He couldn't help looking at her stomach, saw the small bulge he hadn't paid any attention to before, and felt something shift inside him.

"This is not why I told you, Parker. I just figured you should know that I was having your baby."

"Drew . . . ," he began, standing up to face her.

"No. Let me finish, please."

He nodded.

"I know you're not the relationship type of guy, and truth be told, I'm not looking for a commitment either. This wasn't what either of us planned, we both know that now. So fine, we'll do the grown up thing and take care of our child. But that's all there has to be between us. I want you to know that I'm okay with that."

She was intriguing. That's what he'd thought that first time he saw her working at The Crab Pot. Their gazes hadn't met because she'd been delivering drinks and crabs to tables. Her hair had been pulled so that it fell over her right shoulder, leaving the left side of her neck exposed. He liked the smoothness of her skin, the sleek line of her neck, and had imagined kissing her there. And a couple of hours later, he'd hoped he would be doing exactly that. But she hadn't given him that pleasure. Not that time or the many times thereafter. Preston had said Parker loved the chase because he'd never experienced it before. He figured that was true.

Right now, however, seeing this woman standing not four feet away from him, trying to be strong when he sensed she was afraid, giving him the okay to walk away and not feel guilty, he thought it wasn't the thrill of the chase that intrigued him. It was simply the woman.

"You have to eat, Drew. Both of us do. I'm simply suggesting we do it together."

She shook her head. "And I'm declining your offer."

Don't push. Don't push. It's not about the chase. Parker told himself this over and over again until the instinct to simply show up tomorrow with dinner in hand had subsided.

"I understand," he said, shocking himself probably as much as Drew. "But I will call you tomorrow to see how you're doing. We still need to talk about our plans for the future." When her eyes widened, he held up a hand. "Our separate plans, Drew. Separate but together for *our* baby."

They'd both said it, and Parker still couldn't believe it. They were having a baby. He and Drew Sidney were going to be parents.

After he'd left Drew's place and was driving the Suzuki around the streets of town, he thought about how his siblings were going to react to that little announcement.

Chapter 5

Parker walked through the door not knowing what to expect. He'd drawn his gun because the lock had been completely busted. Amateur burglars had been his first instinct, but once inside and using the flashlight from his utility belt, he caught a quick glimpse of the mess that had been made of his apartment. The sofa and leather recliner had been ripped to shreds, miniblinds torn from the window and crushed. As each step brought him deeper into the apartment, more glass crumbled beneath his feet, and he saw that the doors to his entertainment center had been shattered, DVDs and CDs strewn across the floor.

Then he heard a sound coming from the bedroom, and adrenaline pumped loud and fierce in his ears. His blood pulsated and the hunger of the chase ignited a new strength in him. He moved with sure steps, arms raised, gun in hand, ready to shoot the intruder first and ask questions later. With his foot lifted, he kicked open the bedroom door. Then he stepped inside, first to see words scrawled in red on his bedroom wall: "Dead men tell no tales." He almost smiled at the saying, a picture of Johnny Depp and the *Pirates of the Caribbean* immediately coming to mind. *Amateurs,* he thought once more, and was about to lower his weapon when movement from the left caught his eye. Parker took another quick step and turned, aiming his gun in that direction.

A man stood staring at him, the infamous can of spray paint in one hand, a baby in the other.

A baby?

The little cherublike face was scrunched, tears streaming down the plump cheeks as it let out a loud cry. Parker stopped, staring from the baby to the man and then back again. Something wasn't right. The feeling moved along his spine like a snake, sure to bring destruction or at least lots of pain in its wake. He lifted his gun arm again, aimed at the man, and was just about to ask what was going on when he was struck from behind. The next thing he saw was darkness. And a couple of hours later, he'd stared into the eyes of his commanding officer.

Then he'd been suspended from the force, and the next day Gramma had died.

Now, he lay in his bed, one hand still crossed behind his head, the other rubbing down his face as if that action would clear the remnants of the dream. Beside him, resting his head on the pillow to the right, was Rufus, the twenty-four-week-old Lab he'd inherited from his grandmother. After last week's visit to Dr. Bellini, Parker had to force himself not to refer to Rufus as a puppy any longer. At eighteen inches tall and fifty-one pounds, he was almost 75 percent of his adult size. That 75 percent occupied half of Parker's bed as if he were already an adult.

Parker had experienced lots of dreams in the last few weeks, followed by anxiety attacks that almost choked him. Attacks he kept from his family out of embarrassment. Only Rufus knew about the attacks, as the dog had witnessed more than a few of them. When Rufus was around and Parker had an attack, the dog would promptly plant his chin on Parker's knee, looking up at him with chocolate-brown eyes that Parker was told had been blue when he was born. Parker would rub Rufus's broad head with a shaking hand, breathing deeply until the attack finally passed. Afterward, Rufus would almost immediately want to go out and play, a task that Parker found relaxed him as well as accommodated his dog.

When he and his siblings had first learned of their inheritance, The Silver Spoon B&B and restaurant and the Labrador puppies, many of them had been skeptical about keeping them. Gramma had obviously foreseen this and left an out clause in her will—if they didn't want to keep the puppy, they had to at least find it a loving and caring home. To date, none of them had parted with their puppies, even though Preston had tried to put his up for adoption and Savannah cursed hers every day, all day. Parker was very content with Rufus, admitting only to himself that the dog filled a void that had been in his life for far too long.

As for the anxiety attacks, the doctor at Capitol City Hospital had advised Parker to contact someone if the attacks persisted, that maybe he was suffering from post traumatic stress syndrome and needed to be monitored. Parker hadn't thought of doing any such thing. He wasn't sick. Physically injured, yes: From the concussion in his apartment to the shattering of his knee in that stupid accident, his body had been brutally attacked. But there was nothing wrong with his mind.

And apparently other parts of his body worked just fine as well.

Drew Sidney was pregnant with his baby. He'd almost been about to ask himself how that happened, but he knew the answer to that question all too well. Parker had known that night they shared together wasn't going to simply evaporate from his memory, like many of his past sexual exploits. He'd known that morning as he'd made his way back to the B&B that sleeping with Drew Sidney had been different from any other sexual experience he'd ever had.

He'd never thought the difference would result in her becoming pregnant. But they'd both had a few drinks that night and had been caught up in the moment—so caught up, apparently, that they'd forgotten to use protection. He'd remembered that in the morning as well, when he'd arrived back at the B&B and had undressed to take his shower. He'd taken the wallet from his back pants pocket and flipped it open just out of curiosity. There were three condom packs in the back slit where he always kept them. The same three he'd had in his wallet since arriving in Sweetland. He'd cursed, closing his eyes to his irresponsibility, and immediately began thinking of how he'd apologize to Drew for not protecting her.

Dressing after his shower, he'd decided he would visit Drew later that evening down at The Crab Pot. She ran a flower shop, so the last thing she needed was him barging in on her at work. Besides, he was hoping for a repeat performance of the night before, this time without the aid of alcohol.

But that hadn't happened. Drew had totally ignored him at the restaurant and had actually slipped out the back door while he'd waited for her to get off. That had become the first of many times she'd avoided him, up to and including the day earlier this summer when she'd sat in the dining room of the B&B with her mother and acted as if she'd never met him before. If his siblings knew what he'd been through with Drew, they would undoubtedly say he was getting a dose of his own medicine and not liking it one bit. That's precisely why Parker hadn't told any of them. Now the circumstances had changed, drastically. He'd have to

tell his siblings, and he'd have to figure out what he and
Drew were going to do. Because Parker Cantrell was going
to be a father.

Most likely an unemployed father, but a father nonetheless.

"The Marina's grand opening is a few weeks away,"
Michelle said the moment all of them were seated in the
dining room on Sunday afternoon.

Their breakfast buffet had long since been cleaned,
and the Sunday brunch customers had all but filed out of
the Silver Spoon. Michelle had the beginnings of the dinner special—smothered pork chops, red-skinned mashed
potatoes, and asparagus spears—already started in the
kitchen. Customers were light enough in the restaurant
that she felt comfortable leaving Nikki's sister Cordy in
charge for the moment. Since Nikki and Quinn's engagement, the Brockingtons had been like extended family,
and since Cordy's husband, Barry, would be in Iraq until
late October, she'd been spending a lot of time at the
B&B. Her three kids loved the puppies, and the love was
reciprocated each time Josiah, Zyra, and Mimi came over
to play. Cordy had begun filling in at the restaurant when
Lisa, the intern, returned to college.

The *sous-chef* Michelle wanted to hire had already
accepted an internship in Europe, so the thought of help in
the kitchen was also out. Sure, her sister Raine had said she
was staying in Sweetland indefinitely and Savannah
seemed to be content to stay here, but that didn't qualify
either of them to do the jobs she needed done. But she didn't
want to dwell on that at the moment, didn't want to take a
second away from the time that she and all her siblings had
together.

"They're planning a huge party with live entertainment and fireworks," Savannah added. She was sitting in a chair, legs crossed and lips pouting, as usual.

Savannah was the youngest of the Cantrell siblings. She was hands down the prettiest and had proven that point by leaving town the moment she graduated and eventually becoming a world-renowned supermodel. Now, she was back with a chip on her shoulder the size of Mt. Everest, which meant nothing but moody days for whoever had the pleasure of being in her company.

"They're having live entertainment and fireworks without a functional kitchen?" Raine asked. "Didn't they just hire us to cater their meeting with the town council?"

"They're trying to look like they're blending in with the locals," Nikki added.

Nikki had worked at the B&B as an assistant manager until Gramma's death. Then she'd been unanimously named the manager once the siblings inherited the place. The part about her falling in love with Quinn, the oldest Cantrell, and now planning a Christmas wedding with him . . . well, that was fate lending a hand, to Michelle's delight.

"Keeping their enemies close just like we are," Quinn added.

"You're probably right," Preston said from the side of the table where he sat next to his fiancée, Heaven.

Just a few months ago, Heaven had come to town intending to adopt the puppy Preston had inherited, named Coco. The fact that she was still here was a testament to both the town and the power of love. Michelle smiled each time she looked at them.

"And they're pulling out all the stops marketing-wise," Heaven mentioned. "The Hemingways, a very influential Bostonian family and owners of their own cable station, received a personalized invitation to come down for the opening."

Heaven was one of the Boston Montgomerys, or at least she would be until she married Preston; then her mother would probably want to disown her. At any rate, for the time being Heaven was working her social connections to spread the word about The Silver Spoon while Savannah came up with ideas for specialty packages to enhance what the B&B already offered and Preston worked out the legalities to it all. Quinn's part was to assist Nikki in management while Michelle did what she always did, what she'd gone to college to do: cook.

"So they're bringing in the big guns," Preston stated flatly.

"The Hemingways aren't even big enough. They've invited Senator Majette and his family, too," Heaven added.

"Damn! How are we supposed to compete with their corporate money and their political connections?" Savannah questioned. "They're bigger and fancier and giving the customers everything but a gold coin to come stay at their resort. All we're giving people are huge slices of pie and pretty flowers on the table."

The pretty flowers were courtesy of Drew Sidney and her flower shop. Months ago, they'd struck a deal with Drew: She'd provide fresh centerpieces for the dining room every week, and they would prominently display her business cards for guests to connect the lovely arrangements with a place where they could purchase them for themselves. So far it had been working pretty well, as Drew had reported to Michelle just last week.

"It's not about the biggest and the prettiest baubles," Mr. Sylvester said. He'd been the first to arrive in the dining room for their family meeting.

The last meeting he'd almost missed—when they'd had steamed crabs and discussed the new direction of the B&B—Mr. Sylvester hadn't been too happy. He was family because Gramma had loved him. She'd let him permanently rent a room at the B&B, and now that she was gone he'd sort of slipped into her place as the family elder. Michelle hadn't meant to leave him out and swore to never make that mistake again.

"They don't have one thing that we do here at The Silver Spoon," he continued. "The one thing Janet built this place with, and that's love. We're a family-run business. That means we can offer them a more personal touch than a big corporation. We have to play our strengths here, not re-create the wheel," he said emphatically.

For a man in his sixties who never owned a business in his life, who had children who didn't speak to him scattered about the United States, and who had shown up on the doorstep with only a duffel bag and a smile, he was wise and helpful beyond measure.

Michelle nodded. "He's right. We should focus on what we do well. The townspeople know us, so they'll vouch for us. People in the city working fifty-hour weeks want a change, they want to come to a place and relax."

"They want to come to a place and be able to go for a swim," Savannah quipped. "We need to get a pool."

"We're not getting a pool," Quinn reiterated for the billionth time. "I don't think the answer is to disturb our land. It's historical, Savannah, you know that."

"History isn't making us any money," Savannah retorted.

Nikki shook her head. "On the contrary, we're doing really well. The two weddings in August put us well in the black this month. Weddings are definitely a strong point, especially with Michelle's catering."

"So I'm the stupid one for thinking that things like a pool and maybe a gym would be a great addition?" Savannah asked.

"No, honey, that's not what they're saying," Raine said softly, reaching over to touch Savannah's hand. "They're just trying to say that newer doesn't necessarily mean better."

Raine was the peacemaker. She was the middle sister, the teacher, the only one who hadn't inherited their mother's quick temper and sharp tongue or their father's booming voice and tenacious attitude.

"It is what they're saying, Raine!" Savannah yelled. "Nobody ever wants to listen to me. I have something to contribute and I'm part owner of this place. I should be able to make a suggestion and not get slapped down like some pesky insect."

"Who's slapping who in here?" Parker asked, walking into the meeting late.

It was the first time Michelle had seen him since yesterday, when they'd all arrived at the festival together. But Parker had left before any of them, and she hadn't seen him since. Sure, she'd heard some things about him—which wasn't really new where Parker was concerned—but she hadn't seen him. And now, looking at her too-handsome younger brother as he walked over to the dining room table and took a seat beside his twin, she wondered if what she'd heard had any truth to it.

"Nobody's doing any slapping in here, but I heard you got yourself a good whacking when Louisa caught you in the girls' bathroom last night," Mr. Sylvester said, not looking at Parker but lifting his ratty old baseball cap from his head and scratching.

"You were where last night?" Nikki asked Parker.

Preston shook his head. "That's a new place even for you, Parker."

Parker frowned as his siblings ragged on him about Mr. Sylvester's comments. "You were talking about Savannah and her ideas. I think some of them have merit," he began in an attempt to shift the focus away from him and his issues last night.

Unfortunately, in the Cantrell household it just didn't work that way.

"So why were you in the girls' room?" Raine asked quietly.

Savannah let out a hoot of laughter. "Are you seriously asking Double Trouble Cantrell that question? You know why he was in the girls' room, to get with some girl!"

Nikki joined Savannah in laughing. It was to be expected, since those two had been thick as thieves since they were younger girls. Mr. Sylvester shook his head, and Quinn looked seriously at Parker.

"You're a law enforcement officer, tell me that's not what you were doing," he said to Parker.

"I'm a law enforcement officer in Baltimore, which I was so rudely reminded of last night," Parker stated, leading Michelle to believe that something actually may have happened last night.

"So did they arrest you for being in the bathroom?" Preston asked. "And were you in there alone?"

"No. He wasn't alone, Louisa was in there with him like I said before," was Mr. Sylvester's next comment.

"Ewww, you were with Louisa in the bathroom?"

Savannah's face scrunched with her words, which made Nikki laugh a little harder. This time even Parker and Heaven cracked a smile.

"We're not going to get past this, are we?" Parker asked.

Michelle felt sorry for him. Well, not really, but she wished he'd just go ahead and explain so this torture would stop. Then again, she wanted it to last a little longer, because this entire scene brought back memories of when they were younger and Gramma was still alive. They'd shared so much in this house, good times and bad times, and Michelle hadn't wanted to let them go. Standing here today, she realized she still didn't want to let her siblings go.

"All right, yes, I was in the bathroom. But I wasn't with Ms. Louisa. That old busybody followed me in there," he told them.

"And why were you in there? Did you get lost?" were Preston's questions.

Parker frowned at the man sitting beside him who looked a lot like him. "No. I wasn't lost. I followed someone in there."

Michelle held her breath and waited for the rest.

"Who in the world would you follow into the bathroom, and why?" Savannah asked incredulously. Her mood had brightened significantly since the topic of Parker in the girls' room came up.

A few seconds passed in silence, all eyes on Parker as he seemed to be contemplating his next words. Parker was many things, but a liar was not one of them. And for the most part, he owned up to whatever situations he managed to get himself into. Michelle didn't believe this time was any different, but he was hesitating a bit longer than normal. If Gramma or even their father were standing in this room, she'd understand the hesitancy, because neither of them had tolerated Parker's foolishness—not that their discipline had been effective in slowing Parker down any.

Finally, Parker sat back in his chair, his gaze reaching everyone sitting in the room. Michelle couldn't tell if he was looking for allies or simply trying to familiarize himself with his siblings again.

"I followed Drew Sidney into the bathroom to see what was wrong with her. She told me she was pregnant and Louisa barged in," he said as simply as if he'd just recited the day's weather forecast.

And the room went quiet, utterly and amazingly quiet, for a seemingly endless stretch of time, possibly the first time in the last twenty or thirty years.

Chapter 6

"Drew's pregnant?" Heaven asked, looking directly at Quinn.

Parker might have missed the look his future sister-in-law and his older brother shared if he hadn't been avoiding the knowing glare coming from his twin. Of all the people sitting in this room, Preston was the only one who knew about Parker's night with Drew, and that knowledge had been granted to him only recently. Parker had had no choice but to tell him after walking into this very room a couple of months ago to find Drew and her mother sitting in here. They'd come so that Lorrayna could discuss her legal woes with Preston, and Preston—professional that he was—had asked Parker to entertain them while he made some phone calls for the woman.

Drew's reaction to his entering the room sort of said it all; luckily, Preston hadn't seen it. But when they were leaving, as Parker bade Lorrayna good day and attempted to do the same to her daughter, the frigid response from Drew was a dead giveaway. The minute the front door of the B&B closed, Preston turned to him.

"What did you do to her, and when?"

"I don't know what you're talking about," was Parker's knee-jerk reply, because for the first time in their lives Preston's accusatory tone had offended him.

"Before you came down Drew was annoyed with her mother and apologetic to me. Then I leave you alone with her for fifteen minutes and she's irritated and ready to run out of this place as if her life depended on it. And she wouldn't look at you. Any female that doesn't look at you has probably already seen as much as she could stand or as much as you've allowed. Now, I'll ask you again, what did you do to her?"

Preston had that serious litigator tone in his voice. He wanted an answer and he expected the truth. Parker suspected he already knew the truth. He and Preston were fraternal twins, born only minutes apart. They were as close as two people could be without being conjoined. They'd grown up in this town together, doing the same things, chasing girls, and getting into trouble. When they graduated from high school, Preston had immediately headed to the University of Maryland while Parker had gone into the police academy. They'd both moved to Baltimore City, where Preston attended law school and Parker worked his first years as a rookie on the force. Maturity had come for both of them as they settled into their adult lives, still chasing women but this time fighting trouble.

Things had changed since Gramma's passing. Preston had moved back to Sweetland, going into the city only for court appearances his former law partner couldn't handle. He was engaged to a gorgeous woman who loved and respected him. Preston was living the American dream, or the Sweetland dream, Parker corrected himself. And he was looking at his twin brother as if he were wondering why he wasn't doing the same thing.

"I slept with her, okay? Are you satisfied?" Parker finally replied.

His response was a sigh and a shake of his head. "You know how small this town is, Parker. Everybody knows everything, and females here are thinking of that cute little house, two point five kids, and a husband at the dinner table every night. If you're not prepared to do that, you should probably leave them alone. Go back to the city and take care of your urges," Preston told him.

"Like you did?" Parker argued, anger growing at the way his own brother was judging him. "Heaven's not your normal city girl. She has those same plans in her pretty little brown eyes and that didn't stop you from getting her in bed as soon as you could."

Preston looked slightly riled by Parker's words but still remained calm as he continued to chastise his younger brother. "She wasn't living in Sweetland when our relationship began and I didn't leave her high and dry the next morning. But from the way Drew was avoiding any contact with you at all, I'm assuming that's what you did to her."

Parker couldn't deny the obvious, and he hadn't wanted to. What he'd wanted was to scream how he'd been trying like hell to talk to Drew since that night, how he'd wanted nothing more than to see her again, and not just intimately. But Preston wouldn't have understood that because it wasn't the way Parker normally behaved.

"Look, we're both adults. Whatever is between us, stays between us," Parker had told Preston, ending the conversation.

Now, sitting at this table and feeling like one of Preston's defendants on the witness stand, he got the impression that what was between him and Drew was about to become a family matter.

"And why would she tell you she's pregnant, Parker?" Quinn asked, his voice low and subdued.

"Heh, heh, heh," Mr. Sylvester chuckled, slapping his cap on the edge of the table.

"Parker?" Preston prodded.

"Wait!" Savannah screeched. She'd sat up in her chair, palms flat on the table so that her hot-pink-polished nails glistened against the cherrywood of the table. "Did you sleep with her? You did, didn't you? You slept with Drew and now she's pregnant! Oh. My. G—"

"Parker Roland Cantrell," Michelle interrupted, her voice reproachful and stinging. "Of all the people, in all the world, you chose Drewcilla Sidney."

He wanted to leave this room. Really badly. If he could just go back to the last fifteen minutes, where he'd stood on the deck of the restaurant looking through the glass doors to the table where Drew sat with her mother, having their Sunday brunch. She'd looked a lot better than she had last night, rested and refreshed, a smile gracing her face a time or two. Her hair was pulled into a ponytail. She wore faded jeans, a turquoise tank top, and flat sandals with glittering studs across her toes. She drank orange juice and ate Michelle's fluffy waffles with berries and plenty of syrup. Parker didn't care for the berries, but he loved maple syrup on his waffles.

"Well, are you going to answer us or not?" Nikki prodded. "Or I can just waltz into the dining room and ask Drew myself."

Nikki stood, but Quinn touched an arm to her elbow to stop her.

"If Parker has something to tell us, he will," Quinn announced.

Whenever Quinn spoke in that tone, everyone knew it meant someone would be doing exactly what he'd said in the next few seconds. This time the someone was Parker. And he was no longer a child, so being scorned by his big brother—either one of them—wasn't intimidating. At least he planned to act that way.

"Drew is carrying my child," he announced.

"Heh, heh, heh, heh!" This time, Sylvester chuckled so hard that his frail body fell back against the chair, tears eventually beading in the corners of his dark brown eyes.

Michelle rushed around the table to his side. She put her hands on his shoulders, looking over at Parker as she spoke.

"Well, he's probably in a state of shock," she said.

"I think *I'm* in a state of shock," Heaven murmured.

Nikki shook her head. "Cordy's gonna flip when she hears this. All those years she spent wondering what could have been between you two if you hadn't packed up and moved away and she hadn't married Barry, and now you're going to end up with a Sweetland girl after all."

"Great, another Cantrell wedding. Yippeee," Savannah said blandly.

"There isn't going to be a wedding and I'm not ending up with a Sweetland girl," Parker told them. "A woman who lives in Sweetland is carrying my child. End of story."

"Oh my, my, my," Mr. Sylvester wheezed as he spoke, using the backs of his hands to wipe his eyes. "Mary Janet is smiling in her grave, I just know it. She loved her puppies, but she really wanted babies around this here house. She's gonna love this. Heh, heh, heh."

"Look, it's not public knowledge yet, so let's just keep this under wraps for the time being. Drew and I are still trying to figure all this out," Parker continued.

The last thing he wanted was for this news to spread through Sweetland like a deadly disease. He suspected Drew didn't want that, either, and since he was still trying to figure out what he was going to do about the mother of his child, he'd like to stay in her good graces.

"So you're not going to marry her?" Nikki asked, but quickly cut short her next question as Quinn gave her a look.

Quinn shared that look with everyone, then finally

said, "We have more pressing business than Parker's love life. Keeping The Silver Spoon alive and viable in this town while new businesses sprout up all over the place is our priority."

And Parker's latest stunt is his own to get out of. Quinn didn't say that part, but Parker felt the words drifting quietly through the air. All his life he'd gotten into things— the fight in school with Billy Wilder, where Billy left with a broken nose and Parker had to get stitches in his head; the speeding ticket he'd received for driving on the highway and that he and Preston had considered fighting all the way to the Supreme Court; the night he was caught in the Lincolns' garage, a very naked and agreeable Shannon Lincoln lying on a blanket beside him. There seemed to be no end to what Parker Cantrell could get himself into, or so the residents of Sweetland thought. Years later, it appeared his oldest brother still felt the same way.

"Right, we should focus on the B and B. I can take care of my own problems," Parker said, and he walked out, leaving the rest of his siblings to stare after him.

Drew couldn't focus at all.

At brunch with her mother, she'd only half listened to the conversation, very much aware of Parker out on the deck, carrying boxes back and forth. He wore shorts and a sleeveless shirt that molded against his chest like a second skin. Each time he lifted a box, muscles in his arms flexed and Drew's breasts tingled. As he walked, the muscles in his calves were more pronounced, his strength undeniable. At one point he'd stood on the deck, his back to the window where she was looking from the other side. Raine had approached him with a bottle of water. Drew had watched, entranced, as he'd removed the top and put the bottle to his lips, tipping his head slightly and drinking the contents without stopping.

She'd swallowed hard, watching him do the same. Then her mother had said something in a pitch significantly louder than she had been using, and Drew had pulled herself from the enticing daydream that had been forming in her mind. She was physically attracted to Parker Cantrell.

Well, she was a female, so that fact alone wasn't hard to figure out. Every single woman in town was attracted to Parker, and before he'd left Sweetland they had been as well. At that time, he'd been very eager to give the women as much of his attention as he could, or so Drew had heard.

"He's not going to marry you," her mother had said after Drew missed a few more of her questions while staring at Parker.

Her head had jerked around as she'd looked at her mother in shock. "I don't want to marry Parker," she'd countered defensively. Even though she didn't know why she needed to defend her position with her mother. Lorrayna of all people knew exactly how Drew felt about committed relationships and about intimacy, for that matter.

"Well, you want to do something with him," Lorrayna had continued, wiping her hands on the linen napkin and then dropping it onto her still partially filled plate.

Drew had no idea why her mother insisted on having brunch every Sunday when she rarely ate the food. This was definitely not a testament to the cuisine at The Silver Spoon, Drew thought as she chewed another mouthful. No, that was all wrapped in Lorrayna's warped and heartbroken mind. Her mother's heartbreak had played a significant part in Drew's outlook on relationships, as had her third date with Jared Mansfield.

"I can tell by the way you're staring at him like he should be on your plate instead of those waffles. And everybody else in this room can tell, too, so you should really get yourself together," Lorrayna continued to scold her.

"He's the father of my baby, I think I'm going to have to look at him at some point," Drew replied. But she did stop ogling Parker. She focused on her plate and not her mother, who was already beginning to get on her nerves.

Lorrayna tsked. "If he were concerned about being the father of your baby, he would have come in to at least speak to you by now." She shook her head, dull brown curls haloing her face like a snug-fitting cap. "He's nothing like his brothers, I tell you that much. They're so in love they can hardly walk down the street without smiling. Every time I see one of them they're happy as can be. That one," she said with a jerk of her head in the general direction of the deck, "he doesn't seem to know if he's coming or going, unless he's on that godforsaken bike making all that noise. I wish somebody would ban those motorcycles for good."

"You cannot ban motorcycles, Mom. It's a free country, remember?"

Drew had been tired of this conversation ten minutes after they'd sat down, but she didn't have the heart to cancel. Her mother rarely went out except for when she went to work. She stayed at Uncle Walt's house as if it were a shelter from everything, including life, and Drew thought it was sickening. After her father's death, her mother had seemed to shut down completely. Sure, she worked and paid bills and generally took care of herself and now Uncle Walt as well, but that was all she did. No dates. No friends. No other family. No connections to anyone. All Lorrayna seemed to want to do with the rest of her life was bask in widowhood, without ever accepting that her husband was a selfish idiot to do what he'd done to their family.

Lorrayna shook her head. "How's he going to ever take his child anywhere on a bike? It's so childish, Drew. He probably thinks it makes him hot stuff. You know, I heard he used to think he owned this town, or at least all the women in it."

The last remarks her mother had whispered, even though there was no use. Drew had heard the same thing, to some extent. Whenever Parker's name was mentioned, the citizens of Sweetland didn't hesitate to give the same warning speech to Drew they did to every other available female. It was as if they had a presealed warning label ready to administer at a moment's notice. Originally, when the warnings had come from women like Louisa and Marabelle and Mrs. DelVechio at the library, Drew had taken them with a grain of salt. But that was before she'd actually seen Parker. After their first meeting, it had been Diana McCann who had given Drew the next warning.

"He's an ass. A selfish, womanizing ass who doesn't give a crap about anyone but himself. He even left his poor grandmother here to take care of the B and B all by herself," Diana had reported.

To date, there'd been no one to counter those opinions of him. Of course, Drew hadn't asked anyone for fear they'd immediately think she had an interest in Parker. She hadn't wanted to be the subject of a town's ridicule, not again. Yet now here she was, pregnant with the child of a selfish, womanizing ass who rode a bike that surely meant he was the spawn of the devil.

She put her elbows on the table and sighed, listening to her mother go on for another fifteen minutes before their most painful brunch yet was finally declared over.

Then she drove back to her apartment and changed into shorts and a T-shirt. Heading out the back once more, Drew set out to spend some quality time in her garden.

That never failed to relax her. Something about the manual labor tended to take her mind off her issues. It had been that way since after the incident in Stratford. She supposed it was the one positive thing to come out of that horrific time in her life. The mere memory as she stepped outside had her immediately dropping to her knees, pulling at weeds with a vengeance, thinking in her mind that they were someone else from some other time who had caused her more pain that any human should be allowed to endure.

"Rufus would not run away," Parker declared about ten minutes after a frantic Raine bounded into the living room, where he'd been checking his emails on his laptop.

"Then explain where he is, Parker," Raine demanded. She folded her arms across her chest and impatiently tapped a foot on the Aubusson carpet.

Mary Janet Cantrell had a flare for antiques and kept the lower level of the B&B decorated in its signature Victorian glamour. The parlor, living room, and foyer each boasted room-sized rugs with colors that coordinated with the furniture. The living room had a cranberry-and-beige theme that Parker found oddly relaxing. In the weeks that he'd been here, he'd taken to sitting in one of the elegant armchairs near the front window. From there he could look out onto the front porch and just about down the length of Sycamore Lane. Normally, it was a very relaxing act, but he'd just come across an email whose sender had sparked an air of alarm in him. Then in came Raine and now Parker was closing his laptop, standing in front of his sister.

"Rufus loves to play, Raine. I'm sure he's just hiding in a bush somewhere. I'll go out and look for him."

Raine didn't seem convinced, but she fell into step behind Parker as they headed through the parlor toward the kitchen. The puppies, Loki, Lily, and Micah, along with their mother, Ms. Cleo, spent the bulk of their day playing in the yard at The Silver Spoon. In the evenings, Michelle and Raine kept their dogs at their house; Parker and Savannah were the only two siblings living at the B&B, so Rufus and Loki stayed with them. At one point, when the siblings had first come back to Sweetland and had been just getting used to the idea of being owners of an inn and baby Labradors, all the puppies had been housed in kennels in the basement. Parker, however, had immediately taken to Rufus and usually kept the dog with him. In fact, Rufus had been running around near the deck earlier this afternoon while Parker had been unloading supplies. When he'd come in for the family meeting, he'd taken Rufus around and put him inside the pen that kept all the dogs from running down to the water for an impromptu swim in the backyard. And he was certain he'd locked the pen when he'd left.

But as he stepped out into the backyard, he could clearly see the gate to the pen was wide open. Ms. Cleo was leashed to the edge of the restaurant's deck.

"Where's Micah, Lily, and Loki?" Parker looked over his shoulder to ask Raine.

"Savannah took them inside so none of them would get the same idea and wander off," she told him.

"Rufus wouldn't wander off," he said, continuing to look around the yard. When he didn't see him, Parker called the dog's name once, twice, three times, but there was no response.

Labs loved the water and Rufus swam especially well, so that's where Parker headed next. The edge of the Cantrell property was marked by a small slope covered in rocks that led down to a thin patch of sand and the bank of the Miles River. They all took the puppies down there to swim almost daily; maybe Rufus had wanted to take a second dip today. Moving over the rocks gingerly, he looked in both directions. But the water was calm.

"Do you see him?" Preston asked from the top of the slope.

Parker shook his head and started back up. "He wouldn't wander off," he repeated.

"He could have," Preston said. "They're getting bigger, more active, if that's possible. Coco will run all the way to the end of our block before realizing I'm still stepping out onto the porch. He's probably somewhere on Sycamore."

Parker wasn't so certain. "I was sitting at the window. I would have seen him."

"You've got other things on your mind besides your dog," Preston added.

Parker shot him a look. "I told you that was between Drew and me. It's not open for discussion at the moment."

Preston lifted his hands in a surrender position. "Calm down, I'm not trying to pry. You're an adult, you'll handle this situation the best way you see fit."

He said that, but Parker was almost positive his brother didn't actually believe it. None of his siblings believed he'd do the right thing by Drew. And actually, Parker had been thinking of what exactly the right thing was. But that wasn't his biggest concern right now. Finding Rufus was.

Chapter 7

Drew sat back on her heels, wiping her forehead with the back of her hand. It was late afternoon, probably close to six o'clock, but the sun was still beaming as if it were noon. The part of her garden that bordered the wall of her house received the most shade. The farther she moved down toward the end of her yard, the more sun she was exposed to.

Maybe she should have worn a hat, she thought as the section of her skin she'd just wiped felt as if it was pricking with sweat once again. Looking down, she thought she'd done a pretty good job. The red valerian she'd planted down this end was still in full bloom, even though the vibrant color would last only another week or so. Still, it was one of the easiest perennials to maintain. Beside it, the moonbeams would flourish until first frost.

Drew looked down, loving the play of colors in her garden. The intense purple that gave way to a lighter shade of lavender, firelike yellows and reds, soft, calming blues. All of which she'd planted herself, tended to as if they were extensions of her life. She was good at tending flowers, selecting them, arranging them. It was a far cry from the associate of arts degree she'd received in business and her certification in medical coding. Just as sitting here in the backyard of the quaint little house and flower shop she owned in this small Eastern Shore town was a far cry from the apartment in the city she'd dreamed of having. Her life had certainly taken a dramatic turn, one that for a short time she hadn't thought she'd recover from. But now, she thought with another sigh, now, she was content. And she was pregnant, a fact that made her smile.

Then there was a noise and Drew looked around. The first thing she saw was dirt flying into the air in a wicked arch that had her heart stopping. The dirt was coming from the top of her yard, the spot she'd started tending when she'd come out and had just added fresh soil to. With a muted curse, Drew got to her feet and headed for the front of the yard. Dirt splattered her legs as she bent forward, pushing her hands into the shrubs she had planted there so she could see what was going on. Her first thought was a rabbit or a squirrel, but there was too much dirt and they didn't normally kick it up into the air this way. She thought she saw something black before more dirt pelted her, this time in the face.

"Dangit!" she yelled. "Come out of there, you little troublemaker!"

What she received in return was a yelp or a tiny bark, and for a moment she startled. Then she pushed back a huge elephant ear hosta leaf and frowned as chocolate-brown eyes stared back at her—eyes that were on a broad head with ears flopping at the side.

"And just what do you think you're doing in there?" she asked what she now recognized was one of the Cantrell Labradors.

Everyone in town knew that Mary Janet Cantrell owned a beautiful chocolate Lab named Ms. Cleo. Earlier this year, Ms. Cleo had birthed a litter of puppies, two of them black and the remaining four chocolate brown like their mother. The black ones were named Loki and Rufus. Drew couldn't tell which one this was, but he was staring back at her with what looked just like an innocent smile. She didn't smile back.

"You know you're trespassing, right?"

The reply to that was a lift of his head and movement of his nose as he sniffed.

"Don't sniff at me, you're the one playing in the dirt," she scolded. "Come on out of there," she continued, taking hold of his collar and pulling gently until the dog agreed to walk toward her.

"I just worked on this area and here you come making a mess. Do your owners know where you are?" she asked, wondering how the dog had gotten all the way down here. Even though they were growing every day and no longer looked like puppies, they weren't yet mature Labs, so Drew knew the Cantrells had been keeping a close eye on all of them. Well, all of them except this one.

"You certainly don't belong all the way over here by yourself," she continued, thinking she could simply climb into her car and take the dog back to The Silver Spoon. But then she might see Parker again. With a sigh, Drew decided she'd rather not have another confrontation with him so soon.

"Since you've created more work for me, I'm going to tie you up over here while I call someone to come and get you."

She frowned slightly as she realized she was conversing with a dog. A dog that looked as if he might actually be laughing at her and his antics. There was some rope over near her shed and she used it to latch on to the collar and tie the dog to her side gate.

"Now you stay put until someone comes to claim you."

She moved to her back steps, where she'd put a bottle

of water and her cell phone. Holding the phone, Drew punched a stored number key and waited for an answer.

"Hi, Michelle?" she spoke into the phone, watching the puppy dance around in a circle, effectively tangling the rope as he did. "This is Drew. I think I have something that belongs to you," she said, then laughed because in all his turning and rope winding, the dog had lost his balance on his long, gangly legs and fell back on his butt. He looked confused and even had the forethought to shake his head for clarity.

About twenty minutes later, Drew was sitting on her back steps; she had re-soiled the section of the garden that the dog destroyed, patting it down softly after applying a trickle of water to help the soil settle. She'd continued to talk to the dog, who wanted to get loose and had now resorted to giving her the saddest puppy-dog stare she'd ever seen to make that happen. She wouldn't untie him, though, because she didn't want him to run away or to get into her garden again.

"Rufus!" she heard a male voice yell, and hurried to stand.

Drew was brushing down her clothes, frowning at the mess the dirt and sweat had made of her shirt and shorts. With a slight curse, she realized she was brushing over her clothes while still wearing her dirty gloves, which was only making matters worse. She pulled them off, tossing them behind her on the steps. It had never occurred to her that Parker would be the one to come and claim the dog. This had been precisely the scenario she'd hoped to avoid. Since she'd spoken to Michelle, she'd actually expected to see her pull up in the silver minivan she drove. Instead, the very handsome and very clean Parker stepped into her yard, heading straight for the dog, who was now leaping up and down, tongue wagging, ears flapping in excitement to see him.

"What are you doing here, boy? You scared me half to death," Parker said, immediately going to his knees, his hands gripping the dog's broad head as he ruffled his ears. "You're not supposed to leave the yard," he continued, lowering his face until it was close enough to the dog's that Drew thought they might actually kiss.

But while Parker's voice sounded relieved, it was still scolding, and she sensed the dog—Rufus—knew that, too. His tail still wagged, but for the most part he had stopped moving, looking at Parker with those same sad eyes he had been giving her.

"Maybe you should get him a GPS," Drew suggested to lighten the mood.

Even though she'd probably been talking to the dog in the same tone when she'd found him in her garden, she almost felt bad for the poor thing being scolded by Parker, too.

Her comment caught his attention and Parker immediately turned his head in her direction.

"He's never run away before," he said, his gaze locking with hers.

Drew swallowed. Just one look from him and she felt weak at the knees, her overactive imagination remembering bits and pieces of their night together even though it was months ago. The bits and pieces that consisted of his hands on her body, his tongue on her skin, his length filling her so completely. Hell, she swallowed again and used the back of her hand to wipe along her forehead because it was suddenly ten times hotter than it had been before.

"Maybe he just wanted a different scenery," she replied when the silence between them had gone on too long.

Parker stood then, shrugging his broad shoulders. "Maybe. You look like you've been working hard out here.

Maybe you should try for some different scenery as well. Like inside out of this heat with your feet up."

For a minute, Drew had thought he was trying to tell her she looked too bad to be standing out here talking to him. Then she realized he was being considerate—of her pregnancy.

"I was just finishing up when Rufus there showed up and created more work for me."

Parker looked at Rufus, then back to her. "Really? You should have called me sooner. I would have fixed whatever he messed up."

She waved a hand. "It wasn't that much," she lied. It had been more work than she'd wanted to repeat, but she wasn't about to tell Parker that. He was already thinking she needed to be carted off to bed, and not in the way she'd been thinking. "So I thought they were kenneled in the yard or the basement. How did he get out?" she asked.

"I have no idea, but I'm going to keep a closer eye on him now that I know he likes to travel."

They shared a chuckle over that, and for a second Drew felt perfectly comfortable standing there with him. The scene almost seemed right for late on a Sunday afternoon, with her finishing her work in her garden and Parker just back from walking the dog. They almost seemed like a real couple, or a real family.

"I should also keep a closer eye on you to make sure you don't overwork yourself out in this heat," he was saying when Drew finally snapped out of her daydream.

"What?"

"I said I should probably come around more often to make sure you're not working too hard out here. Do you always do all your own gardening as well as working in the shop throughout the week?"

"Ah, yes. I do. I'm the owner of Blossoms and this is my house, my garden. Who else would do the work?"

"Staff, maybe?"

Drew shook her head. "I don't have any staff. Whenever I have a big job, my mother comes over to help. Lately, Heaven's been stopping by after reading at the library. If it gets crowded while she's here, she'll help with packaging. Otherwise, I'm a one-woman show."

He frowned and Drew wondered what she should say to that. Nobody had ever been concerned about how much work she was doing. Her mother was too busy complaining when she was here to notice, and really, she did most of her business during the summer months when tourism was high in Sweetland. The rest of the year she did the occasional anniversary or birthday bouquets. Just recently, she'd begun providing centerpieces for The Silver Spoon and as a result had also contracted with the mayor to provide seasonal bouquets and floral decorations for the many town events. As she ticked off all those things in her mind, she realized an assistant might not be a bad idea, especially in her present condition. But she wasn't about to mention all that to Parker.

"Anyway, I should probably go in now. I still have to come up with ideas for next week's centerpieces at The Silver Spoon."

"And you have to shower and eat dinner and relax before work tomorrow," he added.

By this time, Rufus had walked around Parker's legs so many times, begging for forgiveness, that both of them were tangled in the rope. Parker cursed and tried to unwind himself.

Drew went to them and untied Rufus, letting the end of the rope loose while she helped Parker get his feet free. Rufus jumped up on Drew's legs, and she went down on her knees to ruffle his ears. "You be sure to call before you stop in for a visit next time," she told him with a laugh.

"I'll make sure he calls first," Parker said, tossing the rope to the side. "In the meantime, I can run down to the pizza shop and pick us up some dinner."

And she could go inside and shower and then they'd sit on her couch, watching television and eating pizza. Rufus would doze in the corner and eventually they'd head to bed for the night. And wake up beside each other in the morning. Just like a normal couple.

But they weren't a normal couple. And they weren't working their way toward that goal. He was Parker Cantrell, bad boy and womanizer extraordinaire, and she was just the flower shop owner who'd been irresponsible enough to get pregnant by him.

"No. I'll pass on the pizza," she replied quickly, standing and backing away from Parker and his mischievous, cute-as-a-button dog. "Besides, I have other plans for the evening. But thanks for the offer."

He looked as if he didn't believe her, but Drew didn't care. The last few years of her life had been about self-preservation. She'd been careful to work hard at building the new and improved Drewcilla Sidney so that the towns-people wouldn't have anything negative to say about her. She'd stayed away from men and relationships so the mistake she'd made in Stratford could never be repeated. And in one night she'd done something that could possibly unravel all her hard work. She wasn't about to do anything else to sabotage herself, so fooling herself about Parker Cantrell was a definite no-no.

"I'm not going to bite you, Drew. I think we've already established the fact that we need to talk about things, about our futures," he stated calmly, matter-of-factly, as though he were giving her a rundown of her rights.

"I don't presume you're going to do anything to me, Parker." *Other than what's already been done,* she neglected to say. "I'm just trying to keep us on even ground here. I'm pregnant and you're the father. But there's no reason for either of our lives to change. You can continue on with your career and the life you've built for yourself and I'll continue on with mine."

"And I'll live in Baltimore and you and my child will live here in Sweetland. Tell me, do you even plan to let my sisters see the baby, or will the father of your child become Sweetland's best-kept secret?"

He wasn't happy. Well, that was fine. Keeping Parker happy wasn't a job Drew had applied for.

"Secrets always find their way out," she told him as succinctly as he'd just spoken to her. "And I wouldn't dream of keeping this child away from its family, yours or mine. But what I'm trying to say is that there's no rea-son for you and me to be any different than we were two weeks ago."

He raised a brow. "You mean when you saw me in God-frey's and dropped your honeydew melon to head down the opposite aisle because I came over and spoke to you?"

Drew cleared her throat, talking as she walked back to her steps and picked up her phone and half-empty water bottle. "I mean that we can remain cordial and have a baby together. You don't have to come over here telling me I'm working too hard or that I need to put my feet up. And you certainly don't have to worry about whether or not I'm eating dinner or provide said dinner for me. I can take care of myself."

"And I shouldn't care one way or another if you fall out in the sun from heatstroke or forget to eat because you're working too hard and my baby is born stressed out or permanently damaged because of it."

"How dare you?" she asked, turning quickly to find that he was standing right beside her. Behind her she heard Rufus bark, as if he'd gone up on her steps and waited at the door. He apparently thought he should be let inside her house and her life as well. "You cannot come into town poking your chest out like some bronzed peacock expecting every female to fall at your feet. And you certainly cannot get me pregnant, then presume that means you have some type of control over my life or the way I live it. You, Parker Cantrell, are not the boss of me, and I don't care how big and bad of a cop you are in Baltimore!"

She was gorgeous when she was mad. Color had infused her cheeks, her already pert lips had firmed, brown eyes going fierce as her voice had elevated. Parker had to resist the urge to grab her at the waist, pull her into his chest, and kiss her senseless. He'd had to clamp down on the instant arousal stirring as he'd listened to her words and watched her reaction to what he'd said. All of that was the reason he hadn't been able to stop her from turning and going into the house before slamming the door in his face.

Drew was pissed at him, Rufus was asleep in the passenger seat of Michelle's van, and an hour later, Parker was parked at the pier, looking out to the fishing boats coming in for the day.

Sweetland's reputation rested on its fresh seafood and the unique cuisine prepared with it. In the time he'd been back, he'd witnessed the prosperous results of that reputation as tourists poured in all summer long, staying weeks at a time, crowding the pier to get into The Crab Pot. The Silver Spoon had also seen an increase in business, with most of their rooms consistently booked and Michelle cooking nonstop.

They'd settled into something of a routine, with everyone pitching in with everything from taking shifts serving at the restaurant to changing linens in the rooms. Preston and Heaven were comfortable in their little house, planning the details of their spring wedding. Quinn and Nikki were juggling their managing duties with marketing plans for the B&B and planning their Christmas wedding. As for Parker, it had taken him six weeks to heal from the motorcycle accident that had crushed his leg so badly, he'd been forced to take medical leave from work. And he still wasn't sure how it had occurred.

At least that had been what he'd told his siblings. Nobody knew that he'd been suspended from the police force before he'd ever stepped foot in Sweetland again. And nobody was going to know if he could help it.

That ordeal had been a nightmare, one Parker feared he was still living as he reached for his cell phone. Scrolling through his emails, he saw the message that he'd been just about to open when he'd found out Rufus was missing. The sender's name hadn't been familiar. But the subject line was: Vezina.

Tyrone Vezina had been murdered in an alley in downtown Baltimore one rainy night in early April. He'd been walking down the street, a man about five feet eleven inches wearing blue jeans and a black jacket. His hands had been stuffed into his front jacket pockets, the collar pulled up high on his neck as he hunched over in an attempt to ward off the steady flow of raindrops. He walked fast, as if he was trying to get to his car or to wherever he was going before becoming completely drenched. In the next few steps, he'd hit the corner and was yanked into the alley.

Parker was keeping surveillance of the building a block down and on the opposite side of the street. But he'd noticed Vezina and felt a familiar sensation at the base of his neck. That had been Parker's warning, and it had come only seconds before Vezina was pulled into the dark alley. Parker instantly went into action. He stepped out of his unmarked vehicle, pulling his weapon as he ran across the street. Back against the wall, Parker had peered around the corner just in time to see the flash of the floodlights on the side of the building being shot out. He'd cursed and reached into his pocket to get his cell phone so he could call for backup. That action took him all of fifteen seconds. Then he heard another shot and decided against waiting for the backup he'd just summoned. He turned into the alley, gun raised and aimed. It was dark, so for the most part all he saw were bodies, three of them, Vezina included. The man was standing with his back against the wall, his arms up in the air. Two other men had their backs to Parker. He approached, yelling, "Police! Drop your weapons and get your hands in the air!"

One guy did as he was told. The other lifted his gun higher and fired at Vezina. Parker fired simultaneously. Then both men turned and ran toward Parker. He yelled to them to stop again, then fired his weapon twice more before one of them crashed right into him. Parker fell back, dropping his weapon. Cursing, he grabbed hold of the assailant's shirt and they tussled over the wet ground.

From the end of the alley, the second assailant yelled, "I'm hit! I'm hit! Let's go!"

Parker had rolled his guy onto his back, crashing his fist into his face three times before another shot rang out. Inches, the bullet was mere inches from his temple, and Parker went down to the ground, searching for cover. He was being fired at, and he couldn't find his gun.

"Leave him! Let's get the hell out of here!"

He heard their feet pounding the sidewalk and stood. Parker could hear sirens in the distance and knew that help was on the way. He turned away from the victim then, intending to follow the assailants, the ones that had run him down and shot at him, because at the moment apprehending those assholes was his first priority.

He took only two steps before the voice cried out.

"Help me! Help me!"

It was the victim, and Parker immediately turned back. The assailants were getting away, but this man was apparently alive for the moment.

"Help me!" he cried again.

"I'm here. I'm a cop," Parker said, kneeling on the ground.

The man had been shot in the neck and shoulder. Blood poured from both wounds, but he was still trying to talk.

"Just relax, an ambo will be here in a few seconds," he told him.

The man had lifted a hand then, grabbing Parker's hand and stuffing something into it. "So am I," he whispered about two seconds before his eyes went cold.

In the pouring rain, kneeling in an alley, Parker Cantrell stared down at the police badge in his hand and the dead man on the ground. He should have known then that from that moment on, his life would never be the same.

But he hadn't imagined, hadn't for one second thought that things would go downhill as fast as they had. Preston had been in the middle of a five-defendant murder trial, so he'd been too busy to hear about what had happened or to hear that it had involved Parker. The break-in to Parker's apartment and his suspension had come only weeks later, and by that time Gramma had died. It wasn't the time to dump his problems on his family.

And now that he'd gotten himself into another situation, Parker figured the decision to keep his mouth shut about what happened in Baltimore was even smarter.

His finger hovered over the button that would open the email, his sergeant's words echoing in his mind.

"I told you to stay the hell off the Vezina case, Cantrell. It's not yours to solve."

"He died in my arms," Parker had replied while standing in Sergeant Lawrence Mertz's office.

"Then get a Kleenex and some counseling and move the hell on! But don't let me find out you're working this case or your ass will be out of a job!"

Mertz had never been one to bluff.

Technically, Parker still had a job, he just couldn't go to it, not until the internal investigation was over. Then, there was no telling what his career future would hold.

Still, someone was obviously trying to tell him something about the murder, something Parker desperately wanted to know. A cop had been killed in his city, on his watch. He wanted to know why. And he wanted to find the bastard that had the balls to come into his house to leave him a personal message.

But there was more . . . much more. Parker was now going to be a father. There was another person he had to consider over his own wants and demands. There was a child, his child. Another person Parker needed to protect. He touched the screen of his phone without thought, reading the short message.

Welcome to Sweetland! How sweet will it be when they find out there's a cop killer in town?

Parker gritted his teeth, tossing the phone across the front of the van. Rufus jumped up, barking at the device as it hit the passenger window and fell to the floor. In seconds he was on the floor retrieving it. Not that he planned to give it to Parker, he simply wanted to occupy himself with something else for the moment.

Driving back to the B&B, Parker thought of all the things he'd done in his life. He thought of all the trouble he'd gotten himself and his twin brother into and how many situations his grandmother and his father had gotten him out of. That had been when he was young and earning the Double Trouble Cantrell reputation had been fun. Walking on the wild side, being the bad boy of the town, had been liberating and an adrenaline rush that compared with none other.

Now Parker was an adult, and as an adult he'd be the first to admit that he'd continued to make mistakes. Living a perfectly neat and satisfying life had never been his plan. But things had changed. A lot of things had changed, and Parker knew he'd have to change with them. He'd have to stand up and fix his own problems this time, and he had to do it soon.

Chapter 8

"I remember when I wandered off from St. Louis. Had my bag on my shoulder and my cap on my head. Always wore a cap, since my daddy gave me the first one when I was just a wee little thing. He loved baseball, my dad did. Said it was a thinking man's sport. Some say that's golf, but me and my dad, we liked to move about even when we were thinking. Keeps the mind fresh, Dad used to say."

Sylvester Bynum had begun talking the minute Parker stepped up onto the front porch of the B&B. Holding Rufus under one arm wasn't an easy task, but he'd already told his trusty canine friend that he was on traveling restrictions for the next couple of days, so he planned to keep him close.

Parker hadn't planned on having a conversation on the front porch, especially since it was almost midnight when he'd returned.

"No matter how old a man gets, he always keeps a part of his father, right in here," Sylvester continued, slapping a hand over his heart.

Parker nodded. He, along with the rest of his siblings,

were perfectly aware of Mr. Sylvester's penchant for talking. He'd been their grandmother's closest friend right up
until her death, even keeping Mary Janet's cancer diagnosis a secret from the family at her request. After the funeral, when the siblings thought Mr. Sylvester might pack
his bags and head off, they were pleasantly fooled by the
older man's stubborn persistence to stay right where he
was and help them see Mary Janet's wishes through. He'd
stayed when so many others might have left. Parker had
great respect for the man for that reason alone.

"It's getting late, Mr. Sylvester. You want to head on
inside?" he asked the man as he stood next to the Adirondack chair Mr. Sylvester favored.

Parker had seen him sit on this porch for hours, just
staring off down the street. One of his sisters would peri-
odically bring him a glass of tea or lemonade, maybe a
sandwich or some cookies. Mr. Sylvester favored Michelle's chocolate-chip cookies fresh out of the oven.

"Someday soon I reckon I'll get all the sleep I need.
Right now I'd like to keep my eyes open. You should do
that, too," he said, turning his head to look directly at
Parker for the first time since Parker had come up onto
the porch. "You should keep your eyes open."

Sometimes Mr. Sylvester talked in riddles. That was
the assessment Parker and his brothers had made. His
sisters had given it a more flowery explanation, saying he
was a wise and sentimental man, which wasn't a normal
combination.

"Right, I will, sir," Parker said obligingly.

Mr. Sylvester smiled. "No. You won't," he told Parker.
The older man removed his baseball cap, sat it on his left
knee, and clapped a hand over it. "Men can be stubborn
creatures. We can walk around for years and years with
our eyes open but not really seeing things until they
whack us on the head but good. You got a hard head,

Parker. Janet used to say she never saw anybody as stubborn as you. 'Course, she called it strong-willed because she loved you like only a grandmother can." He chuckled after that.

Rufus picked that moment to wiggle and bark, more than ready to be put down despite Parker's earlier warnings.

"That dog of yours has his eyes open. That's why he walked off like he did. He had a path and he followed it. His owner should be smart enough to do the same," Mr. Sylvester said.

Riddles, Parker thought once more. The man loved to talk in riddles.

"Yeah, Rufus walked off. But he won't be doing that again. Since he's growing up, I think I might have to tighten his rein a bit."

"Hold too tight, you might choke him. Might need to let him go and see where he leads you. It's not beneath a man to follow sometimes."

Parker nodded. "Right. Let's go on in, Mr. Sylvester."

The older man paused a minute, just staring at Parker as if he wanted to say something else. Then he decided against it, heaved a heavy sigh, and stood. His thin legs wobbled a bit, and at one point he held on to the arm of the chair a little longer to steady himself. Parker knew better than to offer his help. Mr. Sylvester was a strong and proud man. Parker gave him the respect he deserved.

He opened the screened door, holding it while Mr. Sylvester made his way through. Once they were both inside, he closed the front door and was about to take another step. He turned back, looking at the gold door handle. If he were in his apartment, he would lock the doors, fasten the bolt he'd had installed years ago, and check his windows before going to bed. He'd remove his weapon, his personal Glock, from the side holster he always carried, placing it on the nightstand right beside his clock and his cell phone. And he'd sleep soundly, knowing he was protected.

Rufus barked again and Parker finally let the dog jump to the floor. He took off the moment he was free. Parker remembered that feeling, too. He'd remembered a lot tonight, possibly too much. Turning from the door, he headed toward his bedroom, not wanting to think another moment about locking doors or grabbing guns for protection. He was in Sweetland, the one place in the world where he'd always felt safe. He was home.

"It looks like a bottle of Pepto-Bismol exploded in here," Heaven said with a chuckle as she entered Blossoms.

Outside, the sun was shining brightly. The storefront window of the florist shop was no match for its intensity, as the showroom almost glowed with light and pink. The opposing color was everything in tissue paper and netting and paper balls, and beneath what seemed like a man-made mountain of the pink was Drew.

"Help!" she squeaked, giving Heaven what she figured was a baleful look. She'd been unpacking the boxes that had just been delivered. "My theme is Falling into You, not Cotton Candy Haven. I can't believe they totally screwed up my order!" she exclaimed.

Heaven stepped forward gingerly, because Drew had been so upset when she'd first opened the box that she'd quickly begun pulling out paper and streamers and tossing them onto the floor in the hopes that at the bottom of one of the many boxes she would discover the burnt-orange and harvest-yellow items she'd ordered. But they were nowhere to be found, and by this point Drew was beyond irritated by that fact.

"So, good, we weren't going for the seven-year-old-girl theme here," Heaven said, then stopped abruptly.

Drew stopped looking in the last box and focused on Heaven. She was what could be referred to as model shaped, tall, long legs, aristocratic facial features, warm smile that touched her eyes every time, and hair that obeyed no matter what the time of year. If Drew's assessment of Heaven Montgomery sounded a little tainted by some envy, it was spot-on! Heaven was gorgeous and educated and successful and in love with a terrific man who promised her the world by way of this small town. Yes, envy was definitely playing with her this morning.

That could possibly be attributed to the fact that she had not been able to button two pairs of jeans this morning. Of course, she had a perfectly valid reason for this and knew that the visible changes to her body were just beginning, but that didn't stop Drew from rolling her eyes at Heaven. The woman was dressed neatly in a crisp white sleeveless shirt, khaki cuffed shorts that displayed perfectly tanned legs, and simple sandals, with her hair pulled up into a efficient and most likely cool ponytail.

And right now she was looking at Drew as though she'd said something wrong or that she hadn't meant to say.

"You okay?" Drew asked.

Heaven blinked. "Ah, yeah, I'm fine. Are you all right?"

"I'm fine. Why wouldn't I be, and why are you looking at me like I have two heads? Is my eyeliner running?" Drew moved back from the counter. She kept a cosmetics bag on the shelf beneath the register. There were other things of importance on that shelf as well, but right now this was the priority.

"No. No. You look great," Heaven rushed to say. "Really great."

Now that was said in a wistful tone, and Drew looked up to see what was going on with her today. With a shake of her head, she reached into the cosmetics bag and found her compact mirror. She looked into it, turning so that she could get a good look at her entire face even though the mirror was too small to take in her whole image at once.

"Nothing's smudged," Drew was saying when Heaven touched her wrist.

She'd crossed the room without Drew really noticing and was now looking at her with teary eyes.

"Okay, Heaven," Drew said, slamming down her mirror and taking both of Heaven's hands in hers. "You tell me what's going on with you right now."

Heaven shook her head and swallowed, as if trying to compose herself before speaking.

"I should be demanding the same thing from you," was Heaven's reply.

She was smiling, so Drew was pretty sure the woman wasn't angry with her for something.

"I'll tell you whatever you want to know if it'll stop you from looking at me like I'm some sort of creature."

"No, not a creature. But I feel like we're somehow connected now," Heaven told her.

Now Drew nodded, calming slightly. "We're friends, Heaven, of course we're connected."

Although Drew had lived in Sweetland for a little more than two years, Heaven had been the first female she'd ever really opened up to. And by open up, Drew didn't mean telling Heaven about her past, because she didn't ever want to have to tell anyone about that horrible time in her life. But she'd opened up enough that she and Heaven had shared some pretty intense conversations about their life's goals and what the future might hold for them. That's how Drew knew how ecstatic Heaven was about marrying Preston and finally being part of a big and caring family.

Heaven shook her head. "Not just that way. I mean like family."

Now a few things started to click. Ms. Louisa had seen her standing on the pier with Parker. Then the old busybody had barged in on them in the ladies' room, just after she'd told Parker about the baby. And now Heaven was standing here practically beaming at her. Drew instantly felt bad for what she was about to say.

"Oh, no, don't let the town's gossip get to you, honey. Despite what tales Louisa might be spinning, Parker and I are not together. She just walked in on a bad moment. No big deal."

At that Heaven cocked her head, staring at Drew quizzically. "So carrying Parker's child is no big deal?"

Drew swallowed. She opened her mouth, then swallowed again. Okay, she hadn't thought that Louisa had heard that much of their conversation. In fact, she was almost sure she hadn't, but then again, this was Louisa Kirk she was talking about.

"Ah, that's what the rumor is? That I'm pregnant with Parker's baby?" she managed to finally ask.

"Are you pregnant with Parker's baby?" was Heaven's reply.

Drew pulled her hands back, lacing her fingers together behind the counter, then releasing them as she took a deep, steady breath. "I didn't think that was public knowledge. And people shouldn't be spreading other people's business around. It's not polite," she said quietly. "No. It's just plain rude, that's what it is. It's nobody's business what I do with my life or who I do it with!"

"Wait a minute, hold on a sec," Heaven said. "Don't get all upset. Parker told us about the baby. It's not like it's the word on the street. Well, I mean, Louisa had told everyone about catching him in the ladies' room with you, but she didn't say anything about the pregnancy."

Drew was shocked. Again. The room swirled around her as she lifted a hand to her forehead.

Heaven was around the other side of the counter in seconds. "Come on, let's sit you down here."

Two wrought-iron-back stools sat at the highboy table that was off to the side of the display case. This was where Drew met with clients when they came in for a full consultation. Now, she was the one sliding onto the chair, trying to get her bearings. Parker had already told his family about the baby. What did that mean? What were his plans where this baby was concerned? As the questions filtered through her brain, she felt like kicking herself, because Parker had been trying to talk to her for two days now about this very subject.

"Parker told you about the baby?" she asked when she thought the words would come out coherently.

Heaven nodded. She'd pulled the other chair close to Drew's and took a seat. Now she reached for Drew's hand.

"He was kind of put on the spot when confronted by Louisa's claims of catching him in the bathroom. Plus, I think he wanted to tell us before anybody else had a chance to. But he hasn't said a word about it since and that's why I'm here. Preston won't talk about it, but I know he's worried and I'm excited and so happy for you and Parker."

Drew smiled softly. Heaven was such a nice person, a nice and slightly naïve person considering her sheltered upbringing in only the correct and polite societies. The real world was a much more daunting place, as Drew had learned the hard way.

"There is no me and Parker, honey. There's Parker, the father of my baby, and then there's me." And that sounded so dismal, Drew actually wanted to cry. Never in her life had she anticipated being a single mother. Actually, if she let herself be completely honest—even if for a moment— she hadn't considered becoming a mother at all after what happened with Jared.

"But you two make a great couple. He's all big, bad cop and you're the street-smart flower girl of the twenty-first century. And you're my friend and he's Preston's twin brother. This is so perfect. We'd be like sisters. I know that sounds silly and really girly, but I'm an only child, so I'm allowed some leverage here."

Drew had to laugh along with Heaven's eternal optimism. For a woman who had come to town to pick up a puppy and start a new life, she'd certainly planted herself firmly in this place and amid the Cantrell family. And Drew was really happy for Heaven and the happy ending she'd found. Unfortunately, happy endings didn't always knock on everyone's door.

"Parker's not that kind of guy," Drew replied. "And I'm not the kind of woman to trap a man or to try and keep one that doesn't want to be kept. We had one night and now we're going to have a baby. It's as simple as that." She shrugged, even though at the moment it didn't feel half as simple as she'd just put it.

"When exactly are you having the baby? Or expected to have the baby?"

"I saw a doctor in Easton, the one Quinn referred me to. He gave a tentative due date of February fourth. But Dr. Lorens has moved here permanently and is going to be sharing office space with Quinn now. She's going to take over my prenatal care."

"So we're having a winter baby, that's terrific. One of the weddings will be over by then. Michelle's already thinking about ideas for a baby shower cake. She was mumbling something about knowing this great baker who specialized in custom designer cakes."

Heaven was talking fast, her eyes bright with excitement as she went on and on about the baby shower, baby names, baby this and baby that. Drew had been trying valiantly to let her have her say. Actually, she'd been trying to feel as excited as Heaven was about the whole "baby in the Cantrell family" thing. But really, she was as nervous about the family knowing as she had been about Parker. Call her crazy, but her family was nowhere near as sane or as supportive as the Cantrells. Add that to the fact that the bowl of raisin bran and skim milk she'd had for breakfast was choosing this moment to disagree with her, and Drew was no longer making an attempt to act as if she were enjoying this conversation. Seconds later, she hopped from the stool and headed toward the bathroom.

"Not again!" Parker roared, slamming the back door behind him. "How did he get out this time? I personally locked that pen when I left this afternoon."

"Maybe instead of going for yet another ride on that death-trap bike of yours, you should have been spending some quality time with your dog. He might be jealous, you know," Savannah said from her perch in a chair at the kitchen table, a bowl of Michelle's homemade macaroni and cheese in front of her.

"The dog is not jealous, Savannah," he said in exasperation.

"Well, then maybe you should be spending time with someone else instead of riding on that bike like some teenager on summer break," she quipped.

"Labor Day marks the unofficial end to summer," was his tart retort.

"Then you're just being a bum, and that's neither attractive nor conducive to a man about to be a father." This time her words were followed by a distinctive twirling of the neck and eye roll that had him considering her the teenager in this conversation.

"She has a point there," Michelle added, making her way into her favorite part of the house. "Have you talked to Drew today? How's she doing? Is she eating right? Having much morning sickness?"

"How the hell should I know?" he yelled at his sisters

without considering that they were his sisters and that yelling at them probably wasn't going to go over too well.

Both females looked at him as if he'd lost his mind, or an ear, or both.

Frustration with Runaway Rufus, the nightmare that had kept him awake half the night, and the meaning behind the baby that now made an appearance in said nightmare had made Parker cranky beyond belief. He'd felt it as he'd pushed the Suzuki for more speed. Then again as he'd yelled at the attendant at the gas station for not initiating the correct pump after he'd already paid, when in actuality Parker had been the one to pull up in front of the wrong pump. He was having a pretty bad day, and the way his sisters were now looking at him wasn't making it any better.

"Look, I can only deal with one crisis at a time," he replied with a deep sigh that was more sincere than either one of them could have imagined.

"So expecting a baby is a crisis?" Michelle asked.

Her back was to him as she loaded dishes into the dishwasher. She was cleaning up after the early dinner rush, which for a lot of Sweetland citizens was between four thirty and six thirty in the evening. They'd eat early, then head back to their homes to sit on the porch while the sun set and the night breeze moved in—when there was a night breeze. For the past couple of weeks, humidity had been their best friend.

"It can be," Savannah muttered.

"No. Having a runaway dog is a crisis, especially when I know I locked him up. And why is it that only Rufus is getting out? Ms. Cleo and the others are going on about their daily business in the yard while my dog acts as if he's got someplace better to be."

With that comment, Michelle slammed the door to the dishwasher. "I certainly remember how that type of

confusion feels. Gramma asked those same questions
about each one of you as you made plans to get out of
Sweetland so fast after high school the sun hadn't a chance
to set the next evening."

And on top of his horrible day, Michelle would proceed
to lay on the guilt like a thick layer of fudge on a sundae.
Parker squeezed the bridge of his nose and silently counted
to ten. No, he didn't make it to ten; somewhere around five
he gave up and pushed through the swinging doors that
led into the parlor so hard, he thought they might actually
fly off the hinges.

Mr. Sylvester was on the porch again as Parker made
his way out the front door. He was playing cards or doing
something solitary, as he usually did this time of day, and
when Parker passed him he heard him mumble something. Definitely not in the mood for Mr. Sylvester's words
of wisdom right now, Parker kept right on walking until he
was once again straddling the Suzuki, loving the familiar
feel of power as he kicked the stand up and started the
engine. In a screech of wheels, he pulled off and headed
down Sycamore toward the town center, where he had a
good idea Runaway Rufus might be.

Chapter 9

Drew had just stepped out of the shower when she heard the noise the first time. It was like a scratching sound, and she chalked it up to the television she'd left playing in her bedroom once she'd come upstairs for the evening. She wasn't working at The Crab Pot tonight; her mother had that shift, thank goodness. Today had been eventful and emotional, from the moment she'd received the boxes from her supplier packed with all the wrong stuff, to the three hours she'd spent with Heaven, talking, crying, listening to Heaven plan an elaborate baby shower, having ice cream down at Scoopalicious, and then coming back to wilted carnations that had finally succumbed to the treacherous heat of the day. At five o'clock, she'd locked up the shop and headed upstairs with the intention of taking a long, soothing bath and then enjoying one of the many frozen chicken pot pies she had stored in her freezer. Drew could cook; having watched her mother do so for many years, she was more than capable of preparing a much better meal for herself. But since it was just her, she usually thought all that ceremony was a waste of time. For that reason her freezer was full of meals that suited her diet just fine. But instead of the long bath, she'd fallen asleep on the couch about three minutes after entering her living room. Hence the shower at seven fifteen.

There was a sitcom on television, something in syndication that she was paying very little attention to, so the sound had been easily brushed off. Then, minutes later, as she stood at her dresser, which was close to the open window, she heard the sound again. Out of curiosity this time, Drew moved to the window, pushing the sheer curtain aside to peer out into her backyard.

Car? Check.

Garden intact? Check.

Dog up on his hind legs, scratching against her back door? Check.

What?

Recognizing Rufus immediately and ready to scold the dog for once again showing up unannounced in her backyard, Drew threw on her nightgown—which was an old New York Yankees shirt that had seen better days and barely scraped her upper thighs—and headed out to confront her trespasser.

By the time Drew made it downstairs to pull open her back door, another unannounced visitor had arrived. Parker's all-too-familiar black-and-silver bike pulled up right beside her Fiesta as if it belonged there. Despite what the older women of the town—her mother and Ms. Louisa came quickly to mind—thought, his bike was surprisingly quiet as it made its approach, the lone headlight casting an eerie glare amid the still bright sunlight.

While she was busy eyeing his owner, Rufus had jumped up on her legs for a cheerful greeting, then pushed right past her and bolted up the stairs. The dog's quick motions combined with the momentary distraction of watching the man on the bike, and feeling the familiar prickles said man on said bike elicited, knocked her off balance. Drew fell back against the door, holding on to the doorknob to keep herself from falling.

Parker was at her side in record time, his strong arms going around her waist and jacking up her already too-short shirt a few more inches so that warmth from the humid air brushed over her lower butt cheeks. Or was that the distinct flush of arousal, since Parker's muscular body was now plastering her smaller body to the door, his dark gaze bearing down on her?

"You okay?"

No! her inner self screamed. *I'm not okay! Your big body is pushing me against the door and all your hard and enticing muscles are doing crazy things to my otherwise dormant hormones, my knees are shaking, and my stomach is dangerously close to growling because I haven't eaten since two o'clock and the two scoops of double chocolate ice cream with chocolate shavings at Scoopalicious!*

Her verbal reply was a simple, "I'm fine."

"Good," was his response. "I'll be right back."

And then he was gone, running up the stairs just as his dog had done a few minutes ago. With a sigh Drew closed her eyes, wondering when exactly her quiet life in this small town had been changed.

"You're not funny," Parker yelled from the center of Drew's living room, where he stood looking around for Rufus. "And I'm losing my patience with this little disappearing act of yours."

"Having trouble with your dog?" Drew asked from the doorway.

Parker turned to her voice and wanted to groan. It wasn't fair. This day could not possibly get any worse, yet as each minute passed, it did.

She looked amazing. Hair in a sloppy ponytail, the

ends a little wet, some matted to her forehead, an adorable flush at her cheeks, and that sexy-ass shirt—even if it
was the freakin' Yankees—teasing him with a generous
view of her legs and not enough of the rest of her. The
moment she'd pulled that door open, his body had tightened with need, his throat constricting with lust. He'd recognized both sensations immediately and quickly tamped
them down. Now was neither the time nor the place. He
was here to retrieve his dog, not to attempt another seduc-
tion of Drew Sidney.

Yet the fates played a cruel game with him. Why have
her come to the door looking so damned doable if she
wasn't, or shouldn't be, or whatever the hell, he was just
having a really bad day!

"My dog is having trouble remembering the rules," he
snapped, looking away from her quickly because that
seemed like his only viable defense.

"It might be the way you're enforcing the rules. I hear
Labs should be trained early on to curtail their behavior,"
she told him.

Parker had just stood up from looking beneath the futon, which was amazingly low to the ground. Rufus could
have squeezed beneath there, but he wouldn't stay in that
cramped space for long. The one thing Parker had learned
about the dog in the time he'd had him was that Rufus
loved space to run and to play with whatever he found
amusing at the moment. He took things, hiding them
from Parker on more than one occasion—the remote control, shoes, even Parker's baton from his utility belt,
which he'd packed and brought with him regardless of his
suspension from work.

"Rufus loves to play," he said, standing and looking
around the room once more.

It was a small apartment that led to her bedroom on

one side and the kitchen on the other. He remembered her bedroom and frowned. Rufus might be in there.

"Do you mind?" he asked her before going in that direction.

"Why don't I have a look?" she countered. "If you're the one he's running from, he might be more amenable to a new face. And since he keeps showing up at my doorstep, he obviously likes me at least a little bit."

Parker wanted to tell her that regardless of his dog's feelings, he liked her more than a little bit. But he refrained. "Fine," he replied tightly.

She disappeared into the bedroom, and Parker moved around her living room once more. This time he stood near a built-in shelving unit where she had more knick-knacks than he thought he'd ever seen in one place. Upon closer inspection, he realized they weren't just knick-knacks, but salt and pepper shakers. There was a set that looked like spooky eyeballs, one that consisted of peas in a pod, a bumblebee and a flower, and many more. He picked up the one of a boy that looked vaguely familiar. The boy was in a boat; he was the pepper shaker. The girl was in the other half of the boat; she was the salt. Holding one in each hand, Parker clasped them together and recognition hit: Darla and Alfalfa from *The Little Rascals*. Gramma loved that show. She used to laugh and laugh sitting in her room and watching the antics of the group of children. On more than one occasion, Parker had been drawn into her bedroom by that laughter. His grandmother worked so hard at helping to raise them when both his parents were around and then by herself after his father's death and his mother's departure. She was always loving and supportive, but she wasn't happy all the time. Yet whenever she sat in her room in front of her nineteen-inch color television set watching an old black-and-white

movie, she'd laugh as if there were nothing in the world
but happiness. Parker liked to remember her that way.

"My favorite is the one of Dorothy's ruby slipper and
the Wicked Witch of the West's black hat."

Parker hurriedly placed the set back in its place on the
shelf and turned to see Drew holding Rufus under one
arm. The action hiked that godforsaken Yankees shirt up
high on her right hip, exposing more of her upper thigh
and a shadow of the curve of her backside. Rufus was giving him a goofy look, as if he knew what Parker was really
staring at, and Drew was looking slightly past him to the
shelves he'd just been exploring.

"Excuse me?" he asked when it dawned on him that
she'd said something.

"The shakers," she said with a nod to her collection.
"The *Wizard of Oz* set is my favorite."

"Oh," he said, looking over his shoulder. "It's quite a
collection you have there. I would have never figured you
for a collector."

She shrugged. "Well, we're not always what we seem."

"No. We're not," he replied, ignoring the clenching in
his chest as she said those words. "I see you've found my
runaway."

"He was under my bed, huddled in a corner."

"Playing games," Parker said. He took a step toward
her, reaching for Rufus, who immediately barked his dis-
content.

"He can stay over if you'd like. I mean, if he insists on
coming here anyway." She nuzzled Rufus as she talked,
and Parker felt a distinct spurt of jealousy.

"I've got a better idea," he said, reaching into his
pocket to retrieve his cell phone. A few minutes later, he'd
ordered two of Amore's Italian feasts with fresh garlic
bread and sodas. The hostess had offered their house
wine when Parker had given his name, but he'd declined,

not mentioning that Drew couldn't have wine because of her condition.

"I'm buying you dinner to repay you for being kind to my disobedient dog," he said. Without waiting for her reply, he moved to that infamous futon, took his seat, and reached for the television remote. "You can pick the movie and Rufus can have his quality time at your house since he thinks for some reason he's entitled to it."

Parker didn't look up because he didn't want to see Drew wrestling with whether she should insist on him leaving or tell him that she'd already eaten—which Parker knew was a lie because the microwave had been beeping intermittently from the kitchen, signaling that something inside it was finished cooking but had not yet been eaten.

She didn't reply but set Rufus down and went back into the bedroom. When she came out again, she'd donned a robe. It was pink and belted at her waist. But it wasn't much longer than her shirt, so Parker's burgeoning arousal would have no reprieve.

It was a dream. She'd had them before and had awakened to wet panties, a quickened pulse, and the kind of breathy delirium that could only come from pure satiation or downing a whole bottle of Scotch by herself.

So when Drew's thighs clenched with the familiar pulse of arousal, she let herself fall deeper into the dream. When her palms flattened over the muscled chest of her dream guy, she sighed at the sensations that went rippling through her body. In her dream, she had complete control over her inhibitions and her fears about intimacy. She could be and do anything without fear of recriminations or that her partner wouldn't agree with her choices. The only other time she'd felt this way was that night. . . .

But even this was different. Drew felt the heavy haze of dreamland weighing down on her just as she felt the hardness of a man beneath her. With that in mind, she spread her legs, rubbing her center over the thick arousal straining to break free. Damn, she wanted it to break free. She wanted it buried deep inside her, pushing her to limits she'd long held firm in her mind but secretly wanted to break through. She circled her hips, coming up onto her knees and giving a little pump. There was a groan, deep and long, and it sent spikes of heat soaring through her body to land with perfect aim in her center. She gasped, the feeling leaving her weak with longing.

Strong hands came to her hips, holding her in place as he thrust upward. He felt so thick and so hot, and she was so hungry for more. In the next instant, Drew was ripping off her robe and her nightshirt. She slipped off of dream guy, hurriedly pushing her panties down her legs and stepping out of them. Before she could return to the futon, dream guy had sat up. He'd taken off his shoes and was now pushing his jeans down very muscled thighs. He pulled his shirt over his head and revealed a toned chest and abs that seemed vaguely familiar to her. Then it was showtime!

His boxers came down slowly, as if he wanted to draw out each and every torturous second. He was long and hard and thick, and Drew's heart beat so fast that she thought she might pass out. Instead she watched entranced as he reached down to the floor and picked up his pants. Inside his wallet he found a condom, tore open the package, and smoothed the latex over his length. Then the strangest thing happened—stranger than her mouth watering at the sight before her. Dream guy spoke.

"Come here, beautiful," he whispered.

It was precisely what she wanted, so she moved closer to him. His hands went to her hips and she felt something strange again. Dream guy leaned forward, kissing her abdomen softly, touching his tongue to her navel, all the while mumbling something she couldn't quite decipher.

Then he looked up to her and she saw his eyes, the deep brown color of his eyes.

Had she ever dreamed in color before?

His gaze was intense and held hers steadily for endless moments, until he lay back on the futon—the black futon. Drew straddled dream guy. She kept her gaze focused on his as he cupped his length, stroked it until the bulbous head looked as if it were ready to explode. With a lick of her lips, Drew lowered herself onto him slowly. He whispered her name.

"Drew. Oh sweet, Drew."

He called her sweet. He knew her name.

When she was completely impaled, he pulled her closer, touched his lips to hers, and kissed her deeply.

"Oh baby, I dreamed of this. So many times since that first night I've dreamed of feeling you again," he whispered against her mouth.

Something about what he said, how he said it, coupled with the night breeze sifting through her living room window, moving the lavender curtains slightly . . .

His touch felt so real; she'd never dreamed this realistically before. Each time she lifted off him and sank down again, her body shook with pleasure. His hands tightened on her bottom, squeezing each cheek in his palms as if she were a ripe melon. Over and over again, he told her how much he'd wanted this . . . again.

"Parker." It was a sigh and a note of recognition. Drew pulled back and looked down at him. His eyes were half-closed, his mouth drawn in a tight line. When he realized she'd stilled, he looked up at her.

"Am I hurting you?" he asked. "The baby?"

Parker. She'd dreamed of him before, but he'd never mentioned a baby and he'd never talked to her. He'd simply made love to her and then gone on his way, just as his reputation dictated. This Parker was looking at her with concern, making love to her with a tender hunger that she felt was genuine and that she'd always longed for.

"No," she whispered in response. "No."

Then Drew closed her eyes. She rode him with the ferocity of a woman starved, refusing to deny herself the pleasure or to think whether this morning after would be a repeat performance of the last time. This wasn't a dream, she thought as she arched her back, Parker holding her tightly, thrusting into her fiercely. He stroked her evenly; she returned his thrusts and cried out his name. It would be just how she'd wanted it for as long as she could have it. Tomorrow, she'd deal with the truth. Right now it was only the pleasure.

Parker had no idea how they'd come to this point. They'd started out watching a movie, something romantic and funny because they'd both laughed a time or two. Eventually they'd both fallen asleep, stretching out on the futon for comfort. Then she'd touched him and she'd shifted, her breast rubbing enticingly against his chest, her leg slipping between his, knee brushing against his erection, and Parker was instantly on fire. He'd wanted her from the moment he'd seen her in that damned Yankees shirt, wanted her even more when she'd attempted to cover said shirt with a frilly little robe that was too sexy for words. She'd straddled him, and Parker thought he'd died and gone to heaven. Then she was stripping and he was following suit, and now . . . now he was about to lose the manhood his reputation had claimed. This joining was intense, the sounds she was making, the feel of her moist heat surrounding him, almost strangling him, he could do nothing else. It was inevitable. Tightening his arms around her, burying his face in the crook of her neck, Parker let go and let pure pleasure wash over him.

Seconds stretched on and they stayed locked together

on the futon. He wondered what she was thinking. The last time they'd made love, they'd both fallen asleep immediately and in the morning he'd left. But he couldn't lift her off him, then set her aside and walk out the door this time. Besides that, with the crack of an eye he could see across the dimly lit room a lump in the middle of the beanbag chair that represented his disobedient dog, relaxing as if he were at a resort. He couldn't leave without retrieving him, and that would likely cause more of a disturbance. No, it seemed he was staying with Drew, at least for a little while longer.

With that in mind, Parker stood, keeping her locked in his arms.

"What are you doing?" she asked almost immediately, attempting to shift so that he almost lost his balance and landed them both on the floor.

"We can't sleep on that thing," he said, referring to the futon with a frown. "It was killing my back."

He was moving across the floor with her still in his arms by then.

"Put me down, I can walk," she protested.

"But I like carrying you," he admitted honestly.

"But your knee, it's not healed completely. And I'm not an invalid, I can walk to my bedroom," she continued.

She was even prettier with her hair completely tousled, her lips still swollen from his kisses, the last remnants of lust still clouding her eyes. He couldn't resist—he kissed the tip of her nose. "Too late, we're already there."

Parker laid her on the bed and she quickly pulled back the comforter and sheets to cover herself. He could leave now. She was in bed, he was standing. All it would take was a quick "Good night" and he could turn around and be out of her house in about ten minutes, including the seconds it would take for him to grab his dog.

"Are you leaving now?"

The sound of her voice quickly pulled him from his thoughts, guilt slapping at him with her questioning glare. Even in the dark of night her room was well lit, courtesy of the half-moon that cast a soft white glow through the thin drapes at the window. She looked almost angelic lying in the bed, pink sheets and fluffy comforter pulled up to her neck even though it wasn't exactly cold in here. She had the air conditioner on, but that simply made it comfortable, certainly not cold enough for her to be bundled up so tightly. The thought that she was hiding from him didn't sit well with Parker. It made him think she was afraid, although of what he wasn't quite certain.

"Are you putting me out?" was his responding question.

She didn't answer immediately, and he thought maybe she was contemplating doing just that. Would he leave if she asked? He'd never been asked to leave a female's apartment before. Never gave them the chance to ask was more like it, and right now he didn't like that this might be the first time.

"I'm giving you permission to do what you know you want to do," she said in a voice that was surprisingly strong and succinct.

In essence, she was putting him out. Parker didn't know how to react to that.

"Look, Parker, I don't want you to feel any obligation here. Especially not because of our new situation. You don't stay with women you sleep with. I guess if I wanted you to stay, I wouldn't have slept with you. So feel free to do what you need to do."

Wow. She was doing more than putting him out. And Parker didn't like it. Not at all.

"First, I need to go to the bathroom. Then, I need to get into this bed and get some sleep. Rufus and I have an early morning tomorrow. Laney Dobson's getting married at the inn tomorrow morning, and if we're not there to set up, Michelle will go ballistic."

He didn't wait for her reply but left the room for the time it took him to handle his business in the bathroom and return.

When he returned, it was to see Drew hadn't moved and still looked at him questioningly. Because he didn't have any more answers, Parker walked around to the other side of the bed, hating the small amount of space between the bed and the window, and remembered falling in the exact spot four months ago. Ignoring that, he pulled back the frilly comforter and sheet on that side of the bed and climbed in, dropping against the pillows without another word.

"Fine. Do whatever you want," Drew snapped, turning over onto her side.

Parker watched as she turned her back to him, moving so close to the edge of the bed that he thought she might actually roll off onto the floor. He thought about following in her direction, wrapping his arm around her waist, and pulling her back close to his front. Something told him they'd both sleep infinitely better if they were touching, continuing the intimacy they'd started in the living room. The stark silence in the room also told him that was out of the question.

He turned on his side, his back facing hers, and pounded a fist into the pillow before settling his head down once more.

See, he could stay with a woman, he could sleep in a bed all night with a female after sex. It wasn't the end of the world, as most would like to think of Parker Cantrell. He wasn't the total womanizing ass they'd portrayed him as. And he wasn't going to get a moment's sleep knowing that Drew was so close and yet so far away.

Chapter 10

Drew lay perfectly still, hands cradled beneath her cheek, legs pulled up to her chest in a fetal position. The bed shifted. Parker was awake. She actually believed he'd been awake for some time now, like the last forty-five minutes, each second that she had also been awake. They both lay in her bed listening to the morning sounds—birds chirping, gulls squawking around the shore, looking for breakfast. Though her windows were closed, living so close to the seashore assured she'd hear whatever sounds were outside regardless. Normally it was a calming sound, the sound of routine and serenity, and she loved it.

This morning it was like a ticking time bomb. Each chirp, each squawk, the sound of a car driving by— probably a fisherman heading down to the dock to his boat—was like a countdown in her head. The countdown for the moment Parker would get up and sneak out of her apartment as he'd done before. Drew wondered if she would let him go this time, as she'd done before. Or should she jump up the moment he did and make him confront her, make him tell her why he was leaving, why he hadn't held her last night, or why he wouldn't have breakfast with her this morning and possibly dinner with her later tonight? She wondered if she should even care that he couldn't commit or that he wouldn't commit. Then she thought of why she shouldn't commit, why a repeat of her past mistakes was not an option for her this time.

When Parker rose from the bed, paused, probably to see if she was awake, then walked across the floor heading to the bathroom, she didn't move.

Drew didn't open her eyes. She didn't speak. She did nothing—just as she had when Jared had spread those vicious lies about her.

He dressed slower this time than he had the last, almost as if he might be trying to wait for her to wake up. She didn't. He made noise this time, knocking into her dresser so that perfume bottles fell on his way out. The glass containers clanked together as he picked them up, probably tried to reposition them. She cracked an eye open, then quickly shut it as he turned and looked directly at her.

Drew heard him moving into the living room. Rufus was also awake, barking until Parker shushed him. Then Parker whistled, probably telling Rufus to come on so they could leave. Instead the dog ran and seconds later had his front paws up on the edge of her bed, his tongue lapping happily over her face. She couldn't remain asleep, or even fake sleep, with all that going on.

"Okay, okay. Good morning to you, too," she said, unable to stifle the giggle that escaped with the dog's exuberant actions. "You are one persistent pup, aren't you?"

She lifted up a little, supporting her weight on her elbows as she looked into the dog's rich brown eyes. "If you weren't such a cutie, I'd have to call the pound to come and take you away for trespassing."

"I'll pay the fine," Parker said from the doorway.

He stood there leaning against the doorjamb, arms folded over his chest.

Tired of being on the sidelines, Rufus jumped onto the bed and settled himself on Drew's side, dropping his head onto her stomach. She patted him, smiling once more. "He's such an attention hog. Maybe he keeps running away because you're not giving him enough time," she told Parker without looking up at him.

"I can't sit and scratch his ears all day long," Parker replied.

She nodded. "Right. Especially not when you return to the city and to your job. What will you do with him then?"

"I haven't thought that far."

"Why?" she asked, looking up this time because she was sure Parker knew every second of what his future held, or at least what he wanted out of it.

He shrugged. "I guess I've been a little preoccupied with the funeral and the B and B and then my accident."

"Are you thinking of not returning to your job because of your accident? I thought you'd healed perfectly." *I thought you did everything perfectly.* The latter echoed in her mind.

"My job's not my life," was his tart reply. "Rufus, come!"

Drew startled at the brisk change in his tone. Rufus's head lifted as the dog looked in Parker's direction, but he did not move.

"Come, Rufus!" He snapped his fingers, but the dog remained still.

Drew pushed at the covers and gently moved Rufus from his perch. She stood and Rufus jumped to the floor beside her, where he stayed. "I apologize if I overstepped. Your life is certainly your business. I was just asking because I'd like to know how to get in contact with you when the baby's born. I mean, if you'd like to know."

He moved fast and so did Rufus. The dog now stood in front of Drew, protectively. Parker was a few inches from her, stopped from coming any closer by Rufus, who couldn't look menacing even if he tried. Instead he just looked as though he couldn't decide which one of them he wanted to pick him up and rub his tummy.

"Let's get this straight once and for all. I will be a part of my baby's life from the moment it takes its first breath." He took a deep breath, clenching his teeth and closing his eyes. "I want to be here for you now and when the baby comes, Drew. So stop standing there looking at me like you expect me to be on the first thing smoking out of town."

"I don't expect anything where you're concerned, Parker. I'm smarter than that," Drew told him just before pushing past him and heading for the bathroom. "You can see yourself out. And pay some attention to your dog so he doesn't keep showing up at my doorstep."

She was gone before Parker cursed and Rufus fell back on his butt, looking up at him reproachfully.

"You trying to kill yourself or chasing demons?" Preston asked Parker the moment he stepped into the basement.

Parker, who had been on his eighty-fifth crunch, spared his brother a weary glance and continued. "I'm working out," he managed to reply.

"You're working off steam," Preston continued, taking a seat on the step. "Rufus giving you some trouble? Maybe you should think about putting him up for adoption."

"Like you did with Coco?" was Parker's retort.

Preston smiled. "Coco's doing just fine with me and Heaven. She loves that crazy little bed with the pink paw prints that Heaven bought her, even though she still thinks she's supposed to jump up in our bed at night."

"Yeah. Real cozy," Parker muttered.

Preston paused, watching as Parker counted off four more crunches. "Maybe you're thinking about Drew and the baby. I know Heaven can't stop talking about baby showers and baby names. You'd think she was the one pregnant."

Parker breathed in through his nose, pulling his knees to his chest once more. "I'm sure you'll be catching up on that pretty soon," he said simply when he released his breath and his legs.

"Yeah, we'd like to have kids of our own," Preston conceded, as if Parker's sarcastic remarks hadn't bothered him. "But since you're the first one of us to experience parenthood, we're all kind of looking to you to see how this works. So she's having the baby in February, huh?"

Parker paused, frowned. "I guess."

Preston nodded. "You gonna stay in Sweetland until then? Sergeant Mertz's not going to like that."

"To hell with Mertz."

Preston stood, then walked over to where Parker was laid out on a mat. He knelt, touching a hand to his brother's shoulder, holding him down so he couldn't complete another crunch.

"You wanna stop the BS and tell me what's really going on with you?"

"I'm trying to work out and you're breaking my flow, that's what's going on," Parker snapped.

Preston shook his head. "You're hiding something. You've been hiding something for months. Now, what I can't tell is if this something has more to do with your accident, your job, or Drew Sidney."

Parker should have known Preston would come at him this way sooner or later. The twins didn't keep secrets from each other—at least they hadn't until the Vezina incident. "My knee and my leg are fine. And Drew's pregnant. I haven't quite figured out what to do with that information. Is that what you want to hear?"

"Okay, well, I know getting her pregnant wasn't in your plan. But it's done and you've got to stand up to it."

"Don't talk to me like you're my father, Pres. You're not. And you've made mistakes, too."

Preston looked shocked for all of ten seconds, then his brows drew close, his jaw clenched, and he looked pissed off.

"Yes, I have made mistakes, Parker. But I was taught just like you to stand up to them, to fix every situation that was in my power to fix."

"I can't change that she's pregnant. All I can do is be a father to my child."

Preston nodded. "That's all I expect you to do."

"Bullshit!" Parker spat, pushing out of Preston's grasp and coming to a stand. "You expect me to pack up and walk away. You expect me to say to hell with this baby and Drew and this small backwards town. That's what everyone expects Parker Cantrell to do!"

Preston seemed to be absorbing Parker's words, and for a second Parker thought of apologizing for the explosion. "Maybe the people of this town that don't know the man you've become expect you to do that," Preston started seriously. "But I know you better. For instance, I know my brother never forgets to use protection when he's with a woman. Ever." He paused. "So what happened with Drew?"

Parker ran his hands down his face, taking a deep breath and then exhaling slowly. He'd asked himself this very question over and over again. The answer still eluded him.

"She came into Charlie's one night when I was there. I

pestered her until she let me buy her a drink. We danced and had another drink and then we went for a ride."

"You were drunk?" Preston asked.

Parker shook his head adamantly. "No. You know I wouldn't drive if I was drunk, not even in this little old town. Besides, I'm still a cop." He said the last with a lot less enthusiasm, but he hoped Preston didn't pick up on it.

"We sat and looked at the stars and the moon, and I guess I just got caught up in the moment. The next thing I knew, we were in her bedroom and then it was morning and I had to get the hell out of there."

"Before she woke up and realized you'd spent the night with her?" Preston continued.

Parker nodded. "I don't spend the night with women, Pres, you know that."

"But you did with Drew."

"I did with Drew twice," he admitted. "Last night when I went looking for Rufus, he was at Drew's house. He keeps running off and ending up there. I don't know why."

"Maybe your dog's got a thing for her, too."

He cut Preston a weary look. "You're joking and I'm trying to figure out how and when my life decided to spring out of control. Thanks a lot, bro."

"Actually, I'm making an observation. You're usually not the type to get thrown off-kilter so easily, Parker. I think what you should be working on deciding is how these new events will affect your future. It doesn't matter when the change came, it's here staring you right in the face. The next step is up to you."

The next step. Parker sighed. Preston had no idea that the next step could also mean life or death for Parker. If he did, he wouldn't have been smiling as he clapped his twin on the back and headed up the stairs.

* * *

"I know it's cliché, but I couldn't resist," Carl Farraway said as he stood in front of Boudoir with his arms extended, two dozen yellow roses thrust in Drew's face.

"Ah, well, not necessarily," she said with a wavering smile. She didn't really know how to react to this gesture—this very open and very public gesture.

"I just wanted to apologize for the other night, you know. Things got a little out of control and I wanted to let you know that I was sorry about my part in it all," Carl continued.

Drew looked up and down the street. There were tourists mulling about, Mr. and Mrs. Brockington had just come out of Godfrey's with grocery bags in tow, and just her luck, sitting in their favorite front window spot at Jana's Java were Louisa and Marabelle, their eyes trained on her.

"This really wasn't necessary, Carl. I was actually speeding, so you were just doing your job," she told him.

She hadn't taken the flowers from him, afraid of what message that would send. But Carl wasn't giving up. He actually stepped forward and lifted her arm so he could set the bouquet within her grasp. Drew held on to them, loving the scent of the flowers but hating the gleam in Carl's eyes as he watched her holding them.

"That yellow looks like pure gold against your skin," he said.

"Wow," Delia replied from her position behind Drew.

Drew had forgotten that she and Delia were on their way over to The Silver Spoon for an early dinner with Savannah and Heaven. All day long, Drew had been looking for things to do to keep her mind off last night with Parker and this morning with Parker. Something had set him off this morning, probably something she'd said, but his rude tone toward her had ticked her off. She wasn't about to stand there and let him talk to her any way he felt like just because he was angry. So she'd walked out on him this time, hopefully leaving him to wonder how he'd apologize to her when she returned. But when she'd returned, Parker was gone. No surprise there.

And now it seemed that Carl was the one coming with an apology. Not Parker.

"Thank you, Carl. I really appreciate the gesture," Drew said, then attempted to turn away.

But Carl followed, walking right beside her as she moved down the street.

"So where are you headed? I know you close your shop up around five, that's why I made sure to come down when you were finished with work. I thought maybe you'd like to get some dinner or something."

He'd been talking really fast, and Drew had tried to walk even faster. She'd looked over her shoulder for Delia and found her right behind her, a smirk on her face.

"Well, I, ah, I'm going to dinner now," Drew told him.

"With me," Delia chimed in. "Just in case you were about to invite yourself, Deputy. She already has dinner plans with me and the girls."

Delia Kincaid was an ex–movie star who'd come to Sweetland just a little while before Drew. They'd clicked instantly. Not because they were similar in any way, since they were actually as different as night and day. Where Drew was more of an introvert and liked quiet nights at home with a good movie and a TV dinner, Delia, with her short-cut hair, almost to the scalp around the sides and spiked with red-frosted tips on top, was a diehard extrovert who laughed heartily and could cut scathingly if necessary. That's probably why Delia hadn't even blinked as she'd quickly cut Carl down.

"Oh, ah, okay . . ." Carl stumbled over his words, looking back at Delia and then to Drew once more. "Um, maybe some other time. Maybe tomorrow or another night, I guess."

"Sure. And Carl, next time don't bring flowers to a florist," Delia called when Carl had begun to walk back in the direction they'd come from.

"That was bad," Drew told her.

"Oh please, that was necessary. He hits on everything with boobs in this town. And doesn't stop with the tourists, either. He's cocky and his shoes squeak when he walks. At the very least, if you're gonna try being a playboy, buy good shoes and stop shopping in the bargain bin."

Delia never pulled any punches, not with anyone. As Drew continued walking, she smiled, wishing she could be a little more like the strikingly gorgeous and seemingly fearless Delia Kincaid. Maybe then she could tell Parker Cantrell where to go and how fast to get there. Instead of falling for this basic thing that was between them every time she saw him, this thing that had created the precious life growing inside of her.

They'd decided to walk to The Silver Spoon. Delia said the exercise would be good for her pregnancy.

"In L.A. pregnant women take Pilates and yoga classes until the day they deliver. They say it makes the labor pains a lot easier to bear and healing goes faster afterwards," she told her while chewing on a Twizzlers.

That was another thing about the perfect Delia. She ate as though she were eight or nine months pregnant and was the size of a sex symbol pixie.

"I don't mind walking. It's the heat I'm beginning to be averse to. It's September, you'd think the humidity would take a hike by now," she complained.

"Heat's good for you. It keeps the blood pumping and other things pumping, too." Delia chuckled as they crossed the street onto Duncan Road.

"You're a sex addict who never has a man at her place or goes on dates," Drew told her, but she couldn't resist laughing herself.

"That's because I know how to do my business and keep it to myself. I learned that living fifteen years in the spotlight."

"But this is Sweetland, there's no paparazzi or reporters around here."

"Are you kidding me? What do you call those nosy old bats Marabelle and Louisa? They may not have the expensive photograph equipment or the byline, but they're just as cutthroat when it comes to gossip as the pros. You see how they were staring across the street at you and Deputy Fly Guy like they were drinking in every word and gesture? I'll bet by the time we get to the B and B, Savannah and Heaven will have heard about Carl's play for you." Delia looked at her and lowered her black sunglasses on her nose so she could peer at her with her lavender contacts. "And his dismal crash and burn as well."

Drew laughed, as she always seemed to do when Delia was around. Next to Heaven, Delia was the closest friend she had in Sweetland. But she wasn't so sure Delia would understand what she was going through with Parker. Delia's whole take on the one-night stand ending in a pregnancy was, "Single mothers are the new family, kiddo. I'm here for you, whatever you need."

She hadn't asked anything else about Parker and didn't really seem to care. Again, Drew wished she could have that type of live-and-let-live motto for her own life. Emotions were messy and complicated, and she knew better. Dammit, she knew better. Yet the moment she stepped onto the front porch of the inn, she longed to see him, longed to watch that lazy smile of his form or his muscled arms cross over his wide chest. She was doomed.

Chapter 11

Savannah Lynn Cantrell was a supermodel. Sure, she'd been in Sweetland for the last five months, helping to run the B&B her family now owned and getting on her older sister Michelle's nerves, but she was a supermodel in every sense of the word. If Drew thought Delia was beautiful—quirky, but still beautiful—then Savannah could be described as nothing less than stunning.

She had a light complexion, lighter than both of her sisters, but the three of them shared the same high cheek-bones and soft jaw. Savannah had great eyes, expressive and wide, and a smile as bright as the sunshine. Drew had heard some men at The Crab Pot saying that about her one night when they'd been more than halfway drunk. She remembered turning to see Savannah, Raine, and Michelle at their corner table, picking their own crabs and oblivious to the attention. Raine said something quietly, Michelle shook her head and smiled, and Savannah laughed. The man, however drunk, was absolutely right: Her smile was like sunshine.

For as pretty as Savannah was, she was just as moody, if not more so. One minute she was laughing and joking, and the next she was sullen and sarcastic. This evening she was stuck somewhere in the middle, playing with the food on her plate and participating distractedly in the conversation.

"Why didn't you mention you'd slept with my brother?" Savannah said suddenly.

Drew almost choked on the raspberry tea she'd been drinking. They'd been talking about Sherry Oglesby's Labor Day outfit—blue- and white-star-covered booty shorts and a red-striped halter top. Savannah hadn't been very chatty all through dinner, but they'd all silently decided to ignore it and not press her for a reason. This outburst took the three of them by surprise, and they looked at her strangely.

"What?" Savannah asked, staring around the table. "I'd like to know when my friends are sleeping with my brothers or if they're using me just to get close to my brothers. Heaven, you don't count, but the Nikki and Quinn thing definitely took me by surprise. And Drew, I didn't think you were interested in men period."

"What?" Drew asked, feeling about to choke again, only this time on nothing because she hadn't gotten over the last words that fell from Savannah's lips.

"I mean, I thought you were like confused or something. Trying to figure out if you were gay or not."

"Savannah!" Heaven squeaked. "Are you serious?"

"What? Why's everyone looking at me like I'm the three-headed monster?" she exclaimed, slamming her palms onto the table.

Another thing Savannah Cantrell was good at was temper tantrums. Normally, Drew thought these acts by anyone over the age of eight or nine were immature, but with Savannah it was like a bad reality show on a channel you couldn't change no matter how much you wanted to.

"First off, I'm not gay, Savannah," Drew whispered.

There were other customers in the restaurant, and the last thing she wanted was for them to hear this conversation.

"And second, I don't have to talk about my sex life with you or anyone else." Drew thought that may have sounded a bit harsh, but she was feeling a little bruised and embarrassed by Savannah's accusation, so she also felt justified. "And it's not like it was an ongoing thing."

"She's right," Delia added. "One night stands don't count. And honey, if you're gonna request that every female come and ask your permission before jumping into bed with one of your brothers, you'd better come up with some sort of database to keep track of that information."

"Well, Preston's off-limits, so she doesn't have to worry about keeping stats on him," Heaven added. "And so is Quinn."

All eyes fell to Drew, who couldn't say the same for Parker.

"We slept together once and I got pregnant," she said in defense. "The next time was just a fluke, and I'm sure it'll never happen again."

The minute the words were out, Drew realized her mistake.

"You slept with Parker a second time?" Heaven asked.

Delia was shaking her head, long gold dangly earrings slapping the side of her face with the motion. "You didn't tell me that."

"Oh, so it's okay for the both of you to expect full disclosure, but I should just sit back and wait for information to flow my way?" Savannah asked, sitting back in her chair with a huff.

Now she was slipping into indignant mode, her lips turned up slightly at the ends as she eyed Drew.

Drew dropped her head into her hands and seriously considered getting up and running all the way home. Then she thought better. These ladies weren't the enemy. Unlike the friends she'd thought she had back in Stratford, Delia and Heaven had been on her side since day one. They were open and friendly and helpful and hadn't judged her when they'd learned she was pregnant by the infamous Double Trouble Cantrell brother. Savannah, on the other hand, well, for the most part Drew thought she was a nice woman. She thought she had some emotional problems that manifested in fits and screaming matches, but she seemed nice enough. If ever there was a time she needed female friends, now would be it.

"Yes. We slept together last night," she admitted.

"Did he leave before you woke again?" Delia asked as she motioned for the waitress to bring her another Scotch on the rocks.

"Probably. Parker's never liked sleeping with anyone, not even Preston when we went on the camping trip that one year. He slept on the cold floor of the tent with only a small fleece blanket because he'd left his sleeping bag home and refused to share the double one Preston had purchased." This was from Savannah, in a tone much lighter than the one she'd been using. She'd been reminiscing a lot lately, getting a faraway look in her eyes whenever she talked about her family and their past adventures.

"But things are different now. There's a baby involved," Heaven countered. "I think he's going to stick this time."

That might have been music to Drew's ears coming from someone else, but Heaven had been in Sweetland and a part of the Cantrell family for only a couple of months; she could hardly be considered knowledgeable on what Parker might or might not do.

"He didn't leave before I woke up. Well, I think he may have if Rufus hadn't come in to say good-bye," she offered.

"So that's where Rufus ran off to yesterday." At that,

Savannah chuckled. "Michelle was about to call the state troopers in to look for that stupid dog."

"Yes, Rufus has been showing up at my doorstep and then Parker follows," Drew admitted.

"You think it's planned? If so, that's a whole lot more original than the stunt Deputy Do Nothing pulled today," Delia replied. Her drink arrived at that moment and she took a sip.

"Deputy who? And what stunt?" Heaven asked.

Drew shook her head. "No. I don't think Parker is making Rufus come to my house just so he can follow. And what Carl did was just ridiculous."

"Carl Farraway's hitting on you, too? Girl, I guess I was wrong and you're not gay," Savannah said with a smile.

"Gee, thanks a lot for that vote of confidence." Drew picked up her glass to take another sip just as Parker walked into the dining room.

"Morning Stud Muffin at three o'clock," Delia stated from beside Drew as if Drew hadn't already seen him.

As Savannah and Heaven were sitting on the other side of the table from them, they both turned to watch him stride across the floor.

"Hey, brother dear, we were just talking about you," Savannah said in a sugary-sweet voice that Parker seemed to ignore.

"I'll just bet you were. Can I borrow Drew for a second, ladies?"

"You can borrow her all night if you promise to cook her breakfast in the morning," Delia replied. "She's partial to waffles and cheese scrambled eggs."

"Stop it!" Drew chided, embarrassed that Parker not only knew they were talking about him, but now, thanks to Delia's comment, undoubtedly knew that she'd told them about last night.

She stood and followed him out onto the deck, because

she wanted to get away from the conversation that she knew was only going to get more out of control. Not because she expected any type of apology from Parker for his rude behavior.

But that's exactly what she received the moment they were alone.

"I'm really sorry for the way I spoke to you this morning. It was uncalled for and way out of line. I've just been under a lot of stress lately and apparently not doing a good job of keeping it under control."

He stood in front of her, thrusting his hands into his pockets as he talked, as if he didn't know what else to do with them.

Well, Drew didn't know what to say. She hadn't imagined this would happen and was accordingly taken off guard.

"I know some great yoga positions for stress relief," was her ultimate reply. Of course, she figured that was the absolute wrong thing to say, but there it was.

He sighed, then smiled. "I might take you up on that sometime. Right now, I just wanted to make sure we were cool."

She nodded. "We're cool."

"Good. So you've already had dinner, I see."

"I did, so you don't need to order me a meal tonight," she replied with a smile.

It seemed a little easier to smile around him now. Since he knew about the baby and hadn't accused her of trying to trap him or, worse, said it wasn't his, she'd felt much more at ease. Being betrayed by a man and the subject of his lies and a town's ridicule wasn't an easy thing to get over, and for the last four months she'd been hoping and praying she wasn't about to go through that all over again.

"In that case, can I walk you home?" he asked, taking her by surprise when he stepped forward and brushed a few strands of hair from her forehead.

It was still humid, so if she took the band from her hair, it would explode like a giant puff ball. Keeping the wisps around her face at ease hadn't been easy, and the product she'd applied so generously had apparently been no help at all.

"I came to have dinner with them. Sort of a girls' night out," she said.

"And by 'them' you mean the ones that are getting up from the table and heading out the front door," he commented with a nod of his head toward the window.

Drew turned, watching in mild annoyance as Heaven, Delia, and Savannah all stood up to leave the restaurant. On their way, Savannah turned to give Drew a wave and another one of her brilliant smiles—the one that made you want to wrap your hands around her neck and squeeze.

"Guess I'm not having a girls' night out after all," she said, reaching for the nonchalant tone over the slightly confused one.

"Then I'll walk you home." He extended a crooked arm to her.

She looked at it for a moment, debating whether physical contact with Parker was wise after last night. Then she decided to go with her gut, since they were in a public place and couldn't possibly end up in the sweaty throes of sex as they'd done in the past. She linked her arm with his and walked beside him.

"Would you rather a ride home? I only have my bike, but Preston's on host duty tonight so his SUV's parked out front. I can grab his keys."

"I like the bike," Drew said quietly. She had been on her feet at the shop all day, getting the flowers together for

Albert Hammond's retirement party. Add that to the walk over here for dinner and she was feeling completely wiped out.

"Ahh, now I see what the real plan was. You and Delia walk over here, she leaves you, and like magic you get another ride on Sexy Susan," he told her as they walked through the grass at the backside of the inn.

It was quiet back here, only the rustle of the water sounding in steady intervals. Night had draped the town, tiny little twinkles in the sky serving as stars. And she was walking hand in hand with Parker. All seemed very well in the world.

"Wait," she said, stopping and almost pulling her arm from his hold. "Who's Susan?"

Parker's lips spread into a full grin. "Jealous?"

She did yank at her arm then, trying to step away from him, but he held on tight.

"Just kidding, Susan's what I call my bike. She's sweet and sexy and always treats me right, no matter how many mistakes I make."

He chuckled when she continued to stare at him, questioning what he'd said a little longer.

"Come on, you're being silly. Why would I mention another female when I'm with you?"

Drew couldn't help it: She shrugged and admitted, "Because you're Parker Cantrell. You have women lined up to be with you here in Sweetland and I know in Baltimore, too. It's highly likely there's a Sexy Susan somewhere in the line."

He stopped walking then and turned her so that she faced him. His hands went to her shoulders, rubbed down her arms, then back up again.

"You're first in every line, Drew. Whenever you think about who I am and what everyone says about me, I want you to remember that."

Parker looked so serious, even in the dark of night. His eyes bored into hers as if he were trying mentally to burn the words into her mind. His fingers had tightened on her arms as he waited for her response. Did she believe him? Could she afford to put herself in the position that believing him would undoubtedly do?

"Are you serious?" was her response instead.

"I've never been more serious about anything in my life," he told her, then moved in closer so that their bodies were touching.

His hands moved up to her shoulders, then grazed over her neck, making their way to her face, which he held gently, tilting her head slightly.

"There's never been anyone like you," he whispered as his lips lowered to hers.

Drew brought her hands up to his wrists just as their lips met. She'd been thinking about pulling away but hadn't been quick enough. Or maybe it was fate that had slowed her movements, made her think twice about resisting the inevitable.

The kiss was so soft and as gentle as the evening breeze. Parker expertly coaxed her lips to open, her head to tilt, as he took them deeper. And Drew felt herself falling. In her mind she was treading water, trying desperately to stay afloat, but it was pointless. Her hands ran the length of his arms, over his muscled shoulders, and to his back as she pulled him closer. His tongue stroked hers longingly and she moaned, her knees going weak.

When he finally pulled back slightly, they were both out of breath. He rested his forehead against hers, and they stayed that way for endless moments.

"I don't know what this is, Parker. I wasn't looking for anything with you, I didn't plan to get pregnant," she began.

Parker shook his head. "You don't have to say that," he

told her, hating the tortured sound in her voice as she spoke. It was as if she was apologizing for what was going on between them, apologizing and keeping her distance at the same time. This was new to Parker, maybe because in the past he'd been the one staying far away, keeping all he had safely locked away, not willing to share even an inch of his soul with a woman.

Now, he felt unwilling to let this woman walk away believing he felt anything different.

"Sometimes things don't go according to a plan," Parker heard himself saying. He almost shook himself after those words, because they sounded more like something his grandmother would have told him. Come to think of it, she probably had at some point in his life.

Drew pulled back, looking up at him. "Do you really believe that?"

"I really do," he replied without a second thought.

"Come on, let's get you home. It's getting chilly out here," he said, taking her hand. They walked until they were in front of the house, at the curb where his bike was parked.

He grabbed the helmet from the backseat and placed it gently on her head, admiring how cute she looked wearing it. This was another first for Parker. He loved his bike and rode it as much as possible in the city, but whenever he went out with a female, he drove his Expedition. Drew was the first female to grace Sexy Susan's backseat. This was her second time riding with him, and damn, she looked good doing so. Parker smiled as he watched her lift a leg and slide onto the seat as if she'd been riding there every day of her life.

He took the long way to her house, heading toward the dock instead of turning in the opposite direction on Duncan. He figured she didn't mind by the way she wrapped her arms tightly around his waist and laid her head on his back as he drove. The humidity was lifting a little, and a thunderstorm had been predicted for later tonight. He could smell it in the air, the soft, dewy scent that accompanied a good summer shower.

"I love this," she said, speaking loudly over the wind as he turned the corner so they were now riding right alongside the dock. It wasn't yet nine o'clock. Charlie's, The Crab Pot, and Amore stayed open until ten, so lights were on and cars were in the parking lot. Some of the decorations from the Bay Day festivities were still there—the large Sweetland banner rippled in the breeze, while puffy red, white, and blue balls still hung on the lampposts. And Sexy Susan purred through the night.

"Hold on," he told Drew over his shoulder.

She did. If it was possible, her arms tightened around his waist even more, her body scooting even closer to his. Normally Parker would have been driving much faster, loving the feel of the wind cutting across his cheeks as he drove. But tonight he was carrying a special package and she was carrying a package even more dear to his heart. So he drove with caution, but with enough energy to satisfy them both on some level.

He finally came to a stop in her yard, pulling up beside her car once more. It was becoming a familiar parking spot for him, but Parker didn't give that any more thought than was necessary.

She hopped off immediately, pulling the helmet from her head. Her hair always seemed tousled, unruly, gorgeous. He'd been with primped and fancy women more times than he could count. He'd also been with women with professional careers and some whose professional careers were to find a man with a good job to marry and train. But he'd never been with a woman who owned her own flower shop in a small town, worked part-time at her uncle's crab shack, collected salt and pepper shakers, and snored softly when she slept.

"That was great!" she exclaimed, her eyes alight with a life he hadn't noticed in her before.

"You like to ride, huh?" he asked, kicking the stand down and stepping off the bike himself. "I would have never figured you for a biker babe."

At that she laughed. "Biker babe. I kind of like the sound to that."

"Well, anytime you want a ride all you have to do is say the word," he told her seriously. He had a flash of Drew and him riding down the open highway on his bike, the wind at their ears, no traffic in sight, and their entire future ahead of them.

"You're not what I expected either," she said, coming to touch a hand to his cheek.

"Then maybe we should release all expectations and see where we go from there."

It was the most honest suggestion he'd ever made to a woman. But Parker figured if there was one woman who should know the real him, shouldn't it be the mother of his child?

"Maybe," she said quietly, dropping her hand from his face.

Then she yawned, lowering her head and lifting a hand to cover her mouth as she tried to hide it from him.

"Tired?" he asked anyway.

She nodded and looked at him once more, a small smile creeping across her face. "I don't know what's wrong with me. More and more I'm ready for bed by eight and dead to the world by nine thirty."

"Your body's going through a lot of changes, preparing to carry the baby for the months ahead. It's normal that you're fatigued in these early months," he told her.

"Wow." Drew laughed. "You sound like a textbook."

"What to Expect When You're Expecting," he told her just a little shyly. "I saw it on your nightstand last night, or rather earlier this morning when I couldn't sleep."

"You couldn't sleep? Why?" she asked, then shook her head. "I mean, why didn't you wake me? We could have watched another movie."

Or made love again.

The words hung between them like a noisy chime. They both heard it, both knew that's precisely what would have happened had he awakened her, and both didn't want to accept what that revelation really meant.

"One film dated before 1960 is my quota for one night," he said lightly. "Come on, let's get you inside so you can get some rest."

Once at the door, Drew pulled her keys out of her pocket and unlocked it. She stepped up onto the step that would take her inside and turned back to look at him.

"Thanks for the ride home and for telling me that Sexy Susan was the name of your bike."

"Thanks for joining me for the ride and for not kicking my ass before I had a chance to explain that Sexy Susan was the name of my bike."

They both laughed at that.

"Good night, Parker," she said finally when Parker thought the silence between them was going to drive him nuts.

"Good night, Drew. Sleep tight."

She smiled then. "You too."

When the door clicked shut and she was out of his sight, Parker stood on the steps, his palms to the door, and lowered his head. She was the mother of his child, and he wanted her. He wanted all of her regardless of what she'd been programmed to think about him. And he was going to prove that his reputation had died the day he'd left Sweetland.

Chapter 12

Rufus was in Parker's room when he returned to the B&B. He'd been keeping close tabs on his dog since last night's runaway incident. For whatever reason, the dog wanted out of the B&B. Parker couldn't figure it out, since Rufus was perfectly content running around the backyard with his mother and siblings all day long. He took his meals, had gone for a swim earlier in the morning with Parker after his morning run, all as he normally had. Yet Parker had been nervous about leaving him in the pen with the others today. So he'd brought him to his room and let him have free rein there.

Looking around now, he figured that might not have been such a great idea. Labs were generally very sociable and playful pets. They needed lots of love and attention, and for the months he'd been here, Parker had been able to give Rufus that. He remembered the day the will had been read and they'd all found out that each would inherit a puppy—Michelle had been the unlucky one to inherit Cleo, the mother, and the pup Lily. Savannah, Parker, and Quinn had been the most averse to keeping their dogs. Gramma had left a clause in the will stating that if they found the puppies a loving and caring home, they could get rid of them, but no one had resorted to that method yet. Parker hadn't even considered it. Sure, he lived in the city and worked long and unpredictable hours, but something about receiving the dog and part ownership of the B&B had just seemed right to him.

Now, standing with hands on his hips, looking around the main sitting room of the space he occupied in the B&B, he was having second thoughts.

On the table where he kept his laptop and the mail that was being forwarded from the city, the cup he'd been drinking out of before he'd left earlier today had been knocked over. There had been water left over in that glass, and Parker cursed, heading in that direction first. He picked up the laptop, turning it over to survey the damage. Luckily, the pile of mail had absorbed most of the water so there wasn't any damage to the laptop. But books that were stacked on one of the end tables had been knocked down, and all the magazines that had been on the lower level of the coffee table now littered the floor. One side of the curtain at the window was lopsided, frayed at the edge.

"I punish you for running away and you trash my room. Not a good decision, Rufus," he said to the dog, who had already taken his leave, heading into the bedroom without so much as a backward glance. "And I know you hear me in there!" Parker roared as he went around the room picking things up.

He fell to his knees, frowning only slightly with the pinch of bending his bad knee and plopping it down on a hard surface. Now and forevermore his knee would be held in place by pins, a fact that had been a little hard for him to swallow immediately after the accident, but one that he'd been slowly getting used to.

Parker found the remote control and yelled Rufus's name. He found a rawhide bone chewed almost to bits and figured at least the dog had made use of it before losing his interest. Then he pulled from beneath the chair a long envelope with his name printed on the front: DETECTIVE PARKER R. CANTRELL.

Parker sat on the couch, trying to remember if he'd seen this envelope in the room before this moment. The fact that he was almost positive he hadn't had him lifting a hand to rub the back of his neck. That was Parker's tic, a quick tingle running down the base of his neck that meant something was out of whack.

Without another thought, he opened the envelope and pulled out the contents. There were pictures, lots of them, some falling to the floor as he reached forward to drop the rest on the table. He leafed through them, his gut clenching at the sight of him and Savannah arm in arm as they'd walked down the steps of the front porch the morning of Gramma's funeral. There were more from inside the church of Michelle and Raine, Preston and Quinn. Candid shots of each of the puppies and Ms. Cleo, one of Mr. Sylvester sitting on that bench he loved in the backyard.

Parker picked up the ones from the floor and cursed, low and fluent. There was a picture of him riding down the highway, one of his bike swerving off the road, and another one of him slamming into the tree that busted his knee open. That one Parker crumpled. He closed his eyes and tried counting down from one hundred to calm the rage boiling steadily inside him. Around ninety-five he gave up and stood, walking with quick strides to his laptop. With quick pecks of the keys, he began the booting process and pulled his cell from his side pocket.

"It's Cantrell. I need you here. Now." That was all he said, all he'd had to say.

She wasn't being silly. It was a natural request, and if he didn't want to go, well, then that would be fine, too. She wasn't going to force him, she'd already sworn she'd never force him to do anything he didn't want to where this baby was concerned.

The fact that it had been over a week—almost two, to be exact—since Parker had kissed her good night on her doorstep made this task a little harder. Still, Drew stepped up onto the front porch and was about to open the screened door when a voice stopped her.

"You walk over here?" Mr. Sylvester asked from his chair, which had been pushed toward the corner so that he was angled to see more of the street.

"Oh," Drew said, startled because she hadn't realized he was there. "Hi, Mr. Sylvester. Yes, I walked." She neglected to tell him that the reason she'd walked was that she was in such a hurry to get away from her mother, she'd left the flower shop through the front door and didn't want to go back inside to go out back to where her car was parked. Lorrayna was watching the shop for the afternoon since Drew had an appointment. Her mother was in one of her moods, so Drew didn't think the flower shop would do much business while she was gone. Lorrayna in a mood was more than enough to scare anyone off, but Drew had no choice; she'd had to ask her to fill in for her. She really needed to think about hiring an assistant, especially as she went further into her pregnancy and would need to take time off for the delivery. But right at this moment, Mr. Sylvester was demanding her attention.

"Should you be doing all that walking in your condition?" he asked when she made another attempt to go inside.

For a minute Drew was about to ask him what condition. To her knowledge, her pregnancy wasn't public knowledge. But the Cantrells knew, and that was most likely why Mr. Sylvester knew. He was like a part of their family.

"Exercise is actually good for my condition," she replied. "And the walk's not that far."

"It's hot out here today," he continued, his thin lips turning down into a frown. "Too hot for you to be waltzing around in the blazing sunlight. I'll bet you're thirsty."

He'd grasped the sides of the chair and was struggling to stand. Drew went to him and grabbed hold of his arm, only to have him pull away.

"I don't need the help. You do. Anybody crazy enough to walk around in this heat needs a lot of help. Come on in here, let me get you something to drink."

Drew could have argued that the walk hadn't affected her. Well, not any more than every other activity she undertook lately. For all that her first trimester had passed with average to sometimes severe morning sickness, her second trimester plagued her with unimaginable fatigue that she was trying desperately to cope with.

Mr. Sylvester, on the other hand, looked a little peaked himself. His brow was sweaty, but that could have been from sitting out here on the porch in ninety-plus temperatures. He managed to get up from the chair and stood still a few seconds before taking another step. He looked shaky, but she wasn't going to attempt to help him walk again for fear he'd snap at her once more. She did, however, stick close to him as they walked into the house together and straight back to the kitchen.

On the way, Drew waved to Natalie, the front desk clerk, who was taking a sip of one of her favored energy drinks. Natalie was probably in her late thirties and used to teach at the elementary school in Easton, but she'd retired early because of a stress-related illness. Uncle Walt had given her the rundown one night when Natalie had come into The Crab Pot with her ex-husband, Bob. They'd ended up arguing, Bob had stormed out, and Natalie had sat at the table crying. Uncle Walt said her sanity had been fragile ever since the breakdown that ended her career and her marriage simultaneously. Drew was happy to see her smile, even though word around town now was that she was addicted to those energy drinks and worked part-time at the B&B so she'd have money to order them in bulk online.

Shaking her head as they entered the kitchen, Drew reprimanded herself for rehashing the town gossip, even if it was just to herself. She knew how hurtful lies and assumptions could be, not only to a person's reputation, but also to the victim's well-being.

"Why don't I fix you something to drink, Mr. Sylvester," she said, moving quickly to the refrigerator and praying he wouldn't argue.

He paused by one of the chairs at the Formica-topped table and vintage chairs that Michelle kept in honor of her grandmother.

"Well, since you're already over there," he mumbled.

Drew heard the chair slide across the floor and assumed he'd taken a seat. She opened the door to one of the Sub-Zero refrigerators—Michelle used one to house most of the supplies for the restaurant and inn and a second one to keep stuff for the family. As Drew had been spending time with Heaven in the last few months, she'd been privy to this information and knew just where the family refrigerator was and that it was okay for her to get herself and Mr. Sylvester something to drink from there.

She was sitting at the table with him, watching as he drank his lemonade slowly, when Michelle came in.

"New guest checking in," she was saying as she entered. "He'll be in the Sunshine Room. Doesn't know how long he's going to stay."

Michelle was speaking to Raine, who came in right

behind her, a notepad and pen in hand, jotting down things as Michelle spoke.

"Oh, hey, Drew. Mr. Sylvester," Michelle said, pausing momentarily.

"He's a Major League Baseball player," Michelle continued. "Wanted me to know that right away since I didn't act like I recognized him, I guess."

"I know who he is," Raine said, lifting her head from writing for a moment. "How are you feeling today, Drew?"

Drew smiled at the sisters as they worked together, looking more like partners every day. Heaven had told Drew how the siblings were just getting to know one another all over again after everyone had been away. The ownership of the B&B and those puppies had formed yet another bond between them that some were still struggling with.

"I'm feeling good," she replied, only partially lying. "You two look busy. Anything I can help with?" She made the offer because she sensed that sitting with Mr. Sylvester would lead to a conversation she didn't want to have—one where he would give her advice she'd have to pretend to be interested in taking.

"New guest came in this morning," Michelle said, pulling boxes out of the B&B refrigerator. "He's got more luggage than Savannah, and you know how Savannah travels."

Raine laughed.

"Should have seen when that girl arrived," Mr. Sylvester chimed in. "The driver was so out of breath by the time he finished bringing in all her bags, I tipped him myself." The older man chuckled.

Drew smiled, loving the homely feel of sitting in this kitchen with them.

"I don't think we'll need help with him per se," Michelle said in response to Drew's question. "But if you're available to help serve tonight, Hoover and his booster club are having their annual meeting here. They're taking all of the deck and some of the yard space to set up their casino games."

"Wow, casino night at The Silver Spoon," Drew remarked. "I wouldn't miss that for the world." Then she remembered her sole reason for coming to The Silver Spoon in the first place—to see if Parker was available this afternoon. "I have a doctor's appointment in about twenty minutes, then I'll come back here."

"What does a man have to do to get some lunch around here?"

The question came from the newest person to enter the kitchen. He was tall, with a slim but muscular build, eyes the color of the sea, golden-blond hair slicked back with precision, a strong jaw, and a deadly smile.

"Jared?" Drew whispered.

"Hold on a minute," Jared called after her.

Drew didn't listen. She was back at the front desk when he reached out and grabbed her arm.

"Let go of me!" she yelled, attempting to pull her arm from his grasp.

"Not until you at least talk to me. Damn, it's been years and you're still running away from me," he told her.

"That's because I don't have anything to say to you! I didn't then and I don't now." She yanked at her arm again, but he had a tight grip.

She remembered that about him and felt a wave of dizziness. Her knees buckled and she would have gone down but for two things: 1) Jared was holding her firmly, so if anything she might have just dangled there if she passed out; and 2) Parker appeared.

"I believe the lady asked you nicely to let her go," Parker said, coming up behind Drew. He'd slipped one arm around her waist, effectively keeping her from crumpling to the floor.

His other arm had extended, his hand wrapping around Jared's wrist.

"I'm not going to be as nice when I tell you to get your goddamned hands off of her," he continued in a lethal tone she'd never heard him use before.

"We were talking," Jared replied, looking at Parker as if he were a fly on the wall.

Drew figured Jared probably shouldn't have done that. In the next instant she was pushed aside, her arm wrenched from Jared's grasp. Parker's right arm moved quickly, his fist connecting with Jared's jaw with a sickening crack. Natalie screamed as Jared fell back against the highboy table that held one of Drew's arrangements and brochures about the inn. Raine, Michelle, and Mr. Sylvester had come into the front desk area by that time, and Raine was moving to Drew's side.

Michelle rushed to Parker, grabbing him and pushing him back when Parker looked as if he'd swing on Jared again.

"You bastard!" Jared roared when he'd managed to stand upright again, one hand gripping his jaw, the other pointing at Natalie. "Call the cops—I want this idiot in jail!"

When Natalie had finally clapped her hand over her mouth to keep from screaming, she looked from Parker to Jared and back to Parker again in question.

"Now!" Jared roared.

"Just wait a minute," Michelle said, extending her arms and standing between both men. "I want to know what's going on here."

"What's going on is I'm about to sue this establishment for allowing its guests to behave in such a reprehensible manner. I was minding my own business when this guy came out of nowhere and hit me," Jared argued.

"He had his hands on Drew and she asked him to remove them. I told him to remove them and he didn't listen. Case closed," Parker said, flexing his fingers at his
side and then going to Drew.

Without a word, he moved Raine out of the way and
touched Drew's shoulders. "Are you okay?"

Still shocked from seeing Jared and having him touch
her again, Drew was trying to regain her composure.
She'd been watching what was going on, at the same time
feeling like an outsider looking in on a really bad television drama episode. Years ago, she'd been the star of that
same show. Now, with her hands still shaking, she wanted
to run, to go as far as she could again, because obviously
the first time she hadn't gone far enough.

"Yes," she finally whispered to Parker. "I have to go."

But he merely tightened his grip, which made her heart
beat wilder. She knew he wasn't Jared, knew quite easily
the differences between these two men. Still, his hands
on her right now wasn't a good thing. "Please," she said,
closing her eyes. "Please let me go, Parker."

He looked hesitant, then he looked angry, but Parker
removed his hands from her shoulders. Drew took a step
back and turned. Then she was moving fast. She was out
the door in no time, the warm air brushing over her face.
Her legs moved, her body followed, but she didn't speak.
And best of all, she didn't cry, not this time.

"So where's your brother?" Deputy Farraway asked Michelle about fifteen minutes later when he'd sauntered into
The Silver Spoon.

Michelle was not in the mood for Carl's foolishness.
When Jared Mansfield had yelled at Natalie one time too
many, the already jittery woman had picked up the phone
and called the sheriff's office before Michelle could convince him that there was no need. Besides, the red bruise

on the man's jaw was a dead giveaway that something had happened.

In no time at all, things at The Silver Spoon had spun out of control. One minute she'd been talking to her family about a new guest, and the next said new guest was chasing after Drew and getting punched by Parker. Now the police were here and both Parker and Drew had stormed out of the house.

"I don't know where he is, Carl," she said, not bothering to mask her irritation that he was in her house at all.

Carl had been present at the Brockington house when Nikki was being questioned by the Easton police a few months back. He'd behaved himself well enough, as it had been Deputy Jonah Lincoln who had been nursing a longtime crush on Nikki, only to be thwarted by Quinn's quick courtship of her. But when Heaven had been kidnapped, Carl had shown his true colors and behaved obnoxiously to Heaven's parents—who rightfully deserved it—then to Preston, Quinn, and Parker (mostly Parker), about the way they'd all ultimately handled the situation. If memory served her right, which for Michelle it always did, Parker and Carl had exchanged pretty heated words a few days after Heaven's rescue, and it had taken Quinn and Preston to hold Parker back from slugging the man then. Jonah had also been there, but he hadn't acted as fast as Quinn and Preston to stop the possible physical altercation. Michelle figured that after being Carl's partner for more than five years, Jonah might feel the man deserved to get hit.

"Do I need to search the house?" Carl pressed.

"Do you have a search warrant?" asked Savannah, who had appeared just as Parker had walked out. She stood there with her hands on her hips, glaring at Carl.

"He left after Drew did. I think you should go out and look for him. He's mighty dangerous and I'm afraid of what he might do to her," Jared said in a tone that even Michelle recognized as fake.

Now, true, about half an hour ago she had swiped this man's credit card and smiled brightly as she'd welcomed him to The Silver Spoon; but at this moment she was ready to get all of his many suitcases and bags and toss them— with their owner—out onto the sidewalk.

"Parker's not going to hurt Drew," Mr. Sylvester said. "That's just plain nonsense. Now, you, on the other hand, I don't know about you, son."

Jared scowled in Mr. Sylvester's direction. "I'm not your son, old man. And you can just mind your business. I'm filing a report for assault and I want this officer to go out and find Drew and bring her back here to me ASAP."

"A report? Really, is that necessary, sir?" Raine asked. "After all, you were physically assaulting Drew. Parker was just defending her and he did ask you nicely to take your hands off of her."

Raine was always the peacemaker. She hadn't even raised her voice as she tried to reason with this jerk, who was not only threatening her brother, but ordering their deputy to do something. Michelle wasn't going to be as diplomatic.

"Mr. Mansfield, I think it's time for you to leave The Silver Spoon," she said sternly. "And Carl, you can follow him out."

"I'm here to make an arrest," Carl said with more pleasure than Michelle cared to hear in his voice.

"Then arrest this idiot and get it over with," Savannah told Carl, moving so that she now stood directly in front of him.

Carl was a man. He was a man who loved women. And all men, especially the ones who had grown up in Sweetland and witnessed the blossoming of Savannah Cantrell, girl to woman, loved Savannah. Today she wore a lavender dress that wrapped around her body in gentle yet alluring folds. Her heels were at least four inches high—Michelle was sure she'd hadn't seen Savannah in flat shoes since she'd turned thirteen—and her hair was pulled back from her face, cascading down her back like a glorious dark mane.

Carl just about drooled when Savannah was right up on him. She didn't touch him because she didn't like him, probably liked him even less now that he was threatening her brother. But Carl was too besotted to figure that out.

"He's not welcome here, Carl. And if you're not careful, you won't be either," she said in a tone just a touch softer than before.

"That's bull!" Jared yelled again.

The man obviously had no problems raising his voice at women and law enforcement. Michelle had thought he had a privileged air to him when he'd checked in, but she'd chalked that up to his being a ballplayer. In her mind she'd also dismissed any privilege he thought he might receive at The Silver Spoon. That wasn't the type of establishment they ran. He would get the same treatment as the couple in the Blue Room that had come up from South Carolina with their two adorable daughters.

"I've paid my money to stay here and I'm not leaving," he continued.

"I can fix that for you right now," Michelle said. She moved around the front desk and quickly ran her fingers over the keyboard. "I'm refunding your money. I suggest you get started removing your bags and call yourself a cab."

"You can't do that!" he yelled back at her.

"She can and she is, sir," Quinn said as he walked into the room. "And I'll warn you against raising your voice at my sister again."

Michelle had no doubt Natalie had also buzzed back to

Nikki's office when all the commotion had kicked off. Nikki would not have hesitated to call her fiancé, who was now standing in the doorway looking and sounding as foreboding as he actually was. As the oldest of the Cantrell siblings, Quinn took his role very seriously. He felt responsible for all his siblings as well as for the success of the B&B. Right now, he was most likely feeling protective of both.

"Fine! I'm sure there's someplace better in this hick-assed town that I can stay!" Jared said. He was about to walk away when he stopped in front of Carl. "I want him arrested and her brought to me."

Carl at least had the guts to push away the finger that Jared had been jabbing into his chest. Glaring at the man, he said, "Assault, of any kind, on an officer is a crime. I'll investigate the incident between you and Parker Cantrell. But as far as Drew goes, I don't want to hear of you bothering her again. We understand each other?" The last was said as Carl's hand moved down to his sidearm and rested on his hip.

Jared followed Carl's movement with a frown and stepped back. "I'll find her myself," he said before walking away.

"What was that all about? Who was that guy and why is he looking for Drew?" Quinn asked.

"I don't know who he is, but Drew definitely knows him. She took off running the moment she saw him. That's when he chased her and that's when Parker intervened," Raine told him.

"Sounds like self-defense to me," Quinn said, eyeing Carl.

"It's self-defense if he assaulted Drew and she was the one to clock him. But if Parker hit him, it's assault and I'm going to bring him in."

Carl made that announcement with a smirk before

turning to leave. "I'll wait for Mr. Mansfield to leave the premises, then I'm going to go find your brother."

He was gone when Quinn cursed.

"What the hell was Parker thinking hitting this guy?" he complained.

"He was probably thinking that some stranger had his hands on the woman he loves, and usually, for a Cantrell man, that's just not acceptable," Savannah said with a smile.

Quinn didn't smile, but Michelle suspected he knew Savannah's assessment was right.

Chapter 13

"How've you been feeling, Drew?" Dr. Amelia Lorens asked as she gently pushed around Drew's abdomen.

Drew was lying on the exam table, staring up at the ceiling light as if it were the light welcoming her to eternity. She was biting on her lower lip, trying desperately to keep her breathing steady, her mind focused on the exam instead of the events that had occurred just before it.

"I've been a little tired," she said, letting out a deep breath.

"Really? Are you eating enough?" she asked.

"I guess. I mean, I'm eating three meals a day now. Before, I'd work straight through lunch, but once the morning sickness kicked in I figured out it was best if I didn't go hungry for too long."

"Right," Dr. Lorens commented. She moved away from Drew, glancing at her chart once more.

Drew noted the woman seemed more than competent. The many degrees and commendations hanging on the wall in her office supported that fact. She looked to be in her early thirties, with a pretty smile and a calm demeanor. Her hair was short and curly, her eyes light brown and

compassionate, and her hands soft; she was a far cry from
Dr. Stallings, whom Drew had seen last year for a strep
throat.

"What about exercise?" she asked just as there was a
knock on the door.

Dr. Lorens looked surprised, then shrugged. "Excuse me."

Drew went back to looking at the ceiling. She could hear
whispering but wasn't paying it much attention. Until Dr.
Lorens spoke to her.

"Drew, there's someone here who says he'd like to
come in. Is that okay with you?"

She turned her head and wasn't half as surprised as
she should have been to see Parker standing in the doorway. As she'd walked toward the doctor's office, she'd
thought a navy-blue SUV had been driving pretty slowly
behind her. But a few times she'd turned back and hadn't
seen the SUV at all. Seeing Parker now connected the
dots. Preston had a navy-blue SUV.

He looked at her imploringly and she nodded her
agreement. After all, hadn't she gone to The Silver Spoon
to ask if he wanted to join her for this appointment?

Now a new anxiety assailed Drew, and she clenched
her fingers in the top of her shirt, which Dr. Lorens had
pushed up above her slightly protruding belly.

"Okay, then let's finish up the exam," Dr. Lorens continued cheerfully, leading Parker inside and closing the
door behind him. "We were just about to listen for the little
one's heartbeat."

"Oh," Drew mumbled. "We weren't able to hear it the
last time because you said it was still too early."

Parker had come to stand right beside her. He didn't
touch her, as she almost thought he would. There was a
war going on inside her where part of her prayed he would
touch her and another part feared the result of that same

action. Her heart was racing, and she hoped they could hear the baby's over her own.

"Let's see," Dr. Lorens said, referring to her chart. "You're at eighteen weeks and three days' gestation today. We should be able to hear the heartbeat loud and clear."

Dr. Lorens reached for a tube off the shelf, then moved back to the table where Drew lay. She applied the cool gel to Drew's stomach, then frowned down at Drew. "A little chilly."

Drew nodded and replied, "A lot chilly."

"Is it painful?" Parker asked.

"No," she answered. "I guess I'm just a little nervous." That was a lie. She was *a lot* nervous. In a few seconds she would hear her baby's heartbeat for the first time. Parker was standing right beside her—looking, of all things, interested. And Jared Mansfield was in Sweetland. Nervous didn't accurately describe what she was feeling.

Parker frowned. "Yeah, I know the feeling."

She looked up at him then, and the frown shifted to an awkward smile before he returned his focus to her stomach.

Dr. Lorens touched a smooth probe to the lubricated area of Drew's stomach, then moved it along slowly. In her other hand, she held what looked like a speaker that was attached to the probe by a spiraled cord. The first sounds were loud, like wind blowing over a telephone connection. Seconds later, it was joined by another sound, a quick rhythm that sounded too fast to be a baby's heartbeat. Drew looked at the doctor, ready to voice her concerns.

Dr. Lorens nodded, a smile spreading quickly. "That's your baby, breathing very strong and steady."

Drew gasped, her fingers clenching in her shirt even tighter. This time Parker did touch her, his hand going to her shoulder.

"That's our baby's heart beating?" he asked, his voice sounding as bewildered as she felt.

Dr. Lorens nodded. "It sure is."

For the next few seconds nobody in the room spoke, they simply listened. Tears welled in Drew's eyes, and Parker moved so that his other hand touched her stomach just above the lubricated area.

"Our baby's in there, breathing strong and steady," he whispered.

"That's right," Dr. Lorens told him as she removed the probe and reached for a tissue to wipe the lubricant from Drew's stomach.

"I'll see you again in four weeks, Drew. But feel free to call me with any questions or concerns in the meantime."

Drew was still grappling with the sound of her baby's heartbeat and her baby's father's hand on her stomach. Emotions swirled inside her like a brewing storm. She felt like crying, then she felt like running again. Fear and elation didn't mix well.

"About the fatigue," Dr. Lorens continued. "I want you to break up your meals into six smaller ones instead of three. Make sure you're staying hydrated, especially since it seems we're not out of summer's clutches just yet. Exercise is good, but don't overdo it. And be sure you're getting enough rest, not too much. The fatigue should subside, but if it doesn't in a couple of weeks, give me a call and we'll see if something else is going on."

"Okay," Drew said.

"You're fatigued?" Parker asked, looking up at her once more.

Drew finally released her grasp on her shirt, pushing the now wrinkled material down to cover her stomach. Parker moved his hand but stayed beside her. When she attempted to sit up, he hurried to help her, and when she slid off the table, he kept her standing right in front of him.

"What's going on?" he continued when she hadn't answered his first question. "Can I help?"

She absolutely loved the way his eyes softened when he looked at her. She'd noticed it that night they'd kissed and the last time they'd slept together. Her heart did something funny in her chest when he looked at her that way, a sort of jump start and then skid to a stop, as if it couldn't possibly be true.

"I've just been really tired. Remember I said I was ready for bed by eight every night," she told him.

"And that's not a bad thing," Dr. Lorens chimed in. She'd been moving around the exam room, replacing the Doppler she'd used and scribbling notes in Drew's file. "I'm sure you're up pretty early before opening the shop. A solid eight hours' sleep is good for everyone. For a pregnant woman a nap at some point during the day might be helpful. Do you have someone who can help you out at the flower shop?"

"I can handle the shop for now," she protested. "But I was thinking of looking for an assistant as the pregnancy proceeded."

"We'll hire someone soon, Dr. Lorens. And she'll get the rest she needs," Parker said adamantly.

Drew looked up at him to protest, then decided it was probably best not to argue in front of Dr. Lorens. The last thing she wanted was word getting out that she and Parker had argued in the doctor's office—even though she was almost positive Dr. Lorens wouldn't be spreading rumors around Sweetland, especially not about her patients. She'd come highly recommended by Quinn, which to Drew meant she was a damned good doctor practicing with the same morals and discretion as the uncle of her child.

But when Parker ushered her out of the room and into the waiting area of the medical center, which from the outside looked like a beautifully restored folk-style Victorian house on the corner of Elm Road, her thoughts about morals and discretion came to a screeching halt.

"Fancy meeting you two here," Marabelle Stanley said, hurriedly getting out of her seat and coming to stand in front of them.

Parker had his hand on Drew's elbow, and she'd been adjusting her purse on her shoulder. Dr. Lorens's office and exam rooms were adjacent to Quinn's. They both shared the same waiting room, the one where Marabelle had been sitting with her husband, who had already pulled the magazine up to cover his face. It was a shame the man hated to be seen with his wife, but considering who his wife was and her reputation around town, Drew couldn't really blame him.

"Hello, Mrs. Stanley," Parker said to her, his smile and charm quickly appearing.

Marabelle smiled in return, blinking her eyes as if that were suddenly going to make her young enough to smile at a man Parker's age. Then she looked at Drew as if just remembering she was there. "Parker and Drewcilla. I would have never thought to run into you here. Did you have an appointment?" she asked, pinning Drew with her too-nice-to-be-true stare.

"Um, we came by to see Quinn," was Drew's quick response. Too bad it was the wrong one.

"Oh, my dear, Dr. Cantrell's office is that way." Marabelle pointed. "And my Sam is next on his appointment list. The receptionist over there said Quinn was running a little late, had to deal with some sort of issue at the B and B. I figured I'd pick up Louisa after I finished here with Sam and we'd go over to see what was going on over

there. But here you are, I can just ask you." She looked at
Parker then. "What's going on at the B and B and why are
you here with her, instead of there with your family?"

Parker's grip tightened on Drew's elbow and she
sucked in a breath. He quickly loosened his hold on her,
slipping his arm around her waist instead. "If you would
excuse us, Mrs. Stanley, Drew and I need to get going."

Just as they were about to walk away, Nora, Dr. Lorens's assistant, came running up to them, two CDs in
hand.

"Oh, Ms. Sidney, I'm glad I caught you. Dr. Lorens
always gives her patients a recording of their baby's first
heartbeat. Here's a copy for you and one for Mr. Cantrell."

Nora was a lovely young girl, hair in one long braid
draped over her right shoulder, eyes shadowed with a
lime-green color today that matched the apples decorating the pink shirt of her scrubs. She was simply doing her
job and very happy that she'd caught Drew before she'd
left. Her smile was honest and genuine because she had
no idea what she'd just done.

Parker took the CDs from Nora. "Thanks," he muttered,
because by now he'd caught on to the fact that Drew was
absolutely speechless. They moved to take another step,
only to find Marabelle still standing there, this time smiling as if she'd just received the award for Best Gossip of
the Year—which she might actually claim once she started
spreading the word that Drew Sidney was pregnant with
Parker Cantrell's baby.

Michelle was a mind reader, Parker was certain of that now.
He was also certain that was another trait his sister had inherited from their grandmother. Gramma always seemed to
know what they needed, just when they needed it.

"I wish I could cook like your sister," Drew said, wiping her hands on a napkin.

She was sitting across from Parker at the small table in her kitchen. About an hour ago, just a few minutes after they'd returned from Dr. Lorens's office, Michelle had appeared at Drew's back door, picnic basket in one hand, jug of summer punch in the other, Rufus standing right beside her as if he'd been trained to do so. Parker had only smiled as he took the jug from her hand and let her and the dog pass him to go up the stairs.

"Everybody wishes they could cook like Michelle," Parker replied.

Drew had sat back in her chair, so he reached across the table and helped himself to another seasoned potato wedge from her plate. Michelle had made crab cakes the size of a fist, six of them, and enough seasoned potato wedges to feed a small army. Before sitting down to eat, Drew had retrieved her own plastic bowls to use for all the food that would have to be consumed later. She'd eaten only half a crab cake and about three wedges. Parker was helping himself to the rest.

"Doc said you should eat more," he told her when he'd finished chewing.

"She said I should eat more frequently, not more in quantity," Drew corrected. She smiled as she pushed her plate toward him so he wouldn't have to reach across the table again.

He liked her smile. It was simple, not dazzling like Savannah's, and it touched her eyes, giving her face a happy and calm look that Parker didn't see her with often. He'd waited patiently for her to voluntarily tell him about the bastard at the B&B and why he'd thought he could put his hands on her. More important he'd waited for Drew to tell him why she was trembling when the man held her and why each time Parker had touched her since, she'd started as if in fear. His instincts said old boyfriend, domestic abuse, the past coming back to haunt her. His instincts also said to kill, but Parker was trying desperately to tamp that down.

"It's been a long day," she started after standing and taking her empty glass to the sink. "I think I'll take a bath and lie down for a while."

Parker used his napkin, then stood to help clean the table. "That sounds like a good idea," he told her.

When they met at the sink, he took her hands in his. It was a gentle motion, one he'd made while keeping eye contact with her. "Do you trust me, Drew?"

She opened her mouth to answer, but Parker was already shaking his head.

"What I'm asking you is do you trust the Parker Cantrell you've come to know over these past months? Not the reputation that preceded me or even what people are saying about me now."

Drew took a deep breath, licked her lips, then replied, "I think I do."

Parker smiled. They weren't the exact words he wanted to hear, yet they touched him with a soft warmth that soothed him.

"I mean, we haven't known each other long. Or rather, we haven't been on speaking terms that long," she corrected.

"I understand. And I want to thank you, even for that." He took a deep breath, still trying to grasp how such simple words could almost take his breath away.

"Parker, I know we got off to a strange start, but I think you'll be a great father," she continued.

And she was going to be a wonderful mother, he thought with the deep compassion he could hear clearly in her voice.

"We're going to be great parents," he continued. "But for right now, I want you to take that bath while I clean up in here. Then when you're finished I want you to sit down and tell me about the man at the B and B and what he's doing here in Sweetland."

As expected, Drew's entire demeanor changed. Her eyes blinked rapidly before she dropped her head and sighed.

Parker cupped a hand to her cheek and prodded until she looked up at him again. "I'm not trying to be pushy, I just want to know what we're dealing with."

"Right," she replied quietly. "I'll be back."

And then she was gone and Parker was left standing alone in her kitchen, wondering how he'd ended up in this place. Earlier this year, he was at the top of his game. He was one of the most renowned detectives in the city, closing murder cases that others hadn't even attempted to investigate. He'd worked alongside other great detectives, had dinner with the mayor, the chief of police, and the state's attorney. Parker had done everything he'd promised himself he would do and thought there was nothing left but to grow old gracefully.

He'd thought wrong. In the last two weeks, as he'd worked secretly with Ryan DelRio, a friend of Preston's who was with the FBI, digging up anything and everything he could about Officer Tyrone Vezina and the cases he was working on, Parker was convinced that what he'd witnessed was a professional hit put out on Vezina. The visit to his apartment by the killer later had been a scare tactic, not a hit, which led Parker to also believe that whoever had started the ball rolling against Vezina suddenly felt that killing another cop might be detrimental. However, intimidating that cop into a fearful silence was not—hence the email and the pictures of his family in Sweetland. He and Ryan had implemented some safety measures around the B&B, and Ryan was staying just outside of town at a hotel where his cameras could keep surveillance of the place. For that reason, Parker had stayed away from Drew for the past couple of weeks. Of course he'd wanted to see her, to check on her, but getting to the bottom of this Vezina thing was a priority that would keep them all safe.

As if that weren't enough for Parker to deal with, he'd walked out of his bedroom to hear raised voices coming from the front desk area. Nothing could have prepared him for the sight of Drew being manhandled by someone Parker didn't know. He'd instantly seen red and reacted. He knew he probably faced assault charges against the guy, but he didn't give a damn. He shouldn't have touched Drew, and he'd better have learned his lesson.

Now, Parker wanted to know who the guy was and why Drew was afraid of him. In his pocket his cell phone vibrated, pulling him from the murderous thoughts he found himself having despite the fact that he was on the opposite side of the law.

"Cantrell," he answered quickly.

"Farraway's looking for you," Quinn said. "Jared Mansfield wants to press charges for you trying to break his jaw."

Parker sighed. He'd figured as much.

"Where's this Mansfield character now?" he asked.

"Packed up and looking for someplace else to stay in Sweetland. He'd just checked in for an indefinite stay, but Michelle reversed his charges and just about tossed him out after he insisted on having you arrested and Drew found and brought to him."

Parker's fist clenched. He walked across the room to keep his composure. "What did he say about Drew?"

"Just that he wanted her found and brought to him immediately. He said that a couple of times until Farraway warned him to stay away from Drew or risk being arrested himself."

"Finally, the dunce supercop does something right," Parker murmured.

"Well, the dunce supercop is out for blood where you're

concerned. I'm guessing it has something to do with your past," Quinn continued. "At any rate, I thought I'd give you a heads-up."

"Thanks," Parker replied.

"Parker?" Quinn continued.

"Yeah?"

"You're a good guy. I know I don't tell you that often enough and I know being here brings back memories of when you weren't such a good guy. But it's not just about you this time around. Drew's carrying your child. You need to think about that first now, before you react."

Parker gritted his teeth. That was precisely what he'd been thinking about these past two weeks. He wanted to end the issue with Vezina's murder and get things straight with his job so he'd be able to support his child—and then he saw the man assaulting Drew and wanted only to protect her. He was doing the right thing despite what people around him thought.

"I hear you," was all he managed to say to his older brother. "And I'll take care of Drew and the baby and everything else."

Parker clicked off the phone before Quinn could say anything else. Then he went back to cleaning the kitchen before the adrenaline pumping through his system incited him to go out and do something else. Something dangerous. Something only the Double Trouble Cantrell brother would do.

"Everybody in town loved Jared. He was tall and handsome and talented. All his life he'd been groomed for the MLB. His father had played for years in Seattle and had moved to the East Coast when Jared was in fifth grade. That's when I met him. He sat behind me in Mrs. Frostburg's math class." Drew sighed, resting her head against the pillows that Parker had piled there.

He was sitting on the edge of her bed. Rufus was right beside her, his head and floppy ears resting on her thigh. She'd started rubbing his head the second the dog joined her and now did so without thought.

"His father was inducted into the Hall of Fame. In his sophomore year Jared took the high school team all the way to the national competition, where scouts began watching him. By the time we graduated he'd had more scholarship offers than anyone else in town. He went to Virginia Tech and came home during the summers. I went to the community college and worked as a waitress at night. We dated our senior year in high school and then broke up when he went away. By the time he graduated and had been drafted to play in Florida, I'd finally finished my business degree at the community college and was planning to take all the money I'd saved and move to the city."

"You wanted to be a city girl?" Parker asked, a small smile on his face.

She could tell he was being extremely patient with her. He wanted to know why Jared was here in Sweetland, not the whole sordid tale of their past. But Drew didn't know the answer to that question. She had to assume the reason was somehow wrapped in their sordid past.

"I wanted to get away from that town. The town where everybody knew everybody and they all knew your business. I was so tired of being there."

He nodded as if he understood. "Why didn't you go away to college?"

"My mother didn't work. My father wanted a traditional family where the wife was a homemaker and the three kids did as they were told. Unfortunately, Mom only had one child, so she tried to make up for that by being the Martha Stewart of Stratford. Still, Dad drank and gambled and basically treated my mother like crap. As for me, he ignored me as much as he possibly could, which I guess was my blessing in disguise."

Drew shrugged, because rehashing all that now didn't give her that same depressing feeling she used to get. Now there was just this kind of sadness for the life her mother had endured and the tragic end Arthur Sidney had inflicted on her.

"So you stayed to help take care of your family?"

She sighed. "Dad had some new business venture, said it would take a year or two to get off the ground. So I gave him some of my savings and I stayed to help with monthly bills and still saved as much as I could. I took online medical encoding classes during that time, hoping to enhance my chances of getting a good job when I finally made it to the city.

"The winter before my dad died, Jared's mother was diagnosed with leukemia. He came home. We went out twice." Drew stopped then, taking a deep breath and willing herself not to crumble in front of Parker. She wasn't a weak person, had known that even in the midst of all the turmoil she'd gone through at that time. No matter what, she would hold her head up high, she would move forward, and she would live her life on her own terms. She'd been doing just fine at that, until now.

"On the third date Jared apparently had more detailed ideas of how it would end. I wanted to go home. He wanted to go to a hotel. I said no and got out of the car to walk. He followed me, pushed me between two buildings, and dared me to scream. I did it anyway because I wanted him to know I wasn't afraid of him. He clamped one hand over my mouth and used the other to rip my shirt off. His hands were down my pants when I bit him and kneed him in the groin simultaneously."

Drew looked down then. She focused on Rufus and his

dark brown eyes. She watched her hand moving mind-lessly over his black fur.

"Did he rape you, Drew?" Parker asked in a voice that sounded so raw with emotion, her head jerked upward so she could stare at him.

A muscle in his jaw twitched, and his lips were pulled in a tight line. She could tell he was angry, but his eyes were warm and compassionate.

She cleared her throat. "No. No. He didn't get the chance to. A car had stopped at the red light and saw us between the buildings. The driver got out to see what was going on. It was the principal from the high school, and when he saw that it was Jared he was so busy asking for an autograph, he hadn't bothered to ask if I were okay. I walked home that night. Went straight to the bathroom and showered for an hour. Then I went to bed and tried to forget.

"But by the next afternoon my mother was already re-ceiving calls about me being caught in a compromising position with 'the' Jared Mansfield. By the end of the week there was talk of a big wedding, of Jared coming back for me and giving me the life of the rich and famous. Then Jared had to leave for spring training. When it be-came obvious that I wasn't going with him, gossip started again. Now, Jared had left me because I wasn't good enough for him. I wasn't pretty enough or smart enough. When I finally told my parents what really happened that night, my mother cried. My dad scowled. We went to the police and they basically laughed at us. To the whole town I was the woman scorned and tried to get revenge by spreading vicious lies about the town's golden boy. Then my dad got sick. The doctors told him he was dying, and rather than linger on like Mrs. Mansfield was still doing, he killed himself, leaving my mother with a mountain of debt and the life insurance company refusing to pay because the death was a suicide." She sighed heavily, having just told a story she'd never told before.

"And that's when you came here?" Parker asked after a few seconds of silence.

She nodded. "We moved to Sweetland almost a year after my dad's death. Mom was going to live with Uncle Walt and I was going to stay until she got settled in."

"Then move to the city?" he asked.

It hurt even to hear him say those words, a quick pang that reminded her of just how much those events had changed her goals and ultimately her life.

"My mother was so distraught. For the entire first year in Sweetland she couldn't even leave the house to go help Uncle Walt at the restaurant. So I helped him as a way of earning her keep. Then I started planting flowers around Uncle Walt's house, taking arrangements to The Crab Pot. Word got around that I was good with flowers and gardening, so I took some side jobs." She shrugged. "Then one day the idea to start my own business just hit me. I never thought I'd make my home in another small town where everybody knew everybody and they all knew everything about you. But Sweetland seemed different. Besides, I figured the people here didn't know everything about me. They didn't know about Jared."

"But now Jared's back." Parker stood after saying that. "He had paid to stay at the B and B, but Michelle gave him his money back. Do you think he knew you were here?"

"I don't know how he could have known," she said, then thought about it. "Uncle Walt was born in Stratford, maybe he connected him. I don't know, and why would he go through the trouble of coming to see me? I haven't spoken to him since that night."

"Did he try to talk to you afterwards?"

"He called a couple of times before he left town. His

mother was really sick, so he spent most of his time with her."

Parker made a noise. "Most of the time that he hadn't spent forcing himself on innocent females."

Drew shook her head. She didn't want to relive this, and she especially didn't want to relive it in the place she'd thought to call her home. "I wish he'd just leave. The last thing I want is for anyone here to find out what happened between us. I mean, hell, it's bad enough the rumor mill's going to be in live-action mode for the next few days as Louisa announces that I'm carrying your child."

"You're worried about that?" Parker asked. He'd been pacing in front of the bed but now stopped to look at her. "Were you planning on keeping it a secret?"

"I was planning on having my baby peacefully. I didn't know what position you were going to take, so all I could do was hope everything would go along quietly."

"You thought things would go quietly in Sweetland? I hate to tell you, but that was never going to happen. They were going to have questions regardless of who the father of your baby was. They just like to know everything."

"And now they're going to want to know what comes next," she said quietly. She'd been kind of wondering that herself.

It was Parker's turn to shrug. "We're having a baby. And I don't care who knows it. I'm not running back to Baltimore and leaving my child behind. In fact," he said, giving her a long look. "How fast can you pack a bag?"

Drew narrowed her eyes at him. "Pack a bag? Am I going somewhere?"

"Didn't you say you wanted to go to the city?" he asked, a playful gleam in his eyes.

Chapter 14

Drew said she was all right with what he'd just done, but Parker wasn't so sure. Still, it was for the best, and he wasn't about to let her sulk any more than she already had over that jackass Mansfield.

The phone call to Carl Farraway was as short and concise as Parker could possibly make it.

"Why don't you come on into the station, Cantrell? We can talk when you get here," Carl said the moment Parker announced who he was on the phone.

"I'm actually on my way out of town, so that's not going to be possible."

Carl tsked. "Running from the law? Now what would your superiors in Baltimore think about that?"

They'd probably think it was the final straw and officially fire him. Funny thing, about six months ago that might have really caused Parker some grief. Now, the thought didn't seem so far away from his reality.

"I still hold a badge of my own, Farraway, so despite what you think, I won't be doing anything illegal. That's actually why I'm calling you," Parker continued without letting Farraway get in another jab. "My brother told me you were at the house looking for me. So I'm calling to give my side of the story."

He proceeded to tell the dunce deputy about Mansfield's history of assaulting Drew and that Drew would be filing for a restraining order the moment they returned to Sweetland and that Farraway should keep an eye on Mansfield as long as he was in town. To his credit, Carl agreed to contact the authorities in Stratford to see about the report Drew had filed years ago. He even agreed with Parker's suggestion that Carl talk to Mansfield again, maybe get him to agree to giving his prints or DNA so they could do a database check and see if there were any other women the man had gotten too friendly with. It was unlikely for a guy to sexually assault one time and then quit cold turkey. No, with the money and the power Mansfield assumed he had, his personality would almost force him to dominate over and over again.

Carl still wanted to talk to Parker when he got back, and Parker was more than happy to agree to that meeting. As long as he had some time alone with Drew first. Some time to show her that not all men dominated and not all reputed bad boys were actually bad.

He let her sit in the passenger seat of Preston's SUV, seat belt intact, seat reclined. She'd requested he turn on the radio, so he did, some station that was playing slow songs that he figured a female would like. In the backseat, Rufus had settled on the fleece blanket that normally lay across his dog bed in Parker's room at the B&B. On the third bench seat were their bags and Rufus's kennel. They were taking a road trip, and Parker felt oddly familial at the thought.

It was just about eleven PM when Parker turned into the entrance for the underground garage to his apartment building. The attendant knew him by face but was taken a little off guard by the vehicle.

"Mr. Cantrell, you're back," said Styles, the twenty-year-old college student who worked part-time in the building.

"Just for a couple of days," Parker told him.

"New vehicle, I see, along with some other new things." Styles gave a wag of his eyebrows at that comment.

The younger man had no problem getting into Parker's business. After all, Parker had been the one to arrest Styles over a year ago for fraudulently using a debit card in the convenience store down the street. He'd also paid Preston to represent the kid in court and was pleased when Preston had negotiated a probation before judgment sentence with community service instead of jail time and the possibility to have the conviction expunged from his record with good behavior. In return for that favor, Styles had been a model citizen since then, and Parker hadn't hesitated to help him get a job as well as get him enrolled in the local community college. "Sometimes, all they need is a chance," Parker could hear his own father telling him as they'd watched the news depicting the rise of violent crime in teenagers years ago.

In his years working on the force, assigned to the inner city, Parker had seen his share of teenagers and adults who weren't going to do the right thing with another chance no matter what. And for those, Parker could only pray for an end to their reign on the streets. He was willing to give people second chances as long as those second chances didn't involve someone else getting hurt or another crime being committed.

"Still paying attention to details, I see," Parker joked with him. "This is Preston's truck. And this is . . ." He hesitated because he really didn't know what to introduce Drew as. And since she was asleep, he went with saying she was a friend and proceeded to his parking spot before Styles took that meaning any further than was necessary.

When he parked the car, he gently nudged Drew to wake

her. Then Rufus, who no doubt had roused the second the truck stopped, barked and Drew jolted.

"Sorry about that. You already know he's insubordinate," he told Drew when she turned her head on the console and looked at him. "We're here," he announced quickly, because the sleepy sluggishness of her eyes, the way her tongue slowly licked her lips, and the lift of her breasts when her arms went over her head while she stretched were making him want to touch her instead of showing her how much of a gentleman he could actually be.

She stepped out of the car without a word and without Parker's help, as he was busy letting Rufus out and then reaching for their bags. "Could you grab these and lock the truck?" he was forced to ask since his hands were full.

"Sure," was all she said as she reached for the keys that were on top of the truck as the nod of his head suggested. "Do you want the alarm on?" she asked.

"Yeah," he replied. "In the city it's best to lock and alarm your vehicle to cut down on theft." In Sweetland they locked the car but rarely used the alarm system.

In the elevator there were two other couples laughing and giggling, clearly having just enjoyed a fun night out on the town. As Parker lived on one of the top floors, they'd gotten off before Drew remarked, "Do people sleep at all in the city?"

Parker laughed. "It's not even midnight yet. And I live in downtown Baltimore. It's likely you'll see people up all night long down here. Those four looked like they were just coming from an Orioles game. We got lucky and had one of the finals games here this year."

"I don't follow baseball," she replied quietly, and Parker wanted to bite off his tongue. Of course she wouldn't follow baseball after what happened.

He decided it was best just to keep quiet after that. They walked down the hall once they were off the elevator, and then he nodded to her once more. "You've got the key."

"Oh." She'd been holding Rufus's leash and the dog had been more than excited by his new surroundings. She wrapped the leash around her wrist so Rufus wouldn't run off while she tried to open the door.

After a few seconds of working with the key, the door opened and Parker nodded her inside. She walked ahead of him, bending to take the leash from Rufus's neck the moment Parker closed the door. Rufus took off, disappearing into one of the back rooms. Parker put down the bags and turned on the lamps in the living room, which was about three feet from the small foyer they'd come through. He watched her look around and remembered when he'd done the same thing in her apartment.

"What do you think?" he asked after a few minutes of watching her walk around, touching this, smiling at that.

"Definitely a bachelor pad," she quipped.

Parker chuckled. "How did I know you were going to say that?"

She laughed with him. "Because you know what your house looks like. There're absolutely no female touches in here."

Parker moved to one of the end tables where the phone and the blinking answering machine were. He pressed rewind and waited. "That's because I'm not a female."

She blinked, then looked as if she thought he were joking. "But surely you have females here, I would think you'd try to at least appeal to them on some level. You know, make them a little more comfortable."

He shook his head. "I don't bring females here."

She was quiet; that was telling. Parker had already pushed the button to listen to the messages, so he didn't look up to see the further extent of her reaction to his words.

"Where's your bathroom? I'll go now while you're listening to your messages," she said.

He did look up then, just as the machine was announcing the date and time of the next message. "Do you have to go to the bathroom now?"

She looked a little wide-eyed at him, then down to the phone and back to him again. "No. I just, um, I was just offering you some privacy to listen to your messages."

What she meant was she was giving him an out. If a female was leaving him a phone message, she wouldn't hold it against him. But she really would, Parker thought. She already was. He took a deep breath and exhaled slowly, reminding himself that this was new for both of them. She'd had a bad experience before, and he did have a reputation. But standing in her kitchen several hours ago, Drew said she thought she trusted him. He'd trust her enough not to get angry at her presumptions that spoke otherwise.

"There's not going to be a female leaving me any messages, Drew. My home address and phone number are personal and off-limits to the women I date."

"But dating is personal, isn't it?" she asked.

Standing in front of the fireplace, stark white walls, cool gray leather furniture, black statues, and gray carpet surrounding her, moonlight streaming through the wall-to-wall windows to the left, she looked lost and a bit out of place. Her eyes wide, her demeanor uncomfortable, she'd asked him a pretty simple question, yet it felt like one of the most important questions he'd ever had to search for an answer to.

"It can be," he said, treading lightly.

Before the conversation could go any further, a familiar voice sounded through the machine and Parker looked away from Drew to the phone as if that person were actually there.

"Cantrell, your name's coming up where it shouldn't

be again. I know you've been out of town, but if you get this message, I need you to get your ass back here, pronto!"

Yes, he'd said "pronto," as if anybody in this day and age still said that.

"He sounds angry," Drew said, stating the obvious. "Maybe you should call him back now."

Parker shook his head. "He's my supervisor and I'll call him in the morning."

"But he asked for you to get back here right away, that has to mean it's urgent."

"If it were really urgent, he would have used my cell or called the inn. He has both numbers." So why hadn't he used them? Parker thought to himself. And what did he mean, Parker's name was coming up where it shouldn't be? He'd been out of town for almost five months now, on suspension. How could his name come up and he wasn't even here?

"Let's get you and Rufus settled," he said, not wanting to deal with any of this tonight.

She followed him into the bedroom, and Parker could almost hear her mind ticking off one question after another. He'd never had to explain himself to anyone before and wasn't sure how it worked. How would she react if he told her he'd been suspended from his job? Would she think he wouldn't be able to support his child? He shook his head, stopping to put the bags down and to shoo Rufus off his bed.

"Off! Now!" he told the dog sternly.

Behind him, Drew snickered. "Did you bring his bed with you?"

Parker groaned. "He's not a baby, and he has that silly blanket that Raine gave him. He'll be fine in the kennel or on the floor over there." He pointed to the spot he was referring to and waited while Rufus trudged over there slowly. Then he felt bad and found himself on his knees, rolling the dog over and scratching his stomach. Rufus laughed . . . well, for all that dogs could laugh: His mouth was open, tongue hanging out. He loved this type of attention and Parker didn't normally mind giving it to him. It's just that these last couple of weeks had been really stressful.

"Five dollars says he ends up in this bed by morning," Drew said.

Parker turned. She'd crossed her arms over her chest and stared at them. She wore yoga pants that rested beneath the bump of her belly and a teal shirt with glittering high-heeled shoes on the front of it. The shirt came to the tops of her thighs, but as she'd lain back in the car, it had risen up, and that's how he'd seen that the yoga pants didn't go over her stomach. But from here, looking up at her, the bump was definitely visible. Their child was growing inside there, and in a couple of months she would be bigger, their baby would be bigger.

"I don't usually take money from females, but for you, Ms. Sidney, I'll make an exception."

"Wow, wait till I tell Heaven and Delia I'm getting special treatment now," Drew said, smiling, heading to the bathroom with her bag.

Parker used that time to undress, moving through the room with vague familiarity. This was his home, had been for the past ten years. Yet it felt as if he were the outsider here. Drew was back before he could further examine that feeling, and they quickly ditched the lights and climbed into bed.

"That was delicious," Drew said, sitting back against the soft, leather-bound booth. "I've never had steak cooked so well."

Parker agreed by nodding his head because he was still chewing the last bite of her steak, which he'd forked after she'd shaken her head in defeat. She was so full, she thought she'd burst. But Parker had already told her they were walking along the harbor as soon as they finished at the restaurant.

He was giving her the complete tourist treatment, showing her around Baltimore City like the seasoned veteran he was. Earlier today, they'd taken a cruise to Fort McHenry and had lunch on the plush green lawn. Afterward, Parker had insisted they return to his place, where they'd gone for a swim at the pool in the apartment building.

"I can't swim," she'd admitted as she'd sat on the side, letting her feet dangle in the four feet section of the water.

"No problem, I'll carry you," Parker had replied.

And thus he had.

At first she'd clasped her legs around his waist, her arms around his neck as he glided through the deep end of the water. Their bodies were warm together, and she laughed like a schoolgirl when he returned to a more shallow part of the water and flipped her off his back so that she plunged into the water. Drew came up sputtering and gasping. That's when he laced his arms around her, pulling her close.

"I really like swimming with you," he whispered about two seconds before his lips grazed hers.

Her body hummed with mounting desire and Drew hungrily kissed him back. Her legs twined around his waist once more, and he backed her up to the wall of the pool. His hands were everywhere, grasping the side curve of her breasts, moving downward to cup the globes of her bottom. Then his fingers were beneath the band of her bathing suit, touching the moistened heat of her center. Drew gasped, barely managing to break the kiss in time to pant, "Stop. We can't do this here."

Parker rested his forehead against hers, his breath

coming as fast, if not faster. His fingers were still touching her, stroking her. "I can't seem to keep my hands off you," was his reply. "No matter where we are."

"Um," she started to say when one finger slipped slowly inside her core. The partial word ended on a moan and Drew had to close her eyes, clamping her teeth down on her bottom lip until she thought she might draw blood, to keep from screaming out her pleasure. "I hope you don't think I'm complaining," she started again, once she felt steady enough to speak real words and not just sounds.

"I'm certainly not complaining," he said, nipping along her cheek down to the line of her jaw. All the while he'd added another finger and was now stroking her gently, coaxing what Drew feared would be a soul-shattering release.

"Parker," she whispered, letting her head loll back against the lip of the pool.

He went for her neck so quickly that if she were of the mind for fanciful thoughts, she might have been afraid he were some breed of vampire. Instead, his tongue lathed along her damp skin, moving downward to her collarbone, then the swell of her breasts. Drew did scream then. It was a low scream, but it echoed throughout the pool area as if she were in a gymnasium.

"Parker, please. Someone . . . might . . . see us," she panted. She was talking, her hips were jerking with the thrust of his hand, her breasts puckering with the touch of his tongue and teeth.

"Later," he whispered against her skin. "Say I can have you later and I'll stop."

Drew didn't think she could say her name, not even if someone stood in front of her holding up flash cards and sounding it out phonetically in her ear. Her eyes rolled in the back of her head, breath coming in heavy gasps. Finally, she couldn't stand it a moment longer.

"Yes!" she declared. "Yes!" The acclamation was for so many different reasons, but she followed with, "You can have me later."

His hand slipped slowly from beneath the bottom of her bathing suit, but his mouth lingered seconds longer over her breasts before she lowered her head and he took her mouth. Their tongues dueled madly in a heated promise that neither of them was likely to forget.

Afterward, they'd returned to the room and to Rufus, who was none too pleased at having been left there. A quick shower and a walk around the downtown streets with Rufus, then they were back in the apartment. As much as Drew wanted to continue on, she was dead tired and Parker knew it. He ordered her to bed, then lay beside her with his laptop while she drifted off to sleep.

Now they'd just finished dinner and Drew was feeling ready for bed again. Ready for sleep, that is. Until Parker touched her again.

He slid closer to her in the booth, as if that were even possible. When they'd first been seated, he'd rearranged the place settings so they could sit side by side instead of across from each other. Now, he reached a hand over and touched her thigh. Not a caress, just sort of resting it there, but every nerve ending in Drew's body went on instant alert.

"You want dessert?" he asked, using his free hand to finish off his glass of wine.

That's what she needed, some wine to relax her nerves. But that was out of the question, so she'd have to keep her insatiable thoughts to a minimum.

"No, I couldn't eat another thing."

"I'm pretty stuffed, too," he added, then asked, "Having fun?" He put his glass down and looked at her.

"I always wanted to see the city," she said wistfully.

He nodded. "And now you are. What do you think?"

"I think its pace is a lot faster than Sweetland. I got an adrenaline rush just watching the people on the streets heading to work this morning. And traffic was insane."

Parker chuckled. "If you think that was something, wait until I take you to New York."

Drew waved a hand. "Oh no, not just yet. One big city at a time, please." She laughed and Parker smiled.

"Okay, I can work that out."

The waitress returned to take away their plates, and Parker requested the check.

"So do you miss it? The city, I mean. Do you miss being here?" she asked, not entirely sure she wanted the answer but willing to take the chance.

He paused, fiddling with the edges of his napkin for a few seconds.

"When I first came back to Sweetland, it was for my grandmother's funeral. Staying there permanently never crossed my mind. Then the will was read and there were all these new responsibilities. Savannah wanted to bolt immediately. Quinn looked like he was going to explode if one more thing were added to his plate. Preston, he's the calm one, but he even looked pressured. Raine accepted because that's what she does. Then everyone looked to me to do what I had no idea."

He took a deep breath, blew it out slowly.

"They wanted to know how I felt about the inn and the dogs and the town and what I planned to do, but I didn't have an answer. Then I guess everyone did what they always do where I'm concerned: They assumed."

"People tend to do that with everyone," she said with a sigh of her own. She'd lowered one of her hands so that it rested on top of his on her thigh. "I think it's instinct for them. If they don't have the whole story, just fill in the blanks. Without even thinking about the consequences of doing such a thing."

Parker nodded. "You're right."

"How did you crash your bike?"

He frowned then, and Drew wished she hadn't asked. Of course crashing into a tree would be a bad memory, not to mention the damage to his knee. She suspected that might be the reason Parker hadn't returned to his job yet, but she wasn't sure. Making him admit that to her might not be such a smart idea, but suddenly, being in this city, *in* his city and in *his* space, she wanted to know as much as she could about Parker, to be as close to him as she possibly could, even if it was temporary.

"One minute I was driving, enjoying the wind against my face. The next someone was there and I was swerving and they kept coming and then . . ." He paused. "Then I crashed."

Drew couldn't believe what she'd just heard. "Are you saying someone drove you off the road?" That's not the way she'd heard about the accident. The story around Sweetland was that the Double Trouble Cantrell had been drinking at Charlie's and went out on his bike, losing control and then crashing into a tree.

"There was definitely somebody out there on the road with me. When the cops came they were gone and I was unconscious, but I remember. I remember the car." He stared off as if he remembered more, but Drew was too startled and too frightened to ask.

The waitress returned and Parker paid their check. They left the restaurant and walked hand in hand along Baltimore's famous Inner Harbor. Huge ships were docked there, and from a distance ahead a trio played music. People mulled about on this early evening, some couples holding hands like them, some families—one with a boy and a girl, the mother holding the girl's hand and the father walking alongside the boy.

They didn't talk anymore, just walked, enjoying the

company without making it necessary to converse. By the time they arrived at his apartment building once more, Drew was once again feeling extremely tired.

"I have a couple of things to work on. I'll stay out here and let you go on to bed," Parker told her.

He'd been distracted since they'd spoken about his accident, and Drew wanted to kick herself for spoiling their wonderful day. Parker had demons of his own to chase. She wondered why she'd never thought that possible before. Some days she felt she was the only one with a past, the only one with problems. It was a naïve thought, of course, but Drew preferred not to think of the other people in the world struggling along in life as she was.

"Hey, Rufus, boy. Come on up here and keep me company while he's in there," she told the dog after she'd changed into her nightshirt.

Rufus had indeed returned to the bed with them last night, causing Parker to lose the five-dollar bet. The dog loved to get on the bed, and if Drew really let herself dream, she'd say Rufus loved to cuddle up on the bed with her. For a while she flicked the channels on the television, then she finally gave in to fatigue, still wondering what Parker was working on and if it would eventually bring him back to this big city for good.

Chapter 15

This time Drew wasn't dreaming. She was wide awake and she was aroused. For the last five to ten minutes, she'd lain on her back wondering what she should do about it.

"I want you, too."

Drew yelped, covering her mouth quickly to stifle the sound. What was Parker doing awake, and what did he mean by "too"?

He rolled over so that he was partially on top of her this time and slowly moved her hand from her mouth. "You must have the best and hottest dreams," he said, looking down at her.

Then he kissed her fingers, one by one.

Drew couldn't move. She wanted to, or at least she thought she did. But his weight was bearing down on the top half of her body, holding her still. The bottom half was tingling, her thighs squeezing tightly together.

"I was asleep and dreaming of touching you," he whispered to her. "I dreamt of cupping your breasts and kissing your lips."

Drew swallowed and blinked, trying hard to focus on the outline of his face. It was dark in the room, except for the light that came from the window with the partially open blinds. And that light was from buildings and street-lights that never went out in the city.

"Then I heard you moan. I thought I was dreaming," he finished.

He hadn't been dreaming. She had moaned. She'd fallen asleep on her side, Rufus cradled in her arms. At some point Parker had come into the room and most likely put Rufus over by his spot on the floor. Then he'd climbed in beside her and Drew had cuddled against him instead. Her leg had been draped over his, her arm over his stom-ach, hand flat on his chest, and the feeling had been sen-sational. She'd moved closer to his body heat, loving the feel of taut muscle beneath her limbs, and she'd begun to dream, only the dream was more real than ever as she found herself panting and needing with urgency. That's when she'd rolled over onto her back and struggled to pull herself together.

"I'm sorry," she said softly. "I'll stay on my side of the bed from now on." That was all she could manage. Em-barrassment infused her cheeks just as another heat rushed to her center. She needed him to move away, to move far, far away, so she could get herself together.

But Parker did not oblige.

"I want you right where you are," was his response as his hands framed her face. "I want you in kissing dis-tance, touching distance, loving distance."

The last words fell over Drew like a soft veil . . . white with lace edging. She closed her eyes, took a deep, come-back-to-reality breath, and whispered his name. "Parker."

"Drew," he replied, his face so close to hers that their lips touched as he spoke.

Damn reality! Drew thought with one last sigh. She kissed him. She pressed her lips to his, thrust her tongue deep inside his mouth, and closed her eyes to the spikes of heat soaring through her body at their contact. This was what she'd felt that night at the park, the night she'd wished on the summer's moon without any thought to where that wish might actually take her. This was what she'd felt that night in her apartment when she'd thought she'd been dreaming but she and Parker were actually having sex again.

This time Drew didn't want to believe the truth was a dream, didn't want to convince herself that what they were doing was because of opportunity or because of this lust that seemed to pull at them like magnets. She wanted to believe exactly what Parker had told her, that he wanted her, too.

He moved until he was completely over her, his arousal pressing persistently into her center.

"Am I hurting you?" he asked in a breathy whisper when he'd finally managed to pull his mouth away from hers.

Only to the extent she thought she might actually die of this slow torture. "No," she whispered, spreading her legs slightly so that he could shift and they could be joined.

But that didn't happen. Instead he came up on his elbows and stared down at her.

"I thought you were beautiful that first night I saw you at Walt's. You were working and moving all over the place, but every glance I caught of you left me a little more breathless than the first time."

She didn't know what to say. She'd noticed him that night and felt waves of nerves attacking her as he'd stayed seated, not ordering anything but not leaving.

"Then I made a point to show up wherever you were, but you never even noticed," he told her.

She shook her head. "I noticed," she admitted.

He smiled. "Playing hard to get, huh?"

"No," she said with a tentative smile of her own. "Playing it safe."

Parker sobered. "I won't hurt you, Drew. Despite what you've heard about me, I could never hurt you."

"Why me?" she asked, because that question had plagued her mind for weeks now. Why of all the women in Sweetland had Parker Cantrell set his sights on her? And why, after all these years, had the thought of being intimate with a man not scared her to the point of staying locked in her apartment, as it had so many times before?

He shook his head. "I've been asking myself for days now why you would get yourself tangled with a guy like me. Gossip and controversy are the last things I know you want in your life, and those two things follow me around like a dark cloud."

"And now your dog is following me around," she said lightly. "We're some pair, huh?"

"Yeah." He smiled. "We're some pair."

His lips found hers again in a kiss so deep, they were both out of breath when he pulled away, trailing hot, wet kisses down her neck, stopping only when he'd pushed her nightgown up and over her head and his mouth found one puckered nipple. He palmed the other mound while suckling the first, and Drew arched her back to the pleasure. Then he was kissing down her torso to her navel.

Drew was on fire—she was going to explode if release didn't come fast. Parker, on the other hand, didn't seem to be in any hurry. He cupped her juncture, holding his hand still there for endless seconds. Drew's legs spread wider, her breaths coming quicker. When his fingers finally parted her nether lips, touching the warm, moistened folds, she gasped. He touched her there with his hands, with his tongue, and Drew held on to every second in her mind and in her heart.

This was beyond anything she'd ever experienced, any

connection she'd ever dreamed of making with a man. Her body trembled and she arched up off the bed as he said her name softly.

In the next moments, Parker was moving. Drew heard a drawer open and close, heard the rip of the wrapper, and knew he was sheathing himself. Her fingers clenched the sheet beneath her as she waited impatiently for him to return to her. When he did, when he lifted her legs, placing an ankle onto each shoulder, and then guided his length into her one torturous inch at a time, she screamed his name.

The moment he was completely inside her, Parker knew. He knew without any doubts or recriminations that Drew was the one.

The tightness in his chest he'd felt a little each time he saw her was so intense now, for a moment he'd thought he was having a heart attack. But then she'd smile, she'd laugh while playing with Rufus, and the intensity would subside slightly. He watched her as she slept, saw the peaceful look on her face, watched the steady flow of her breathing, and remembered the sound of his baby's heartbeat as well. His baby that she was carrying. And the clutching in his chest grew intense again.

He moved over her now, looking down into her lust filled eyes, heard the soft sound of her whispering his name. She was giving him a part of her Parker suspected Drew hadn't willingly given before. That thought held a magnitude Parker could not match. She was giving and he was taking, but what was he offering her in return?

Parker lowered her legs from his shoulders, pulling out of her slowly. She looked up at him in question as he lay down beside her. Before she could speak, he was gathering her in his arms, hugging her so close and so tight that he feared he might crush her. With that thought, he lessened his hold, whispering to her once more, "I won't hurt you, Drew."

"I know you won't, Parker," she replied. "I know how it feels to have people misjudge you. But you're not the man they say you are."

Parker heard her words and cared for her even more deeply because he knew she wouldn't say them unless she really meant them.

"The thing is, I've done some things in my past that I'm not proud of. I played to the reputation because it was easier that way."

"And I packed up and left Stratford because it was easier for me, too. It seems we both like to take the easy route," she said with a slight chuckle.

She was rubbing her hands up and down his back as they both lay on their sides, face-to-face.

"Getting involved with me might not be safe," he admitted, although it pained him to give her the choice. What if she thought he wasn't worth it? What if, as they'd both done in the past, she decided to take the safe route?

What she did next not only startled Parker, but effectively sealed his fate.

Drew lifted a leg and wrapped it around his waist as she slid closer to him.

"I'm willing to take the chance if you are," she whispered before her lips touched his.

Parker hesitated only a millisecond before replying, "I'm willing."

The kiss deepened, and Parker moved until he was once again sheathed by her warmth, held steady by her tightness and her embrace. And when they both reached their release, it was with a feeling Parker had never experienced but was profoundly grateful to have shared with Drew.

* * *

"Do you want a girl or a boy?" he asked her later into the night, or earlier into the morning.

They'd showered and climbed back into bed, bodies still entwined as if they were afraid the mental connection would break without the physical.

Drew thought about his question, loving the feel of his hand over the soft curve of her belly. "I'd love a little boy to run around and play with Rufus," she replied.

Then, when he would have asked something else, she continued, "Or a little girl Savannah could spoil and spend her time dressing up like a princess."

To that, Parker chuckled. "And that's precisely what Savannah would do."

"Oh, I know, she already told me," Drew joined in with a smile. "Savannah and Delia are firm on wanting a girl, while Heaven, Michelle, and Raine think a boy, a mini-Parker, would be sweet."

"A mini-Parker, huh? I don't think we want to go that far," he said. "I'd like a daughter so I could spoil her myself and teach her about all the bad guys out there in the world."

"But she'd be surrounded by so many good guys," Drew countered, because she didn't want Parker to feel that his own reputation would somehow hinder his daughter. "You and Preston. Mr. Sylvester and Quinn and Uncle Walt. All of you would protect her and teach her. She'll probably be forty by the time she gets her first boyfriend." She patted his chest while laughing to lighten the mood.

"Hey, I'm not going to argue that last point. Besides, I think forty's a good solid age for her to enter the dating arena."

"It is not," Drew chastised him.

"What does your mother think about this?" he asked when they'd been silent a few seconds.

To that, Drew sighed.

"I think she likes the idea of a grandchild, but the rest, I'm not entirely sure."

"The rest being me as the father of said grandchild."

"You know, Parker, I don't even think it's just that with my mother. She's still so wrapped up in her grief over losing my father I don't think she sees relationships or marriages the same anymore. And as far as becoming a grandparent, well, Mr. Sylvester talks about it much more than she does."

"Mr. Sylvester talks about everything much more than everyone does," Parker replied.

Drew nodded. "Yes, that's true. But he means well."

"Yeah, he does. I don't think his health is doing too good, though. I'm going to talk to Quinn when we get back about seeing if he can get him to come in for a physical."

"That's a good idea. I noticed he was moving a little slower when I was there the other day."

The silence returned, and Drew figured she'd go ahead and get the next question out of the way.

"Are you going to be arrested for hitting Jared? Is that why we came to the city?"

Parker shifted, propping his head on his arm as he looked down at her. "I gave a statement. But if Jared wants to press charges, yes, I can be arrested."

She let out a breath. "I'm so sorry. I never meant for any of that to happen."

He stroked her cheek with the back of his hand. "And it wasn't your fault that it did. Jared was out of line, and I could have taken a deep breath or counted to three thousand before deciding to slug him." He shrugged. "But what's done is done, and I'll go back to Sweetland and deal with it. I don't want you worrying about Jared or anything else."

"I hope he's gone when we get back," she admitted.

Parker pulled her into his arms and settled them both back in a lying position. She curled into him as if this had been the way they'd slept for years and years. As he pulled the sheets up over them, he kissed the top of her head. "All I want you to worry about is finding an assistant to help you at the flower shop so you and our daughter can get plenty of rest."

"*Our* daughter," Drew whispered, letting her eyes close, her cheek pressed against his chest. "I like the sound of that."

Drew's new assistant, at least for the time being, turned out to be Parker. The morning after they returned to Sweetland and every day that followed that entire week, Parker and Rufus showed up at her back door, usually carrying some sort of breakfast sent to her by Michelle, so she didn't argue their appearance.

They waited while she dressed, and all went down with her as she opened the shop. Parker handled the deliveries and some of the packing, although he was horrible with tissue paper. Drew joked that the soft lavender sheets of paper were just too dainty for the big bad cop to handle. To that Parker snarled and ripped another sheet in half.

For his part, Rufus roamed around the shop until Drew took him out back and let him run around in the yard. He was leashed, of course, because she didn't want him attacking her flowers, nor did she want him running off again.

The routine had been so easy to slip into that she didn't think twice about it as Parker headed over to The Marina to deliver the arrangements she'd made for their front lobby. The big grand opening was this weekend, so they'd wanted something extra big and extra splashy, which to Drew had translated as extra expensive.

"I don't know how much I like the idea of you working for the enemy," Parker complained as he hefted one of the large pots onto the back of Caleb Brockington's pickup truck.

On Tuesday, Parker had showed up with the truck, explaining that he'd asked Nikki's brother if he could borrow it during the day. Since Caleb worked at the fire department with his father and brother Brad during the day, he'd agreed.

"It's business, Parker. And with this little one coming, I've got to make sure I keep this business in the black," was her reply.

He looked at her for a moment, and Drew thought maybe she'd said something wrong. Then he gave her that smirk. "The Redlings are still enemies to the Cantrells."

"They're competition, not enemies," she corrected while handing him a smaller arrangement to load. "And actually, Lillian Beasley and her granddaughter Emily were in here yesterday afternoon talking about how big and formidable The Marina looked. They think it's an eyesore and would much rather have the quaint cuteness of The Silver Spoon. That's why Lillian said she recommended The Silver Spoon for their family reunion venue next summer."

Parker looked over his shoulder at that comment. "Really? She said that?"

Drew nodded. "She did. And it just so happened that I have Silver Spoon brochures and business cards sitting right on the counter near the cash register now. The new design Nikki and Quinn came up with is absolutely lovely. Taking a picture of Ms. Cleo with the puppies all lounging on the porch was brilliant. Anyway, Lillian said she was going to call Nikki first thing this morning to get the ball rolling."

Parker jumped off the truck, grabbed her by the shoulders, and gave her a very loud and very public kiss. "Welcome to the family!" he exclaimed.

Drew could only smile as she swatted him away. "Go, make the delivery," she told him as she moved back into the store.

She needed a moment to compose herself. Parker had just told her she was a part of his family.

He'd pulled off by the time she'd made it all the way to the stool behind the register. Parker had brought the stool over from the meeting area, so she wouldn't have to stand all day. He was very thoughtful like that, she thought as she put her elbows up on the counter, staring at absolutely nothing.

That's how Diana McCann found her when she bounced in. The normally regal, sedate, and snobbish Diana moved with a certain air of happiness today, which should have been warning enough for Drew. Instead, wrapped up in her own state of euphoria, Drew was caught off guard.

"I've been told to order whatever I want," Diana began instantly.

No "Good afternoon," "Hello," "Hey, Drew, how are you?"

"So I want some of these, and a bunch of those, and yes, these too because I love yellow. This is horrible. And roses, yes, I must absolutely have roses," she continued, moving about the shop, touching the flowers she wanted, frowning at others she didn't.

She wore a purple-and-red straight printed dress, a thin purple belt cinched tight at her waist. Her heels were purple, as were the bangle bracelets at her arm and the earrings dangling from her ears. Her strawberry-blond hair was pulled up tightly in a Grace Kelly style, and she carried a purple snakeskin bag that was big enough to fit a bowling ball inside.

"Will this be a handheld arrangement or would you

like to pick out a vase?" Drew asked, slipping into her professional mode, since obviously that's where Diana was today.

Diana turned to Drew as if Drew had somehow reached across the room and slapped her. "That's your job! Or should I go someplace where there's actually a florist and not a tramp that specializes in trapping men?"

Diana's words were spoken so viciously, Drew reeled back as if she'd been hit. "Excuse me?" she finally managed to ask.

"Oh, you need more than excusing. First, you try to ruin Jared's career, then you run away to Sweetland, where you wait ever so patiently until the next prospect shows up. And here comes Parker returning to his hometown and unsuspectingly walks right into your clutches. Tell me, don't you feel stupid that you managed to get pregnant by the now unemployed ex-cop instead of the star major league ballplayer?"

Drew's heart beat rapidly, her palms were sweating, and she felt the urge to hit something, or someone. How dared Diana come into her place of business and start hurling insults! For all that Drew had tried to remain a peaceful citizen of Sweetland, she wasn't about to become a doormat for anyone.

"First of all, Diana, if you'd like to place an order, you are welcome to do so. Select your vase and your flowers and I'll arrange them for you."

Diana took a step forward, opening her mouth as if she planned to say something else. Drew gave one quick shake of her head that stopped her, then continued to talk.

"Next, if you have something to say to me on a personal level, then you can address me woman to woman. But don't come in here tossing insults at me in the hopes of getting some type of rise out of me, not while I'm at my place of business." Even though Drew was afraid

Diana had partially achieved that task. She was beyond pissed off.

Diana had the audacity to laugh at that. "Business? Is that what you call this? The only ones hiring you are the Cantrells and that's only because you're sleeping with Parker. But let me just inform you of one thing, honey—I've known Parker for a long time and you are definitely not his type. Not the keeping type, I mean."

Diana stood right across from Drew at the counter now, hoping that her closeness would further intimidate Drew. Oh, how wrong she was. Drew squared her shoulders and stared Diana directly in the sea-green eye contacts she wore.

"Apparently you weren't even the one-night-stand type for Parker. I wonder how that makes you feel?" she countered.

Diana frowned, her lips thinning to a straight line. Her cheeks were already covered in a pale pink blush, but now they turned ruby red, her eyes closing to slits as she glared at Drew.

"Ready yet, babe?"

Both women turned to the male voice coming through the front door. Diana melted. Drew seethed.

It was Jared.

Chapter 16

"So wait a minute, let me get this straight," Savannah said as Drew sat on the front porch with her, Michelle, Heaven, and Raine.

Delia's shop had been swamped with customers after Drew had shut down the flower shop and barged in there. She'd left before Delia could see her for fear her friend would put all her customers out to see what was bothering her. Instead she returned to the flower shop, went out the back door to her car, and drove to The Silver Spoon. She hadn't known where else to turn.

"Jared Mansfield's a sexual-assaulting bastard, in addition to being an arrogant jerk, and now he's sleeping with Diana McCann?" Savannah continued with a combined baffled and disgusted look on her face.

At the far end of the porch, there was a swing. Drew sat there with Heaven beside her, holding her hand. Michelle and Raine sat in the Adirondack chairs while Savannah sat on the railing, with half her profile to them and the other half to anyone so blessed enough to walk by.

"That sums it up about right," Drew murmured, shaking her head. "I mean, I'm not jealous by any means. She can certainly have Jared. But why did he have to come here, and why is he still here? And why does she have to be such a bitch about everything?"

Michelle waved a hand. "Diana's been a bitch all her life, because according to her she was born into the wrong family. She's wanted to be a Fitzgerald so she could walk around acting as if she owned the entire town. Instead, she's a Bellmont, which is still pretty close to royalty around here. Unfortunately, close just isn't good enough for her."

"Then there's the fact that Parker turned her down," Raine added in her quiet voice.

"He turned her down numerous times," Savannah added with satisfaction. "That's because Parker has taste and can see the totally classless even when they're busy pushing their C-cups up in his face."

"She accused me of trapping Parker the same way I tried to trap Jared. I can't believe he told her that," Drew continued.

"Oh, believe it, honey. Diana's as nasty as they come," Heaven told her. "She tried to make me believe Preston had wanted her but she'd wanted Parker. There are no limits to how low she'll stoop to get the desired results."

"Well, I didn't have a meltdown. I barely blinked when Jared walked in and put his arm around her. I know he wanted me to say something, but I refused. Just told them both they could leave."

"You didn't sell her the arrangement?" Raine asked.

"Hell no, she didn't sell that witch anything! She should have selected a vase and whacked her over the head with it," was Savannah's next contribution to the conversation.

Michelle and Heaven laughed, nodding in agreement. Raine shook her head.

"I was just thinking that business is business. The personal needs to stand on its own," Raine continued.

"You're right," Drew said. "I just needed both of them

to get as far away from me as they could before I did reach out and hit one of them."

"Well, I'm just glad Jared came to his senses and decided not to press charges against Parker," Michelle added.

Heaven spoke up. "Oh, that's because Parker ran a background check on Jared and found out he was just as dirty as Drew already knew. Since he's been with the MLB there've been more than fifteen complaints about harassment and sexual assault on females. Most of the cases were kept quiet and Jared paid them off, that's why it was never in the news."

"I'm not surprised," Drew said. She wasn't surprised by Jared's criminal record, but she was surprised that Parker had him investigated and didn't bother to tell her. And what was that about Parker being unemployed?

"Carl said as long as there were no complaints about his behavior he wouldn't chase Jared out of town," Heaven continued.

Savannah chuckled. "Carl can't chase his own daddy out of that sheriff's chair. How does he think he's going to chase a man like Jared out of Sweetland? The press would love that."

"Sweetland would get tons of publicity, though," Raine added. "The connection to Parker and The Silver Spoon would be mentioned. More exposure for us."

"Way to think about the positive side to all this, sis," Savannah quipped.

"There is no positive side," Drew said with a sigh.

"Sure there is," Michelle offered. "Jared apparently got the hint that he needs to stay away from you. So if he wants to go around spending his time with opportunistic Diana, let him go right ahead. You have better things to worry about, like what we're going to have on the menu at your baby shower."

Drew couldn't help laughing at that. Instead of running a B&B, the Cantrell sisters should be in the business of event planning. They'd worked on the Bay Day celebration and the Labor Day events, and Raine had already mentioned something about the Winter Wonderland Dance in a couple of months. In addition, they were planning two weddings. It was no wonder they were more than happy to add a baby shower to their repertoire.

"It doesn't really matter," Drew said nonchalantly.

"Of course it matters," Michelle chided her. "This is the first Cantrell grandbaby, we have to do something special."

"Special would be if that baby shower turned into a wedding as well," Mr. Sylvester added, stepping slowly up onto the porch.

Drew wanted to lower her head into her lap or disappear, whichever would be easier. She did not want to talk about her relationship with Parker with his family and definitely not with Mr. Sylvester.

"We've got enough weddings going on around here for the moment, Mr. Sylvester," Heaven said while squeezing Drew's hand.

Mr. Sylvester eyed the two of them, then shook his head. "Never too many weddings. Some folk wait too long to get hitched to the one they belong with. Next thing you know, it's too late."

He was inside the house, the screened door closing behind him before any of them could respond. It was probably for the best, since they knew he'd been speaking of himself and Mrs. Cantrell. He'd been in love with her and she'd passed away before they could make their union official. For the rest of the evening, Drew could think of nothing else but love lost and love wasted and why Parker hadn't told her about his investigation of Jared.

*   *   *

"Looks like a ghost town out there," Parker said when Drew opened the back door for him the next morning.

She'd half expected him to come by last night. A part of her longed for another candlelight dinner and night of lovemaking like they'd had in Baltimore. Another part of her was banking its anger about the Jared situation. Rufus knew his way around now, and instead of going upstairs he headed straight toward the shop, where he liked to sit in the window and look at the passersby on the street.

"The Marina's having that breakfast and balloon lift at nine," she said sort of absently as they took the stairs.

"Yeah, Nikki and Raine were getting dressed to head over there this morning. Savannah refused to go and volunteered to work the front desk at the inn for the entire day."

Drew paused once they were in the kitchen. "Hmmm, Savannah and Michelle in the house together all day, that might not go too well."

"And Mr. Sylvester wasn't feeling well this morning. Michelle was taking him tea and toast when I left."

Parker talked while moving around the kitchen. He had cups from Jana's Java and what smelled like blueberry muffins. She'd already had a bowl of watermelon this morning, as she'd awakened feeling a little queasy. Crackers and tea didn't really work for her; instead she craved cool and sweet, which seemed to be the best remedy.

"He's been looking a little tired lately," she added. "Did you talk to Quinn about taking a look at him yet?"

Parker met her back at the table, placing a cup in front of her as she took a seat. "Yeah, he's going to stop by to see him before he joins Nikki at The Marina."

She nodded, thinking that was a good idea. "So all of you are going to The Marina today to have a look?"

"That was the original plan. Now, they're all going in intervals so it doesn't seem too obvious. I opted to visit you instead."

"Like nobody from town is going to notice the Cantrells at The Marina," she said, deciding to downplay the fact that he wanted to be with her instead of with his family staking out their competition. "You know Louisa and Marabelle will have a lot to say about their attendance," she finished, reaching for her cup and taking off the lid. There was only a small frown when she realized it was hot chocolate and not her favored caramel latte.

"Jana said there's less caffeine in the hot chocolate," he said when he caught the slight frown.

"How did she know who you were buying it for and why it needed less caffeine?" Drew asked cautiously.

Parker took a sip from his cup and handed her a muffin. "The same way I know that Jared and Diana paid you a visit yesterday. Louisa and Marabelle were already sitting at their favorite table when I came in."

Drew sighed. "So the entire town knows now. I should have known this would happen."

"Drew, I hate to be the one to break this to you, but you're starting to show. There's no way you were going to keep this pregnancy a secret."

"And no way I was going to keep the parentage secret either, not in Sweetland," she quipped.

Drew broke off a piece of her muffin and stuffed it into her mouth, chewing without really tasting it. Parker toyed with the paper that had wrapped his muffin, not looking up at her. Then he cleared his throat and said, "Would you rather move to the city?"

She almost choked. Coughing, she picked up her cup

of hot chocolate to take a sip. It was delicious, and she frowned again. "Why would you ask me that?"

He shrugged and looked over to her. "You worked so hard to get your education and your goal was to move to the city to work. Then you ended up here running a flower shop. Last weekend when we were in the city you enjoyed everything from the National Aquarium to riding on the subway. Besides, there's a sense of anonymity you can achieve there that is practically impossible here."

"When are you going back?" she asked quietly. Drew had known this moment would come. Her mother had told her, Louisa and Marabelle had told her, and even Diana McCann had said so yesterday. Parker wouldn't stay in Sweetland, and he wouldn't stay with her.

He didn't get a chance to answer, as the bell to the flower shop buzzed throughout the kitchen. Uncle Walt had wired it so that she could hear it from any location in the building. She jumped at the sound, and Parker frowned.

"Expecting company this early?"

"Ah, no, well, it could be the deliveryman." She stood and so did Parker. He walked in front of her and by the time they were downstairs had moved to open the door after they both saw the UPS truck parked in front.

Drew signed for the delivery while Parker carried the boxes inside. When the driver was gone, Drew noticed it was only a few minutes until nine, so she kept the door unlocked. No sense in locking it when it was just about opening time.

"Another big job?" Parker asked.

"The window display," she told him as she moved around the counter where he stood. She had to reach past him to retrieve the scissors, then cut into the first box. "The previous order was all wrong."

Drew smiled as this time she pulled out the burnt

orange and brown decorations. "The judging starts on Monday and the winner will be announced the following week. I'll have to work through the weekend to get everything ready."

"Work through the weekend doing what?" Parker asked.

He'd leaned forward and was also looking inside the box. He pulled out two fluffy balls of yellow, looking at them as if they were foreign weapons.

"Designing my window so it'll beat Delia's. She's doing a Midsummer Night's Dream theme that sounds fabulous, so my Falling into You has to be just as good," she told him. "I'll need the ladder from the back and that fish wire that's on the big spool beneath the sink."

She was already giving orders, and in no time she and Parker were in the front window—working around Rufus, who refused to move from his perch. A few familiar faces walked past, waving to her and to Parker as they moved by. When a customer came in, Drew stopped and handled their business. Parker, who had finally caught on to her idea, measured netting, strung the fluffy balls he still commented were weird looking onto the fish wire, and hung them from the top of the window seal as she'd instructed.

In anticipation of receiving the rest of her supplies, Drew had dyed her flowers yesterday. After setting the stems into the different vases of colored water, she had let them sit overnight. Now she went into the back storage area to retrieve them herself. She'd chosen Gerber daisies, carnations, and baby roses. They'd all absorbed enough dye so that the petals were the perfect shades of rich browns, exuberant yellows, and pert oranges. She would use some white as well, but these colors were really going to pop on a bright, sunny day, which she prayed Monday would be.

They worked side by side for hours without any interruption, which was a good and bad thing, since apparently she wasn't doing any business today. Around four o'clock, Parker suggested they call it a day.

"Let's go out and grab an early dinner. Walt stopped by with a delivery for Michelle this morning and mentioned he had some fresh oysters and flounder as the special today," he told her.

"I kind of want to finish this," was her reply.

She was surprised to feel his hands at her waist. There had been no touches, no kisses, since they'd returned from Baltimore. What there had been were lots of deep silences where she'd wondered what Parker was thinking. There had been moments when he would stare off, or he'd spend time looking out the front window. She'd wanted to ask but refused to, not really certain whether she should pry.

So the warm tingles that rippled up and down her spine at his touch startled her momentarily. She turned in to him just to make conversing more convenient, but she wasn't looking for anything more, didn't want to be disappointed if the intimacy with him she'd secretly craved didn't come.

"We can finish up when we get back. I'm hungry and I'm sure you and our daughter are as well. So let's go out for a while and work later. Besides, there's supposed to be a storm tonight, so we can stay in and watch those old movies you love so much."

Drew smiled; she couldn't help it. Not only did he remember she liked old movies, but he was offering to watch them with her, which meant two things—one, he was definitely paying attention, which was better than the physical intimacy she'd been thinking about a few seconds ago; and two, he was planning on staying with her tonight instead of heading right back to the inn after the shop was closed.

"Well, since you put it that way, I guess we can take a break now," she replied.

A very happy Rufus danced around their feet, jumping up only once and then stopping when Parker gave him a hand signal. Rufus immediately sat, looking up at the two of them expectantly. From his pocket Parker pulled a dog treat and offered it to him. It was the silliest thing, but Drew was touched. She knelt down, rubbing Rufus behind the ears.

"Good boy, Rufus," she said a couple of times.

"All right, all right, don't spoil him," Parker scolded her. "Let's get the place locked up."

"I'll get the keys from behind the counter," she said as Parker pushed the boxes they'd emptied up against the wall and moved to the door.

"Toss 'em over," he said. But when Drew turned to do that, she stopped to watch Parker staring out the door as if he'd seen a ghost or something equally devastating.

She quickly came from around the counter and went to stand behind him. She didn't see anything, but it did sound as though a car had just passed by. Across the street two women were walking toward Godfrey's Market, but Parker was looking in the opposite direction, closer to the coffee shop.

"What is it?" she asked, putting a hand on his shoulder.

He was tense and stood perfectly still, and he didn't answer her.

"Parker? Did you see something or somebody? Was it Jared? Because I can call Carl. I told him yesterday about Jared and Diana's little visit and he said he'd speak to Jared again about bothering me."

Parker turned at that. "You told Carl that Jared had come to see you but you didn't tell me?"

She opened her mouth to speak, then closed it quickly because she didn't know what to say.

Parker took the key from her hand and locked the door. Then he walked past her, saying only, "I'll be out back in the truck. Rufus, come."

Drew wondered if he meant for her to follow as meekly and obediently as the dog had. If that was the case, he was sadly mistaken. She went upstairs to freshen up first, joining him in the truck almost twenty minutes later.

Parker wasn't crazy, although he was pretty certain Drew was probably thinking he was. This had been a strange week, and although he'd tried to act as if all were normal, he knew she was beginning to pick up on the fact that it might not be true. It was a fact that had been hard for Parker to swallow as well. But today had sealed the deal: He was being followed.

"Hey, pretty girl, you're still hanging with this bum, I see," Walt Newsome said by way of greeting as Parker walked into The Crab Pot with Drew at his side.

Walt was a tall, burly-looking man. His graying beard and bushy eyebrows gave his face a menacing quality, while his booming voice and beady-eyed gaze put you in mind of Bluto, the not-so-tough bully from the *Popeye* comics. Drew stepped into his towering embrace immediately, and the old man stuck his tongue out at Parker as he hugged his niece tightly.

"What's good today, Walt?" Parker asked when Drew was once again at his side.

"Everything's good here all the time, you know that, Cantrell. Take a seat over there by the window and I'll have Wendy bring you some drinks."

That's how it worked at Walt's, when he knew you. There was no sense taking out the menus or even asking about the daily specials as Parker had just done, simply to tick him off. Walt would call back to the kitchen what he wanted and he'd put it on the table. It was either eaten and enjoyed or hated and the diner possibly banned from The Crab Pot forevermore. There wasn't a thing that Parker hadn't eaten on the many occasions he'd come through that door.

He held the chair for Drew to sit and she did, but she didn't say anything to him. A female's famous silent treatment, oh goody.

Sitting down, Parker figured he might actually deserve the silent treatment this time, so he decided to go ahead and get started with the groveling.

"I'm sorry I snapped at you," he said, sitting back in his chair.

She sat forward, dropping her elbows onto the table and crossing her arms. "Why didn't you tell me you'd had Jared investigated? Did you think I was lying about the assault?"

Silence or lethal candor, Parker wondered which was worse.

"No. I believed every word you told me. I had him investigated because experience warns that a sexual assailant rarely strikes only once."

Her look told him that was something she hadn't thought about, then she toyed with the cutlery that was so elegantly wrapped in a white paper napkin and held together with a strip of Scotch tape.

"Well, did he do it again?" she finally asked quietly.

Parker nodded. "He did."

She looked up immediately. "Has anyone told Diana about this?"

"Glad we're back to that point." Parker leaned forward. "Why didn't you tell me Jared and Diana had come by the flower shop?"

"I," she began, then stopped. Yanking her hands away from the table as if she hated the idea of fidgeting with the cutlery, she sat back and huffed. "I'm not used to having someone to run to. I called Carl because legally I want Jared to stay away from me. Then I went to Delia, but she was busy with customers." She hunched her shoulders. "Next thing I know, I was at the B and B talking to your sisters."

"All those people you could turn to and I wasn't one of them." He hadn't wanted to make her feel guilty, but he'd been pretty sore about that fact all morning. Actually, it had begun last night when Mr. Sylvester had come into his room like an old-school gangster getting in his face about not protecting his woman.

"You've got my cell number and my private phone at the B and B. I'd give you the number to my apartment, but that's futile since I'm here. I'd really like it if you could move me up on the totem pole the next time something like that happens." That was as cordial as he could manage. He'd really wanted to demand she tell him everything all the time, but something told him that wasn't going to work.

They were halfway through their bowls of cream of crab soup, warm bread, and side of fresh-shucked oysters when the fun really began.

Marabelle and Louisa came in with a bustle of complaints that had Walt arguing back and forth with the two women. Walt may have been one of only a few who dared to go that route with Marabelle and Louisa, but he didn't seem to mind one bit.

"Your sign says dollar crab night. I want ten dollars' worth of crabs and don't bring me those puny ones with nothing in 'em," Louisa yelled as Walt walked away from the table by the window the waitress had led them to.

"You get what I give you and nothing more," Walt yelled back.

"That's poor customer service, you old coot!" was Louisa's next reply.

"They'll fight for the next hour," Drew said with a roll of her eyes. "I can't say I've missed that in the weeks I haven't been here."

Parker chuckled. "Your uncle's time enough for her. And you said yourself how tired you are after you close the shop. Walt telling you not to come back to work here until you had the baby is a good thing."

When she only shrugged at that comment but glanced over to Louisa and Marabelle's table once more, Parker continued.

"They won't even have time to notice we're here. I mean, if you're still worried about people talking."

Drew looked over to him then, the tension between them having dissipated throughout dinner. "It doesn't matter. If they're not talking about us, they'll talk about someone else. It's the way of the world, I guess."

"I guess you're right," Parker replied, and ordered them another round of sodas while they waited for their dessert.

It just couldn't be enough that Sweetland's gossip central were eyeing them every couple of seconds. No, when things in Sweetland went downhill, it was usually with a quick plop into the river and a fall to the bottom, as if rocks were tied to your ankles.

Dollar night was a huge hit on a regular basis, but tonight it as if Walt were giving away food for free. Hoover came in with his drunken stagger and some choice words for Louisa, who'd commented on his wife's criminal history.

"She was a loudmouth thief and you married her!"

Louisa tossed across the room to where Hoover had taken a seat at the bar.

Hoover swiveled on the bar stool, almost falling off before catching himself sloppily. "And you're an old battle-ax!" was his retort.

"Oh, pipe down, Hoover. You've had one too many again," Marabelle added in her sweet but vinegar-tinged voice. "I'll bet your liver looks like a raisin by now."

"If you think I'm plastered, what do you think Stan and Grange are doing every night? Hell, being married to you two, they can't wait till you old hens come home so they can come out and play. They need a good drink every night just like I do." Hoover laughed at himself as he picked up his glass and downed his first drink—the first drink he'd had at Walt's, because it was clear Hoover was already plastered.

"Some things never change," Parker commented with a shake of his head.

"I don't know, I think they like giving each other a hard time," Drew added.

"I think they're all miserable and that's why they give everybody else a hard time."

She nodded. "Could be."

They were just about to get up, Parker had already put his cash on the table. Drew had stood and was pulling her purse onto her shoulders when Parker heard the shots. Glass rained all around them as he dove over the table, knocking Drew to the floor.

Screams erupted as more shots were fired, more glass was broken, and thunder erupted that was so loud, the entire dockside restaurant seemed to shake. When Parker turned to look toward the windows, all he saw was a thick bolt of lightning crackling through the sky and all he felt was the rush of adrenaline he'd had that night in the alley when Vezina was shot.

Without another thought, he reached down and pulled out the gun he'd had strapped to his left ankle. "Stay here and stay down," he whispered in Drew's ear. Then he was gone through the front door and out into the night, where another lunatic with a gun awaited.

Chapter 17

Outside, rain fell in big fat drops, pelting Parker as he made his way around to the parking lot, where he presumed the shots had come from. By this time there was chaos going on around him. He heard more screaming, then feet running down the stairs of the restaurant, over the asphalt, and down the pier. In the distance there was the sound of sirens, probably the cops and the fire department.

Parker made note of it and left it all behind in his pursuit. He moved through the night, looking at every parked car, underneath, over, and around, until a hand on his shoulder stopped him.

"He's gone," Ryan DelRio said. Ryan was a couple of inches taller than Parker, his frame only slightly thinner. He'd drawn his gun as well. "I was out of my truck the moment he got the first shot off. He stood right down there." Ryan pointed toward the water, where a hill of rocks created about a ten-foot drop to the river.

Parker looked back at the restaurant. "A clear view of the windows of the restaurant."

"A clear view of you and Drew. I could see you from

where I was sitting. He'd have had an advantage standing up on those rocks."

"And you couldn't catch him?" Parker asked with more irritation than he'd intended. Hell, he'd intended a lot of irritation because he was pissed. Someone had been shooting at him!

"Not when he had a boat waiting for him. I told you after you sent the text about being followed it was time to call in for more backup," Ryan reminded him. "You're a sitting duck in this small naïve town. Nobody locks their doors, nobody's looking over their shoulders. He's probably staying at that big fancy resort on the other side of town, participating in the festivities or going down to have ice cream."

Parker frowned. "This doesn't happen in Sweetland!" he yelled. "It just doesn't happen."

"It is happening, Parker! It happened tonight, and if his aim hadn't been worth crap, you'd be lying on that floor with a bullet in your brain."

Parker turned away, rubbing a hand down his face. But Ryan wasn't finished; he yanked Parker's arm until he turned around.

"Worse, Drew could be lying on that floor with a bullet in her head," he said calmly but seriously. "Now I know you're used to thinking you're Superman and walking through a hail of bullets might be the norm for you. But think about that woman, the one that's carrying your child. Think about her, Parker!"

"I am, dammit! I am!" Parker yelled back. And when he was just about to say something else, he looked over Ryan's shoulder to see her running toward him.

He cursed again, pushing Ryan out of the way. Drew fell into his arms before he could even extend them to her. She wrapped her arms around his neck, holding him so

tight that Parker almost choked. Instead he wrapped his
hands around her waist, holding her just as tightly against
him. His heart pounded in his chest, and sweat sprinkled
his forehead, even though it was most likely lost in the
downpour that was now drenching them both.

What he'd said to Ryan was absolutely correct. He
couldn't think of anything but Drew and his baby now
and the fact that he had to protect them no matter what.
Damn his sergeant's orders, damn his reputation and his
plan to prove everyone wrong. It was only about keeping
Drew and his daughter safe, that was all.

An hour later, they were at the inn. Drew and his sisters
were in the kitchen, making tea or hot chocolate or something. Parker was in the living room, his brothers, Ryan,
and the Sweetland police accompanying him.

"We're spending more and more time over here talking to you boys about some sort of trouble," Sherriff Kyle
Farraway said in his raspy voice. "Almost seems like old
times," he finished, looking over at Parker.

He stood by the window. Michelle had drawn all the
drapes when they'd come in, but Parker used a finger to
separate them, peeping outside. Sycamore Drive was
completely quiet. The rain was still falling, creating small
puddles in some places, a glossy sheen on the sidewalk in
others.

"Yeah, but in the old days we all knew what was going
on and we had time to get our stories straight before you
arrived," Quinn commented solemnly.

Parker took a deep breath and turned to face the firing
squad. It was no shock that every gaze in the room was on
him. Exactly like the old days. Only this time he didn't
have Gramma standing in the room ready to defend him
to the death. And he didn't have his dad looking stern but
sure to defend him as well, at least until the police left

and he'd be able to scold him in private. No, this wasn't seventeen years ago; Parker was no longer a mischievous teenager. He was a grown man and he was on his own this time.

"About six months ago I witnessed a murder," he began. "A cop was killed and I saw the killers. A week later they paid me a visit and left the message that I should back off the investigation. Then I got the call that Gramma died and I came to Sweetland." There was more, but Parker didn't want the sheriff and his two deputies to hear it. He'd tell his brothers after they were gone; he still had a bit of pride left to swallow.

"You're a witness in a murder case and you didn't tell me?" Preston asked immediately. "Why didn't you say something before now?"

Parker shook his head. "It wasn't exactly the right time to dump more on the family, Pres."

"Bullshit, Parker! We're brothers!" The words exploded from Preston, and Parker frowned. It was a rare time when Preston lost his cool. Most recently it had been when Heaven had been kidnapped. Very rarely it had been with Parker.

"I know, I should have told you," he admitted. "I should have told both of you the minute I came back. I thought I'd left it all in Baltimore, until the accident."

"When you ran your bike into a tree?" Carl asked, a tinge of humor in his voice.

Both his father and Jonah, the other deputy, shot him disapproving looks.

"I didn't run into a tree. I was run off the road. I saw the car just before it swerved in front of me."

"Another secret, Parker? You could have died in that accident." Preston was in rare form tonight. Guilt ate at Parker with ferocious hunger.

"Parker told me about his suspicions when I came here

to help out with Heaven's situation," Ryan interjected. His words took Preston's heated gaze from Parker for about ten seconds.

"You told Ryan? You told the goddamned FBI and you didn't think to tell your family?" Preston asked.

Quinn walked over to Preston then, putting a hand on his shoulder. "I'm sure Parker had a good reason for his actions. In retrospect we'll all agree now that he should have told us, but that's not getting us anywhere tonight."

"He's right," the sheriff added. "I want to know everything you two know." He looked from Parker to Ryan.

"I have a file back in my hotel room. How about we meet tomorrow morning at the station and go over everything?" Ryan suggested.

Kyle nodded. "Sounds good. Now, for tonight I want you boys to lock this house down good. Michelle said you don't have any guests checking in until tomorrow, but Jonah will keep patrol tonight."

"I can handle the patrol," Carl protested.

Kyle didn't even look at his son when he said, "Jonah will take tonight's patrol. Ryan, you headed back to your hotel?"

Ryan nodded. "I am. I'm also going to email my commander with a report. My jurisdiction's limited on this one. I've just been giving Parker a hand with some investigative work. But with tonight's incident, I've got to call it in."

"Right," Kyle said with a nod. "What about you, Parker? You calling your sergeant tonight or do you want me to do it in the morning?"

Parker swallowed. "I'll call him in the morning. I've got some other things to take care of tonight."

The women came into the room at that moment, passing out mugs and setting a plate of cookies on one of the tables. It was weird and somewhat comforting to watch all the women migrate to their partners—Nikki to Quinn and Heaven to Preston. Michelle, Savannah, and Raine stood close together, everyone needing a little extra support. Drew took her time after handing Jonah and Kyle their cups. When she turned, she came in Parker's direction but didn't get as close as Nikki and Heaven did to his brothers. That was the only signal Carl needed.

He stepped close to Drew. "I'll take you home now, Drew."

Quinn and Ryan immediately looked at Parker. He didn't need their nudge, he'd already decided what he was going to do.

"Thanks, but it's okay, Carl," he said, moving close enough to Drew to place a hand on her shoulder. "I'll take care of Drew." He wanted her to stay at the inn with him tonight, wanted her close just as he wanted his family close. After all, she was his family now, too. But he didn't want to say that in front of everyone.

"I think it's better if I take her home, out of harm's way. I can stake out in front of her building for the night since Jonah's doing the patrol here," Carl continued.

"You'll be at the station, Deputy, handling the paperwork from tonight's events," Kyle said.

"Fine," Carl replied tightly. "But I'll take Drew home first."

"No, thank you, Carl. Parker will see me home," Drew said in a quiet voice.

Parker let out a secret sigh. He wasn't sure how Drew was feeling about him at the moment. Sure, she'd hugged him tightly outside the restaurant, but that was before the revelation that whoever had shot out all Walt's windows had done so because of him. They hadn't had a chance to talk alone about what had happened, and he so desperately wanted the opportunity to do so.

Carl looked dejected, again. But Parker didn't give a

damn. As a man, Carl was out of line. He was making a play for Drew right in front of Parker, and that wasn't cool. As a cop, he was apparently pissing off his father and his superior. That, Parker didn't want to get into at all.

"Then let's all get a good night's rest. Everything will look better in the morning," Michelle said. "I'll walk you to the door, Sheriff, Deputies."

"Y'all have a good night," Jonah added in his always polite voice. He'd taken off his police hat and now tipped it to the women as he slipped it back on and headed for the door.

"We'll meet at the station nine AM sharp. Parker, I expect to see you there," Kyle told them. "And lock this place up tight."

"Yes, sir," Parker heard himself saying. Kyle Farraway had always been a fair man. Even when he was grabbing Parker by the collar and dragging him away from whatever trouble he'd gotten into, he was fair and he was solid. He'd been married to Esterine Farraway for what had to be more than thirty years, and his only son, Carl, had followed in his footsteps. If there was any other man in Sweetland that Parker had looked up to outside of his father, it was Kyle Farraway.

Carl stormed out first, not muttering a word to Parker or any of them. "Boy's never gonna grow up," Kyle admitted.

Parker stood with Drew as they filed out.

"I want to talk to you," Preston said to Parker.

"Not tonight," Quinn added. "We've all had enough for tonight. And since there's nobody in the rooms, we'll all just stay here. That way Michelle won't worry for the next eight hours about where we are and if we're all safe."

Michelle shook her head. "I wouldn't worry," she told them. "I'd just call your cell phones every hour on the hour."

Nikki laughed at that. "I don't doubt it for one moment. Come on, Quinn, we'll take the Blue Room."

Heaven wrapped her arms around Preston's waist. "And we'll take the Sunshine Room. It'll be like old times," she offered him a smile. When he didn't immediately return it, she nudged him and kissed his cheek. "Everything's going to be fine, we'll deal with all of this in the morning."

Preston went with her reluctantly, without looking back at Parker. He was beyond pissed off, and Parker hurt for the rift he'd created between them. It was stupid not to tell at least Preston what was going on. But it wasn't the first stupid thing he'd done in his life.

"Are you two staying here tonight?" Raine asked when she came to stand in front of Parker and Drew.

"Yes," he answered for them, pulling Drew closer. He needed her tonight more than he'd ever needed anything in his life. If she pulled away, if she refused, Parker had no idea how he'd handle it. Luckily for him, she didn't.

"I'll take the dogs down to the basement and get them all settled," Drew offered.

She moved away before anyone could stop her, and Parker was left alone in the living room with Savannah, Raine, and Michelle.

"I think Carl's got a thing for Drew," Savannah told Parker.

Michelle tsked, moving around the room to collect the cups that everyone had left. "Carl's got a thing for every female he sees."

"But he isn't buying flowers for every female he sees," Savannah added as she plopped down into a chair. "He gave Drew flowers and asked her out to dinner."

"When?" Parker asked tightly.

Savannah smiled, crossing her legs. "Weeks ago, I think. Delia got her out of the date, but Carl's been hanging around the flower shop a lot lately."

"Stop it, Savannah," Raine admonished her. "Tonight is not the night to get Parker all riled up with jealousy. He has a gun, you know?"

"A gun he'd better keep locked up while he's in this house," Michelle added.

"How's he gonna protect us if that lunatic comes back to finish the job if his gun is locked up? Really, Michelle, don't be such a grandmother."

Everybody froze at Savannah's words, looking at her as if she'd spoken another language.

"What? You all know she's walking around here acting like Gramma, nitpicking everything and telling us all what to do," Savannah continued.

"Stop it," Parker said finally. "Just stop it. There's enough going on around here without us fighting with each other. If Carl has a thing for Drew, I'll be sure to set him straight. I'll keep the gun close to me, Michelle, but out of sight. Okay?"

Michelle nodded.

"Let's get some rest," he said, and started to walk out of the room.

"Parker?"

He turned to Michelle's voice. "We're here for you, no matter what. Don't you ever forget that."

He looked at his sisters, each one of them, even the pouty one on the couch, and smiled. "I know, and thank you. It's about time I started being here for everyone as well."

Parker left the room then, heading down to the basement to find Drew. There was a lot he needed to come clean about, and he wanted her to be the first to hear his confessions.

"So there's a very good chance that I may lose my job," Parker said to Drew when they were seated on the couch in the sitting room of the caretaker's suite.

Rufus was lying in his dog bed, even though Drew didn't expect that to last for long. He hadn't wanted to stay down in the basement, crying and scratching against his kennel as she'd taken that first step in attempting to leave him. Then she'd looked up and seen Parker standing at the top of the stairs. Drew hadn't known what to do—run to him or away from him. Instead she'd turned back, unlocked the kennel, and pulled Rufus into her arms. Tonight, he'd serve as the buffer between her and his owner.

Around them the house was quiet, but she still heard the gun shots and the shattering of glass. She sat leaning forward with her legs pulled close together, her elbows resting on her knees, hands clasped together.

For the last half hour she'd been sitting in silence while Parker talked. He had a lot to say, a lot she hadn't known and had wondered about. And when he finished, it seemed there should be more. Mainly because now he was sitting quietly, waiting for her response, no doubt, and Drew had no idea what that response was supposed to be.

Parker had been suspended from his job for investigating a case his commander explicitly told him not to investigate. He'd come to Sweetland for his grandmother's funeral and someone had followed him here—most likely the person who'd come to his apartment to issue a warning. But why hadn't that person just killed Parker? Apparently he'd tried that day on the highway; why hadn't he managed to get the job done yet?

And why was she thinking of Parker being killed?

She dropped her head, took a steadying breath, and that's when she felt it. A flutter in her abdomen that made her gasp and sit up straight.

"What's the matter?" Parker asked immediately. "What is it?"

Drew didn't speak for fear he'd think she was crazy and,

worse, that it wouldn't happen again and she'd think she was crazy. But it did happen again, a fluttering across the front part of her abdomen. Her hands went there immediately, and Parker moved closer to her on the couch, his arm going instantly around her shoulders. "Drew, are you okay? Do I need to call Quinn or Dr. Lorens?"

"No," she whispered, shaking her head. "I think she moved."

And as if on cue, the sensation erupted again and she sat back in the chair, smiling, hand still on her stomach. "Our baby moved."

Parker didn't speak at first, but Drew locked gazes with him, saw the corners of his mouth lift into a smile. He covered her hand with his and looked down. "She moved, huh?"

Drew nodded. "Yes, three times. I felt it and it was like, it was so soft and so quick and . . ." She sighed. "So real. It's real, Parker. I'm going to have our baby."

Parker was nodding as well, still looking down at her stomach, at their hands on her stomach. "You're close to twenty-one weeks now, so yes, it's normal. Some women feel what's called a quickening as early as fourteen and fifteen weeks. But first-time mothers sometimes take a little longer to feel first movements or to actually decipher what they are."

He was babbling, and Drew thought it was so cute that she laughed. "You must read a little more of that book each time you're at my apartment. Maybe I should just buy you your own."

He looked up at her then and they both shared a smile. "I'm going to be a good father, Drew. I promise. Regardless of what's going on now or what I've done in the past. Even given the fact that I may not have a job, my first priority is to be a good father to our daughter."

"I know, Parker," she told him. It was the first concise

thought she'd had, feeling she'd experienced, since they'd come into his room. "I know you're going to be good to our child. And you'll find a way to fix what's going on now. I believe everything is going to work out just fine. I don't know why I believe it, I just do."

He lifted both her hands from her stomach then, bringing them to his mouth for two gentle kisses. "Gramma would call it having faith," he said quietly. "And if you believe it, Drew, then so do I. If you think we can make this work, then I know we will."

She watched him lean forward then, knowing he would kiss her. She expected and anticipated that kiss, loving the warmth that spread throughout her body as his lips touched hers. In no time he was moving over her, pushing her back on the couch.

"Tell me if I'm hurting you," he whispered, his hands cupping her face.

Drew shook her head. "I'm fine. Just fine," she told him, pulling his head down for another kiss.

Parker kissed her as if he'd been dying of thirst and she was there to quench it. His tongue moved slowly over hers, his hands moving down her neck to her shoulders. He moaned as he shifted some of his weight off of her, not believing that his body lying completely on hers could not be causing some sort of discomfort, considering he outweighed her by at least eighty pounds. She moved with him, twining her legs with his, grabbing handfuls of his shirt at her shoulders.

In his mind, all he wanted to do was whatever made her happy. If that meant working side by side in a flower shop, dammit, he was willing to do that. Whatever it took so that he could see her each day, touch her, talk to her, be with his child, Parker was willing to do it.

"Drew . . ." He pulled back, chest heaving, feeling the

need to tell her all that was going through his mind at this moment.

"Shhh, Parker. Not now," she whispered in return, yanking at his shirt and pushing it up over his chest.

He ducked out of the shirt, heard it hit the table and knock something over. She kissed along his bare chest, her teeth nipping lightly at his skin. It took much more strength to keep from ravishing her than it did to hold himself over her so that she could have her way with him. The feel of her flattened palms were like liquid fire as they moved over his pectorals down to his abs, then around his back to cup his buttocks.

"Off. Now!" she stated clearly and a bit loudly.

His ego wouldn't let his smile stay at bay. "Tell me what you want and I'll give it to you," he replied.

She lifted a brow. "Off. Now." And this time she followed it with a nod of her head toward his pants.

With a grin that threatened to split his face, Parker eased off the chair and removed his pants, shoes, socks, boxers. Before he could return, she pointed to the pants he'd thrown on the floor and he backtracked, reaching into his pocket for his wallet and a condom. Drew held out an upturned hand and he dropped the packet there.

She tore it open, then crooked a finger for him to come closer. Sitting up on the couch, she pulled him closer by his hips until his erection was perfectly aligned with her face and her mouth. Parker let his head fall back and moaned. No way could he watch what was coming next. Not and remain standing and possibly breathing—there was just no way.

Light as a feather, she kissed the tip of his shaft and Parker sucked in a breath. In long, slow strokes, her tongue moved up and down his length, and he wanted to yell out in pleasure. Next were her hands, cupping him, stroking him from hilt to tip, long, slow, delicious. The latex touched his skin seconds later, and she rolled it down inch by inch, slowly. He finally had enough strength to look down at her and was none too pleased to see her smiling with satisfaction.

"You okay there?" she asked, her eyes twinkling with mischief.

"Yeah, pretty pleased with yourself, aren't you?" he asked, his hands on his hips. "So what else do you want?"

Drew let her hands fall to her sides and began lifting the hem of her shirt.

"Would you like me to do that?" he asked, eager to get his hands on her again.

But she shook her head. "No. I want you to watch and don't touch."

He frowned like a child, clenching and unclenching his fingers at his side. "So torture is the name of this game," he replied with a nod.

Drew continued to smile as she removed her bra. She'd worn sandals, so it was easy to slip them off her feet, and the long skirt that he could now see was pulled over the swell of her belly and slipped to the floor silently. When her panties followed, Parker knew he was screwed. There was no way in hell he could keep his hands off her.

He stepped forward and placed both palms on her stomach, which he would swear grew more every day. "She's going to rule the world," he whispered.

"Just like her mother," Drew replied, leaning forward to kiss Parker's neck.

He pulled her closer, loving the feel of her naked body in his arms. Then he picked her up, kissing her lightly along the neck and shoulders as he walked them into the bedroom. Just as they were about to cross the threshold, he turned back to whisper a command to Rufus. "Stay."

* * *

Drew lay back on the bed, knowing Parker would soon follow. She ached for him. The whole "do what I say" foreplay she'd instigated in the living room had pushed her well beyond her threshold of desire. Her thighs were quivering and her center was already moist. She was ready for him now.

But Parker apparently had other ideas. He started at her feet, massaging them both until she was moaning in pure bliss. He kissed each arch, stopping only when she begged him to, then moved to massage her calves. Drew wanted to sink into the mattress, she felt so relaxed and so aroused. When he touched the inside of her thighs, she bit her bottom lip to keep from screaming. He touched her there, right along the plump folds of her center. A soft touch before he leaned forward, blowing on the tightened bud of her. There was a moan, then a groan, then she thought, *To hell with it all,* and screamed, "Parker!"

She knew he was smiling, knew he was feeling smug in his idea of getting back at her, but right now Drew wasn't to be played with. Instead, she moved and maneuvered until she'd wrestled him over and was straddling him.

"Well. Well. Well. You can dish it out, but you can't take it. That's very nice to know," he said with a smirk.

"Shut up and make love to me," Drew insisted.

"Whatever you say, Ms. Sidney." His hands went to her waist, lifting her until she was leveraged directly over his length.

She reached between them to grasp his erection, guiding him as he lowered her onto his rigid arousal. Their joining was once again like liquid fire, easily ignited and burning brightly as they moved. And boy, did they move. They'd started out in one position and ended with her standing, leaning over the bed, and Parker thrusting deep inside her from behind. All that physical exertion coupled with the events of this evening had them both running to shower afterward and then back to bed, where they fell asleep almost instantly.

Just before dawn, Drew awoke to the sound of a car door slamming. She jolted so fast and hard that it woke Parker.

"What is it?"

She sat straight up in the bed. "I think somebody's outside," she whispered.

Parker was up and out of the bed instantly. She barely saw him reach over the side of the bed to retrieve his weapon. But she saw it plainly as he pressed against the wall and leaned over to look out the window. He looked like one of those actors on television, holding his gun in both hands, arms upward, bent at the elbow, ready to shoot. Except for the fact that he was totally naked, he looked absolutely dangerous.

Then he pulled back, flattened himself including his head against the wall, and sighed. "It's your uncle Walt. Sometimes he delivers shipments to Michelle early in the morning after he comes from fishing."

"Oh, right," she said, feeling like an idiot. "I'm sorry. I just heard the sounds and . . ." She trailed off.

Parker sat beside her on the bed, putting his gun on the bedside table. "It's okay. It's natural to still be shaken up after last night. It's not like you get shot at every day."

"No," she said softly, reaching up to run her hand along a scar that she'd just noticed on his left side. "But you do."

He frowned down at the scar, then looked back up at her. "That was actually a knife wound from some wannabe gang thug that couldn't aim worth crap. He'd been trying to kill me, no doubt, but he'd barely grazed me before I body-slammed him and his knife to the ground."

She winced and he ran his fingers over her cheek. "It's

okay. I'm not a beat cop anymore. Most of the time I'm sitting behind a desk going through case files. When I finally get out into the field, the shooting has already been done."

"Like that cop that died in your arms?" she asked, knowing that was a scene that would never stop replaying in Parker's mind.

Parker sighed. "I keep thinking I was there for a reason, at that specific time and in that place, I had to be there for a reason. But Vezina died anyway, so I don't know what that reason is. I didn't save him and the perpetrators got away. What was the point?"

"Hey, I think you're being too hard on yourself. Despite what the rumors say, you're not Superman. You can't know all and defeat all and get up to do it again the next day. That's just not how it works in the real world."

He smiled down at her. "I guess you're right. But knowing that doesn't take away the questions, it doesn't make me not think about this or even dream about it over and over again. I hope you can understand that."

"I understand that you need closure," she said with a sigh of her own. "I've been thinking that I need that, too. I figured bad things are going to happen in our lives, but it's how we deal with them that will determine how we go on. Years ago I let that town demolish me with their rumors, and I let Jared walk away like a hero. When what I should have done was bury his phony ass in court."

Parker leaned forward and kissed her forehead. "You're a lot tougher than you look, Drew Sidney. I can't believe nobody's realized that by now."

"Maybe I'm just realizing it," she told him. "Look, Parker, I know that you're going to keep investigating that Vezina case until you find out what happened and why. I also know that as long as you do, you're in danger. And as much as I want you to stay safe, I care about you too much to ask you to give up what you do best. This is your career, and it's your life. I can accept that."

There was a moment of silence in which Parker seemed to be struggling to say something. Finally, he simply shook his head, kissing her lips once, then twice. "I don't know what I've done to deserve you, to deserve this gift you're giving to me. But I don't want to lose it. I don't want to do anything to jeopardize it."

"Then close this case and put this incident behind you. We have a daughter to prepare for."

He smiled. "More orders. Man, you're a bossy one. But I think I can handle that. I'm meeting Ryan and the sheriff at the police station this morning to go over what we have so far. I'd like for you to stay here so that you're not alone."

Drew was already shaking her head. "I have to get to the shop. Michelle needs new centerpieces for the restaurant tomorrow."

"I'm sure she'll understand. Or maybe you can bring your work here. When I finish at the station I can go over and pack the stuff up for you and bring it here."

"Remember just a few minutes ago when I was telling you how I respected your job even though it was dangerous and all that?"

Parker looked over his shoulder at her.

"Well, the flower shop is my job. And this contract I have with the inn is important. Just because I'm carrying your child doesn't mean I'm going to take that for granted." He wasn't looking as if he agreed, but Drew climbed out of bed and kept on talking. "So I'm going to get dressed, see if I can help Michelle with anything before I head over to the shop. Then I have some closure of my own to deal with."

"What?" he asked in a slow voice. "What do you mean by some closure of your own to deal with?"

Drew took a deep breath as she pulled a shirt he'd tossed to her over her head. It touched her midthigh and hid her baby bump, not that she was trying to. And when she looked up at him, she knew this wasn't going to be easy. Despite the fact that she'd just about given him permission to go out and chase after a killer, she had a sneaking suspicion Parker wasn't going to be all smiles and agreement with what she was about to say.

"I want to talk to Jared."

He opened his mouth to speak, but she held up her hand to stop him.

"I want this over with, Parker. For years I've been hesitant about relationships and scared to death of creating more town gossip. Now, I'm sick of both. I want us to move forward with our lives and to raise our child here in Sweetland. I don't want to worry about gossip because I know it'll circulate regardless and I don't want to keep running from Jared and what he did to me. It's probably too late to press charges, but at the very least I can just stand up to him, once and for all."

"I don't want him near you," Parker began.

"I know, but—"

He shook his head. "No! I don't want him near you and I definitely do not want you left alone with him. You're asking too much of me, Drew. This is just not something I can allow."

She nodded, hating that this was exactly how she'd figured this conversation would end.

"It's my life, Parker. You can't 'allow' me to do anything," she told him before pushing past him and heading for the bathroom.

Chapter 18

"I want to see my daughter right now! You cannot hold her hostage here," Lorrayna Sidney yelled after all but busting through the front door of the B&B.

Her brother Walt was standing right beside her, holding one of her arms to keep her from running throughout the house. "Calm down, Lorrayna. The Cantrells don't hold people hostage."

"No, but they do have people shooting at them. You know it's true, Walt, just look at your restaurant. Who's going to pay for all that damage? I bet the Cantrells won't." Lorrayna continued on her rampage until Michelle and Nikki came out of the kitchen to see what was going on.

"Morning, Walt. Hi, Lorrayna. What can I do for you so early in the morning?" Michelle asked, wondering what could be so important that the two of them were here before eight o'clock in the morning.

Normally this would be the time Walt would make his deliveries, but she didn't see any boxes or crates, and Walt usually came in through the back door so he could put everything right in the freezer for her.

"I want to see my daughter right now!" Lorrayna all but yelled in Michelle's face.

Michelle took a step back and looked to Walt. "Is there a problem?"

"She thinks you're holding Drew in some kind of protective custody because of the shooting last night," Walt told her with a shake of his head.

Nikki chuckled. "Holding her? Really, Mrs. Sidney, is that what you think?"

"Don't get sassy with me. Just because you're shacking up with one of those Cantrells doesn't mean that Drew has to," she said to Nikki with unmasked disgust.

"With all due respect, ma'am, I'm engaged to Quinn and Drew is pregnant by Parker," Nikki stated.

Michelle put a hand to Nikki's shoulder to keep her future sister-in-law calm.

"Drew is here. She spent the night because Parker wanted to make sure she was safe," Michelle explained to Lorrayna.

But Lorrayna was unfortunately too far gone for reasonable explanations. "She would have been safe if he'd stayed away from her completely. Waltzing into town on that death bike of his, thinking he was hot stuff. He maneuvered her and used her just like that other animal. But I'm not going to let her fall this time. I'm not going to let her down, I'm going to be right by her side through this whole ordeal."

"What ordeal are you talking about?" Michelle asked her.

"Lorrayna," Walt said, trying to reason with his sister again. He'd stepped in front of her and was now holding her by the shoulders. "Look, you've got to calm down. This isn't like Stratford. Drew's safe here."

Lorrayna shook her head. "No. No, she isn't. I saw him in town just yesterday, walking around proud as a peacock with that silly McCann girl on his arm. He's here to hurt Drew again and I'm not going to let him this time."

"Now who does she think is hurting Drew?" Nikki whispered to Michelle.

"I think she's talking about Jared Mansfield," Michelle whispered back without taking her eyes off Lorrayna and Walt.

"What's going on out here?" Parker asked, entering the living room.

"That's him! That's him! Call the cops, Walt! He's the one that's kidnapped my baby!" Lorrayna yelled.

At the same time, Savannah came down the steps in her usual slow gait so that everyone could see what she was wearing and how good it looked on her. But when she heard Lorrayna's tirade, she moved a little faster into the living room.

"What in the world is going on down here? And why are you in my house yelling like a banshee at the crack of dawn?" Savannah asked Lorrayna.

"I don't want to talk to these people. I don't want to talk to anyone but Drew! Please, Walt, just find my baby. Just find her, please," Lorrayna wailed.

"What in the world is going on out here?" Mr. Sylvester said, coming into the room leaning heavily on his cane this morning. "Sounds like a bag of screeching cats."

"She's flipping out," Savannah quipped.

Michelle nudged her to be quiet, and Walt rolled his eyes skyward.

"I'm awfully sorry about the intrusion, Michelle. I know what happened last night wasn't Parker's fault. If she could just see Drew, maybe she'll calm down." Walt talked calmly, which was out of character for him.

Mr. Sylvester had made his way completely into the room and was now standing about a foot from where Walt held on to Lorrayna.

"Nonsense, last night was nobody's fault but that fool that had the gun. Now you come on over here and sit down a spell. Get her some tea to calm her nerves," he directed Michelle and Lorrayna at the same time.

Michelle looked to Savannah, afraid to leave this particular group of people alone in the room. Savannah huffed.

"Fine, I'll get it." But she wouldn't be happy about it, Michelle was positive of that.

Mr. Sylvester took a seat on the couch, patting the spot beside him for Lorrayna, who was steadily wringing her hands and making weeping sounds, although no tears were being shed. In Michelle's opinion, the woman was doing more than flipping out, she was giving an awesome performance. She'd seen Lorrayna on occasion throughout town, holding on to Drew as if her life depended on it while shopping in Godfrey's or even walking along Main. On Sundays when she and Drew came in for brunch, Michelle always picked up on the tension at their table and the way Drew looked for any possible escape.

Between Drew's relationship with her mother and Heaven's estranged relationship with hers, Michelle counted herself lucky that Patricia Cantrell had packed her bags and left Sweetland only days after they'd buried their father. It saved her a lot of time and grief trying to deal with a woman too selfish to have children.

Lorrayna all but fell onto the couch next to Mr. Sylvester, waving a hand like a substitute fan over her face. It was cooler in this house than it was outside, and it was pretty cool outside, considering it was still early in the morning and last night's storm had done a great job of knocking down the temperature and the humidity. The fanning was another part of Lorrayna's act.

"I just want to see my baby. I want to make sure she's all right," Lorrayna said in a baleful voice.

"She's just fine, ma'am," Parker told her. "Drew was taking a shower when I left her. She'll be dressed and out in a few minutes, then she's going down to the flower shop. Everything's all right, Mrs. Sidney, I promise you."

Lorrayna shook her head. "You can't keep promises, young man. I know all about you. Undependable trouble-maker, that's what they told me, and so far that's all I've seen. Just look what you've gotten my daughter into."

Parker opened his mouth to speak, but Michelle touched his arm, shaking her head for him to refrain. "I beg your pardon, Mrs. Sidney," she said. "Parker and Drew are very happy together. Nobody could have predicted what happened last night."

Lorrayna continued to shake her head. "Ever since you Cantrell boys came back to town, things have been happening. Sweetland used to be so quiet and so peaceful. Since you've been here we've had murders and fires and motorcycle accidents. It's terrible!"

"It's life, that's what it is," Mr. Sylvester interrupted. "Things happen and we don't plan 'em and we can't predict 'em. It just is. Sure, there's been some bad things happening around town lately, but you know what? It's about time things got stirred up a bit around here. Can't live in a fantasy world all your life. But I can promise you this, whatever comes with these boys, they handle it right quick. And they don't mean any harm to anybody. This boy would no more hurt your girl than he would his own sister."

"Her reputation's ruined here, just like it was back home. Every time Drew gets mixed up with a man it ruins her reputation. Now she's going to have this baby out of wedlock and raise it on her own while he gallivants around town like a peacock on that noisy bike or goes back to the big city with those fancy women. It's just not right." Lorrayna sobbed.

Michelle looked to Parker, whose frown had deepened

significantly. He turned and walked back through the house toward the kitchen, and she let him go.

"What ain't right is you judging a man solely by what you've heard. I suspect whatever ruined your daughter's reputation in your former home wasn't true. Especially since I've had occasion to meet your daughter and she seems like a lovely gal to me." Mr. Sylvester took one of Lorrayna's shaking hands in his. "You didn't want people judging your girl by rumors, yet you sit here and do the same to my boy. He don't deserve that, not from you or anybody else. He's a good man and he's going to do the right thing by your daughter."

Now Michelle felt bad for letting Parker walk away. If there was one thing she knew her brother needed to hear, it was another man standing up for him. It was somebody saying that he was as good as Michelle knew him to be.

Lorrayna lowered her head, her shoulders hunching as she continued that fake-cry episode. Then the only other person who could possibly calm the woman down entered the room, and the tension grew so thick that Michelle almost choked.

"Hello, Mother," Drew said in a quietly exasperated voice.

"You're not going to like this," Ryan began once they were all assembled in the front room of the building that had long since housed Sweetland's police department.

It wasn't a large building, and from the outside it looked more like a warehouse than a police station. There was a shield on the front of both swinging glass doors and the sheriff's name printed in bold block letters beneath it. The front room was like a sitting area, with functional office chairs lined up along the front and side walls. There was a table in the center of the room that held all sorts of brochures, from the local restaurant menus to the town's event schedule and maps highlighting where to go in Sweetland. Across the room was the front desk, where Esterine Farraway, Kyle's wife, sat serving as the dispatcher and receptionist for going on thirty-five years. If Parker remembered correctly, that was how Kyle and Esterine had met.

This morning, Kyle had sent Esterine back to his office. Jonah, Ryan, Preston, and the sheriff sat in the room with Parker, all of them looking equal parts exhausted and concerned.

"I already don't like it," Kyle replied to Ryan's remark. "All this shooting and sneaking around in my town's not sitting well with me or the mayor. I'm meeting with her later this afternoon," he informed them.

Parker cleared his throat. "I apologize for bringing my troubles to Sweetland."

"Actually," Ryan began, "it looks like Sweetland's been hiding a little bit of trouble of its own."

"You mean Inez King? Yeah, she was robbing us blind and working with that embezzler guy that they thought Nikki Brockington shot." Kyle scratched the top of his head, the spot where hair used to be. "We took care of all that."

Ryan shook his head. "It seems Inez and Randall Davis were connected in more ways than one."

Preston flattened his palms on his knees. "We already know that. The PI I hired months back to help us figure out what was going on with the past due tax bill reported that Inez King had secret meetings with Randall Davis and that the investment firm Inez was working with was A.W. Investments, owned by Aaron Witherspoon, Randall's boss."

"Right," Ryan said with a nod. "Witherspoon's just recently been indicted on federal charges of fraud and embezzlement. In the investigation it was uncovered that

Witherspoon was working with some lower-level street hustlers. Somehow those lower-level hustlers were tipped off that their names were appearing on our radar and they began to tie up loose ends."

"Okay, what does this have to do with what's going on here now?" Jonah asked.

Jonah was around Parker's age, a good-looking man, if quiet and introverted. He'd lived in Sweetland all his life and for as far back as Parker could remember had wanted to be a cop.

Ryan looked to Parker to continue with his part of the explanation. "The murder I witnessed was of Tyrone Vezina. He was a PG County cop and one of the players in Witherspoon's franchise. After the murder I pulled some of Vezina's cases, the ones I could get access to. He was in Narcotics, which sort of confirmed what I'd initially thought about the murder, that it was an ordered hit for a drug deal gone bad."

"So this cop was selling drugs?" Kyle asked.

Parker ran a hand down his face. "That's what I originally thought, but then after a few discreet meetings with some of Vezina's informants, I realized he wasn't just running drugs. There was an elite operation going throughout the state that included drugs, bribes, forged documents, conspiracy. With this information I had more names and I ran some reports. The next day my apartment was broken into. Then I was suspended from the force. My sergeant said I needed a break, possibly a permanent break."

It wasn't easy admitting to that in front of these men, but Parker had chucked his pride at the door the moment Drew and his child's life had been put at risk.

"So whoever is after you wants to shut you up," Jonah started. "Then why haven't they killed you yet?"

When Preston and Ryan looked at him with heated expressions, Jonah backtracked.

"Hear me out here," he said. "This Vezina guy was a cop, and they killed him in cold blood. You start snooping, they break into your house, then follow you here to Sweetland, run you off the road, and shoot out an entire restaurant you were in. But you're still alive. It doesn't click."

Kyle nodded. "He's right. If they really wanted you dead, I suspect you'd be in a pine box by now."

"I think they want to recruit me instead," Parker said quietly. He'd received another email when he'd checked his in-box this morning. It had only said: *We need to talk.*

The men continued to talk, throwing out ideas, suggestions, trying to come up with a plan, a strategy to put an end to a situation that had gotten completely out of control. All because Parker had been in the wrong place at the wrong time, or had it been the right place at the right time? Vezina's murder had put certain things into motion, events that brought him here, to Drew. He wondered how smart it was to curse the very situation that had led him to the happiest he'd ever been in his life.

"Your dog's gone again and your woman's still at work," Savannah stated the moment Parker walked through the front door. She was headed up the steps, no doubt going to take her afternoon rest. She'd been trying to squeeze in a lot of naps lately. Parker wondered at that but wondered more about where his damned dog was for the third time.

But before he could turn around and head back out of the house, he was stopped by a voice coming from the living room.

"You gotta wonder why that dog of yours keeps running off when all the others are content to stay right where they are."

Parker sighed. He'd been talking all morning and a

good part of the afternoon down at the police station. The
other part of the afternoon he'd been riding around
Sweetland. All he'd wanted was to come home, get a hot
shower and a nice dinner, then sit and enjoy the evening
with Drew. The last thing he felt like was more talking.
But his upbringing wouldn't allow him to be rude, so he
walked into the living room to see Mr. Sylvester's legs
propped up on the couch, cane leaning against the side,
glass of water on the table beside him, magazines tossed
across his lap. He looked as if he were on vacation. Either
that or he wasn't feeling well. The latter had Parker eyeing him suspiciously.

"Hey, Mr. Sylvester. How are you feeling today?"

Sylvester looked at him with eyes that watered naturally
and pinned a person fast and hard. "I'm just fine. What I
was wondering was how long it was going to take you to
come to your senses."

Parker took a seat, knowing instinctively this would
take a while. "I think I'm getting things together," he replied, admitting to himself that the man had a small point.

When he'd first returned to Sweetland, his life had
been turning upside down. His career was uncertain, he
was back with a family he wasn't sure he knew any longer,
and his grandmother was gone. Things weren't good several months ago, and now, well, now they'd seemed to become only more trying.

"One of the first things Janet told me about you was
that you were the first of the siblings to walk. You talked
early, too, she said. And from that moment on, you were
on the go."

"That sounds more like Savannah than me."

Sylvester shook his head. "No. She said, 'Parker's the
one who's always been going, trying to get to something
when he doesn't even know what that something is.' I think
she was right."

Parker sat back, recalling the man's words for a moment. "That sounds like Gramma."

"Sure it does," Mr. Sylvester told him, then stopped to cough.

Parker didn't move, but he raised a brow. Mr. Sylvester was definitely not well. Funny how that thought caused a pang in Parker's chest. He'd met the man only about six months ago, hadn't even known there was a man living here with his grandmother before then. Yet he didn't want him to be sick, didn't want him to possibly die as Gramma had, not yet.

Mr. Sylvester reached for his glass, took a long gulp, then drew a few steadying breaths.

"What you've been looking for is right in front of your eyes," he said.

Parker smiled. "Right now I should be looking for my dog, I suppose."

Mr. Sylvester nodded. "Right in front of your eyes, son. All you've got to do is open them up and you'll see everything you've been searching for."

Hours later, Parker would replay Mr. Sylvester's words in his mind. But for the immediate moment, he slipped out of the living room once Michelle came in to bring Mr. Sylvester a bowl of soup and a glass of tea. He had a good idea where Rufus was and drove his bike in that direction, thinking that maybe Rufus was falling in love with Drew, too.

It had taken Drew all morning to gather the courage to actually call The Marina in search of Jared. Her mind went back and forth on the reasoning behind this meeting. She wanted closure, that was plain and simple.

There was something more brewing between her and Parker; she could feel it. No, it wasn't just the baby that she'd felt moving inside her last night—even though she'd felt her move twice today as well. There was an additional something between them now, feelings, caring. Being with Parker now was distinctively different from when she'd been with him that first night. She knew him better, which was a start. She knew what he'd gone through, had a glimpse into the life that everyone in Sweetland had assumed was glamorous and full of fun. For Parker, it had been dangerous and emotionally draining. The entire time he'd been in Sweetland, he'd been struggling with guilt and now had to worry about the lurking danger that the simple act of doing his job had brought on. It couldn't have been easy for him, and she felt bad that he'd had to go through that and the loss of his grandmother, all while living in the shadow of this bogus reputation.

She'd lived in a shadow herself, for far too long. But now she was going to put that behind her.

While she waited for Jared, she made a few calls, put an ad in the *Sweetland Gazette* advertising the opening for a shop assistant and/or manager. She'd spent a good chunk of the morning outlining the daily functioning of the flower shop, her small but growing contracted client list, and more details she thought would be valuable to the person coming in to take her place when she went out to deliver. In the next couple of months, she planned to cut her hours to allow more time to prepare for the baby. She was also thinking of looking for a bigger apartment or maybe purchasing a small house for her and the baby; the apartment upstairs was not going to be big enough to accommodate both of them comfortably. Of course, the cost was a little daunting, with her only income coming from the flower shop, but maybe if she rented out her apartment upstairs, that would help.

Her mind was obviously elsewhere when the chimes

over the door jingled, signaling someone had arrived. Standing up, she was preparing to get this little meeting over with when she felt a wave of nausea at the sight of Jared again.

She took a deep breath and cleared her throat. "Hello, Jared."

"Drewcilla," he said in that deep voice that rubbed right along her skin. The first time she'd heard his voice, it had felt like the warm bubbles of a sauna, relaxing and soothing every nerve in her body. The night he'd had her trapped against a brick wall, his hand thrust into her panties while he whispered crude remarks in her ear, his voice had vibrated through her body like a murderous screech.

Now, there was simply nothing.

"Thank you for coming alone," she continued, closing the spiral book she'd been writing in and sticking the pen in its side.

"You expected me to bring that simpering Diana with me when you called requesting to see me? I have much better sense then that." He talked as he moved closer, stopping at the front desk just barely a foot away from Drew.

She sincerely doubted his "smart" remark but declined to comment on it.

"I want to know why you came to Sweetland," she said, figuring it was best to get this over with as quickly as possible.

Jared leaned over the counter, looking up at her with dreamy blue eyes and a killer smile. "I wanted to see you."

"How did you know I was here?"

"Come on, Drew, you know how people talk in Stratford. All I had to do was go back home and mention your name. They were more than happy to tell me where you and your mom moved to."

Drew didn't doubt that for one second.

"Why would you even mention my name after what happened?"

He reached out then, tried to touch her hand, but Drew stepped back, keeping her hands at her sides.

"I wanted to apologize," he admitted seriously.

She eyed him suspiciously. How many nights had she lain in her bed all those years ago, wishing Jared would call to say those exact words to her?

"Apologize for what?" she asked, the soft ache of needing that apology having hardened over the years.

"For how things turned out, the misunderstanding. You do know it was all a misunderstanding, right?"

Drew shook her head. "I understand you had a hard time taking no for an answer."

He stood up straight then, shaking his head as he smiled. Yes, he was actually smiling while this conversation was happening. The thought had Drew's fists clenching at her sides.

"Things got a little out of hand, I'll admit that much. But you were really overdramatic about the entire situation. I mean, convincing your parents you needed to go to the police to file a complaint. Who files a complaint about the bad ending to a date?"

He looked incredulous at that statement, as though he really believed that was all that had happened that night. It took three deep breaths to steady herself enough before Drew could speak again.

"You tried to rape me, Jared. You sexually assaulted me. I think that's pretty damned dramatic."

"Whoa, there you go with that word and those accusations again. See, that's why things got out of hand. You don't know what to say out of your mouth."

"And you have no idea how to be a real man!" she

shouted back, her resolve slipping. She slammed her palms on the counter and leaned forward. "You made a move, I said no. It should have ended there. I tried to get away, but you followed me. You pushed me into that alley and put your hands on me, ignoring my protests. *That* is sexual assault, you asshole!"

He did have the decency to lose that damned smile. Crossing his arms over his chest, he gave her a deadpan look that said he still thought she was being "overdramatic."

"It's in the past, Drew. Time to move on," he stated blandly. "You ran from one small town to another, hiding from life, using me as your excuse. When really it's your fault for not moving on."

She wanted to hit him. Or she wanted to scream her frustration. Then she thought better of doing both.

"You are scum. You may make a lot of money and have millions of women falling all over you, but you're still scum. And when you go to bed at night, you know what I'm saying is absolutely true. I don't need to live in a big city to know that." She spoke with calmness and a sense of relief she'd never felt before. If a person was an addict, he wouldn't seek help until he admitted his addiction, no matter how many interventions were staged. Drunks stayed drunk until they wanted to get sober. Scumbag bullies like Jared would stay scumbag bullies until they wanted to change. But she did not have to remain on his level.

"I want you out of my shop and out of my life for good, Jared. If you so much as think of coming near me again, I will press charges for stalking, harassment, any charge they have on the books that will stick, I'll bring them. And this time I won't back down. I'll continue until you are buried in a jail, gossip and your major league contract be damned."

He was quick when he moved, his front slamming against the counter about two seconds before Drew moved to the side. She was about to reach for something to serve as a weapon when she heard barking. Then yelling, as Jared reared back and almost fell against her geranium display.

"Oh, Rufus!" she yelled, watching the little black dog grab hold of Jared's pant leg, tugging with all his strength.

Jared kicked at him, and Drew picked up the yardstick she used to measure ribbon and slapped Jared over the back of his head.

"Down, Rufus! Down!" she yelled while she kept whacking at Jared, who was doing some weird rendition of a line dance across the front of the shop.

Rufus finally let Jared's pant leg go, moving to put his snarling body in front of Drew.

"Now I'm going to press charges against you and your unruly dog!" Jared yelled, pointing a finger at Drew.

"Can't do that," Carl Farraway said as he walked through the front door with Parker right behind him.

"What? Why the hell not?" Jared demanded. "That stupid dog attacked me just like that idiot over there did and you're telling me I can't press charges! That's a lot of bull!"

Carl simply shook his head. "Ms. Sidney reported you and Ms. McCann as trespassers in her place of business a couple of days ago. As long as that report is active, you have no right being on this property."

"She called me here!" Jared insisted.

"And you attempted to harm her," Carl stated. "I saw it myself from across the street through the window. You jumped and the dog came to the rescue. Now, if Ms. Sidney wants to press charges against you, I'd be happy to take that report."

"This is bullshit! This whole town is ridiculous, with

your crazy animals and dangerous innkeepers and cops that see through windows! I'll have my lawyers in here so fast all your country-time heads'll spin."

Parker shook his head. "You really don't want to do that. You see, my brother's a lawyer. A really good lawyer that will most likely eat your lawyer for breakfast and spit him out in your face. Now, I warned you about bothering Drew before."

Carl stood between Jared and Parker, facing Jared. "It'd be real smart if you just left town, Mr. Mansfield. This situation doesn't look like it's going to end in your favor."

"She called me here! I was minding my own business and she called me. You stupid—" Jared's words were cut off as he turned to lunge for Drew once more.

This time Parker moved faster. He pushed past Carl, grabbing Jared by his shirt collar and clipping him at the ankles, bringing the taller man to his knees while pulling an arm back so far that Jared yelled once more. By this time, Carl had drawn his weapon.

"Jared Mansfield, you are under arrest," Carl began, reading Jared his rights.

Once he was cuffed and Carl was pushing him into the police cruiser out front, Drew breathed a sigh of relief that had been a long time coming. How many times had she dreamed of seeing Jared Mansfield in handcuffs, being punished for the things he'd done to her? Now, of course, he might not actually be brought up on the sexual assault charges—she'd have to talk to Preston about that—but she would definitely press charges for the attempted assault and intimidation and anything else they said she could, just as she'd warned Jared she would.

"I told you not to meet with him," was the first thing Parker said to her. "Now sit down before you pass out," was the next.

When she sat Rufus jumped up into her lap and she took comfort in knowing he was there, that he'd been there just in time. For the moment, that meant she would ignore the strong tone Parker had used with her, considering he'd probably been right in the first place.

Chapter 19

"I'm not going to be bullied by you, Parker Cantrell, or anybody else, anymore," Drew stated adamantly. "I do not need to stay at your place when there's nothing wrong with my apartment."

"Did you already forget about the shooting incident? Or no, maybe you've forgotten about the crazy stalker that just tried to assault you again, this time in front of witnesses!" Parker yelled.

"Well, that certainly wasn't going to happen with big bad Parker Cantrell in the building." He jerked as though she'd slapped him with her words, and Drew sighed. She was angry and she was agitated. Her back had begun hurting when she'd hurried to get away from Jared. And this scene with Parker was giving her a headache. But none of that was any reason for her to be mean.

"Look, I know you mean well. I know you think you're trying to protect me, and yes, maybe a part of me understands the logic behind staying with you at the B and B again tonight. But I can't."

They were in her apartment. She sat down heavily on the futon because she felt that if she didn't get off her feet soon, she'd collapse. Then Parker would simply scoop her up and carry her to the B&B. She dropped her head into her hands, then looked up at him, determined not to crumble.

"I want to be alone, Parker. I've endured a lot of memories today, a lot of emotional turmoil, and I just want to be alone with my thoughts," she told him calmly.

He ran a hand down his face. "And I want you to be safe. So if it makes you feel any better, I can call Michelle and see if one of the rooms are available. You don't have to stay in the room with me, but at least you'll be close enough for me to protect you if necessary."

So he was trying to compromise as well. Didn't they make a perfect pair?

Drew simply shook her head. "Jonah said he'd drive by my house repeatedly throughout the night. I don't know why Sheriff Farraway won't let Carl do it, but remind me to thank him profusely in the morning. Jared's in jail and you said yourself that gunman was after you, not me. So I'll be just fine."

"I want—"

Drew held up a hand to stop his words. "Parker, please. I cannot take another man telling me what he 'wants' from me right now. I know you're not Jared, but right now you're pushing just as hard as he did."

Again Parker looked as if she'd struck him. He clenched his teeth until a muscle twitched in his jaw.

"I won't even bother to ask if I can stay here with you," he said, and held his hand up to keep her from commenting this time. "Rufus stays with you, and I'm going to talk to Jonah about the frequency of his drive-bys. And keep your cell phone on and close."

He was giving her more orders, even if they were orders for her safety. Drew didn't have the strength to argue. Instead she simply nodded.

"And understand this, Drew," he told her, coming close and kneeling so that they were face-to-face. "I'm not trying to bully you at all. I'm just trying to keep you and our little one safe. If I'm wrong for that, if that makes me big and bad or even an ass in your book, then so be it. As long as there's danger out there, I won't stop doing any of the above."

Drew felt like an idiot, a very tired and overwhelmed idiot at the moment, but one just the same. "I understand and I appreciate you giving me some room to breathe. I also appreciate you leaving Rufus. He was so fierce today."

"Yeah, out of character for his breed. Then again, running away and coming to the same location is out of character for his breed as well. I think I might be able to write a book on the ins and outs of a twenty-first-century Labrador."

They both chuckled lightly at that comment. Then Parker took her hands and brought them both up to his lips to kiss. "I want you to lock the doors and the windows. Keep that phone and Rufus close. And if anything, I mean anything, seems out of the ordinary to you, call me."

Drew nodded. "I'll do exactly that."

He leaned in then and she followed suit. He kissed her softly at first, then pressed a little for more. She welcomed it and him, letting herself fall into the kiss as if she knew she'd fallen in love with him. That was the biggest reason Drew felt she needed space. She'd fallen in love with Parker and had realized it the moment Jared Mansfield walked into her shop.

At one point he'd been the man she'd thought she might spend the rest of her life with. Jared had been the man to take her away from the small town and show her the world. He'd turned out to be the man who would take from her the ability to let go and love someone else. Only he hadn't taken that completely away from her.

She was in love with Parker Cantrell. As surely as she'd just moaned at the touch of his tongue on hers, she knew that she loved him and the baby they'd made together. What she was going to do with that knowledge, Drew had no idea. All she knew for sure was that she wanted to take her time, to not jump before walking—even though it seemed they'd already done that with the pregnancy. She wanted to know Parker and to know that he loved her, too, not just because she was carrying his child, but because he really wanted to be with her.

She needed time and space to figure out how she was going to accomplish that great feat. So with great reluctance, she lifted her hands and pushed lightly at his shoulders until the kiss was broken.

"I'll come by early to bring you and Rufus breakfast," he said softly, his forehead resting against hers.

"Okay," was her reply.

She walked Parker to the door, assuring him that she would lock it immediately behind him. But before he would leave Parker turned to her again, whispering her name.

"I just, I just don't know how this happened," he continued as he pulled her into his arms, hugging her tightly. "But I'll fix it. I promise you, I'll fix it."

Drew hugged him tight, closing her eyes to the pain that seemed to emanate from him. "Everything is going to work out just fine, Parker. I promise you it will."

He seemed to take her word for it and walked out the door, turning before he'd cleared the steps only to have her say, "I know, lock the door."

He only nodded, then waited until she'd closed the door and clicked the locks into place before climbing on his motorcycle and pulling off. Drew walked up the steps, feeling perfectly safe and completely in love.

* * *

Just off Elm Road, all the way down to where the street
came to a dead end that consisted of a light line of trees
and a four-foot drop to the water, sat a little blue house
nestled in brightly colored flowers and a white picket
fence. During a sunny day, the pale blue sky and golden
sunlight framed the house like a Hallmark card. A more
perfect sight one would never see.

As it was just a little after seven in the evening and the
sun had just set, the house looked even more homely,
more perfect, especially when Parker opened the pristine
white fence and Coco, with her Hershey Bar brown fur,
poked her head between two bushes to greet him.

"Hey, girl, how ya doing over there?" Parker spoke to
the beautiful dog, who immediately came forward to greet
him.

Coco walked him up onto the porch, but she didn't go
in, simply moved a few feet to the side over to a huge pink-
and-brown polka-dotted pillow. Laying herself down on
the pillow, Coco gave him a look that said, *Enter at your
own risk.* Parker only smiled at the dog and lifted his
hand to knock.

Heaven had bought this house a few months ago, and
soon after that Preston had moved in. Now the two of
them lived here happily—he supposed—with Heaven doing her research work from the back room she'd turned
into an office and Preston handling the remainder of his
old cases from the city and the new ones he'd acquired
here in Sweetland, using what would have been a guest
bedroom. Preston was resisting the logical urge to turn
that room into his home office.

"Well, hello there. What brings you down this way?"
Heaven asked when she'd opened the door, leaning forward to give Parker a hug.

Heaven Montgomery had been like a gentle breeze
blowing into Sweetland, looking to adopt a puppy and

then settling like a ray of sunshine over the uptight and
tense Preston. Parker noted how much more his brother
smiled now that Heaven was in his life, how relaxed and
content he looked, how absolutely fantastic the proverbial
"happily ever after" looked on this particular Cantrell
brother. And envy reared its ugly head.

Giving Heaven an extra-tight hug, Parker cleared his
throat. "I actually came to see Preston. Is he here?"

Pulling back, she looked up into his face. "Yes. He's in
his office acting like he's working when really he's just
brooding."

Heaven closed the door behind them and Parker
stopped just inside the small living room. They'd added
more furniture since he'd been here last, which was only
about a week or two ago. But now there were thin curtains at the front window, draped in a fashion that reminded him of homes he'd seen in a magazine. The sofa
and two armchairs were a soft gray color and looked beyond comfortable with the oversize charcoal pillows. The
walls had been painted some color that was a mixture of
gray and blue. Pictures adorned the walls, pictures taken
here in Sweetland at the Bay Day celebration and the Labor Day Festival, some of Coco by the water and some
of a serious-faced Preston with a smiling Heaven by his
side.

"You hire someone to take those pictures?" Parker
asked, pointing to the ones of Preston and Heaven.

Heaven nodded. "Yes, you know Kraig Bellini, the
vet? He has a sister named Alana and she was here for a
visit a couple weeks ago. I was talking about wedding
plans when I took Coco in to see the doctor and he mentioned his sister was a wedding photographer. These were
her sample shots and our official engagement shot for the
newspapers. My father requested one and my mother
shouted for about twenty minutes when we sent the beach

photo with Coco included. Alana did a great job, so we've already hired her for the wedding," she told him.

"Alana lives in Baltimore, doesn't she?" Parker vaguely remembered the pretty, exotic-looking female.

"Right, with her daughter. But Kraig's trying to get her to come back here."

"What is it about Sweetland that people either never leave or they always come back?" he asked as they walked through the living room to the hallway that led to the windows. If they'd gone in the other direction, there was a dining room and kitchen, then the enclosed back porch that looked right onto the Miles River.

Heaven stopped and turned to him. Her smile was genuine and gorgeous, and each time Parker saw it he knew precisely why Preston had given up the law practice he'd built in Baltimore.

"Love brings you back, Parker. No matter how far you run or try to hide, it will always bring you back."

Parker smiled at the nostalgic sound in Heaven's voice because she hadn't been born here, but damn if she hadn't adopted the town along with Coco and the rest of the Cantrell family when she'd arrived.

"Go on in and talk to him, he's still pretty upset," she told him once they were standing in front of the door to the room where Preston was in hideout mode.

"Right. I've got a lot of apologizing to do."

Heaven shook her head. "Not necessarily. Just explaining. He feels like the two of you have lost touch, and he blames himself a little for that."

Parker frowned, shaking his head. "That's nonsense. He's always been there for me. Always. No matter if he wasn't physically there, I knew I could turn to him for anything."

She touched a hand to his shoulder. "But not this time, huh?"

He sighed. "Yeah, not this time."

After another hug from his future sister-in-law, Parker knocked quickly and waited for his brother's voice to allow him to enter. Preston was sitting at a light oak desk, his high-backed leather office chair looking only slightly out of place in the contemporary-decorated cottage. His back was to the door as he stared out the window, all pretense of work given up.

"What's up?" Parker said, trying for lightness as he closed the door behind him.

Preston turned in the chair, the frown slow to build on his face. It was times like this that the two looked most alike; even Parker knew that without looking in a mirror. Their key differences had always been their personalities—Preston the more serious, Parker the more laid-back. But as they'd grown into manhood, the differences had grown with them. Preston was extremely focused, steady as a rock, and dependable as air. Parker loved the adrenaline rush, the spontaneous lifestyle of a cop, and he lived his personal life in the same way. Yet today, at this moment they were both serious, both concerned, and both hurting on some level.

"What are you doing here?" Preston asked, leaning his elbows on the desk and looking at Parker with a slight frown.

His thick eyebrows furrowed, and Parker felt his own doing the same in response.

"I owe you an apology," Parker started. "I should have told you about the Vezina situation when it first happened."

"Why didn't you?" Preston asked immediately, clearly not willing to cut Parker any slack.

Parker rubbed his hands down his face. "It all happened so fast. Before I knew what was going on, Mertz had me in his office warning me to stay off this case. I couldn't

figure out why. It was a cop killing. You know how seriously we take that."

Preston nodded slightly.

"I investigated anyway. You know I don't take orders
well," he said grimly. "The next thing I know, I get home
and there's someone else there. But they don't kill me.
Why is that, Pres? Why am I still alive?"

"I suspect there are a lot of people asking themselves
that right now."

"Yeah." Parker sighed. "Namely me. They didn't kill
me that night in my apartment, but weeks later they try to
run me off the road. Then last night they shoot up an entire restaurant trying to get at me."

"But they miss," Preston said.

"Yeah, they missed. But what if they hadn't?"

"We wouldn't be having this conversation," his brother
replied stoically.

Parker frowned. "I don't want to always be known as
the Cantrell that messes up. The one that doesn't listen
and makes a mess for his family to clean up."

"Wait, are we talking about you or Savannah?" Preston asked.

Parker almost smiled. "Savannah doesn't mess up, she
just doesn't listen. Ever."

The two shared a knowing chuckle about their youngest sister.

"You were busy with your case and I didn't want to
distract you with this business. Then Gramma died and I
didn't want to add to that trauma for any of us. I just wanted
to sit here in Sweetland and forget about the shooting,
forget about the man who died in my arms and his family,
who cried hopelessly at his funeral."

"That's why you never talked about when you were going back."

Parker shrugged. "I guess I wasn't looking forward to

going back. I mean, this suspension has been close to six months now. The odds of me getting my job back are looking kind of bleak."

"And yet you're here about to start a family with Drew."

His brother was making one clever observation after another. Parker frowned at how consistently this attorney-at-law hit his mark and how calmly he did so.

"That wasn't a part of the plan. It just happened. And now I've put her and my baby at risk. I've got to clean this up fast, because if something happens to her . . ." He trailed off.

Preston stood then and walked over to Parker, putting a hand on his shoulder and squeezing hard. "Nothing's going to happen to her. We're not going to let anything happen to her, just like we're not going to let anything happen to you. Ryan's got some backup coming in tonight, and one of the numbers on Vezina's cell phone bill turned out to be from an international suspect on the FBI's Most Wanted list, so now he has complete jurisdiction."

"And he didn't tell me?" Parker asked.

"He tried to call you earlier. When he didn't get an answer, he called me."

"I had some issues down at Drew's shop."

"What? Is she okay?"

"She's fine, just that asshole Mansfield. He had the audacity to try and go after her right in front of me. I wanted to put my fist down his throat, the conceited bastard!"

Preston groaned. "I hope you didn't hit that man again."

"I subdued him, with Rufus's help," Parker replied. "Besides, Carl was there and he arrested him. So I at least feel better about that situation."

"Well, this other situation is going to resolve itself, too."

"Cantrells to the rescue." Parker sighed glumly.

"Hey," Preston said, moving so that he stood in Parker's face. "That's what we do, Park, you know that. We're all in this together. Gramma wanted us back here in Sweetland together for reasons just like this. When your back is to the wall, we're here for you, always. And it's not because you're trouble or trouble is always following you. It's because we love you."

Parker's chest clenched, his lips drawing in a tight line. "I guess I forgot for a while what family I was from."

Preston smiled. "I think we all did. That's why it was good that we all came back for the funeral and that we're all still here."

"But how do I stay here without a job, without a way to support my family? I mean, I have a good savings, and thanks to you, I made some really sound investments over the years, so I'm not completely broke."

Preston was already shaking his head. "It will all work out. Just follow your heart."

"Is that what you did?" Parker asked.

Preston smiled, looking toward his desk where a picture of him and Heaven sat prominently facing his chair. "That's what I'm still doing."

"Home alone?" Mr. Sylvester asked Parker when he returned to the B&B.

Parker noted the man was sitting in the exact place he'd been when Parker had left earlier. His cane was still propped against the chair, but this time Parker noticed something else. When Rufus had begun running off, Parker had purchased a new collar for him, one with a GPS chip embedded inside. The collar was black leather with Rufus's name in red, and it was now looped around Mr. Sylvester's cane.

"Rufus was at Drew's," Parker said slowly, taking a seat in one of the twin Victorian chairs near the window.

Mr. Sylvester only nodded. "Funny how he keeps ending up there."

"Yeah," Parker added, rubbing his hand over his chin. "That sure is a funny thing."

"Must be something over there for him," he said.

"Since he's been over there so much, she bought a box of those doggie treats he likes. Maybe that's why he keeps breaking out of the pen and going all the way over to her place."

The older man reached for his glass—a new glass that Michelle had no doubt brought to him—took a slow sip, then set it down as he smacked his thin lips. "That gal makes some damned good lemonade. Some lucky man's gonna snatch her up one day and y'all are gonna miss her hanging around here so much."

Parker continued to watch him closely, thinking about the last couple of weeks and some of the things that had happened and that were said in that time. "Michelle's never leaving Sweetland or The Silver Spoon, they're both a part of her."

Sylvester shook his head. "Don't be so sure. Love makes you do strange things."

"Really? I wouldn't know."

Sylvester fluffed a pillow behind his head and crossed his legs at the ankles. "I think you know more than you want to admit."

Parker took in a deep breath, then sighed. He did know more now than he had twenty minutes ago, and he wasn't sure how he felt about the new revelations. "You've been letting Rufus out of the pen, haven't you?"

"Janet left those dogs to you kids," he began. "She wanted you to take care of them and love them."

"I know that, Mr. Sylvester. That's not what I asked you." Parker was trying not to sound as testy as he was feeling. He hadn't liked leaving Drew alone in her apartment. Sure, he'd left Rufus there, and yes, Rufus had attacked Jared's ankles earlier today, but he was no vicious killer guard dog. He wasn't going to bite some assailant in the nuts or the jugular to save Drew's life. And as good a cop as he thought Jonah was, drive-bys every half hour just weren't enough protection for him.

"Let me ask you something," Sylvester countered. "Why do you think your dog spends more time with the mother of your child than you do? Why do you think your dog *wants* to spend more time with the mother of your child than you do?"

Parker leaned forward, resting his elbows on his knees, looking Mr. Sylvester right in the eye. "I think my dog was being purposely let out of the pen and taken to Drew's house as someone's way of trying to tell me something."

Sylvester was quiet for a moment. Then another moment. He blinked, then closed his eyes. And his eyes didn't open again. Parker got nervous and went to Mr. Sylvester's side, touching his chest. "Mr. Sylvester? . . . Mr. Sylvester, can you hear me?"

His eyes remained closed, and Parker was just about to call for Michelle when a hand grabbed his wrist. Mr. Sylvester's eyes shot open then, wider than he'd ever seen them before.

"Did you hear what you just said? About someone trying to tell you something? It's a shame a person has to go through all these dramatics to get you to open your eyes."

Parker sighed at his words, closing his own eyes and counting to ten as he tried to steady the quick beating of his heart. He'd thought the man had had a heart attack or stroke or something and died right there in front of him. Not that Parker had never seen a dead body before; he had on too many occasions to count. But he didn't want Mr. Sylvester to be counted as one of them.

"You took Rufus to Drew's so I'd follow him over

there. You wanted me to be with Drew. That's a pretty elaborate matchmaking scheme," he said quietly, pulling his arm from Mr. Sylvester's grasp.

"Ha!" the old man laughed. "Did it work?"

Parker went back to his chair and dropped down. "I don't need a matchmaker."

"No, you need a knock on your head. Not a bullet, just a good hard knock so you can come to your senses." He was sitting up in the chair now, mimicking Parker's stance, elbows resting on his knees.

"Everything happens for a reason, Parker. God does not make mistakes."

"Gramma used to say that."

Mr. Sylvester nodded. "True. And she was right. So don't go thinking that the baby Drew's carrying is a mistake. It's not. It was a soft knock on the head for you. Rufus running away was another soft knock. Those bullets flying like hail the other night, that was the hard knock you needed to get your butt in gear. Now you get yourself a nice house, marry that girl, have a healthy baby, and keep your dog in your own yard. That's what I wanted to tell you."

Mr. Sylvester reached for his cane, pulled the collar from it, and tossed it over to Parker. "Good night," he said, and walked out of the room with more energy than Parker had seen in him in weeks.

Footsteps on the stairs. That's what Drew heard in her sleep. Try as she might, she could not stop dreaming. Just one night she'd like a blissful rest without any intrusions. Tonight was obviously not meant to be the night.

She rolled over and felt the warmth of Rufus at her chest. His soft fur brushed across her cheek.

More footsteps.

Rufus moved and Drew reached out to cuddle him closer. He barked and she jumped.

The footsteps were no longer on the steps, but closer.

Sitting up in bed, Drew stared at the doorway leading from her bedroom into the living room—where she could swear she heard more footsteps. She reached for Rufus, but he'd already jumped down from the bed and was barking his way into the living room.

"Dammit!" she cursed, pushing back the sheets and getting out of bed herself.

Something crashed to the floor in the living room. There was a curse. A man's curse, and Rufus barked louder. Searching for something to use as a weapon, she settled on the autographed Cal Ripken baseball bat that had belonged to her father and which she kept hidden behind her door instead of selling because her mother said it was worth something. Clutching the bat in both hands, she entered the living room, only to be faced with a splash of spray in her face.

"Jared, you bastard!" Drew screamed, and dropped the bat. She fell to her knees, her eyes burning, lungs stinging as she tried to breathe.

She heard more footsteps, more things falling, and then the intruder was going down the steps. Drew knew her little apartment like the back of her hand, so even though she couldn't see a damned thing and could barely get a breath out without wheezing, she crawled across the living room floor, banging into the lamp that had fallen and what she figured was the pillow from the futon, until she got to the steps.

Rufus appeared at her side then, and Drew turned backward to crawl down the steps. She figured this way was safer since she couldn't see. Rufus must have agreed because he stuck close to her as she moved. By the time she

reached the bottom—she'd been counting as she went—
Drew was groping blindly for the railing when there was
a loud noise. Everything around her shook and she was
tossed backward until she landed flat on her back, the little
bit of breath she'd had knocked completely out of her.
Then her eyes weren't burning anymore, her back wasn't
hurting, and her lungs didn't feel as if they were about to
explode.

And for the first time in Drew's life, she slept, without
dreaming, without anything but the blackness that had
engulfed her.

Parker's cell phone rang just after midnight. He was awake
instantly, not bothering to look at the screen.

"Cantrell," he answered.

"This is Sheriff Farraway. There's been an explosion."

Parker disconnected the call before Kyle could finish.
He called Preston and Quinn as he ran out of the house
and to his bike. Then he was gone, heading over to Drew's
because he knew Farraway would not have called him
unless that's where this explosion had occurred.

The normally ten-minute ride seemed to take triple the
amount of time no matter how much gas he applied to his
Suzuki. He cut corners, almost ran up on the sidewalk,
and barely missed the tables and chairs and umbrellas
sitting out front of Jana's Java as he turned quickly onto
Main Street. All he could think about was Drew. Drew
being alone. Drew being hurt. Their baby being hurt. His
chest felt heavy as he jumped off the bike and applied the
kickstand. But he quickly came to a stop.

Caleb Brockington, a six-foot-five-inch tall, 220-pound
man dressed in a fireman's uniform, pressed a hand into
Parker's chest, halting his motion almost immediately.

"Fire's still burning pretty hot in there, Parker. I can't
let you go in," he told him.

Parker moved so that he could see around the man. There were other firemen, one holding a hose, the other heading inside the building slowly. Kyle and Jonah were also standing on the sidewalk, glass and debris all around them. Kyle came over the minute he saw Parker.

"I've got 'im, Caleb. You get back over there and keep that fire from spreading," Farraway told him. "I can't believe we have another fire in Sweetland. The last one had fatalities, let's hope this one doesn't."

"Drew?" Parker yelled. "Where's Drew?"

Kyle held on to Parker even though it was a struggle. The bigger, rounder man was clearly getting old, and for that reason Parker tried to rein in his anger.

"Where the hell is Drew?"

"Calm down, son. She's already on her way to the hospital. She and that dog of yours were trying to get out the back. That's where Jonah found them, lying in her flowers."

Chapter 20

Parker had never wanted to walk these halls again. Even though the last time he was here he hadn't actually walked. He'd been pushed to the front entrance, where he'd waited, feeling like a colossal ass for being in a wheelchair and angry beyond words at the car that had run him off the road.

Now he was back at Easton Memorial Hospital, walking toward the emergency room with his heart beating wildly and sweat beading at his forehead. He'd driven the Suzuki faster than ever before, not giving a damn about speeding tickets or crashing or anything beyond getting here to see Drew.

"Drewcilla Sidney?" he asked the nurse a second before he actually made it all the way to the front desk.

She looked a little startled, this older woman with silver hair and warm gray eyes. "Did she walk in or was she an ambo delivery?" the woman asked calmly.

"Ambulance," Parker told her. "Should have been just in the last ten or fifteen minutes. She's pregnant and there was an explosion and—"

"Okay. Okay. I think I've got it," she said, looking

down at something and then back up to Parker. "They just took her down to exam room four."

Parker had already turned away from the desk and begun walking when the nurse hurried behind him, grabbing him by the arm.

"Sir, you cannot just go back there."

"Why can't I?" Parker asked, daring her to stand there and try to stop him.

"For one, because exam room four is that way," she told him, pointing down another hall through a different set of double doors. "And because I have no idea who you are and why you're looking for this patient."

"Look, I don't have time for this. Let me go back and see Drew and I'll answer all your questions. Hell, I'll even give you some blood!" he yelled, frustrated, worried, and impatient.

The nurse simply shook her head. "The doctors are with her, and at this moment they are the most important persons back there. You can take two seconds to tell me what your relation is to the patient and to offer any health background if you can."

She was pulling him back to the desk while she talked. If it were a male, Parker might have punched him. If it were a younger female, he might have charmed her. As it stood, he found himself walking back with her and keeping his curses to himself.

"Now, who are you and how do you know the patient?" she asked in a no-nonsense tone.

"My name is Parker Cantrell and I'm . . . I'm . . . ah, I'm the father of her baby," he finally managed, hating the distant sound of that title.

Drew was so much more to him than the mother of his child. She meant more than just the vessel for his baby to be brought into this world. And though Parker didn't think he'd ever had one before, not a real and serious one, for that matter, he thought that Drew might even be more than his girlfriend. But he didn't know how to say that, not even to this stranger.

The nurse simply nodded at him. "I see. And how far along in her pregnancy is she?"

"Ah, what's today?" Parker thought aloud. "She's twenty-one weeks."

She smiled at him then, and Parker blinked in confusion.

"Room four is through those double doors and to your right, Mr. Cantrell."

While sighing his relief, Parker managed a smile. "Thank you, ma'am. Thank you very much." He was about to walk away, then he turned back to her. "I'm Drew Sidney's boyfriend," he added to his earlier statement.

"We're giving her oxygen and she's to keep the padding on her eyes for the next ten to fifteen minutes, then we'll check her again," Dr. Emil Rogers told Parker when he'd made his way back to exam room four.

Dr. Rogers had been coming out of the room when Parker approached, and after asking who he was and just about requiring identification to prove that point, the doctor had given Parker the prognosis.

"There was no smoke inhalation, but the pepper spray she was exposed to has caused some breathing problems for her."

"Is the baby still breathing?" Parker asked around the lump that had formed in his throat.

Dr. Rogers smiled, closing his chart and holding it at his chest while he crossed his arms. "The baby is doing just fine. I've called for an OB to come down and do an exam to be absolutely sure."

"Why wouldn't you be sure on your own? What aren't you telling me?" he asked, because Parker knew doctors had a knack for keeping the worst to themselves for as long as they possibly could. Hadn't that doctor kept Gramma's cancer diagnosis a secret until months after the funeral?

Rogers nodded as if he understood where Parker's questions were coming from, even though Parker doubted that was actually the case.

"I'm a little concerned about the fall. She said she'd already cleared the last step, then I'm guessing the explosion hit and she ended up in the backyard. I'm guessing that's a pretty good distance."

"A couple of feet," Parker answered worriedly. "But she doesn't have any broken bones or anything like that?"

"No broken bones, no internal bleeding as far as I can tell without performing a scan. I don't think it's worth the risk to the baby to perform one, so I'm just going to admit her and watch her for a day or so, to err on the side of caution."

Parker nodded. Caution was key, because if anything happened to Drew or the baby . . .

"You can go in and see her now. But let's try to keep her calm. Her pressure was on the high side when she came in. I suspect it's because of the explosion and not because she has hypertension or anything more serious."

"No. Her last visit with Dr. Lorens went perfectly. She's not sick at all," he heard himself saying. Babbling. He quickly clamped his lips shut. "I'll see her now."

Dr. Rogers smiled and stepped out of the way. Parker pushed through the door and held his breath.

He wasn't prepared to see her lying there looking so frail and so small. Surrounded by all the white bedding, she looked a little angelic. Two things caught his attention, the lump of her belly sticking up through the sheets tucked tightly around her and the mask that covered half her face. Taking a deep breath, he moved closer and noticed that in addition to the oxygen mask there was a thick white cloth over her eyes.

Parker was speechless, and he stood like that for who knew how long. Then finally he reached for her hand, holding it while he did what he could not to weep.

"Drew," he whispered. "It's me, Parker."

Her fingers grasped his, holding tightly. With her free hand she reached for the oxygen mask in an attempt to move it from her mouth.

Parker took her other hand, now holding both of them. "No. Don't take that off yet. You and the baby need it for a while longer."

She held on to his hands, telling him she didn't like it with that action.

"I know. It's no fun being in the hospital. But Dr. Rogers is simply trying to make sure everything is all right before he lets you come home."

Home, Parker thought. Where was their home?

He had an apartment in Baltimore that he didn't want to return to, a room at the B&B that was lovely but possessed no privacy and no space for a growing dog like Rufus to live in. And Drew, well, she had a one-bedroom apartment that now probably had smoke damage from the explosion in the downstairs shop. Her flower shop. How was he supposed to tell her that it too was gone?

"When you get out of here, I'm going to take you to The Silver Spoon so Michelle and Savannah can wait on you hand and foot. Mr. Sylvester will come in and talk to you, and Rufus will sit on the bed with you," he told her.

Rufus, whom Kyle had put in the back of his car amid the dog's protests to climb into the ambulance with Drew. Dr. Bellini had been called, and Kyle had assured him he'd have Rufus taken care of and back home by the time Parker finished at the hospital.

"You won't have to lift a finger," he continued.

Drew held on to his hands tightly and he brought them to his lips to kiss them.

"After dinner we can sit out in the yard. There's a bench there that Gramma and Mr. Sylvester used to sit on all the time. We can watch the sunset and the boats coming in. Rufus loves to run around out there, he and the other dogs. They all love it at The Silver Spoon. But I was thinking, Drew, that maybe we could find our own place in Sweetland." He swallowed deeply at the words that had been rumbling around in his head but hadn't really formulated until this moment. "Maybe you and I can find a house where we can raise our daughter and so Rufus won't have to come and visit you so often because he'll already be with you every day."

Her hands went still in his, her breathing hitching a bit. Then she sat up, letting the cloth at her eyes fall away. She looked at him through puffy red eyes, the oxygen mask slipping slightly down her pert little nose.

"Are you serious?" she asked, her voice coming over the whir of the oxygen.

Parker squeezed her hands and nodded. "I'm very serious."

She didn't speak, but tears fell from her eyes. Now, these could very well be remnants of the pepper spray she'd endured, or she could be emotionally moved by the giant leap their relationship had just taken. Since Parker's heart was beating so fast that he felt he might need that oxygen mask in a moment, he decided it was the latter; that way, he wasn't going through the emotions all on his own.

"Do you want us to find a house together to raise our family in?"

She blinked and nodded. "Yes, Parker. Yes, I think that's a great idea."

Now he did move the oxygen mask, right after dropping her hands and leaning close. "Just for a second," he told her as his lips touched hers. "Just for one second more." He kissed her again, and Drew wrapped her arms around him.

Chapter 21

"Oh dear, now he's put the baby in danger," Lorrayna began the minute she entered the bedroom at the B&B, where Parker had not an hour ago tucked Drew into bed.

"If you lose this baby, I'll sue that awful ass of a man. Come to think of it, I don't want you staying here." Lorrayna pulled back the sheets, then turned to the partially unpacked suitcase across the room. "Let's get you dressed and I'll get Walt to pick us up and take us home. The poor thing has been working so hard to get his place back in shape."

Drew closed her eyes to the drone of her mother's voice. She'd stayed in the hospital for two days, during which time she'd been moved to the labor and delivery ward, where Dr. Lorens kept a close eye on the spotting that had started only hours after her initial admission. Her heart still beat wildly at the thought, tears welling in her eyes as she considered the implications. Dr. Lorens had commented that the spotting might have been brought on by stress or the fall after the explosion.

Yes, the explosion. She remembered hearing footsteps on the stairs, stinging in her eyes, then the jolt of the house and grabbing Rufus in her arms. The next thing she knew, she was awake and Parker was holding her hands, asking her to find a house for them to live. A house, because hers had been destroyed, along with her flower shop and the life she'd spent nearly three years building.

But she wouldn't cry. No. Tears didn't fix anything, and she'd shed more than her share as she lay in the hospital bed, praying desperately for her baby to live. By the afternoon of day two, the spotting had ceased and there was no trace of any contractions. The next morning, Dr. Lorens discharged her with strict instructions: "Complete bed rest until you deliver."

So in Parker's bed she would rest, until they found their own or until her mother drove her absolutely insane and they found a psychiatric institution that would allow her to give birth there instead.

"I'm not going anywhere, Mama," Drew said quietly, reaching out to pull the sheet back over her legs. It was mid-October, and summer had eased into fall. That normally brought the temperatures down from the high nineties to the seventies. When they'd arrived at the B&B, the thermostat in the burgundy truck Parker had picked her up in read the mid-eighties. It was Parker's truck, the one he'd had transported from Baltimore.

"What do you mean you're not going anywhere?" Lorrayna asked after slamming the suitcase shut and coming back to stand beside the bed. "He almost got you killed and now the baby is in danger. It's not smart to stay with him, Drew. It's downright ridiculous. Everyone in town is talking about you two. It's not bad enough you're pregnant by him, but now you're shacking up with him. It's deplorable!"

Really? Who says "deplorable" anymore? Drew thought with a sigh. One of Dr. Lorens's other instructions had been to cut down on stress, which Parker had assured

her would be done. He'd sworn Michelle and Mr. Sylvester would keep her so occupied that she wouldn't have to
worry about anything else. Apparently that hadn't started
yet.

"Mama, listen to me. I'm going to stay here and I'm
going to get the rest Dr. Lorens prescribed. The baby is
going to be just fine." That was about as calm as Drew
could manage the words, and even then she'd been gripping the sheets.

"He's no good! Where is he now? Why isn't he here
taking care of you?" she demanded.

"He's taking care of business."

"What business? I hear he doesn't even have that fancy
job in Baltimore anymore." Lorrayna had the audacity to
nod her head curtly at the end of that sentence as if she
were giving Drew a breaking news update. "And now you
don't even have a shop. I tell you this is worse than the
situation in Stratford, and we cannot keep running, Drewcilla. It just doesn't make sense. We had it so good here
in Sweetland until he came back here smiling and riding
around town like he were some type of god. Well, he's
not! He's just a man, and who the hell needs them!" she
yelled.

Drew sat up in bed, her temples throbbing, hands clutching the sheets so hard that her knuckles whitened.

"It wasn't my idea to leave Stratford and come to Sweetland, Mama. Do you recall whose idea that was?" Drew
didn't give her mother a chance to answer. "I had plans
for my life, plans that would have taken me to the city,
where I would have worked in a professional setting and
bought a nice place to stay. I would have been away from
Stratford and the unfortunate 'situation' you referred to
so delicately. But no, your husband had a plan, he had a
business venture that took every dime he'd managed to save
in twenty years, which wasn't much since he gambled just

about his entire paycheck every week. I stayed for you. I gave him my money for your sake. Then he goes and kills himself, the selfish bastard! As if he hadn't done enough to disgrace us in Stratford. That business collapsed and we never got a dime from the insurance company. And you couldn't handle any of that, so we came to Sweetland to save your life so I wouldn't have to bury both my parents before my thirtieth birthday!"

Her chest was heaving, tears welling in her eyes, as she spoke to her mother in a tone she had never dared before. But she couldn't stop now; she doubted anything but a muzzle would keep all that she'd kept pent up for years from breaking loose now.

Drew untangled her legs from the sheet and tossed them over the side of the bed. She was standing before she could stop herself.

"I worked for you, I paid your bills even when it took the last of my savings. I started from scratch here in Sweetland so I wouldn't upset you by leaving. I like it here, I've made it my home." She blinked away the first of the tears to fall as she stared at her mother's shocked and pale face. "And I love Parker Cantrell. He is the father of my child and we are going to buy our own house and raise our daughter there. That's for me, Mama. That's what I want to do with my life at this point, for me!"

"Drewcilla!" Lorrayna finally gasped. "You have never been so disrespectful in your life. I can only blame these ill-mannered people you've been hanging around."

Drew shook her head. "Don't do that, Mama. Don't make this about anybody else but us. For years I've been walking on eggshells, afraid I'd set off some ticking time bomb in your head. I've watched you whittle away your life because of what he did to you, and I'm sick of it. I won't watch it anymore. If you want to walk around pining away and banking your pain behind sarcasm and complaints, you go right ahead. But I won't do it with you any longer. I won't listen to it and I won't let you drench my baby in it either." Drew was crying full force now, sucking in air as she talked, and fighting the spiking pain at her temples as she breathed.

Lorrayna shook her head. "You would choose him over me? You would choose this man that hasn't promised you anything but the moment over your mother who gave birth to you and who cared for you all your life—"

"And who put her love and dedication for a drunken gambler over my best interests time after time," Drew finished the sentence for her mother. "Whatever he said you did, whatever he wanted you made sure happened. You asked me to give him my money, you told me it was my duty. Well, it wasn't my duty, Mother. It was his duty to take care of us!"

Like a child, Lorrayna lifted her hands to her ears. Drew reached out and pulled them down, holding her mother's hands at her sides. "You will listen to every word I have to say, because if you still want to carry on with this charade you call a life, then it'll be the last time I talk to you."

Lorrayna blinked and looked away.

"I did everything I did because I loved you and I cared for your well-being. Now, it's your turn, Mama. Now, it's time for you to stop being so selfish and put aside your sordid thoughts and fears for me. Parker is not like Daddy and he's not like Jared Mansfield. He's a better man than both of them rolled up together and we're going to be together for as long as it lasts. I'm not going to think beyond that, or spend my time worrying about the second it's over or if he'll walk away. I just won't live like that—not now or ever again!"

"Drew!" Delia yelled the moment she walked into the bedroom.

Parker's suite at the inn had a sitting room and a small kitchen that had to be passed before a person arrived at the bedroom. So Drew hadn't heard the outer door open, but she sighed with relief that someone had interrupted this scene. Her heart couldn't take another moment of breaking at the sheer look of sadness in her mother's eyes.

"You belong in bed," Delia said, crossing the room until she was next to Drew. "Let go," she told her as she grabbed Drew's wrists, shaking them so that she would let go of her hold on Lorrayna.

Drew felt as though that might be the last connection to her mother she ever had, the last time they actually touched each other, and she lost her breath at the thought. For as much of a pain in the butt that Lorrayna had been over the years, it had been just the two of them for so long. They'd stood together against the Jared incident, her father's death, the move, finding out she was pregnant, everything. And now that might be over.

"Here, get yourself back into this bed and I'll get you some water." Delia pushed past Lorrayna and was back in seconds with a glass of cold water and a wet cloth she used to wipe Drew's face.

As for Lorrayna, she had backed up quietly until she was totally out of the room. Drew closed her eyes to that sight, but she didn't cry. Not again. It was done. She'd stood up to her mother, said some things that probably sounded pretty awful but were necessary.

"She'll get over it," Delia said as she sat on the bed beside Drew, rubbing her belly. "Or she'll miss the very best thing to ever happen to her."

Drew nodded, a part of her hoping Delia was right. Another part of her hating that she might be wrong.

"Hey there, sleepyhead," Parker said softly, gently moving hair from Drew's blinking eyes.

For the last twenty minutes or so, he'd been watching her sleep. Waning rays of sunlight filtered through the half-closed blinds, casting a shadow over part of her body and face. Her hands were pulled up to cradle beneath her cheek and she'd been breathing in and out evenly, melodiously.

"Hi," she murmured, then rolled onto her back and stretched. "How long have I been asleep?"

She was trying to sit up now, and Parker helped her by rearranging the pillows and making sure she was comfortable, which earned him a smile from her. A smile that reached right into his chest and wrapped tight fingers around his heart.

"I've only been back for about a half hour and you were asleep when I came in."

"Oh, really? I still feel really tired," she said with another yawn.

"Dr. Lorens said you'd been through a very traumatic experience so you were bound to be exhausted. She also sent over a bottle of iron pills that she wants you to take once a day."

"Wow, a doctor that really does house calls." She chuckled.

"Not really. I stopped by to see Quinn and she was there. She asked how you were doing and said you should try the pills for a little more energy."

"I guess I really don't need energy considering I can only get out of the bed to visit the bathroom."

She didn't look too happy about that prospect and Parker couldn't really blame her, but it was for the best.

"Where have you been all day? Michelle said she thought you were going to the police station."

The worry was clear in her eyes, and Parker wished he could wipe it all away. Actually, he could and planned to do just that tonight. But he had to talk to her about that first.

"I did, but I stopped by your place first."

Another statement that brought sadness to Drew's face. Hurriedly, Parker moved to the chair across from the bed where he'd dropped the bags he'd brought from her apartment and the flower shop.

"I found the safe you said held all your insurance documents and other important paperwork," he told her, nodding behind him to the spot on the floor where he'd placed it when he came in.

The bags he put on the bed next to her. "These were some things that hadn't been broken and weren't damaged by the fire and smoke. Nikki's dad said there was some extensive smoke damage throughout the entire building, but he thinks it's salvageable. We can call the insurance company tomorrow morning and get them down here to start the claim process."

He'd been talking really fast, hoping something in those bags would make her smile again. She pulled out two things, holding one in each hand, and looked up at Parker with tears in her eyes.

"You saved these for me?"

Parker stared down at the salt and pepper shakers—Dorothy's ruby slipper and the Wicked Witch of the West's black hat. He nodded. "Yeah, you said they were your favorites."

Drew nodded. "They are."

"I'm really sorry this happened," Parker said the moment one tear slipped down her cheek. "If I could go back in time, I'd do so many things different, Drew. I would have listened to my supervisor. I would have gone back to Baltimore after I knew someone had tried to run me off the road. I wouldn't have involved you at all." He said the last quietly.

It was the truth. Of all the things Parker had done in his life, this one was what he most regretted. Not spending that night with Drew and having a baby develop from that union, but all the rest. Witnessing the Vezina murder, investigating when he was told to leave it alone, thinking he was invincible when a bullet could kill him just as easily as a Molotov cocktail thrown through the front window of Drew's shop could have killed her.

"Regrets are useless," she told him. "Totally useless and a waste of time. You did what you thought was right at the time. Now that you've told Ryan and Sheriff Farraway what's going on, I'm sure they'll catch Jared and put him under the jail for breaking into my place and then torching it, and they'll find whoever is behind the attacks on you."

"When you gave your statement to the sheriff at the hospital, you said Jared had been the one to break into your apartment. What makes you so sure it was Jared?" Parker asked, keeping his voice as level and as calm as possible.

Drew still held the shakers in her hands, rubbing her thumbs over each of them. "The baseball cap. I saw it the moment I stepped out of the bedroom," she told him.

"But you didn't actually see his face?" he prodded.

Drew looked at him, then frowned as she contemplated his question. "No. I didn't actually see his face. I just saw the hat and I lifted my arms to swing the bat I was holding. Then he sprayed me and I went down. Wait a minute, how did Jared get out of jail? Carl said he was locking him up earlier that day. How could he have gotten out of jail and come right back to my place in the span of just hours?"

"Right," Parker told her. "Jared's fancy lawyer didn't get here to post bail for him until the next morning. He was in jail the entire night of the explosion."

The shakers slid slowly from her grasp, clanking together as they met on top of the sheet that covered her legs.

"Then who was it? Who came into my apartment and touched my things and then blew up my flower shop?"

Parker took a deep breath then and reached for her hands. He held them both tightly, closing his eyes and silently giving thanks that she hadn't pulled away from him.

"Jonah was just about to make his next circle around your block when a car sped past him. That same car almost hit Hoover King just a block away from city hall. Miracle of miracles was that Hoover remembered the license plate. He reported it to Jonah the next morning because he thought the sedan might be trying to horn in on his taxi business around town. Hoover's description of the car matched the one Jonah remembered seeing, and he ran the tag."

He paused, hating to have to say this about as much as he'd hated it when Kyle and Jonah had told him, Preston, and Ryan earlier today.

"The car's registered to the Baltimore City Police Department. When Kyle called the station to find out who had signed the car out, he was given my name."

"What?" she gasped. "You *were not* driving that car that night. You *did not* break into my house, then throw a bomb through the front window and speed off!"

Her voice grew louder with each word, it seemed, her cheeks flushed with the emotion rippling through her. Emotion that Parker wasn't certain she would feel once he revealed these things to her. He'd thought she'd be disgusted and say she was leaving, say she didn't want her child growing up around such a colossal jerk, not to mention a moving target that was now being framed.

"No. I didn't. And lucky for me I have an alibi. Mr. Sylvester talked to me for at least forty-five minutes that night, and then Savannah saw me going into my bedroom just before midnight. Jonah called in the explosion at nine minutes after twelve. There's no way I could have run from here to your place, tossed a bomb, then been back here in bed by twelve fifteen when Kyle called me to tell me about the explosion."

"Right, but everyone already knew that, didn't they? I mean, you weren't really considered a suspect?"

She sounded incredulous, her eyes filling with growing concern.

"I don't think anybody here thought I did anything wrong. But now that Kyle made that call, my supervisor back in Baltimore has been alerted to what's going on. He told Kyle he would investigate my involvement in signing out the car and the Vezina murder."

"There is no involvement, and he's an idiot if he believes anything else! A big, stupid idiot!"

Parker couldn't help smiling at the quick rise in temper she was showing at his defense. "Remind me to take you with me when I go before the review board."

"Are they the ones that are going to give you your job back?"

And because Parker seriously doubted that he would get his job in Baltimore back, and because he was almost 85 percent positive that he didn't want his job in Baltimore back, he could only look at Drew sorrowfully.

"What's more important is that since the car is the property of the police department, it has a GPS tracker beneath the engine."

"Great," Drew said, letting out a sigh of relief. "That means you can track it, find out where it is, and go get the asshole that destroyed my shop."

"Right, baby. That's exactly what I plan to do tonight."

Route 33 led out of Sweetland and directly into Easton. To the west was Queenstown and to the east, Cambridge. Parker had traveled in all directions more times than he could count. But tonight he drove in the back of one of two white SUVs with tinted windows and FBI agents in the driver's seats. At his back he felt the weight of his nine-millimeter, its twin at his right ankle. His mood was grim as they traveled, his mind on Drew and how she'd looked after he'd showered and dressed before Preston came to pick him up.

She'd watched with interest as he'd strapped on his first weapon, then slipped the second behind his back, her breath hitching as he'd checked the clip and the safety first. He'd said everything he knew to reassure her, never having had to reassure anyone before when he set out on a case.

"I won't be alone," he'd told her as he sat beside her on the bed. "Ryan has a whole unit with him now, and Sheriff Farraway's coming along. We've already notified the Easton police, even though this is solely an FBI investigation at this point."

She'd nodded but hadn't spoken.

He'd cupped her face in his hands then, leaning forward to kiss first her forehead, then the tip of her nose, and then her lips.

She'd sighed as he'd pulled back slightly.

"Come back," she'd whispered.

There it was again, that tight clenching in his chest that made Parker feel almost like weeping. Instead he'd lowered his forehead to hers and closed his eyes. "I promise."

"I love you," she'd said in a voice so quiet, he'd almost thought he'd been hearing things.

His eyes had shot open, meeting hers as she'd looked back at him tentatively.

Parker had sighed, unable to use the excuse that he didn't know what that clenching in his chest meant or that he simply wasn't sure what this foreign emotion was he carried around for her. "I love you too, baby."

That had been almost two hours ago, and Parker missed her already. He missed her scent, the way she looked at him when she was about to question something he did or said, and especially the way she looked at him when she said she loved him and he returned the words. He'd held her so tight before leaving that he'd thought he might crush her, and when he'd finally left the house he'd made Preston wait a few minutes before pulling off, praying with every bit of faith his grandmother had instilled in him that he would come back to her and his child.

"We're here," Preston's composed tone announced.

Parker continued to stare out the window as the SUV came to a stop just off a dark road. Up ahead there were lights, a parking lot, and the motel where the sedan had been traced. He heard doors opening and closing quietly, watched through the window as the agents in the vehicle in front climbed out, Kevlar vests on, weapons already in hand. But Parker didn't move.

"You don't have to go in if you don't want to," Preston said, a hand on Parker's shoulder.

Preston would stay in the SUV because he wasn't a law enforcement officer. He could shoot and had a license to carry a concealed weapon, but he didn't like gunfire much. Of course, none of that had stopped him from running into that abandoned house to save Heaven from her kidnappers. This time, Preston had been along to offer advice on how to preserve this case so that it wouldn't fall through the legal cracks when it came time to prosecute.

"Right now BCPD considers you a suspect. You're not an official investigator on this case," Preston continued.

And those facts gave Parker an official reason not to go in. It gave him a valid excuse in case they all returned home and everyone asked what happened—he could report that he'd stayed in the vehicle with Preston. It was his way out.

There always seemed to be a way out for Parker, another choice that would be easier and likely less of a risk. But he never took it. Never even considered it. He did the dangerous things, took the highest risks, played the worst odds. But that was before Drew, before his unborn child's life had been threatened, before the "happily ever after" in Sweetland looked so appealing to him.

"I'm going," he said solemnly, and got out of the SUV. Ryan came up behind him instantly, as if the man had been waiting for him to step out of the vehicle.

"Stick close and let me or one of the other agents take him down. The more your name stays out of the official reports, the better chance you'll have at keeping your job," Ryan told him with a firm nod.

Parker shook his head. "All I care about is bringing this bastard down. Nothing else matters besides eliminating the threat to my family."

With that they covered the ground from the vehicles to the side of the motel. Four agents had run across the parking lot, one standing with a thumbs-up next to a sedan that matched the description Jonah and Hoover had given. Two more agents went to the door of the room directly across from where the car was parked. The parking lot was basically empty except for another car that was closer to the front entrance. Add that to the fact that only this room had a light on, and they had a pretty good indication that this was where they would find the driver of the vehicle.

Once the two at the door gave the nod, Ryan and Parker ran with two other agents at their back to the door of the room. Ryan did a silent countdown with his fingers, then nodded as his hand went into a fist. The agent to the right of the door turned and kicked the door in. From that point on, there was a lot of shouting as the agents and Parker went into the room. Parker held his gun with both hands, arms raised, finger perfectly calm on the trigger, his eyes trained on the wall where the first two agents now held a man.

His face was pressed to the wall, his boxers wrinkled and crunched between his thighs. A white undershirt and socks completed his ensemble.

"Turn 'im around," Ryan yelled.

And when they did, Parker felt the entire room spinning around him.

Chapter 22

"Will?" Parker finally managed, his throat dry with the one word. "What the hell are you doing here?"

Will Tinley was a fifteen-year veteran of the Baltimore City Police Department, and in the last two of those years he'd been Parker's partner.

"You just couldn't leave it alone, could you, Cantrell?" asked Will, a six-foot-tall man with low-cut hair and a scar on his neck from where a suspect had taken a shot at him and barely missed killing him. "Even after the sergeant told you to back down, you just kept right on going. Always the hero," he finished with a shake of his head.

Parker lowered his gun, closing his eyes to what he was now seeing as the reality of this situation. "Give him five minutes to tell me why he did this to me and to my family," he said, barely banking the anger.

"Talk!" ordered the agent who had a death grip on Will's arm, twisting it behind his back until the man cursed.

"It's bigger than you can imagine. You think it'll stop if you drag me away from here in cuffs? It won't! They've got people everywhere, they're gonna keep going no matter what."

"Who?"

Will shook his head. "Doesn't matter. They want you dead just like Vezina."

"And they sent you to take care of that?" Parker asked, looking in disgust at the man he'd spent countless hours with.

"You're lucky they sent me," Will told him. Then he shook his head again, closing his eyes as his chest heaved. "I couldn't kill you. No matter how much money was on the line, I just couldn't do it. They're gonna come for me now."

"You'll be in federal custody," Parker told him.

"They're everywhere, man. Every damned where! I didn't want to get mixed up with them, but I couldn't say no."

"You could have. If you needed money, you could have come to me," Parker told him, still trying to understand why all of this was happening.

Will was married, with twin eight-year-old daughters. He had a family and a career, he had it all. How had that man turned into this thin and pale creature he now stared at?

"You don't have to hold me so tight, dude. I'm not trying to run. There's nowhere for me to go. Nowhere they won't find me," Will said, his voice laced with defeat.

Ryan gave a nod and the two agents who had been holding Will released their hold on him but still stood close.

"Get dressed," Ryan told Will. "Who is paying you? What do they want?"

Will shook his head as he was allowed to move to the bed, where pants and a T-shirt were lying as if he'd just taken them off. He pulled on the pants, looking at Ryan as he buttoned them.

"I guess it doesn't matter now if I tell you everything I know. Is that what you're hoping for?" Will asked.

"It'll go a long way to helping you as far as jail time. We already have info on Witherspoon and parts of his organization. Maybe if you cooperate," Ryan told him.

Will laughed. "If I cooperate, what?" He pulled his shirt over his head, then sat on the bed to put on his shoes. "You'll give me a cleaner cell to live out the rest of my life in?"

Ryan didn't reply.

Will looked over to Parker then, the two locking gazes, their entire history flashing before Parker's eyes. The cases they'd handled and solved together, the cookouts Parker had attended at Will's house. The smile on the face of Will's wife, Beth, whenever Parker teased her about how sappy Will got when he talked about her. It made his temples throb.

"They will kill Beth and the girls. You know it and I know it," Will said solemnly.

"We can protect them," Parker offered. "Right, Ryan? They can all go into protective custody until this is over."

"That's right. Once we get back to the vehicle I can radio in for them to be picked up," Ryan confirmed.

"And they live their lives in secret, hiding from everyone they know and love, all because of me." Will shook his head and bent down to pick up his shoe. "I can't let that happen. I just can't."

The next moments played out in horrific slow motion for Parker. As Will straightened from supposedly picking up the black tennis shoe that had been sitting right by his feet, Parker noticed the gun he'd retrieved instead.

"Gun!" one of the agents yelled, the sound a slurring of the one-syllable word.

Parker's arm rose instinctively just as Will locked gazes with him once more.

"Tell Beth I love her. I always loved her," Will said two

seconds before he raised his arm, pointed the gun to his temple, and fired.

Parker jerked as if the bullet had somehow penetrated his body instead. He dropped his gun instantly, his heart beating a rhythm so fast that it drummed loudly in his ears. Around him there was cursing and movement and in moments the blare of police sirens and probably an EMT. People came in and out of the room, moving all about, talking, shaking their heads. None of which Parker acknowledged. He stood rooted to that spot, staring at the bed where the body of a man he'd once admired for his happiness and contentment lay dead.

"You couldn't have stopped him," Drew said, her voice quiet in the silence of the bedroom later that night.

Parker had returned to the inn, showered, and immediately climbed into bed, pulling Drew into his arms. He'd hugged her for a long time before finally explaining to her what had happened. Now, he simply kept his arms around her, while her head rested on his chest, the swell of her stomach grazing his thigh.

"He was in too deep, that's what Ryan said as we drove home. He probably felt like this was the best solution rather than have a hit put out on him and his family. He died for them," he told her with emotion still thick in his chest.

"When my father took his life, people came to the house saying that same thing to my mother. 'He did it for you and Drew. He wanted to spare you both the expense and the pain of treatment when he was just going to die anyway.'" Drew shook her head, her hair brushing against Parker's chin. "He wasn't going to die anyway, at least not in six months like that doctor had predicted. But my father didn't know that. He didn't wait to find out. He just decided this was best for us and he did it."

She was quiet for a second.

"I don't know if Will Tinley did this for his family or if it was best for his family. All I know is that those daughters will grow up knowing he left them, that he chose to leave them. His wife will bear the brunt of not having insurance premiums paid because of the suicide and struggling financially, publicly, and emotionally in an attempt to reconcile with his decision. He probably felt like he was making a selfless sacrifice, but it may not turn out that way for them."

"I didn't want him to die," Parker admitted. "Even after I realized he'd been the one to bomb your place, shooting at us, running me off the road, I still didn't want him dead."

"He didn't want you dead either."

Parker heard her words, replayed them with Will's own confession that he couldn't kill Parker. He should be happy for that fact, he should take solace in knowing that Will wasn't 100 percent corrupt, because if he had been, there was no doubt Parker, Drew, and their unborn child would be dead.

That thought had him hugging her closer and kissing the top of her head. She'd wrapped her arms around his waist, lifted a leg to slip between his. He loved the warmth of having her close, the comfort in knowing that she was safe right there in his arms. He simply loved her and—

Parker felt something against his side. He froze, and the thumping sensation was there again.

"She kicked?" It was sort of a question and a declaration, his voice sounding incredulous even to his own ears.

Drew rose slightly, pulling one of his hands to lay it over her stomach.

Parker smiled. "She kicked again." He sighed.

"I think she knows your voice. Before you came home we were both sleeping. Then we were in your arms and we were both wide awake," Drew told him.

He couldn't stop smiling, couldn't move his hand from her stomach, from the movement of his child.

"I love you so much," he told her. "So much that I'll never decide to leave you and our family."

Drew kissed his chest. "Thank you, Parker. I love you, too."

"So Miranda sent these over this morning. I couldn't wait to close up the shop to bring them over here for you to see."

Delia sat cross-legged on the bed next to Drew as she pulled pictures out of a purse that could easily double for carry-on luggage. It was navy-blue leather, soft and expensive and so absolutely Delia's style. Miranda Winslow was a friend of Delia's from L.A. and a couture designer. Delia, who was currently living out her second life as a boutique owner, leaving her acting life behind, had talked Heaven into letting her design her bridesmaid dresses if she could get Miranda to agree to design the wedding dress.

Of course, Savannah had squawked about having a novice design her dress versus Heaven having the couture design.

"I've worn Vera Wang originals," Savannah had claimed.

"And now you'll be the first to wear a Design by Delia," Delia had told her with a smile and a pat on the top of her head as if she were a child or a kitten.

This had caused Savannah to scowl and the other women to laugh.

"Oh, goodness, Delia. They're gorgeous!" Heaven squealed as she flipped from one picture to the next. "Absolutely gorgeous."

"Thanks. I'm pretty pumped to see them actually on a real person," Delia said, handing Drew the pictures after Heaven had seen them.

Drew sighed inwardly at the pictures of beautiful peach-colored gowns. Savannah, Raine, and Michelle would be bridesmaids in Heaven's wedding, while Heaven wore a lovely eggshell-colored gown of pure lace.

As for Nikki and Quinn's wedding, which was coming up first in December, Nikki was wearing an updated rendition of her mother's wedding gown, while Cordy, Savannah, and Michelle would be dressed in gowns the color of evergreen Christmas trees.

Thus the mood at the inn was very festive, even a week after a man had killed himself in Easton. Drew, on the other hand, hadn't been feeling very festive. Because of the explosion, she'd been disqualified from the window decoration contest. She was sick and tired of being hurt over her mother's decision to stay out of her life and depressed because the business she'd built from nothing was now gone and pissed off because she couldn't get out of this damned bed. So she'd decided to be angry about the window contest instead; it seemed to make sense at the time.

Now, with all these smiles and wedding dresses and talk of receptions and menus and everything else wedding oriented, she was slowly slipping into a pissed-off mood for another reason.

"And, I've even got something for you, Ms. Sidney."

Delia nudged her and dug into her purse once more. Drew tried to look interested even though she really wasn't. Whatever Delia had in that suitcase-sized purse of hers, Drew wasn't interested. What she'd much rather be doing on this lovely fall Saturday afternoon was playing in the yard with Rufus. For days now, she'd had to settle for watching him play ball in the yard with Parker or with Raine, who spent an unusual amount of time outside with the puppies, in Drew's estimation.

"Look, isn't it lovely?" Delia asked, putting a sheet of paper directly in Drew's line of vision.

Reluctantly, Drew took the paper. She looked at it, then at Delia, then back at the paper once more. "What is it?" she asked.

Heaven laughed and leaned over the bed to snatch the paper from Drew. "It's a dress, silly. And it's lovely. You'll look wonderful at Cupid's Cabaret wearing this."

Cupid's Cabaret was Sweetland's version of a Valentine's Day dance for grown-ups. It was a big affair that gave the townspeople another reason to get together and eat, dress up and eat—and, of course, fellowship. Last year Drew was supposed to go with her mother and Uncle Walt, but Lorrayna had begged off. So Drew ended up sitting at a corner table nursing a glass of bad red wine, while Delia danced around in the skimpiest red outfit she could find. That was another thing: Everyone wore red to the cabaret. Fun, huh?

"Did you forget that I'll be just about ready to deliver in February?" Drew asked, falling back on her pillows. She stared up at the ceiling, wondering how much it would take to bribe Michelle to let her at least have breakfast at the kitchen table tomorrow. She'd probably have to come up with a sum for Mr. Sylvester, too, as he made a point to have his morning cup of coffee in the room with her, chatting about what things he had planned for the day. They usually amounted to him sitting on the porch, walking around back to sit on the bench, then ending the afternoon sitting in the living room reading the paper. Drew thought he was probably happy just to have someone else in this house to sit with.

"The cabaret is on the seventh this year because the town hall is undergoing renovations beginning the tenth and won't be finished by the fourteenth," Heaven reported.

"Mayor Fitzgerald wants all the renovations on that building and city hall complete before next year's Bay Day festivities."

"Man, she's really getting into all this public relations crap around here," Delia said, referring to Heaven. "I thought you were only supposed to focus on your research and making connections for the inn."

Heaven waved a hand at Delia. "What I'm doing is networking. I go to the mayor's meetings, the ones that aren't private. I talk to the town council and the president of our Chamber of Commerce. This way they all know my name and that I'm affiliated with the inn. And when one of their colleagues or social groups need a place to stay in Sweetland, who do you think they're going to call? Their connection to the inn—which happens to be me!"

Drew couldn't help smiling at Heaven's overly chipper rendition of her job duties here at The Silver Spoon. "It didn't take her long to become as whacky as all the other residents of Sweetland," Drew quipped.

"Now, back to this dress," Heaven said, eyeing Drew and the paper once more. "It'll look lovely on you. And it's designed to have room since you'll be in your final weeks of pregnancy."

"I'm not going to that event dressed up like a red candy apple," Drew protested.

"You'll look lovely and radiant," Heaven added.

Delia snatched the paper from Heaven. "Plus I designed this specifically for you. Miranda's going to have it cut and ready for us to see in a couple of weeks. The only thing that's going to keep you from wearing this dress is if you're in a hospital gown instead," she warned.

"Did you forget I'm on house arrest? Michelle's not letting me out of her sight, and I surely won't be able to hide in that bright red dress!" Drew continued, even though the idea of getting out of the house sounded wonderful to her.

"You'll be close to delivering then, so it won't matter if you go into labor at the cabaret," Heaven said.

Delia laughed at that. "Wouldn't that be something if she did go into labor at the cabaret. Then they could name the baby Cupid."

"Not funny," Drew told them. But eventually she started to laugh herself, as the two of them were having such a good time at her expense.

On Sunday evening, the Redling brothers showed up at The Silver Spoon. With them was Diana McCann and a woman by the name of Evelyn Woodby, who Savannah reported was engaged to Phillip Redling, the older brother. Steven Redling was the goofy one in the expensive suit who was so brainwashed by Diana that he'd seemed to completely forgive her romp with the now free-on-bail Jared Mansfield.

Earlier there'd been an impromptu town council meeting, as four of the council members had gathered after the children's pageant at the church to talk about the amount of traffic and the comings and goings of some of the guests at The Marina. As it was in Sweetland, word traveled quickly, and when those very same four council members ended up at The Silver Spoon for an early dinner, the remaining three members of the council inevitably showed up. Then someone must have also tipped off the Redlings that they were the subject of conversation, so here they were, walking through the door, overdressed and marginally unwelcome.

"Good to see you again, Steven, Phillip," Preston greeted the brothers at the doorway.

"Preston, right?" Steven asked with a smirk. "I can never tell those twins apart."

"You're right, darling. Preston's the tall, thin one. Parker's the bulky superhero one. He's probably laid up in hiding with his pregnant flower girl."

Of course this was Diana—and of course Savannah was standing right beside Preston, ready and waiting for Diana to pounce.

"Actually, Diana, Parker is helping out at the restaurant tonight. His fiancée is resting," Savannah said in a sugary-sweet tone.

Diana's bright pink-tinted lips thinned as she glared at Savannah. Apparently the silly woman was still holding a torch for Parker, and the man on her arm didn't have the good sense to take that as a hint.

Phillip spoke up next. "We hear you're having a meeting about us and figured it made sense for us to at least be here to defend ourselves."

Preston shook his head. "This is a restaurant, Phillip. You know that. And as far as I know, there are no official meetings on hand for tonight."

To that, both Redling brothers looked at each other, then back to Preston, who was more than willing to throw the four of them out without another word. He'd had enough with the snarky remarks from the citizens of Sweetland. This week they'd run the gamut from reminding him of his transplant fiancée who brought kidnappers and the FBI to town to his brothers inciting fires and explosions and knocking up innocent girls. He was ready to tell them all to go to hell, and if he was feeling that way, he could only imagine how Parker was feeling.

"In that case we'll take a table for four," Phillip countered. "And lucky us—I see one right over there near some of the prestigious town council members."

This could potentially end badly, Preston knew. But the Redlings were asking for it.

"Savannah, show the Redlings to their table," Preston

told his sister, then immediately excused himself from the group.

On the way out of the restaurant, he ran right into the person he'd wanted to see.

"Before you go back in there, let me give you a recap," he began, blocking Parker's view and entrance into the restaurant. "Town council's up in arms about the increase in traffic to and from The Marina. A huge complaint is that The Marina has so many amenities on their property that the town won't see as much predicted revenue."

"That sounds like good news for us, so why do you look like it's the exact opposite?" Parker asked.

His brother had most likely just come from checking on Drew for the billionth time tonight. If ever there was a man in love with his pregnant girlfriend, Parker would be it. Now, he probably wouldn't be happy to know that Savannah had just indicated to Diana and the Redlings that Parker was actually going to marry Drew, but that was another argument for another time.

"The Redlings somehow got wind of the discussion and they just showed up requesting a table near the town council members. The Redlings also have Diana and some transplant with them that Savannah says is Phillip's fiancée. Marabelle and Louisa are also in there having their Sunday dinner as usual. Put all that together and I'm guessing we're about to have one exciting evening," Preston said with a frown.

Chapter 23

Parker folded his arms across his chest, his brow furrowing as he thought about Preston's words. Considering all the players his brother had just announced, they definitely had the makings of a major storm brewing in the restaurant.

"Where's Michelle?" he asked Preston.

"She's in the kitchen. Quinn and Nikki are at the Brockingtons' having dinner and going over the guest list for the wedding. Raine and Savannah are in the dining room, and Mr. Sylvester's on the front porch. That accounts for just about everybody," Preston quipped.

Parker only nodded at his brother's sarcasm. "Let's get them served and out of here as quickly as possible," he said. "That's all we can really do."

Preston agreed and the two of them entered the restaurant prepared for whatever went down. Or at least they thought they were prepared.

The argument was in full swing by the time Parker and Preston made their way to the tables where the Redlings and the town council members sat.

"You said our shops would make money, but you have

a spa, a coffee shop, a diner complete with an ice-cream parlor, and a hairdresser right behind your big golden gates!" protested Jeannie Nelson, whose father had been town council president for ten years before he'd died of a heart attack last year.

Jeannie was about four feet eleven in heels, with a head full of fiery red hair and a personality to match. She was as feisty as two pit bulls, and right now she had the Redlings firmly in her grasp.

"We have a full-scale resort, precisely what we pitched to the town council last year. The plans were approved and we built our facility. The fact that you have complaints now is a little too late," Steven countered, his hands flat on the table as he leaned forward toward Jeannie, who had come to stand in front of them.

"That deal was made by Inez Hoover, the cheating criminal that's now in jail!" Jeannie added.

Phillip shook his head. "Not our problem."

"If you ask me," Louisa interrupted from her table across the room, "they shouldn't have allowed any of these big-city folk into our town. None of them know how to be productive citizens. All they do is bring ruckus and mayhem to us good people."

Parker's gaze immediately went to Louisa, knowing the woman had more than one meaning behind her words. The fact that she gave him a curt nod at his glance confirmed that for him.

"It's a free country, you old bat," Diana chimed in. "Leave it to you and your blood sister there we would never have any semblance of progress in this town. None of you people want progress. You want to stay in this small-town rut you've created forever."

"Funny you say that, Diana. You were born in this small-town rut, then ran off to marry some guy you said was rich enough to take you away from this pitiful place.

And yet you're right back here living off one of our founders and causing trouble just like you always did. You're sniffing out money just like a street pup," Jeannie told her.

Diana stood, dropping her napkin onto the table. "Now, you wait just a minute. You're divorced, too! And you're loud and obnoxious, just like your daddy was, God rest his pitiful drunkard soul!"

With that, Jeannie's lithe body was in motion. She cleared that table and had her hands wrapped around Diana's neck in about five seconds, much faster than either Parker or Preston could have moved. Glass fell to the floor and the chaos officially began.

Steven grabbed Diana around the waist, while Phillip tried unsuccessfully to pull Jeannie off her. Evelyn Woodby stood screaming after a glass of red wine had been spilled on her off-white sundress. The remaining town council members, including Hoover King, charged the Redling brothers like a cavalry. Louisa and Marabelle stood up, wrapping their leftover food in napkins and hurriedly sticking it into their purses while shaking their heads in dismay.

That's when Parker felt a hand on his shoulder.

"Looks like you've got yourself a situation here," Sheriff Farraway said.

"Yeah, you got some extra cuffs with you?" he asked, keeping his eyes on the commotion going on.

Kyle nodded. "Sure do, and Jonah's coming in right behind me, so we've got two cruisers to take them in with."

"Too many for two cruisers. I'll use my truck to transport the rest. Let's just get them out of my restaurant now!"

It took Parker, Preston, Kyle, and Jonah about a half hour to subdue, handcuff, and threaten the Redlings, the town council members, and the gossip queens of Sweet-land. They'd decided to separate the quarreling parties, so the Redlings were led out of the restaurant entrance door by Jonah and Preston, while Kyle wrangled up the two town council members who hadn't backed down when he'd told them to, Jeannie being one of them, and Parker secured his favorites, Louisa and Marabelle.

He hadn't cuffed the two women, but damn, he wished he'd muzzled them. They traveled through the house heading to the front door, the two women still complaining and arguing to the point Parker wanted to strangle both of them. It was when they made it into the living room, Kyle and Jeannie coming up right behind him, that Parker's patience finally broke.

Louisa had been walking in front, Marabelle in the center, dressed in her floral creation of the day, and Parker bringing up the rear. Louisa turned and bumped her expansive body into Marabelle's. Parker had been alert enough to take a step back, yelling, "Whoa!" as a warning to Kyle and Jeannie, who were behind him. "Where do you think you're going?" he asked.

"You can't put me out of this place!" Louisa began yelling. "It's a historical monument, and as a citizen of this town I have a right to be here."

Parker sighed. "It's my property and I'm putting you out. If you keep running your mouth, it'll be a permanent ban."

"I'm not afraid of you, Parker Cantrell. If Mary Janet were alive, she'd be embarrassed to the tips of her toes at the way you've been behaving since you came back here!" Louisa continued on this new tirade.

"Isn't it enough you've got that gal locked up some-where in this house? She's having your baby and you're running around here like you're the law, getting people killed or almost blown up! That poor baseball player's probably going to sue our town after you hit him and then had him arrested, of all the stupid things! I won't stand for this treatment from you! I just won't!"

Louisa had barreled past Marabelle until the other woman was pressed against the sofa table by the wall, knocking over one of the lamps. Parker was sure Quinn would have a fit over that.

"That's about enough from you, Louisa," Kyle interjected. He'd moved around the threesome, sending Jeannie out onto the front porch, where Jonah had come to see what was going on. The other town council member watched with interest as he was escorted out as well. Kyle immediately went to Louisa, taking one of her hands.

"I can cuff you and arrest you for disturbing the peace, if that's what you want, Louisa," he told her.

"Why, you should be cuffing this reprobate and looking for Drew. He's probably got her handcuffed somewhere. You know those city folk like all those sordid sex games."

To that comment from Louisa, even Marabelle gasped.

Parker took a step forward, his fists clenching at his side, temples throbbing. "Mrs. Kirk, I'd advise you to shut your mouth and get out of my house right now!"

"Not until I know that gal is all right. Her poor mother's about to lose her mind and nobody seems to care but me! Now Kyle, I want you to turn me loose so I can look for Drewcilla."

"Not turning you loose until we get to the station, Louisa. You're under arrest," Kyle told her.

"Wait."

They all turned to the female voice, Parker shaking his head as he saw her approach.

"I want to say something to her first," Drew stated, walking all the way into the living room.

"What are you doing out here?" Parker asked as he moved to her side.

She held up a hand. "I'm fine. But this has been brewing for a while. She's not going to stop until somebody stops her."

Drew talked to Parker but kept her gaze on Louisa.

"Look at her, heavy with child like she's gonna pop any day now," Louisa said with a smirk. "Absolutely shameful. He won't marry you, you know. Just plans to keep you locked away until you have that baby, then it's over for you. Wise up now and get out while you can."

Marabelle's gaze had softened as she looked at Drew in her very pregnant state.

"Whatever Parker and I do is our business, Mrs. Kirk. Do you understand what that means? It means that you don't have a say, that your opinion does not count in this relationship or even in this house," Drew pointed out.

"Now, the other people in this town might be afraid of you. They might let you snicker behind their backs and spread your vicious rumors. But I'm here right now to tell you that it will stop as far as I and my family are concerned. If you so much as utter our names, I'll slap you with a gag and harassment order. Do I make myself clear?"

Drew had spoken in a clear and concise tone. She'd stood with her back ramrod straight, her stomach protruding through the knee-length nightgown she wore. Her hair was pulled back into a semineat ponytail, flat in the back from lying down. The only show of emotion was the flush of heat at her cheeks.

And Parker had never loved her more.

He wrapped his arm around her waist, looking to the shocked, speechless Louisa and the stunned and now nervous Marabelle with a large measure of pride.

"I'll put these two in my car. You can take the town council members in," Kyle told Parker.

"No. No. I'll go home if it's all the same to you," Marabelle started. "Parker, give my apologies to Michelle and the rest of the family."

He'd never seen Marabelle move so fast as she hustled to get out the front door. She hadn't even spared Louisa a backward glance. As for Louisa, she still held her frown, too stubborn to know when she'd been beaten. Kyle shrugged, slipping the temporary cuffs around her wrists.

"Off we go," he stated, turning and giving a tip of his police hat to Parker and Drew.

When they were alone, Parker immediately pulled Drew into his arms. "I should shake you for getting out of that bed and coming out here," he told her.

"You were making so much noise there was no way I could get an ounce of rest. Besides, I'd heard enough from Louisa Kirk to last me a lifetime. I'm not about to continue on living in Sweetland with her commenting on everything I do from blinking an eye to squatting in town hall and giving birth. The woman's a menace."

Now she was flaring with emotion, her eyes dancing, lips thinning. Lips that Parker leaned in instantly to kiss.

"I love you," he told her.

She melted against him instantly. "I'm beginning to like the sound of that."

"Good, because I'm going to keep telling you, but only if you get yourself back into that bed."

"Join me?"

He rubbed his hands up and down her back, smile and arousal spreading quickly. "I've never heard a better invitation," he told her. "But I've gotta take these people down to the police station."

When Drew looked as if she were about to frown, he added, "But I'll be right back. Wait for me?"

She touched a finger to his jaw, then his bottom lip. "I don't have much of a choice, now, do I?"

"No. You don't," he told her, and then watched her walk back into the bedroom.

With a groan of anticipated pleasure, Parker finally turned away from Drew's swaying backside and headed out the front door to take care of the town council members as quickly as possible. He had something scrumptious waiting for him upon his return.

Granger Kirk left the police station with his face fixed in a scowl. He'd come to claim his wife after Kyle had called him to say he was going to charge Louisa formally if Granger didn't pick her up and keep her on a tight leash for the next thirty days. Granger hadn't looked happy when he'd walked into the station. The only change in emotion Parker had noted was when he'd seen his wife sitting in the temporary cell, looking as if she were about to explode. Granger had almost cracked a smile.

"This station hasn't seen this much action in thirty years," Kyle told Parker when they sat alone in his office.

Parker frowned. "I apologize for bringing my baggage down here with me. But I talked to Ryan last night and that's all finished. With Witherspoon and now his key men in custody, Ryan doubts there'll be any more ordered hits. He filed his final report on Friday and now all that's left is to await the trial."

Kyle nodded. "I gotta hand it to you Cantrell boys, you make a mess, you clean it up. I'm talking about Preston and those kidnappers and Quinn with Nikki's legal woes. You're a good bunch," he finished.

"I think I should say thank you," Parker commented wryly.

To that, Kyle chuckled heartily.

"I've got a proposition for you, Parker."

Parker sat back in the chair, not sure what to expect from the sheriff, who was looking at him with a bit of a gleam in his eye.

"I'm thinking of retiring next year. Or rather Esterine has declared that both of us will be retiring next year." He ended with another of his deep-gutted chuckles. "I guess it's time, we've been doing this for too long. In the last couple of months I've realized that."

Parker lifted a brow. "You mean since me and my brothers returned to Sweetland you've had an influx of crime and figure now it's too much for you."

"Whoa, hold on there, son. You're getting ahead of yourself," Kyle told him. He leaned forward, thick elbows planted on the desk. "I've been a cop for more than forty years. I've worked in this town all my life, but I've seen some things in and around Sweetland. I can handle my town just fine."

Kyle sighed then, and Parker continued to watch him steadily.

"When I met Esterine I thought, Man, the heavens have sure smiled on me. Didn't think I was worth a plug nickel until Esterine gave me her heart. Then we had Carl and I thought, This is the best life possible. At home I had the sweetest, prettiest wife and a growing boy to carry on my legacy, and at work I had had the sweetest, prettiest receptionist and eventually a young man wearing the uniform just as I had.

"But things change, Parker. You know that. Some things just run their course, and Esterine and I feel like running the police station has run its course for us."

Parker nodded. "I understand, Sheriff. I understand more than you know."

Kyle nodded. "I talked to Sergeant Mertz on Friday." He let that sentence hang in the air while Parker frowned.

"Seems like being a cop in the big city has run its course for you, also," Kyle continued.

Parker hadn't told anyone that he'd resigned. He'd planned on telling Drew first, then the rest of his family, but he hadn't found the right moment yet. Something told him that moment was coming soon.

"It was time," he said to Kyle. "Nothing was going to be the same after this investigation. They thought I was a cop killer, were investigating me and getting ready to seek an indictment for my arrest. Had the FBI not gotten involved, I would probably be incarcerated right now. I don't begin to know how to work there again."

"Yeah, I can see that. For the record, Mertz said he had his doubts about the evidence against you," Kyle offered.

Parker shrugged. "Not strong enough doubts. Look, I'm not holding a grudge, life's too short for that. I guess I'm just moving on."

"Which brings me to why I came to see you this evening in the first place. Sure, I wanted a piece of Michelle's custard pie, but I wanted to talk to you about something."

"And you ended up handcuffing a bunch of your residents. I think I could probably get Michelle to send you a slice of pie," Parker said with a smile, glad they were no longer talking about his resignation.

"Well now, that would be good except Esterine's sort of got this thing about desserts lately. Said they look better on someone else."

They both laughed at that.

"I want you to take over as sheriff of Sweetland, Parker," Kyle said after sobering. "And before you ask, you've got more experience than Jonah and Carl. Jonah's a good cop, he's got good instincts and truly cares about the people of this town and their safety. Carl, on the other hand, well, Carl has his own path to walk, I guess."

"And you don't think that path's one day going to lead him to become sheriff?"

Kyle shook his head. "No. It won't. Carl's not a leader. He's not a follower, either, just wants to go his own way, do his own thing. You and I know that doesn't work out in the long haul."

"You're right about that," Parker admitted, enjoying for a moment the feeling of his past reputation taking a backseat to his present actions.

"He told his mother he's thinking about moving to L.A. I'm thinking about wishing him well," Kyle continued. "I may be old, but I'm not stupid enough to demand he be what I want him to be."

"That sounds smart."

"Oh, it is," Kyle said, poking his chest out. "And if you're lucky, when your baby grows up you'll make a smart decision like this, too. Not every child is the same, and no matter what you want for their lives, at some point they're gonna have to go their own way. Makes sense that parents just love and support them."

"I'm hope I'm as smart a father as you are," Parker said, and realized that he meant it.

Most fathers wanted their sons to either follow in their footsteps or be what they planned for them; not a lot of dads could step back and say, Do what you want. But Kyle was going to do that for Carl because, Parker suspected, he knew deep down that Carl would come back to Sweetland just as they all seemed to do.

Chapter 24

December

The Cantrell family had just finished cleaning up after one wedding when another was about to take place. It was eleven thirty-seven on New Year's Eve, and this time, the already married Quinn and the spring groom-to-be, Preston, were helping Parker get into his tuxedo. They were in Parker's rooms at the inn, with Mr. Sylvester sitting in a recliner across from the brothers.

"I can't believe she said yes," Preston said, handing Parker his jacket.

"What?" Parker asked in surprise. "Why wouldn't she say yes?"

"Because you were slow as molasses figuring out you should have been marrying her from the start," Mr. Sylvester chimed in.

The brothers looked fondly at the older man, marveling at how much his health had seemed to improve over the last couple of weeks. Quinn had finally convinced Mr. Sylvester to come into the office for a physical. It was then that they found out he was anemic and had been suffering from extreme fatigue as a result. With Michelle changing a few things in his diet, adding plenty of iron-rich foods, and Quinn prescribing a multivitamin as well as an iron supplement, Mr. Sylvester had perked right up. Not that his talking and advice giving had suffered one moment from his ailment.

"I wasn't that slow," Parker told him.

"You did sort of take your time," Quinn added, moving close to help straighten the bow tie Parker had just completed. "I mean, once you decided to bring her to the inn to stay and then quit your job, you would have thought the proposal would have been next."

"I like to do things in my own time," Parker replied, thinking back to the conversation he'd had with Kyle months ago about men walking their own path.

"So you proposed on Christmas Eve instead, making everyone have to go into mad rush mode to get this thing set up for you two," Preston told him.

"Not to mention keeping me and my lovely wife from going on our honeymoon," Quinn added.

"Come on, you can't blame that one on me. The ice storm grounded all planes at BWI, you weren't going to get to Aspen anyway. So actually having the wedding tonight is accommodating your first-thing-tomorrow-morning flight time," Parker told his big brother with a smile.

"Whatever you say, man," Quinn said with a laugh.

"Well, come on, you don't want to keep that gal waiting any longer," Mr. Sylvester told them as he stood and reached for his cane.

Michelle came in at that moment, carrying boutonnieres and going around to pin them on the lapels of each man there.

"I'm sick of wearing monkey suits and flowers already, and I'm not even up to bat yet," Preston commented when she'd finished.

"That's your nerves talking. You and Heaven are a

great couple and your wedding will be perfect just like
Nikki and Quinn's was and just like Parker and Drew's
will be once he gets his butt out there," Michelle quipped.

That made her move to him next, pinning on his bou-
tonniere and then looking up at him. "Never thought you'd
get married," she whispered, tears welling in her eyes.

"Don't do that," Parker warned. "I won't make it out
there if you cry, Michelle."

She shook her head. "I'm not going to cry," she vowed.
"I'm just so happy for the three of you, happy that you
found your way back home and you found someone to
share your lives with."

Parker touched his sister's cheek. "You're gonna find
that same thing, Michelle. If any of us are meant to be
married and starting a family, it's you."

"Oh no, bite your tongue. I'm the last one that needs to
be tied down to a man and children. How would I manage
all of you and another family?"

With that, Michelle moved to Quinn and then finally
to Mr. Sylvester, who escorted her out of the room and to
the living room.

Fifteen minutes later, Parker stood at the base of the
steps, the thick oak stairway on which banister he'd slid
down more times than he could remember. He waited
patiently as the CD playing the theme song from one of
Drew's favorite movies, *A Love Affair,* was started. About
thirty seconds into the song, Drew appeared at the top of
the stairs. Standing right beside her was Lorrayna, smiling through misty eyes.

The two women walked down the stairs, Lorrayna
holding on to Drew's arm while Drew used the railing to
keep her steady. She'd fussed only a little about the gown
Delia had found for her to wear at the last minute. It was
ecru—that's the color she'd told Parker the day after

Christmas, after she and the other females of the family had been locked in their room for hours. The neck was scooped, sleeves short, and the soft material flared out from just beneath her breasts to fall to the floor. She looked ethereal, a vision in motherly glory. Parker was speechless.

When they stopped on the last step, Parker reached for Drew's hand. Lorrayna touched her hand to his instead.

"I trust you to take care of my daughter, Parker," Lorrayna said in a quiet voice. "I expect you to respect and love her and to respect and love your children."

"Yes, ma'am," Parker replied. "I will."

Several moments later, after the minister had them repeating their vows, Parker heard himself saying those two words again. "I will."

And the moment the clock in the living room of The Silver Spoon struck midnight, he was married. Parker Cantrell, the Double Trouble Cantrell brother, was married to Drewcilla Sidney, the love of his life.

"The shop's reconstruction will be finished in a couple of weeks. It would have been sooner, but that ice storm put a halt to a lot of things," Parker talked as he lay in bed, Drew curled up beside him. "Dr. Lorens said you'll be far enough along in the pregnancy to go over and see the final results."

"Yeah, the minute I got the okay to get out of bed, Delia was draping more material on me for the dress she wants me to wear to the cabaret," Drew said around yet another yawn.

Today, or rather yesterday, had been a busy day. Truth be told, the last couple of months had been extremely busy. After her confrontation with Louisa, Parker had returned to their room at the inn to tell her that he'd resigned from his position in Baltimore and had accepted

Sheriff Farraway's offer to take over his job once he retired. Of course, that was a year from now, but Parker had
assured her that they were financially secure. Over the
years he'd apparently followed Preston's investment advice and made himself a good amount of money. That
didn't include his personal savings account, which Parker
immediately sacrificed to add to the amount the insurance company shelled out for the damage to her building.

They were rebuilding Blossoms, expanding it to the
second floor, where Drew could have an office and two
meeting rooms. There would be no need for her to live in
the apartment any longer since the week before Thanksgiving they'd put in a contract for one of the newly built
Cape Cod homes near Yates Passage.

Now, in the wee morning hours of New Year's Day,
they lay in their brand-new king-sized bed on their first
night in their new home together.

"Thank you," Drew whispered.

"What are you thanking me for? You're the one who
agreed to marry me with only five days' notice of when
the wedding would take place. You're the one who was
patient with me while I figured out that I should have proposed to you from the start. And you're the one," he finished by letting his hands fall to her now very full and
very round seven-and-a-half-month-pregnant stomach.
"You're the one who's going to make me even more happy
and proud by bringing our daughter safely into this
world."

Drew loved when he touched her stomach. At night he
always lay on his side, cuddled up close to her, his one
arm draped over her stomach. His palm rested there all
night while the baby moved against her father's touch.
Drew slept soundly and for the most part dreamlessly in
bed each night beside Parker. She wondered if it was because all her dreams had finally come true.

"But you're the one who gave up his savings to buy us this house and to help fix up my shop. You're the one who went to my mother and convinced her to come over and have dinner with us on Thanksgiving Day. You're the one who loves me despite all my baggage."

Parker smiled at that. "We're some pair, huh?"

"Yes," Drew replied. "We're some happy pair starting the new year in our new life."

"Happy New Year, Mrs. Cantrell," he said, leaning forward to kiss her stomach. "And Happy New Year to you, little princess Cantrell."

Epilogue

February

Drew felt like a giant apple in the red satin dress Delia had designed for her. Her friend in L.A. had taken Delia's sketch and turned it into the soft sheath Drew was now wearing. After a while of being stubborn, Drew had admitted that on paper the design had been pretty, but hanging beneath the plastic on the back of Drew's bedroom door for the past two days, it had been beautiful. Now, on Drew, as she stood at the floor-length mirror in the master bedroom of her house, the dress looked like a shiny covering . . . to an apple.

"You look gorgeous," Parker said, coming up behind her.

"You don't lie well," she snapped. "If Heaven hadn't helped plan this insane party, I'd be staying home tonight watching Cary Grant."

Parker groaned. "Oh please, not more of Cary Grant. That man spends more time with you than I do."

His hands had come around Drew's protruding belly, stopping a few inches before his fingers could touch near her navel, and Drew's heart melted. She would never get tired of seeing Parker's hands on her stomach, on their baby. Especially Parker's left hand, third finger, where he now wore a wedding band. Instinctively Drew covered her hands over Parker's, and the quick sparkle from her wedding ring joining with his caused them both to smile.

"I love you, Drewcilla Cantrell," Parker whispered in her ear.

"Let's see if you'll say that in a couple hours when I fall into the bed with my swollen feet and legs," she teased.

Parker would say exactly that later this evening after he'd helped her into their king-sized sleigh bed and made sure she had her glass of water filled with crushed ice on the bedside table. Then he'd climb into bed beside her, wait until she'd managed to turn onto her side, and wrap his arms around her once more. They would sleep intertwined until morning, a ritual Drew would never grow tired of.

A half hour later, they were walking into the town hall's lower level, where the Cupid's Cabaret was being held. The room had been decorated from floor to ceiling in red and white crepe paper, balloons, and flowers that Drew's new assistant, Ginger, had arranged in the bud vases that hadn't been destroyed by the explosion. There were twinkle lights hanging from the beams overhead, candles adorning each red cloth-covered table. On one side of the room was a row of tables that held the buffet meal, and on the other was the band that Heaven had hired to come all the way from Annapolis. It was a festive event, to say the least.

But Drew wasn't in the mood to be festive. She was tired of carrying around all this extra weight, tired of going to the bathroom, and even more tired of feeling as if she would explode at any moment. Her feet were already swollen, her hands, too, and her back had begun to ache on the ride over. All of that meant she was awarded a seat

at a table near the bathroom the minute she arrived and after everyone had the opportunity to lie to her face, telling her how beautiful she looked and denying that the red gave her a fruit appeal.

After an hour of watching people mingle, Drew's gaze settled on Mr. Sylvester, who was in the middle of the floor doing his version of the Forbidden Dance with her mother, a line of females, young and old, forming to get their chance to dance with Sweetland's newest popular bachelor. It made Drew smile to see her mother happy for a change. Then, suddenly, a sharp pain to her lower abdomen made her gasp. She'd been holding a glass of punch, and when the next pain came about two seconds later, it fell from her hand, crashing to the floor. This time she let out a little sound, or at least she thought the sound was little until it seemed everyone in the room stopped. In the background the music still played, but nobody was dancing now. They were all staring at her.

Heaven was at her side first.

"You all right?"

The next pain was sharp enough that Drew couldn't even speak. Then her water broke and words were no longer necessary.

"Parker!" she heard Heaven yell.

The next moments went by in a blur. Parker's strong arms were around her, lifting her from the floor and carrying her to his SUV. Heaven, Michelle, Raine, Savannah, and Delia were a bustle of activity, all chattering and squealing as they hit the parking lot looking for their vehicles. Quinn had come up to the truck as Parker belted her in.

"I've already called Dr. Lorens. She'll meet you at the hospital. We're going to follow you there," he told Parker, clapping him on his shoulder when Parker nodded.

They were silent in the truck but for Drew's gasps and

low moans of pain. Parker maneuvered the truck, all the while holding Drew's hand, murmuring how much he loved her and how proud he was of her.

The hospital in Easton brought back memories, and Drew tried not to panic. This wasn't like before. She wasn't coming here praying that she would live, that her child would live. They hadn't both just been through an explosion. No, this time was different. This time she was going to have her baby, to welcome the little life that had been growing inside her for the last nine months. She gripped the handle of the wheelchair with the next pain, clenching her teeth at the duration.

Once in a room, she was stripped naked and put into one of those ridiculous gowns that allowed room for zero modesty. Parker had been helping her so Drew could focus only on the pain radiating throughout her lower body. It seemed such a short time from the moment her water broke to the second the pain intensified and her eyes watered. Now, she was panting, gripping Parker's hand with each pain, and trying like hell to breathe normally.

"Hello, Drew, Parker," Dr. Lorens spoke as she entered the room. "We made it!" she announced, pulling plastic gloves onto her hands.

"We did," Parker agreed. "Thirty-seven weeks."

They both grew quiet as Drew endured another contraction. "Yes, thirty-seven weeks," she hissed. "Now can it come out?"

Dr. Lorens nodded. "It looks like that's the plan."

She sat on a stool with wheels and came to the bottom of the bed, touching Drew's legs. "Let's just do an exam to see how far along we are. I'll wait for your next contraction to pass."

And pass it did! Drew closed her eyes to the pain that dominated every thought she had for the next minute.

"Well," Dr. Lorens said with a giggle. "We're ready!"

Drew looked to Parker, who looked as afraid as she was but smiled at her nonetheless.

"Right now?" she asked. Then another pain hit and she screamed, "Right now!"

"It's a girl!" Parker announced in the waiting room twenty minutes later, his voice still a little shaky after seeing and holding his daughter in his arms for the first time. "Mackenzie," he said with a surreal sigh. "We named her Mary Mackenzie Janet Cantrell."

Since its founding, the first female born to couples in Sweetland were named Mary, after Mary Fitzgerald, the wife of the town's founder, Buford Fitzgerald. With that announcement, Michelle went to Parker first, wrapping her arms around him and pulling him close. She held him so tight that Parker almost cried, again. "She's beautiful," he whispered to his older sister.

"I'm sure she is. And she's the luckiest little girl in the world to have you for a father."

"I'm going to make her proud," he vowed. "I'm going to do everything in my power to make her proud that I'm her father and not ashamed."

Michelle shook her head, pulling back so she could look into his eyes. "I'm proud that you're my brother. I'm proud that you're going to be the new sheriff of Sweetland. And I'm elated that you're home, finally home."

This was exactly what Michelle had wanted, what Parker knew his sister had prayed for. She wanted them all back in Sweetland just as Gramma had. So far they were four for six, Savannah and Raine being the only two who hadn't declared their residency in Sweetland. In that instant, Parker wanted nothing more than for that to happen. He wanted all his family together, for his daughter to grow up with his brothers' children and his sisters' children, for the Cantrells to be together once again.

The Silver Spoon Recipes

Cantrell Crab Cakes

1	pound fresh jumbo lump crabmeat
2	large eggs
1½	tablespoons ground mustard
1	teaspoon yellow mustard
1½	tablespoons mayonnaise
1½	cups finely shredded bread crumbs
½	teaspoon Worcestershire sauce
½	teaspoon salt
½	teaspoon ground black pepper
2	tablespoons Old Bay Seasoning

Directions

1. Pick crabmeat in a bowl, removing any remaining shells.
2. In a separate bowl, mix eggs well. Add ground mustard, yellow mustard, mayonnaise, bread crumbs, Worcestershire sauce, salt, pepper, and Old Bay Seasoning.
3. Combine contents of both bowls by hand to limit crumbling of crabmeat lumps.
   Pan-fry in skillet with Canola oil, or broil.

Makes 8 medium-sized crab cakes.

Don't miss the first two novels in this heartwarming
series by
Lacey Baker

"Huge doses of charm, romance, and humor."
—*RT Book Reviews*

Homecoming

Just Like Heaven

Available from St. Martin's Paperbacks

www.laceybakerbooks.com
www.sweetlandromance.com